That expression, that demeanor, that voice—they shook Garfiel to the very core of his being. After all, standing there was—

"—Mom?"

That raspy voice was all that spilled out from his throat in response to this reunion that should never have happened.

Re:ZERO -Starting Life in Another World-

The only ability Subaru Natsuki gets when he's summoned to another world is time travel via his own death. But to save her, he'll die as many times as it takes.

CONTENTS

Chapter 1
Casually Comparing Answers
001

Chapter 2
A Showdown of Fire and Ice
043

Chapter 3
Witch Cult Disaster Response HQ
097

Chapter 4
Gorgeous Tiger
133

Chapter 5
The Operation to Retake City Hall
193

-Starting Life in Another World-

VOLUME 17

TAPPEI NAGATSUKI
ILLUSTRATION: SHINICHIROU OTSUKA

New York

Re:ZERO Vol. 17
TAPPEI NAGATSUKI

Translation by Jeremiah Bourque
Cover art by Shinichirou Otsuka

This book is a work of fiction. Names, characters, places, and incidents are the product of the author's imagination or are used fictitiously. Any resemblance to actual events, locales, or persons, living or dead, is coincidental.

Re:ZERO KARA HAJIMERU ISEKAI SEIKATSU Vol. 17
© Tappei Nagatsuki 2018
First published in Japan in 2018 by KADOKAWA CORPORATION, Tokyo.
English translation rights reserved by YEN PRESS, LLC under the license from KADOKAWA CORPORATION, Tokyo, through Tuttle-Mori Agency, Inc., Tokyo.

English translation © 2021 by Yen Press, LLC

Yen Press, LLC supports the right to free expression and the value of copyright. The purpose of copyright is to encourage writers and artists to produce the creative works that enrich our culture.

The scanning, uploading, and distribution of this book without permission is a theft of the author's intellectual property. If you would like permission to use material from the book (other than for review purposes), please contact the publisher. Thank you for your support of the author's rights.

Yen On
150 West 30th Street, 6th Floor
New York, NY 10001

Visit us at yenpress.com
facebook.com/yenpress
twitter.com/yenpress
yenpress.tumblr.com
instagram.com/yenpress

First Yen On Edition: November 2021

Yen On is an imprint of Yen Press, LLC.
The Yen On name and logo are trademarks of Yen Press, LLC.

The publisher is not responsible for websites (or their content) that are not owned by the publisher.

Library of Congress Cataloging-in-Publication Data
Names: Nagatsuki, Tappei, 1987– author. | Otsuka, Shinichirou, illustrator. | ZephyrRz, translator. | Bourque, Jeremiah, translator.
Title: Re:ZERO starting life in another world / Tappei Nagatsuki ; illustration by Shinichirou Otsuka ; translation by ZephyrRz ; translation by Bourque, Jeremiah
Other titles: Re:ZERO kara hajimeru isekai seikatsu. English
Description: First Yen On edition. | New York, NY : Yen On, 2016– |
Audience: Ages 13 & up.
Identifiers: LCCN 2016031562 | ISBN 9780316315302 (v. 1 : pbk.) |
ISBN 9780316398374 (v. 2 : pbk.) | ISBN 9780316398404 (v. 3 : pbk.) |
ISBN 9780316398428 (v. 4 : pbk.) | ISBN 9780316398459 (v. 5 : pbk.) |
ISBN 9780316398473 (v. 6 : pbk.) | ISBN 9780316398497 (v. 7 : pbk.) |
ISBN 9781975301934 (v. 8 : pbk.) | ISBN 9781975356293 (v. 9 : pbk.) |
ISBN 9781975383169 (v. 10 : pbk.) | ISBN 9781975383183 (v. 11 : pbk.) |
ISBN 9781975383206 (v. 12 : pbk.) | ISBN 9781975383220 (v. 13 : pbk.) |
ISBN 9781975383244 (v. 14 : pbk.) | ISBN 9781975383268 (v. 15 : pbk.) |
ISBN 9781975383282 (v. 16 : pbk.) | ISBN 9781975335250 (v. 17 : pbk.)
Subjects: CYAC: Science fiction. | Time travel—Fiction.
Classification: LCC PZ7.1.N34 Re 2016 | DDC [Fic]—dc23
LC record available at https://lccn.loc.gov/2016031562

ISBNs: 978-1-9753-3525-0 (paperback)
978-1-9753-3526-7 (ebook)

3 5 7 9 10 8 6 4

TPA

Printed in South Korea

CHAPTER 1
CASUALLY COMPARING ANSWERS

1

—First came the unstoppable impact that rocked his brain to its core.

"____"

His heart pounded like it was pumping confusion through his entire body. He wheezed painfully, forgetting how to even breathe. Convulsions racked his chest, and a heavy sheen of sweat coated his back.

The urge to throw up wouldn't go away. All he could hear was an incessant ringing and the cacophony of his own racing pulse. His vision flickered between black and red, as if his fragmented mind was sea-foam rocking on the surface of the water.

He had no idea where he was or what he was doing—

"—ru."

For a moment, he heard an unknown sound pierce the veil of hazy oblivion clouding his senses.

He blindly searched for the source like someone swimming in the ocean at night, groping around in the murk. Ever so slowly, his thoughts broke the surface of his consciousness, and—

"—Subaru!"

The voice sounded like a silver bell. It called out to him again and pulled the loose pieces of his being back to reality.

"—Ah."

After his consciousness returned, Subaru Natsuki rebooted.

As he gradually recovered from his blue screen and his eyes turned back on, the first thing he noticed was two dazzling violet jewels—or rather, violet eyes—staring at him. He saw the concern in Emilia's face as she gazed at him.

She gently stroked his cheek with her hand.

"_____"

The light touch of her slender fingers urged Subaru's senses to recall their purpose.

He could see the garden overflowing with green, smell the hint of flowers on the soft breeze, and hear the playful babbling of the nearby fountain. With these details coloring in the blanks, he finally regained a firm grip on reality.

This was the moment that Subaru noticed he had been holding on to someone's hand the whole time.

It was small, warm, and familiar. When he turned to his side, he was met with a pair of round eyes.

"Bea...trice..."

"Have you managed to calm down, I wonder? You were worrying me."

Beatrice let out a soft breath of relief as she continued holding Subaru's hand. Seeing that she was sitting on the grass, Subaru belatedly realized he was on the ground as well.

This was also the moment that he realized there were two others present besides Emilia and Beatrice.

"Pheeew, you gave us a real scare, Master Subaru. For a moment there, I was worried *I* wouldn't make it. Your humble Liliana still has not learned many funeral hymns, you see..."

Liliana the Songstress was expressing her delight at Subaru's apparent recovery with a rather peculiar choice of words. With one hand, she braced her beloved lyulyre against her hip as if to visibly illustrate her incredibly unique concern.

Standing beside her was Priscilla, who was wearing an expression that didn't show a single shred of acknowledgment regarding Subaru's poor state. She casually fanned herself with the idle composure of someone who was wholly unconcerned. That was so in character for her that it ironically set him at ease.

"＿＿＿"

After taking stock of everyone around him, Subaru slowly rose to his feet.

His head felt leaden. It was almost like his eyes, ears, nose, and skin were trying to keep up with someone suddenly changing the channel while only his soul stayed behind, still tuned to the old one.

That sensation lingered as Subaru took in a deep breath. There was something he had to confirm for himself.

"Subaru, are you sure you don't want to rest a bit more? You really don't look well…"

"I'm all right. Just a little dizzy from standing up. More importantly, Emilia-tan…weren't you going to have Liliana sing another song right about now?"

"Wha?! Why is that the first thing you want to know?! Not only did you have no reaction to what I said, but now I'm also being utterly ignored! You wound me, sir! I demand restitution! Restitution for my heart!!"

When Liliana grasped his sleeve with the force of someone determined to drag him off to court, Subaru immediately brushed her aside. The Songstress cried with a "Gaaah!" as she was flung away, but Subaru paid her no heed and looked straight at Emilia.

Picking up on the intensity of Subaru's gaze, Emilia nodded.

"Yes, that's right. Just now, we were talking about asking Liliana to sing the song we haven't had a chance to hear yet. That's when you and Liliana started whispering about something, and…"

"Which brings us to the present. Got it. Tha…"

Thank you, and sorry.

Right as he was about to thank Emilia for her explanation, something echoed in the back of Subaru's mind.

"_____"

It was the verbal tic of the bandaged maniac who appeared at the time tower—Sirius Romanée-Conti.

In most cases, those magic words were used to convey gratitude and show consideration for others. But for the moment, Subaru couldn't think of them as anything other than the sinister incantation of some dark sorcery.

When he recalled what that basket case had done while reciting those magic words, all he could think of was—

"...Oh. That's right; I..."

Subaru stumbled upon a sudden realization.

One moment, he was trapped in Wrath's crazed delusions, and in the next, he was back with Emilia and the others. It wasn't because he had miraculously managed to escape in one piece. No, quite the opposite.

At some point in the madness and the chaos, Subaru Natsuki had shuffled off this mortal coil. He had died again.

And in death, Subaru Natsuki had returned, so that he might challenge fate once more.

"Shit..."

Coming to terms with that fact, Subaru's breast burned with relief—and nigh-unendurable anger.

Over a year ago, Subaru refused to willfully hurl himself into the jaws of death, instead resolving to challenge whatever hardship or ordeal that barred his path with every iota of strength he could muster. That was the answer he had reached during the Witch's Trial in the Sanctuary.

Despite his big talk, he had failed spectacularly. Never mind resisting death; he'd actually run straight into its waiting embrace without even realizing what he was doing.

"—Ah."

And now another revelation dawned on him. He didn't even have time to feel self-loathing as an eruption of shame consumed him.

It had taken him this long to notice. His grasp on the flow of events, his situational awareness, his thoughts—all of them had been lacking and superficial.

Liliana's second song, the tension that hung over Emilia and Priscilla, Subaru running off to buy them snacks—all those things immediately preceded his encounter with the cryptic stranger, at which point he lost his life and promptly Returned by Death.

Coming back to this moment in time could only mean one thing.

Barely fifteen minutes remained until that eccentric's nightmarish speech would begin again.

"This can't be real…"

Still in shock, Subaru didn't know how to even begin dealing with his new reality.

As soon as he realized what situation he'd landed in, he was so overwhelmed by sheer urgency that it felt like his eyes were swimming. His reaction was completely understandable. Never before had his return point been so close to his demise.

To date, Subaru had been given loop times ranging from several hours to several days. It had been Subaru Natsuki's fight to make the most of that time limit and change any dead-end futures.

For this go-around, that time limit was short—extremely, painfully short.

What in the world could Subaru accomplish with a mere fifteen minutes?

"…Am I an idiot? No, of course I am. There's no time to screw around. I gotta be the one to put a stop to it."

As he bemoaned the incredibly harsh limitations he'd been saddled with, Subaru reprimanded himself to force his thoughts back on track.

This was an opportunity that no one except Subaru was granted more than once to begin with. It was too much to ask for his second chances to be tailored for his convenience.

He had to do his best according to the conditions granted to him. He could complain all he wanted after his life was snuffed out if it came to that point.

"Beatrice! Come with me and…"

"…And what, I wonder?"

Subaru impetuously turned around, ready to charge ahead when his words caught in his throat. Beatrice cocked her head in confusion.

The enemy was an Archbishop of the Seven Deadly Sins. Asking Beatrice for help and fighting together with her was the right choice—without her, Subaru's options dwindled, and his combat strength wouldn't even amount to half of what it could be.

Even though he knew this full well, Subaru hesitated to seek Beatrice's cooperation.

It wasn't because he was afraid of exposing Beatrice to danger or because of other sentimental reasons. His relationship with Beatrice had crossed that line of resolve long ago.

Then what was causing Subaru to waver?

It was Emilia. She was there.

"_____"

That eccentric had called herself Sirius Romanée-Conti, the Witch Cult's Archbishop of Wrath.

Petelgeuse, also an Archbishop, had doggedly targeted Emilia. Wasn't it safer to assume that Emilia would also be in Sirius's sights as well? That worry had a stranglehold on Subaru's heart.

He was afraid of leaving Emilia by herself.

It terrified him to even think about letting someone precious to him out of his sight. The tragedy of never-ending sleep that had befallen Rem had struck Subaru with a strain of cowardice that he could not shake off.

That's why—

"Beatrice, are you…"

"Am I…?"

"…fine with getting the same sweets as everyone else?"

Subaru was still wearing a deadly serious expression when he posed that trivial question. Of course, that didn't sit well with Beatrice as Subaru drew closer to her suspicious face.

"—Could you stay with Emilia? I'll rest easier if I know you're with her."

"...I suppose there is yet another thing you cannot share even with Betty."

"Sorry, but when something comes up, you're the first person I count on."

Though he knew it was low of him, Subaru was relying on Beatrice while withholding details about what was going on. She sighed at his reply as Subaru turned toward Emilia.

"I'm gonna go for a little run and buy some drinks while getting some air. You can just chill here and listen to the dangerous Songstress's song while looking graceful as always, all right?"

Somehow managing to flash a smile, Subaru spoke in a laid-back tone as he tried to take his leave.

But then—

"Wait."

—right before he was about to break into a run, he felt someone tugging at his clothes and stopped. When he checked to see who it was, Subaru found Emilia grasping the sleeve of his jacket, gazing at Subaru as if she wanted to say something.

He'd been incredibly sloppy. Of course Emilia was suspicious.

Therefore—

"Subaru, please, *please* be careful. Don't do anything rash."

Emilia swallowed her doubts and only asked that he keep his wits about him. Her thoughtfulness made him happy.

"Yeah, of course. Just sit tight and trust me. I'll protect you?"

"Okay. Take care."

With that final comment, she let go of his sleeve, blushing a little.

"I have it. Please listen: *Show me your mettle.*"

"All right, I'm off! I'll be right back...or at least, it'll feel like I'll be right back!"

Ignoring the Songstress taking inspiration from the scene to fuel her creative juices, Subaru properly broke into a run.

Approximately ten minutes remained until the nightmarish speech began—a time limit short enough to make him cry.

2

It didn't even take five minutes to sprint to the square that contained the time tower where everything would go down.

Since it had taken him some time to confirm the situation after Returning by Death, he had left the park later than his previous time going there. Skipping the shopping trip let him make up some of the lost time, but—

"With a limit of fifteen minutes, there's no telling how fatal it might be to show up a few seconds late."

That was even truer because he currently had an overwhelming lack of information. The worst of it was that Subaru didn't know what caused Return by Death—in other words, he hadn't isolated what killed him.

The circumstances surrounding his latest death were simply that bizarre.

An Archbishop of the Seven Deadly Sins had appeared atop a time tower and somehow convinced the audience—Subaru included—to joyfully listen to her mad speech. In the end, even when Sirius hurled an innocent boy from the top of the tower, Subaru and the others only reacted with eager applause as they watched the young child's head shatter against the ground.

That was when his consciousness cut out, followed by Return by Death immediately after, so all he could gather from that was…

"Do I know anything other than the fact that I basically lost my mind?"

Sirius had created an anomaly, but everyone present had accepted it like nothing was out of the ordinary. Many would find it tempting to consider it a type of madness or perhaps some sort of mental corruption.

What memories Subaru was able to retain after coming back were heavily influenced by his state during the instant he died. Considering his mental condition at the time, he felt compelled to question the reliability of his memories.

"Man, I already made it."

Arriving at the square with labored breaths, Subaru surveyed his surroundings.

The familiar time tower was deeper inside the square, and lots of foot traffic flowed by its base. This area was part of the most prosperous district in the city. There were far more people than Subaru remembered, and they were streaming around the place without pause.

Fortunately, he couldn't spot any groups or even a single individual clad in a telltale black outfit among them. He hadn't seen any Witch Cultists around Sirius during the speech, either. Perhaps Sirius was acting alone.

Even if that was true, it didn't mean that the threat posed by the Archbishop was diminished in the slightest.

"Now, what should I do? Evacuating the square…would be tough. I'd need way more help to go around convincing people. Besides, doing something like that might tip off Sirius."

For an instant, he considered causing a commotion to forestall the tragedy that was about to take place, but he quickly decided that was probably a really bad idea.

To begin with, Sirius's heinous actions had not targeted anyone in particular. It was indiscriminate terrorism if anything. If he let her get away, she'd eventually just do the same thing somewhere else. That would be a hollow victory.

The Archbishops of the Seven Deadly Sins were creatures of pure evil that had to be rooted out at the source.

"If only I had time to head back to that Japanese-style inn and get one or two people to help… Damn it all!"

After griping about some wishful thinking, Subaru slapped his cheeks with both hands. Then he gazed forward with a firm look of resolve, glaring at the ominous time tower.

In a few more minutes, Sirius would appear at the top of that white tower and raise the curtain on her wicked performance.

That meant she must already be lurking inside it at this very moment. Of course, Lusbel, her young captive, would be in there as well.

"The hell? It's unlocked..."

He noticed that the entrance was an old iron door set unobtrusively in the rear of the time tower. When he tentatively put a hand on it, the unlocked door swung open with ease. Hesitating for only a second, Subaru quietly stepped into the belly of the yawning structure.

"———"

The interior was dark. The putrid air was cold and reeked of dust.

Though they functioned much like a clock tower, time towers were magic crystal timekeepers and did not have any clockwork mechanisms whatsoever. The tower's interior contained only a support pillar at its center and a spiraling staircase, which climbed upward along the walls. Thanks to that, the inside of the tower was quiet and still. Subaru winced at how audible his footsteps were here.

"...Nnngh, mmm, hngh."

Then a faint, crying voice abruptly broke through the veil of silence.

Subaru craned his neck to look higher. The noises of distress were coming from the upper part of the tower. He was sure it sounded like the voice of a child crying while being dragged along—

"—Don't cry, don't wail, and don't make a fuss. You truly are a good child. A strong child who protected someone precious to you. Surely your family, and even your younger brothers and sisters you have never set eyes upon, will always think of you with pride."

He could hear a sinister voice.

Those words were undoubtedly directed at the sobbing child. They sounded like both a blessing and a curse overflowing with resentment, an intense mix of love and hate.

This was twisted. That one utterance was enough for Subaru to tell that the speaker did not possess a sound mind.

"———"

They were above him. The moment he knew that for certain, Subaru let out a heavy breath, then went still.

Putting a hand over his racing heart, Subaru stepped onto the spiral stairs. Fortunately, walking silently was one of the skills that his mentor, Clind, had instilled in him over this past year. Leading with his heels before slowly shifting his body weight forward, Subaru inched toward the top of the tower with stealthy steps.

At the topmost floor, there was a window that allowed for inspection of the magic crystal timepiece and was accessed via a loft that served as a maintenance space. Cautiously, he peered into that room from midway up the stairs, managing to catch sight of some silhouettes wriggling in the darkness.

There was no sign of anyone else in the vicinity. He was almost certain that these figures were Sirius and the hostage.

"_____"

Seeing his chance, Subaru moved a hand behind his hip and slowly drew his weapon—a whip—from its holster.

It shared a deep resemblance with the bullwhip that was favored by a certain archaeologist who often raided old ruins in a world-famous series of films. The main difference was that Subaru's whip was longer, which naturally made it more difficult to use.

However, under Clind's strict tutelage, Subaru had somehow managed to rise to an acceptable level of mastery over the last year. The whip that Subaru held now was a custom gift he'd received from his mentor as a sort of graduation present.

Taking inspiration from the name of the demon beast that had provided the materials, Subaru had dubbed it the Guilty Whip.

It was perfect for tricks and feints—and that was precisely why Subaru had chosen the whip from among numerous other weapons. Subaru had laid eyes upon many swordsmen since his arrival. The world of martial arts was not so forgiving that he could match a professional overnight.

Furthermore, if he had anything to be proud of, it was his cunning. And thanks to his mentor's tutelage, now even Subaru had cards he could play in a situation like this.

"Looks like it's about a dozen or so feet."

Eyeballing the distance between the end of the stairs and the shifting silhouettes, he could see that his target was right at the edge of his whip's range. He needed a step or at least half a step closer to guarantee a hit.

Either way, a whip didn't pack enough punch to land a one-hit knockout. If he was going to use a whiplash as his opening gambit, he couldn't rely on brute force—so instead, he'd make use of height.

He took a shallow breath, then held it.

He decided to attack from a range where he could hit for certain. Surging forward, he wound up his right hand to ready his whip as he cleared the stairs. The silhouettes still weren't looking in his direction. The initiative was his for the taking.

"!"

Taking half a step forward, he swung his right arm like he was circling it overhead. That sidearm motion emphasized speed over force.

As it took flight, the whip was too fast to track with the naked eye. This was another reason Subaru had chosen the weapon: It gave him the ability to quickly land a blow against opponents far stronger than he.

At this rate, the whip would reach the defenseless back of his target, wrapping around her neck and giving him a chance to hurl her down the—

"—Why are you so angry?"

Right as he thought his attack would connect, his target suddenly posed a question, back still facing him.

Almost simultaneously, the silhouette swung her hand without even turning around. With incredible speed and accuracy, the chain that was wrapped around that hand collided with Subaru's whip, robbing it of all momentum and knocking it down.

Subaru's eyes shot open, but the moment he felt his whip make contact with the chain, he yanked his arm back hard.

"Oh my."

The hook hanging from the chain's end had gotten tangled with Subaru's whip, giving him a chance to throw Sirius off-balance. Subaru followed up quickly with a ferocious charge, ramming her with his shoulder.

"Uraaaaah!" "Wah!"

Raising a delicate cry, Sirius's unexpectedly light body went over the railing, turning halfway before vanishing from sight. Just as he'd planned, she fell from the landing and was hurtling straight down to ground level. It was more than a sixty-foot drop from the top floor, tall enough to crack open a child's head like it was an overly ripe fruit.

"You okay, Lusbel?!"

Not staying to watch the strange woman twist and fall to her death, Subaru raced over to the other person still on the landing. It was Lusbel, the pitiable boy who was fated to be hurled from the tower.

His body was already wrapped in a set of chains, which tightly bound his lower half. He looked like he was in pain, but the most repulsive detail was how the boy was gripping the end of the chain that was wrapped around his own body.

There was only one thing that could mean.

"She made him chain himself...?!"

Subaru seethed as he realized the demented events that must have led to this moment.

This young boy had been forced to sign his own death warrant. Just how much fear and horror had Lusbel endured while doing this? Simply imagining it made Subaru sick to his stomach.

"It's all right! You've done enough! You don't need to put up with this anymo..."

"B-but...if I don't keep my promise, Tina will... Tina will...!"

When Subaru tried to undo the chain, Lusbel resisted with tears in his eyes. The name on his lips—the name of the boy's childhood friend whom Sirius had mentioned previously—made Subaru draw a sharp breath.

This boy had accepted a deal with the devil to spare his childhood friend from a terrible fate. Even while enduring such a harrowing ordeal—legs shaking, teeth chattering, and tears coursing from his eyes—his main concern was still his friend.

"It's...all right. There's...lots of dependable people in this city, so...!"

Subaru did his best to console him.

He wanted to be as emphatic as possible to reassure the young boy. At the moment, the Sword Saint, the Sword Devil, and the Finest of Knights were all in the same city. The kingdom's greatest healer was also present. Losing didn't seem possible with all of them a stone's throw away.

That's why there was no need to be afraid. Evil would not triumph here. It was true. It had to be true.

There was absolutely no need to be afraid. None whatsoever.

"That's why…my legs need to quit shaking already!!"

Subaru raised a frantic yell as he fell to his knees in front of Lusbel, whose eyes had shot open in fear.

Subaru's voice cracked, carrying notes of grief and terror. It almost felt as if some alien revulsion was coiling around his entire body and refusing to let go.

"—Urhkgh!"

Before his eyes, Lusbel writhed, then bent over and vomited, spewing yellow stomach fluids. Convulsing like he was having a seizure, the boy collapsed onto a pool of his own sick. When Subaru tried to brace him, Subaru was suddenly assailed by the sensation of something clawing at his own insides and he also threw up on the spot.

Subaru promptly pitched forward just like Lusbel had—

"—That you are so afraid is proof of your kind heart."

"Ngh, gaaaah!!"

The same moment he heard that voice, Subaru screamed from the searing pain that struck his left shoulder. With a powerful yank, he was dragged backward until he collided with a railing and flipped over it.

He went into a tailspin and was hurtling to his death—only to suddenly stop halfway, suspended in midair.

"Wha…?!!"

"Thank you. And I'm sorry."

Having cleared the railing and fallen, Subaru had no way to answer.

The reason was physical rather than emotional. After all, a chain was wrapped around his neck, while the hook on its end dug deep into his left shoulder.

When Sirius twisted and fell earlier, she had apparently thrown her chain to drag Subaru down and used the resulting force to propel herself back up. Now she was the one looking down with a smile at Subaru, who was suspended by the chain around his neck.

Subaru flailed as he kicked his legs in the air and vomit trickled from his constricted throat. As she watched Subaru struggle for his life, Sirius nodded several times with visible delight.

"People can understand one another. People have the ability to become one. Kindness is not for our own sake. It is for the sake of others. Kindness shines brightest when it is offered freely. To be kind to oneself is mere selfishness. A far cry from true kindness! As such, your concern for others makes your kindness bright as the sun! Ahh, ahh, ahh! In other words, it is love!"

"*Ugh, agh, bngh...*"

"Please savor the feeling. Please show me your love, the chains of your limitless kindness, your noble desire to save young Lusbel!"

As blood and vomit continued to spill from Subaru, Sirius embraced the filth-covered Lusbel before her. She rubbed her cheek against Lusbel's, marring her white bandages with the boy's yellow stomach fluids in the process.

"Your gentle soul felt Lusbel's fear. Through you, young Lusbel experienced your fears that had been born from his. And then that additional fear that young Lusbel felt flowed back into you. In this manner, you shall feel the same joy, sadness, terror, and even the pain of being wrung by the neck, until by the loving embrace of death do you part—"

Those rambling words rained down on Subaru from above. In that moment, he was far too preoccupied to dismiss her words as delusional and nonsense. The reason was that everything, from voices to the very air itself, had become an object of fear for Subaru. The entire world scared him. If everything that he laid eyes on was scary, then he should have just closed his eyes, but when he realized that darkness itself was terrifying, this thought combined with the worry that he might never see light again if he closed his eyes, making his entire body freeze stiff, because comprehending that fear made him afraid that he couldn't comprehend fear anymore, which was a terrifying thought in and of itself, because if the whole world was made up of terrifying things and fear was the only truth of the world, then fear gave way to fear that would make fear fear's— "Oh my. It would seem you are at your limit. Compassionate people who love and feel deeply are beautiful but at times fragile… Ahh, people love, and so they suffer. But it is because of love that people's lives have meaning. What a very complicated thing. Well then, I shall borrow little Tina's strength next. Young Lusbel, young man, you two have earned your rest." —reason that dulls the value of life which allows creatures to defy their natural instincts and functions meaning fear is necessary so it's only natural for people to feel fear so it's nothing to be ashamed of and if anything it'd be pointless to not be afraid but it would probably be through thought experiments like this that he'd challenge the fear that gripped his entire body because otherwise why was subaru even scared scared scary scared scary scary i dont feel so goobebebebabababababababaabararadagaddagagadaradadada—

3

"After the song, we'll have a pleasant chat, so could you prepare some snacks, Master Natsuki? Do you not think that sweets will make everyone happy and bring us all closer together?"

The moment he blinked, the world changed before his eyes. Subaru immediately lost his balance, smashing his head into the girl who was winking and holding out an expectant hand toward him.

"Waaaghaaa?!" "Agh!!"

A hard *thunk* echoed as Subaru saw stars in his eyes.

The sharp pain sent Subaru reeling, leaving him wondering what happened as he took a step back. Something crashed onto the grass in front of him, but Subaru paid it no heed as he rubbed his own head.

"Wh-what just…?"

"What are you muttering about, Subaru?! You just headbutted Liliana out of nowhere! You can't do that. Even if you're upset, you need to at least warn them beforehand."

"That's right. Before you resorted to violence, should you not have admonished her right around the time she made that clumsy wink, I wonder?"

"Was it really that bad?!"

Offended, Liliana leaped back to her feet. Emilia and Beatrice traded looks, seemingly pondering how to reply to her question as she recovered from her fall.

Struck by shock at the silent pause, Liliana flopped down and splayed out once more.

"What a ridiculous farce. Do not infringe upon my little bird, peasant. I will not overlook it a second time."

Unexpectedly, Priscilla actually sided with Liliana. She had apparently taken quite a liking to the Songstress, if the sharp look in her eyes was anything to judge by.

But Priscilla's warning did not elicit a single word from Subaru as he checked the state of his own body.

"…Makes me sick."

That was all Subaru could gloomily muster after his second run-in with that walking enigma, who hadn't changed in the slightest.

4

Upon his second Return by Death, unprecedented fatigue ate away at Subaru's psyche.

Experiencing two deaths in a short time frame was undoubtedly a large burden, but the greatest source of his distress was the fact that he had lost his mind twice over. Though both episodes had their differences, he'd tasted mental collapse via mania and psychosis in rapid succession. During the second instance, he'd experienced his very sense of self break down. He never wanted to go through that again.

He wondered if the ultimate cause of his second death was cardiac arrest from extreme terror or simple suffocation from being strung up by his neck. Either way, he'd paid a high price for trying to save Lusbel by himself.

However, Subaru hadn't died twice in a mere thirty minutes without getting anything out of it.

Sirius had been kind enough to explain what was happening to Subaru as his life came to an end, perhaps as a sort of morbid farewell gift.

"Fear heightening as it passes back and forth between people... like a kind of resonance, maybe?"

Subaru had felt Lusbel's fear, and in turn, Lusbel had felt Subaru's. With each subsequent pass, that sensation grew stronger and stronger, culminating in an absolute, all-consuming dread that ultimately led to death.

Based on Sirius's statements and his own mental collapse, Subaru deduced that this was his opponent's Authority. He was also finally able to infer the cause of his manic episode during his first visit to the time-tower square.

That time, all the anger and disgust in the crowd had been overwritten with joy and delight. And inside the tower, the fear that Lusbel felt had passed back and forth between him and his would-be savior, shattering Subaru's mind.

In other words, Sirius's Authority of Wrath—

"It lets her toy with other people's feelings however she likes. Shit, that's bad news."

Just like Petelgeuse's Unseen Hands, it was an Authority, a special power not subject to the world's normal rules of magic. Befitting the title of Wrath, that sinister ability was closely tied to human emotion.

In the end, that was all his second death allowed him to deduce with any confidence. The biggest issue was that he still had no idea what conditions were required for activating this Authority, and he didn't have a single lead on how to resolve this situation.

It was fair to say that the strategy he employed against Petelgeuse had heavily depended upon luck.

Unseen Hands was the Authority of Sloth, and Petelgeuse himself was an evil spirit who had the powerful ability to possess the bodies of others. Subaru just happened to have ways of countering both.

However, setting his means of resisting possession aside, Subaru still didn't know what let him see Unseen Hands. At some point since then, he'd learned a skill he called Invisible Providence, which greatly resembled Unseen Hands, but his suspicions remained just that.

"Since Return by Death seems to have something to do with the Witch, I'd hoped it meant the Witch Cult's rule-breaking tricks wouldn't work on me or something, but…"

He had no choice but to discard that line of thinking after Wrath's power had affected him so deeply.

On top of that, based on what he could gather so far, the worst-case scenario was that Sirius's Authority simply activated upon contact. It was a distinct possibility that hearing her voice or seeing her in person was enough for him to become ensnared.

In that case, the most reliable strategy against Sirius was to blow her up along with the entire building before she emerged from the top of the time tower. That way, she would have no chance to use her Authority. This plan was only possible because Subaru knew Sirius's exact location due to the short time limit imposed by his Return by Death.

If he acted immediately, Sirius could be defeated for sure—so long as he turned a blind eye and accepted the sacrifice of one little boy.

"—As if I'd ever let that happen."

There was no way he'd ever invoke phrases like *necessary sacrifices*.

For Subaru, even if it meant exchanging one life to save many, losing that one life was like giving up the entire world. If he had already made up his mind to not sacrifice himself, how could he reduce the lives of others to mere numbers? That was the act of a god or a devil, and Subaru had no intention of turning into either.

"I'll save Lusbel and beat Sirius. Gotta make both happen somehow, huh? Man, being Emilia-tan's knight is tough."

And yet if he couldn't do that, Subaru Natsuki had no value

whatsoever. Naturally, he knew full well that the kind people around him would surely forgive such weakness.

That's why he had to do it. Subaru wanted to stand proudly beside the people he cared about. If seeing this through was what it took to make that happen, then so be it. That was Subaru's way.

"I challenged her alone and lost pathetically. It's painfully obvious I don't have enough combat power… I need to borrow someone's strength."

The ideal recruit was someone with so much pure combat power that they could overwhelm Sirius. It would have to be a person who'd believe Subaru's words implicitly and agree to cooperate with him. On top of that, they had to be able to resist Sirius's Authority.

He needed a powerful character who met all those conditions and who was close enough to reach the time tower in under ten minutes. Subaru almost laughed at himself for wanting such a convenient ally.

"Oh, right."

He tried to laugh, but then it dawned on him. There was a certain memory.

His first time in the square, he'd come across a particular man. Since that person had also been influenced by Wrath's Authority, he was far from the perfect counter against Sirius, but even so—

"—Reinhard!!"

Right as Subaru began to feel ridiculous for seeking out a wildly convenient answer to his problems, he was finally able to remember that a man who was the epitome of overpowered really did exist.

5

He wasn't trying to make excuses for himself, but Subaru's two very quick deaths were a major part of why he had completely forgotten Reinhard's existence—and the fact that Lachins, who had been present in the square, was connected to him.

—Subaru had experienced death right after experiencing death, and that made it twice that his psyche had collapsed.

It went without saying that going through this unprecedented experience in the short span of thirty minutes had left Subaru rattled. He felt nothing but astonishment at how little time this loop gave him and how it didn't leave any breathing room to calmly figure things out.

Accordingly, Subaru had been forced to run ahead at full speed until he rammed into something barring his way forward. Desperately trying to come up with a way to persuade a certain man was no exception.

"I finally found you! You're not getting away! Please call Reinhard over right now! It's an emergency!"

"Like hell I am! I don't wanna hear another damn word of complaint outta that redheaded bastard! Get lost!"

The shouting match that erupted in the middle of the street made passersby glance at one another as they wondered what was up.

The atmosphere resembled a sporting match as several curious onlookers hurled jeers at them. It annoyed Subaru, but he didn't have the luxury of paying them any heed.

After recovering from the shock of Return by Death, Subaru was following up on his earlier conclusion with swift action.

Asking Beatrice to guard Emilia just like last time, Subaru left the park, ostensibly to go shopping—when in reality, he was looking for Lachins in the square to convey the imminent emergency.

But Subaru had gotten off to a bad start and wasn't making any progress. It had taken him so long to find Lachins that Subaru had accidentally grabbed the man's shoulder the moment he happened upon him. He'd apologized several times, but still.

"Anyway, I need you to calm down and listen to me. I'm not joking around. If you don't want to die, get in touch with Reinhard right now."

"Huh? You think a snivelin' brat like you can do me in? I don't need Reinhard for this. I can pay ya back right here, right now."

"Damn it, you thick-skulled…"

Taking Subaru's words as a taunt, Lachins let his anger grow even hotter.

It was difficult to call Subaru and Lachins's relationship favorable to begin with. On top of that, Lachins seemed to dislike Reinhard a great deal, which apparently made him reluctant to rely upon the knight.

Of course, that stubbornness didn't even compare with the threat that the Archbishop of the Seven Deadly Sins posed, but Subaru had good reason to not reveal all the details about the current turn of events. That said, at the rate things were going, the situation would only deteriorate, which didn't leave him much of a choice.

Suppressing his instinctual fear, Subaru touched his hand to his chest.

"Lachins, this isn't a joke. I want you to call Reinhard because someone who neither of us can lay a hand on is up to no good."

"What are you goin' on about? Talk sense, man."

Lachins snorted, treating Subaru's plea like it was nonsense.

The look on his face made Subaru lower his eyes and breathe deeply— *Stay away*, he prayed privately as he opened his mouth.

"—The people coming…might be from the Witch Cult."

There, I said it, thought Subaru as he let out his breath. Lachins's expression stiffened almost instantly.

A moment after he spoke, Subaru looked down at his chest, but nothing had happened. Even though he'd divulged a piece of information gained via Return by Death, no penalty had occurred.

"Nothing this time, huh? …Well, shit, that's bad for my heart in more than one way."

Grasping his own collar, Subaru was flooded with relief as he cursed with minor irritation.

It had been a year since he'd experienced Return by Death, but Subaru continued to be regularly tormented by the various penalties that he incurred whenever he'd attempted to divulge the existence of his unusual power.

In one notable example, he'd decided to reveal everything to Beatrice once and for all, only to experience truly hellish suffering like never before.

It was a special present from the Witch of Jealousy—the culprit who stood behind those black hands. The penalty almost seemed to say, *Forget about everything that transpired when we parted back at the Witch's Tea Party in the Sanctuary.*

Given the circumstances, Subaru still had yet to disclose the existence of Return by Death to Beatrice or anyone else.

Of course, so long as it didn't call abject suffering down on himself, he fully intended to tell his partner Beatrice everything that he could. He'd spent a long time trying before reluctantly giving up.

Either way, the important part was that he'd been able to convey to Lachins the coming Witch Cult attack without activating the penalty—

"Hey, brat, how serious are you about what you just said? This ain't some kinda ruse, right?"

"It's Subaru Natsuki. Stop calling me 'brat' already, Lachins."

Lachins, who had lowered his voice, clicked his tongue as he received Subaru's reply.

In this world, invoking the names of the Witch of Jealousy and the Witch Cult was indescribably serious, enough that even Lachins had changed his expression as he instantly grasped the gravity of the impending situation.

"Subaru, you piece of shit, where the hell did you hear about somethin' like…? Aww, crap. That's right. You're the one who killed the Witch Cult's Sloth guy, huh? Guess you do have some credibility…"

Flicking his tongue piercing with a finger, Lachins tried to figure out how to treat Subaru's statement. Lachins made some speculation that was a little at odds with the facts, but Subaru's exploits were apparently enough to convince him to play along.

"Anyway, are ya saying those guys are gonna show up in this city? Or right here in this damned square?"

"So you believe me?"

"You're the one who said ya ain't playin' around. Look, I hate that redheaded bastard's lectures, but I like starin' death in the face even less. If you get it, then watch what you say and how you say it."

It wasn't exactly trust or faith, but Lachins had made an unexpectedly logical decision. Subaru responded with a quick "Gotcha!" and a vigorous nod.

"All right, I'll keep that mind. To properly explain, it's the Witch Cult's Archbishop of Wrath who's coming. She's gonna poke her face out at the top of the time tower in this square. There's no particular target, so she's gonna aim for everyone here."

"That sounds just like the Witch Cult, don't it? Shit, how much time do we got?"

"Probably less than five minutes. So I'd really like to call him now."

"Five minutes?! The hell?! Why didn't ya say that sooner?!"

"That's why I've been asking you since five minutes ago!"

Lachins raised his voice as he suddenly realized how urgent the situation was, but the time limit was a curse that Subaru could not be more aware of. If he had any other choice, Subaru wouldn't be relying on casting a net out like this, either.

"Hey! This ain't a sideshow! Get lost, ya damn tourists!"

Lachins had judged that you couldn't make an omelet without breaking a few eggs. Rudely howling at the people crowding around his and Subaru's argument at a distance, he thrust his right hand toward the sky.

"Lettin' magic fly inside the city with nothing goin' on is against city regs. Ya better be there with me to explain."

"I'll do that much any day. I'll lick someone's boots if I have to."

"And you call yourself a knight?!"

An instant after Subaru's reply left Lachins dumbfounded, Lachins unleashed a red light from his palm toward the sky. The flare spread in the middle of the sky, making the heavens glow and glimmer as if he'd launched some small, cheap fireworks.

To be blunt, it was hard to expect much from something so puny, but it was surely enough to summon that hero.

"Gotta say, though, never thought I'd be working together with Larry toward the same goal like this..."

Subaru wanted to believe that such deep sentiment was a sign he'd made the right decision. If this brought Reinhard running, then surely it would drastically change the situation.

—That vague sense of relief had caused Subaru to forget a natural concern.

That moment, he had a thought that would have never occurred to him fifteen minutes ago—back during the second go-around.

"―――"

The people in the square looked up at the light in the sky, raising voices of surprise and wonder.

Accordingly—

"—My. A ball of fire off in the distance. It glows so prettily. Thank you."

Naturally, when she heard the fuss outside, the bandaged enigma came out into the open.

6

Leaning her body forward from the top of the white tower, Sirius seemed to be in a very good mood. Even if the bandages kept her expression hidden, her voice overflowed with emotion.

Sirius savored the red, magical glow floating in the blue sky before clapping.

"Yes! Now then, everyone, so sorry to interrupt. Good day to you all!"

The thundering sound of her clap echoed loudly, and the audience, which had been focusing on the Goa spell that Lachins had unleashed, reflexively turned toward Sirius.

"No, don't look!!"

Worried that this was the condition for her Authority activating, Subaru yelled out in warning. However, no one heeded his words and averted their gazes. Of course not—Subaru himself had done the exact same thing that they did upon coming into contact with Sirius for the first time.

The eccentric was instinctually provocative. Her words and actions made you unable to look away.

"My. You have gone quiet far sooner than I thought. It is surely because these two drew everyone's attention before I came out. Thank you. Applause, please!"

Clapping as she spoke, Sirius indicated Subaru and Lachins with her chain-wrapped hands.

Amid sparse applause, Subaru endured the terrible chill running up his back as he desperately turned his head away in the hopes of escaping from the effects of her Authority. However, it was probably too late for that.

After all, Subaru already found himself unable to cover his ears.

Subaru had deduced that the condition for Sirius activating her Authority was for a potential victim to see her or hear her voice. Therefore, at first, he thought that maybe averting his eyes or plugging his ears might be enough—but what did he need to cover his ears for anyway? After all, Sirius's voice was so soothing.

"—Ah."

Before he realized it, Subaru had turned back around, staring right at Sirius.

For Sirius's part, she swayed her body with delight when she noticed Subaru was gazing up at her. The hooks at the tips of her chains clattered as they scraped along the floor, and this metallic sound pierced Subaru's mind.

"Yes! It took nineteen seconds until all of you looked in my direction. I'm so sorry, but this is joyous indeed. Also, it would appear there is a child here thinking of me with much more intensity than I expected. Now, I should introduce myself."

As the massive audience gazed up at her in silence, Sirius politely bowed her head. As she did so, she peered down upon the square with only one eye uncovered.

"I am the Witch Cult's Archbishop of Wrath—my name is Sirius Romanée-Conti."

Normally, the repulsive being invoking that terrifying name would be regarded as an object of fear and hatred.

And yet the throng of people accepted it as if it were the name of a neighbor whom everyone knew. Sirius gently acknowledged this mild reaction, smiling and nodding like a benevolent mother.

"Tee-hee, thank you. I am so sorry to make all of you spare time for me like this. But rest easy, for it will be over in short order."

Gently, like that of a mother reading a picture book in her child's bedroom, Sirius's voice had a lulling effect.

All they wanted was to hear her voice more. That impulse was so strong that—

"—Oh, really now? In that case, I should finish this sooner rather than later."

This new voice was deeper and more caring than Sirius's hollow affections. The emotions that had been sinking deep into the bodies and minds of Subaru and the others in the square were shaken.

"_____"

Sirius opened her eye wide while Subaru and the rest of the audience joined her in turning toward the edge of the square as one.

Their gazes fell on a waterway flowing behind the square. The normally gentle stream of water was flowing backward as *something* was moving through it with incredible force, kicking up a spray of water in its wake.

His vivid red hair blazed like a beautiful, flickering flame.

He had eyes that seemed like a polished cut of a magnificent blue sky.

He was built so handsomely that any manner of being might fall for him.

—This man was the epitome of what all people pictured in their hearts when they heard the word *hero*.

"Looking for the shortest route took some time. I'm sorry I'm late."

The hero apologized for running over in thirty seconds rather than five.

The Sword Saint stood in the square after taking a path that no one else could as his so-called shortcut—or, more specifically, having accomplished the superhuman feat of running upstream. Then when he caught sight of Wrath, who was standing atop the time tower, he took a breath.

As he hardened his blue eyes, a short "I see…" was all that emerged from the Sword Saint—Reinhard.

"I understand why you called me here. You made the right decision, Lachins. Or was it you who summoned me, Subaru?"

Slowly, Reinhard walked over and patted Subaru and Lachins both on the shoulder. Instantly, strength returned to their totally immobilized bodies.

"R-Reinhard…?"

"Yes, it is I. This seems to be quite a predicament. That's an Archbishop of the Seven Deadly Sins, isn't it?"

As Subaru called out to him in an unsteady voice, Reinhard nodded firmly. The palpable wariness visible in his serene blue eyes showed that Reinhard had instantly realized the danger that Sirius posed with a single glance.

Gulping at how quickly he'd understood, Subaru replied with an awkward nod of his own.

"She…she has the power to brainwash other people. Seems like we're okay for now, but it happens when you hear her voice or look at her."

"No, it's not only her voice and appearance. It would seem that anyone who merely knows she exists is affected. It's possible that I won't be able to maintain my composure for very long."

"No way, even you…?!"

Subaru was stunned seeing Reinhard acting so meek.

Though he had no basis for his belief, he'd thought that Reinhard of all people would be all right. If even he wasn't immune to Sirius's Authority, then Subaru's plan was already falling apart.

And during this exchange between the two, Sirius reacted as well. The bandaged eccentric gazed steadily at Reinhard with a purple eye.

"Could it be…? You with the red hair, are you the famous Sword Saint?"

"That's correct. I am Reinhard van Astrea, current holder of the title of Sword Saint. Unfortunately, I have yet to merit such a lofty title."

Reinhard boldly confirmed Sirius's suspicions. Coming face-to-face with the most powerful being to set foot in that square, Sirius was far from being afraid and actually cried out with an "Ah-ha!"

She shouted and squirmed in place. The eccentric's cracked, high-pitched laughter echoed toward the sky.

"Ah-ha! Ah-ha-ha! Ahh, what a splendid turn of events! What a fortuitous day it is for you to have come like this! You are known as the most splendid knight in all the land! Everyone loves you, and you love everyone! You are the living manifestation of the hope, the very love that I preach!"

"I wonder about that…"

Sirius writhed with emotion, getting incredibly worked up as she flew into what was truly a wild dance of mad delight. Meanwhile, Reinhard was still engaging in conversation with Sirius, who continued rambling, though he didn't so much as look in her direction.

This was far too risky against an opponent with an Authority that joined minds in mutual madness.

"W-wait, Reinhard… It's not a good idea to keep talking with her. It has to be bad. I think…it's bad. I'm not really sure why, though, but…"

"…So it would seem. Putting my own interests aside, this is not something that should be drawn out for long."

"Reinhard?"

"—I will do what you called me to do. It's time to deal with the issue."

With those final words, Reinhard took a single step forward, slightly bent his knees, and leaped up.

His stance made it seem as if he were just jumping over a puddle in front of him—but the resulting gale-force winds, the tremors that shot through the ground, and the shock wave left in his wake made everyone in the square draw in their breaths.

As astonishment rippled across the crowd that he left behind him, Reinhard used that explosive power to rise high into the air.

"Hee-hee-hee! Ahh, how extraordinary!!"

As the Sword Saint shot out a kick at her from below, Sirius crossed her arms to shield against the blow. Her body was easily launched far into the sky above the tower.

"Wh-what in the…?"

—Isn't…isn't this basically aerial combat…?

After taking flight to attack Sirius on the high ground, Reinhard followed up by leaping off the edge of the time tower to pursue his opponent, whom he'd already kicked even higher.

"Hee-hee!! Ahh, what overwhelming power!"

As she watched the hero soar after her from below, Sirius swung her arms as her voice trembled with delight. Hooked chains flew toward Reinhard, slicing through the air with more of a roar than a whistle.

Those razor-sharp hooks could easily punch through the human body, and the sinister chains were no less dangerous, as they could shatter bone on impact. The cacophony of chains rattling seemed to make the very air groan, conducting a symphony of violence and destruction as they snaked toward the Sword Saint.

Sirius exhibited incredible skill as she freely manipulated the flight path of her chains in midair. There was no mistaking that Sirius's mastery was beyond the ability of any ordinary human. One look was all it took for anyone to grasp this.

—That was why what happened next shocked everyone.

"Chains? How troublesome."

The Sword Saint frowned, focusing on the chains that rattled sinisterly as they homed in on him.

Then the spectators were left dumbfounded at how the grimacing Sword Saint dealt with them.

"Hee-hee-hee!!"

Sirius laughed. It was unclear whether the laugh was an expression of enjoyment or desperation.

But for everyone else watching, what could they do but laugh as well?

She slammed her chains down in a hail of blows—but Reinhard did not draw his sword.

According to what Subaru had heard once, it wasn't that he chose to not draw his sword. He simply couldn't. The holy sword that

Reinhard possessed was designed to be impossible to draw except against a worthy opponent.

As such, Reinhard was challenging Sirius unarmed. Even Reinhard should have difficulty fighting her under such circumstances—or so Subaru thought, but that was proof that he didn't truly understand Reinhard yet.

"____"

The raging chains attacked in concert, letting out high-pitched cracks as they were thrown back one after another.

The sight of the resulting shock waves and scattering sparks was such a ferocious display, it made Subaru and the others on the ground feel like lightning was crackling above them.

Reinhard was holding his ground with footwork that surpassed all comprehension.

He met the first strike with the sole of his shoe, purposefully wrapping the oncoming chain around his ankle, instantly gaining control of the hook on the end and using it to knock down each and every subsequent attack.

All that happened in the span of less than a second, meaning the only ones capable of tracking Reinhard's unconventional movements were the few seasoned warriors present. As soon as they realized what they had just witnessed, they would abandon any attempts to understand what was going on.

The audience was suddenly struck with the impulse to laugh. They released the breath they had been holding and let the tension drain from their shoulders. It was good that Reinhard was on their side. If he'd been an enemy, that scene would have left them with buckled knees and weakened bladders.

"Hee-hee, hee-hee-hee! Ah-ha-ha-hee-hee-hee!!"

Seized by a totally different impulse, Sirius kept on laughing.

Of the two sets of chains wrapped around the eccentric's hands, one remained coiled around Reinhard's foot. With her options dwindling, Sirius launched a wild flurry of attacks with her left hand to try and beat the hero down, only for her attacks to fail in a shower of sparks.

The erupting fireworks showed no sign of stopping or slowing. The blue sky seemed to be burning white. But before the air itself was reduced to smoke and ash, the Sword Saint finally closed in on his mysterious attacker.

"To think you would push me this far! Incredible!!"

"You are quite skilled yourself. I can't help but be disappointed all the more seeing you use your talents for wicked deeds."

The instant the two crossed paths, they traded words as well as mighty blows.

Reinhard pulled his right foot back, replacing it with his left hand in a chop. Sirius counterattacked with a downswing that had such force, her golden chain seemed ready to split the sky itself in half.

—Seeing that solid metal chain being severed with a single hand chop was nothing short of astonishing.

A long time ago, Subaru had seen someone use a chopstick to slice a bag of chopsticks as a sort of party trick. If it were Reinhard, he was sure the man could do the same thing to a steel sword like it was made of paper.

Reinhard's hand strike was so sharp and beautiful that Subaru believed that with all his heart.

The twirling golden chain that Reinhard had severed twirled around, breaking through the time tower's wall and whirling somewhere within. It was when Subaru saw smoke and rubble falling down onto the square that he finally came to his senses.

"I'm such an idiot. This isn't the time to gawk. If Reinhard has her pinned down, then…!"

At that very moment, the boy held captive inside the time tower was out of Sirius's sight.

Pulling himself out of his dazed state, Subaru darted through a gap in the crowd and raced toward the time tower. He'd free the hostage—Lusbel—and get rid of his worries in one fell swoop.

He also needed to make sure that Reinhard didn't have to deal with Lusbel being used as a human shield.

Even inside the damp and murky air of the time tower, the battle between superhumans was just as audible inside as it was outside.

Focusing on the task at hand, Subaru dashed up the long, spiraling stairs.

"Lusbel!"

"Ngh! Mnnngh!!"

On the topmost floor, Subaru spotted a young child chained up right beside the inspection window. When Subaru picked up the hysterically sobbing Lusbel, the boy desperately shook his head and struggled.

Subaru knew he'd taken the place of his childhood friend out of concern for her well-being.

"Don't worry, I'm on your side. That bandaged freak is our enemy, and right now, she's got her hands full with a superhero outside. That's why I'm getting you out of here while I can."

Patiently explaining the situation to the writhing boy, Subaru seemed to get through, as Lusbel stopped flailing. When Subaru saw reason rather than fear gradually return to the boy's eyes, he nodded reassuringly.

"You just wait. I'm gonna get those chains off right now."

The still-anxious boy nodded in acknowledgment as Subaru carefully unraveled the chains binding him. When he finally freed him from the chains, which stretched from shoulder to ankle, and removed the one that was serving as a gag, relief finally appeared on Lusbel's face.

"Good, they're off. Can you stand on your own? If not, I'll carry you."

"I-I'm all right... Tha-thank you very much...!"

Rising on trembling legs, Lusbel summoned his courage and thanked Subaru. His face was still marred by tears, but Subaru had seen his bravery several times now. It was worthy of praise.

Nodding in respect, Subaru turned his attention beyond the window to the ferocious battle still raging outside the tower.

"One wrong move, and this whole place might go down. Let's get outta here. You hurt anywhere?"

"Earlier, my left hand got a little..."

Lusbel grimaced as he showed Subaru his injury. The boy's left arm sported a dark bruise and a cruel laceration, like a snake had been wrapped around it. Seeing how the wound seeped with blood, Subaru twisted his face in anguish.

"Did that asshole really have to hurt a little kid like this? Tying one up wasn't enough?"

"No, that's not it. This…started hurting all of a sudden when I was tied up earlier."

"Wait, what?"

Lusbel's words made Subaru furrow his brows.

He recalled that Lusbel's body had been completely ensnared from his shoulders down to his ankles. If the boy's arm hadn't been injured before being tied up, there was no way it could have been injured afterward.

—The contradiction left Subaru's chest throbbing with a deep foreboding.

"…Let's go. Either way, we can't stay here."

Leading Lusbel by his uninjured right hand, Subaru raced back down the spiral stairway of the tower. The two descended down to the lowest floor and proceeded outside.

The instant the two emerged, the scene unfolding in the square before them was—

"_____"

"—Kill! Kill! Kill! Kill!"

There were thunderous calls for murder. The crowd screamed for blood, for the execution of the stranger who was on the ropes.

Their eyes were bloodshot, and their teeth were bared. Their hatred was born from the physiological revulsion that accompanied enmity, and every one of their negative emotions culminated in an all-consuming desire to kill.

—The sum of these phenomena was wrath.

"—Kill! Kill! Kill! Kill!"

Standing shoulder to shoulder with complete strangers, they raised their voices for a single purpose.

"—Kill! Kill! Kill! Kill!"

Before this ordeal, their hearts had coalesced into one, all sense of good and evil superseded by the demands of extraordinary circumstances.

"—Kill! Kill! Kill! Kill!"

This union, this simple honesty, this pure act of will, this was—

"—Kill! Kill! Kill! Kill!"

"—To become one—is that not love? If so, then this is nothing short of a utopia that gives rise to true love!"

In a scene straight out of Hell, Sirius spoke in a voice that was tinged with ecstasy as the crowd continued braying for blood.

With her back against the time tower, the maverick stood on the ground, finally cornered by the hero. The nearby crowd demanded her death, as though their screams would empower the Sword Saint, whom they had entrusted with their bloodthirsty intent.

Sirius had apparently completely lost the chain on her left arm at some point in the time that Subaru had spent in the tower. That meant both fighters were now equally unarmed, but not a single person present thought she could beat Reinhard in a fair fight.

She was clearly in mortal peril—and yet Sirius continued to laugh, her demeanor wholly unchanged.

"Do you have any last words?"

"Thank you for your thoughtfulness, and my apologies. I shall share a warning. The other Archbishops are not as polite as I. Should you ask them for their last words, a terrible fate shall surely befall you."

"—I will take your warning to heart."

In response to Reinhard's charity, Sirius offered a provocative message that seemed to be coming from a place of genuine concern. The Sword Saint dutifully acknowledged her as he raised a flat hand to carry out her execution.

"—Kill! Kill! Kill! Kill!"

The voltage of the audience rose even higher as Sirius's life seemed to be nearing its end.

And yet Subaru, still standing at the entrance of the tower, couldn't ignore the terrible chill stirring in his chest.

He desperately searched for an explanation, a clue of some sort, but he simply couldn't think of the right thing to say. If he opened his mouth now, that incomprehensible misgiving would cause a flood of words to pour out.

"To understand one another. To yield to one another. To accept one another. To forgive one another. To become one like this is the purest form of love."

Heedless of the anxiety gripping Subaru, Sirius opened her mouth to recite her creed.

On the surface, what she said sounded correct, but the instant he thought about Sirius's ways, they mutated into the logic of an abominable heretic. This incorrigible distortion was the Witch Cultists' true nature.

Reinhard seemed to have reached the same conclusion as Subaru.

Deciding there was nothing left to say, Reinhard stepped forward. Sirius simply laughed, stretching her arms toward the sky. The next moment, chains shot out from the sleeves of her robe as if fired out of a cannon—when the chains hidden inside her surged forth, they bit into the walls of the tower as they wrapped around the eccentric's body all at once.

During that shameless attempt to flee, Reinhard closed the distance, effortlessly slipping through the air.

Leaving footprints behind on the paving stones, the red flame chased the fugitive into the sky. His raised, flat hand was an instant-kill weapon equal to a holy sword or a demonic blade—the instant it connected, Sirius's life would be forfeit.

"—Kill! Kill! Kill! Kill!"

The throng's cries would be answered.

Unspeakable terror raced up Subaru's spine with incredible force, a harbinger of something irrevocable.

"Reinhard!!"

Obeying his instinct, Subaru called out the name of the hero.

And then with equal force, he shouted:

"—Kill her!!"

Reinhard's open hand shot forward.

Tracing a white line, he neatly bisected Sirius's body from the left shoulder to the right flank.

The blow was so keen that it took several seconds until the body noticed that it had been split in two. Belatedly, blood gushed from the massive wound as Sirius's severed lower half fell away.

"…Ahh, what a kind world."

Sirius whispered deliriously as she split apart, her innards spilling out.

With chains still wrapped around it, her upper body scattered gore and viscera as it sailed through the sky, while the lower half trailed blood like a gushing fountain as it spun down toward the square.

It was a terrible spectacle that would make most want to avert their eyes. But not a soul in the square did.

They could not.

"…No…"

Turning back, Reinhard stiffened as a word of utter shock trickled out.

His blue eyes swayed with confusion and remorse. Subaru saw the despair spreading across his beautiful face.

And that was the last thing Subaru saw.

"_____"

Subaru and the other spectators had all been cleaved in two, transforming the square into a lake of carnage.

Each of them bore a wound like a filleted fish, all neatly severed from the left shoulder to the right flank.

His blood and organs scattered about, Subaru's mind vanished without any idea of what had just happened.

But in his final moment, he thought he felt something.

The right hand of the boy… The right hand of the boy, who had been severed in half just like Subaru, seemed to faintly grasp Subaru's left hand in search of salvation.

He thought he felt that.

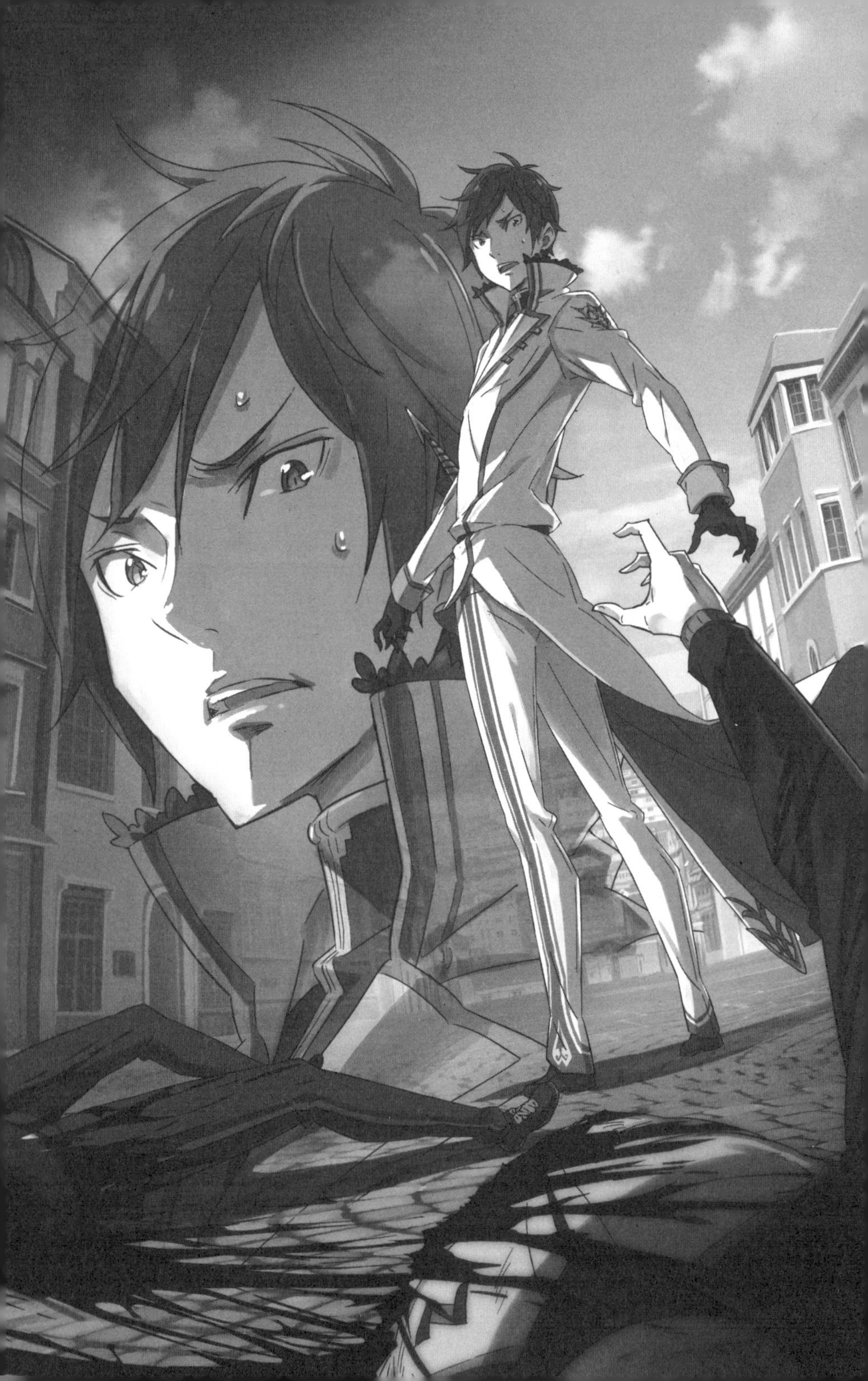

7

"After the song, we'll have a pleasant chat, so could you prepare some snacks, Master Natsuki? Do you not think that sweets will make everyone happy and bring us all closer together?"

"!"

"Oww! Owww! That hurts! That hurts, Subaru!"

A moment after he blinked, a certain voice made Subaru jump in shock.

He had been using every bit of strength he could muster to answer the hand that sought comfort from him—from right before his consciousness had gone out—while squeezing Beatrice's little hand.

Subaru's sudden act of violence made Beatrice kick his shin with tears in her eyes. With that tiny spike of pain bringing him back to his senses, Subaru released Beatrice and stepped back.

"Wh-wh-what is the matter? To suddenly try and break Lady Moppet's hand... What a poor way to treat such a lovely hand. I might even offer to lick it, *hoo-haaah*..."

"Is that not quite unnecessary, I wonder?! Do not suddenly draw so close with such a repulsive demeanor about you!"

When Liliana tried to rub the injured hand against her cheek, Beatrice shook her off and immediately hid behind Subaru. The inexplicable attack on her hand hadn't dented Subaru and Beatrice's bond in the slightest.

Sadly, there was no time to find relief in that happy observation.

"Subaru, are you all right? Your face has suddenly gotten very pale."

"E-Emilia-tan..."

Coming near, Emilia gently touched a hand to Subaru's cheek with a look of distinct concern. Subaru drew a sharp breath when he saw himself reflected in her violet eyes, which were rimmed by long eyelashes.

He'd returned once again.

"_____"

He patted his shoulder and side, checking to see if he was still in one piece.

He'd experienced terrible deaths before, including getting his belly torn open and his head smashed apart, but this was the first time he'd died from a proper slashing. At the instant of his death, a sense of surprise and loss won out over pain.

But that hadn't been the only cause of his enormous sense of loss—

"This is the first…or, actually, the second time I got done in completely due to friendly fire, right?"

As Subaru tried to make sense of the memories he'd returned with, his death demanded his recognition and acknowledgment of what had happened. And this time, when Subaru looked back at what had occurred in his final moments, he was able to grasp exactly what had brought about his demise.

"But that's just broken…"

Subaru's death was identical to how Sirius had died only moments earlier.

They had been killed the exact same way. That incomprehensible fact explained his first death when he watched Lusbel fall to his doom.

When they saw Lusbel plummet to his death, Subaru and the onlookers suffered the same fate all at once. In other words, Sirius's Authority not only created a resonance of emotions but also transferred physical conditions.

"What am I supposed to do…?"

Reinhard joining the fight had certainly fulfilled Subaru's goal of striking down Sirius—at the cost of a great deal of lives in the square, rendering all their efforts meaningless.

Leaving things up to Reinhard had looked like the right choice at first, but knowing what he knew now, it had clearly been a mistake.

"Subaru…"

"Ah."

Emilia and the others looked on in concern as they watched Subaru fall into silence with a difficult expression on his face. For the moment, his priority was to avoid needlessly worrying them further about the Witch Cult being in the city.

With that in mind, Subaru quickly recomposed himself.

"Ah, yeah, uh, it's nothing, really. I'm just a little... Oh, I know! That *daisukiyaki* we had this morning came back with a vengeance, and it's giving me some serious heartburn."

"Ahh, I completely understand that feeling. The same thing happens to me quite a lot. Sometimes, when I mean to burp, I throw up instead, and other times, I pass a little gas the wrong way, and..."

"You don't need to finish that thought. You're technically a young lady, you know? Please never bring that up again."

Stopping Liliana in the middle of what was clearly supposed to be an outrageous joke, Subaru flashed Emilia a smile. For the briefest of moments, that charming smile made Emilia's lips tremble before she replied:

"If you insist, I'll take you at your word, Subaru... But only this time, okay?"

"Yeah, I hear you. Thanks... Anyway, I'm gonna follow Liliana's suggestion and go play errand boy for a bit. You just sit back and enjoy her song, all right, Emilia-tan?"

Appreciative of Emilia's thoughtfulness, Subaru saluted as he played the fool. Then Subaru took Beatrice's hand in a natural fashion while she hid behind him.

"Beako, you're on shopping detail with me. We can be lovey-dovey the whole way there."

"Wh-what are you saying all of a—? Yes, I understand."

Beatrice's face instantly went red as she instinctively got ready to make some retort, but she calmed down immediately instead the moment she saw Subaru's expression. She'd deduced something when she noticed in his gaze the hope that he could rely on her.

"Emilia-tan—I'll be back soon."

"...Mm-hmm."

With Beatrice in tow, Subaru said his farewell to Emilia before setting off from the park.

He was unspeakably worried about leaving her by herself. At the same time, he could no longer think of any other way to break out of the dead end that he found himself trapped in—without borrowing Beatrice's strength.

It was in that darkness with no way out in sight that Subaru ran alongside his partner.

"—Hmph."

Little did he know, a certain red-eyed girl stared intensely after them as they left.

CHAPTER 2
A SHOWDOWN OF FIRE AND ICE

1

"And? Would you finally explain what is going on, I wonder?"

After putting a fair amount of distance between themselves and the park, Beatrice determined that Emilia and the others were no longer within sight or earshot. Only then did she relax her pace and ask him about the situation, their hands still joined.

As Beatrice tried to stop walking to hold a proper conversation, Subaru said "Sorry" as he pulled her along.

"Subaru?"

"If I could, I'd really like to have a nice, long chat about this in a place without anyone around, but there's no time. We don't even have fifteen minutes."

"...Very well. May we at least discuss it while walking, I wonder?"

Seeing the obvious apprehension in Subaru's expression, Beatrice did as he asked without a word of complaint.

Relieved by just how quickly his partner had adapted and adjusted, Subaru hurried over to the square as he tried to explain the jumble of thoughts in his mind.

"Right now, we're heading toward a place where a Witch Cultist is about to show up. We've gotta stop 'em."

"The Witch Cult…"

As Beatrice drew in her breath, Subaru carefully tried to choose his next words.

What made that difficult was the penalty for divulging information related to Return by Death. As long as he only shared the same details that he told Lachins, there shouldn't be any problems. The fact that he didn't know this for certain was one of the things Subaru really hated about the Witch's curse that bound him.

Whenever he tried to share information about Return by Death, evil black hands would come to inflict a penalty—the severity of which seemed to be based not only on the details contained in Subaru's words, but also whom he decided to tell them to.

In other words, the degree of information he could convey depended entirely upon the Witch's whims.

If that wasn't the case, what else could've been responsible for crushing Emilia's heart after he revealed the secret to her? He never, ever wanted to go through that again.

If someone had to get hurt, then better it be Subaru. Of course, the thought of that frightened him, but it wasn't unendurable—and it was far better than watching those terrifying hands turning on someone other than him.

Even if the Witch held back somewhat with Subaru, she showed no mercy to anyone else. That was why he was being incredibly careful.

"—There's no need to make such a worried face."

"Beatrice…"

"You clearly cannot disclose where you came by such timely information…but do I even need to know, I wonder? If Subaru says it is true, that is enough for Betty to believe."

When Beatrice gently squeezed his hand and gave him a bold smile, Subaru's eyes went wide.

"…Damn it, Beatrice. You really are a lifesaver."

The best partner he could ever ask for was supporting his spineless self, assuring him he wasn't alone.

"Heh-heh. Is that not obvious, I wonder? Now, let's start with whatever you *can* share."

"Right. First, the Archbishop of Wrath is gonna show up…and she's a pervert."

"…If you think that is the piece of information you absolutely needed to share first, I suppose I have no choice but to immediately take back what I said earlier."

"I'm still trying to figure out what's safe to tell you. Looks like talking about occupation and perversion doesn't come with a punishment. Well, next is her Authority… It's like…resonance between senses and emotions."

"What does that mean?"

Cocking her head quizzically, Beatrice's eyes made it clear that she didn't understand.

She could hardly be blamed. Despite having actually experienced it, Subaru still found it mind-boggling himself.

"…I can't see what kind of threat a synchronization of senses and emotions might pose."

"Basically, you stop thinking that dangerous things are dangerous. Anyone affected has their emotions go haywire and can't properly judge situations or act… I've had my fill of that one."

He remembered how the crowd had raised both arms high to welcome the screams of a boy who didn't want to die.

From any objective observer's standpoint, that hellish scene must have been utterly revolting. But what was truly terrifying was that everyone there thought they were in some kind of heaven.

"…I suppose I understand the resonance of emotions somewhat. What is this resonance of senses, then?"

"If the other person feels pain, you feel it, too. Cut off the Archbishop's head, and everyone watching will lose their heads, too… Insane, right?"

When he said it aloud, the hopelessness of it left him practically in awe.

Even if they managed to kill their target, they would die, too. Put bluntly, it was hard to think of an ability that was better at making an opponent hesitate. Because of Return by Death, Subaru had a unique chance to discuss countermeasures beforehand, but it was simply unacceptable to take great pains to win the battle only to get dragged down by the vanquished in the end.

"It's pathetic, but I don't have a single card to play. That's why I want to borrow your strength and intellect."

"...Well, of course you do. If anything, isn't relying on Betty the natural thing to do, I wonder?" As she gradually came to grips with the situation, Beatrice assuaged Subaru's concerns.

"I guess you're right… We could also play Reinhard as a wild card, but…"

He revealed to her the possibility that Reinhard might be their one ray of hope.

"…if Reinhard's there, we don't have to worry about him losing to any enemy. But if the Archbishop dies at his hands, the problem is that everyone else is gonna get annihilated because they'll die the same way."

That was exactly how Subaru had lost his life last time.

The possibility of capturing Sirius alive occurred to him, but with no way to convey the finer details of such a plan to Reinhard, Subaru couldn't eliminate the danger of Sirius's resonance kicking in if she was knocked out. If they made even the slightest mistake in neutralizing her, the entire kingdom might very well be destroyed by her sinister "soulwashing" ability.

As Subaru mulled over how to make use of Reinhard, Beatrice raised a tiny hand.

"Subaru, there's something I must tell you. It's bad news."

"…Seriously? I don't really wanna hear any more bad news than I already have if I can help it…"

"I suppose I understand what you mean. Still, I must mention it nonetheless… Should Reinhard and I stand upon the same battlefield, your Betty will likely be reduced to simply being an adorable girl."

"Huh?"

Beatrice's sudden announcement stopped Subaru in his tracks.

"You don't mean that you won't be able to do anything because you'll be too busy swooning at him, right?"

"This is no time for jokes... Is it a physical characteristic of his, I wonder? Reinhard is the epitome of abnormalities in this world. His mere presence causes nearby mana to blindly follow suit. Wouldn't any magic user or spirit caught up in that cease to function normally, I wonder?"

"Wh-what the hell? Is that even...?"

Possible was what Subaru had been about to say when he recalled what had transpired at the Water Raiment the day before.

Right after his first reunion with Reinhard in ages, Beatrice had been particularly wary of him. If that hero really did have such an abnormal constitution, then everything suddenly made sense.

"If it's something Reinhard had any control over, Betty would indulge him and play the adorable little girl. However, if it is not an issue Reinhard can resolve by himself—"

"Then a choice that leaves Beako unable to act ain't much of a choice at all, huh?"

The appearance of a new, immense obstacle shattered one of Subaru's sources of hope.

As usual, Reinhard defied all convention. Unfortunately, that aspect of him was incredibly inconvenient.

"This is bad... Never mind asking him for help. Him showing up would just make things even more difficult..."

It wasn't anyone's fault in particular. The cards in Subaru's hand just happened to be terribly mismatched.

Emilia, Beatrice, Reinhard—any one of them was powerful individually, but if they stood together, their conflicting characteristics and the enemy's Authority would prevent them from acting at full strength.

All his allies were formidable in their own right. It was Subaru's failure and his alone that he couldn't come up with a strategy that let them reach their true potential.

At this rate, he'd end up confronting the eccentric again without so much as a plan—

"—Subaru, just maybe... I suppose I might have an idea."

When Beatrice said that right as they were on the verge of

reaching the square, Subaru felt like those words were sent straight from heaven.

"Really?! You have a plan?!"

"In the end, it is merely a possibility. If the Archbishop's Authority is as you describe, does that not sound very similar to the high-level spell Nekt, I wonder?"

"Nekt! Yeah, now that you mention it, that spell's effect really does resemble Wrath's Authority!"

Seeing Subaru shouting in surprise, Beatrice raised a finger, wagging it as she nodded.

"Ordinarily, I suppose Nekt is a spell for conveying messages between allies without requiring words. To employ it in this manner… It would be the highest of heresies. Is there anything more unforgivable, I wonder?"

Beatrice took great pride in her magic, so it was natural that she was disturbed by the thought of someone misusing it.

Now that she mentioned it, Subaru recalled relying upon Nekt to fight at Julius's side once, though he would've preferred to forget that episode if he could. That was because sharing his vision had been the only way to grant Julius the ability to see Petelgeuse's Unseen Hands.

This was the proper application of Nekt. It was never supposed to be used as a power to bind others like a curse.

"Moreover, Nekt is not magic that works on just anyone. At minimum, I suppose you would need complete harmony between both subjects of the spell. The Archbishop's Authority clearly disregards that requirement."

"It's probably an Authority that forces people to link together. More importantly…"

"You want to know a way to counter it, I suppose? Put simply, this is Shamak's time to shine."

"It's Shamak time! As per usual, it's way more useful than it should be!"

Beatrice's explanation made Subaru unwittingly shout and clench his fist in celebration.

That was how great the existence of the spell called Shamak was to Subaru. In times of suffering, times of bitterness, times of danger, and times of distress—Shamak had been there with Subaru through it all.

Before he'd formed a pact with Beatrice, it was no exaggeration to say that Shamak had lent its strength to the powerless Subaru just as much as Rem and Patlash had.

After Subaru had wrecked his Gate and was unable to use magic on his own, he'd assumed his relationship with Shamak had come to an end—but was Shamak now going to come riding to Subaru's aid once again?

"I see… Shamak, huh…? If we use Shamak, I'm sure it'll manage to come through for us somehow…!"

"Even though it is a beginner-level spell with precious few uses, why do you have such a mysterious level of faith in it, I wonder…?"

"Hold up! I won't let anyone trash-talk Shamak, even if it's you, Beako…!"

"In all seriousness, what happened to make Subaru this obsessed…?"

Sighing deeply, Beatrice thrust the tip of her finger at Subaru's face even as he got all worked up.

"Shamak forcibly prevents the spell's target from sensing the world around them. The strength of the effect scales with the skill of the caster, but for Betty, casting it on anyone is a simple matter."

"Meaning…?"

"I suppose I could put every person within the enemy's range under Shamak's influence. If our opponent compels comprehension and resonance, then Betty simply needs to sow incomprehension and chaos among them."

"Hearing you put it that way makes it sound kind of terrible…but I get what you mean now!"

Subaru slapped his knees, completely convinced by Beatrice's reasoning. Her solution had addressed every single one of Subaru's concerns, and she was proud of herself for suggesting it.

"Okay, let's go! If we can nullify that ability, the battle will swing in our favor. After that… Uh, what comes after?"

"The only remaining task would be vanquishing the Archbishop of the Seven Deadly Sins without Reinhard, no?"

"_____"

The point that Beatrice bluntly raised pressed Subaru into silence.

"Just so you know, Betty will be focused on using Shamak, and it will also be necessary to cast Shamak upon anyone fighting the Archbishop the moment the enemy is defeated. Won't I be too preoccupied to do anything else, I wonder?"

"Damn, okay. Well, this ain't good. We're back where we started."

Having come this far, the initial hurdle had reappeared—Subaru lacked combat strength.

With Beatrice as Subaru's only backup, even if they could block the soulwashing, defeating Sirius on his own was out of the question. It irked him that the whip he'd practiced with so much would be of little use.

"I'll just have to talk to the people in the square when we... Nah, there's no way to know if they'd buy it. I just happen to know his face, so I managed to convince Lachins to hear me out, but..."

There were several people who seemed like capable fighters at the time-tower square. Unfortunately, the real difficulty was persuading them to cooperate.

"In the first place, how do I get them to help when I don't even know what they're capable of? I need to think of something better than that..."

"—If that's the case, since you know what I can do and you can be sure I'll listen to whatever you have to say, maybe it's my time to shine?"

"?!!"

The sound of a voice like a silver bell totally wrecked Subaru's train of thought in the span of an instant.

The all-too-familiar voice made Subaru and Beatrice turn around with looks of surprise. Behind them, a beautiful silver-haired girl was standing there with her hands on her hips.

Her completely unanticipated presence made Subaru draw in a sharp breath, his lips quivering as he raised a question.

"E-Emilia-tan? What are you doing here…?"

"You were acting really strange, so I assumed you were involved in something awful. I think it's a bad habit of yours to keep me out of the loop when things like this come up, Subaru."

Emilia glared at Subaru as she scolded him like he was a naughty child. Subaru was too surprised by her sudden appearance to muster a proper response.

"Didn't you agree to wait in the park? Are you a naughty girl, I wonder?"

Seeing as how Subaru was still in a state of shock, Beatrice answered instead as she peered up at Emilia. Emilia prefaced her reply with a "Sorry" before she continued:

"I really did intend to wait. But then Priscilla said…"

"The girl in red?"

"She said that if I didn't go after Subaru right away, I would regret it. If nothing was wrong, I planned to go right back…but I can't leave now after seeing you two talk so seriously this whole time."

Subaru wanted to curse Priscilla, the culprit who'd gone and pressured Emilia to take action.

She really did like to stir situations up. This was how she complicated things as if she'd planned it all out in advance. Thanks to her, the situation Subaru had wanted to avoid the most had just come together like it was scripted.

"Emilia, I'm happy you feel that way. I really am, but right now…"

"The Witch Cult is going to show up, right? I caught a little part of your conversation… Subaru, I won't go back even if you ask me to. I'm not exactly uninvolved when it comes to dealing with the Witch Cult."

"Emilia!"

Subaru inadvertently raised his voice as he tried to somehow convince Emilia to change her mind.

It wasn't as if Subaru wanted to push Emilia away without good reason. If the opponent wasn't the Witch Cult, he would've immediately asked Emilia for her help.

But given who they were facing this time, that was not an option.

He didn't need logic or reasoning. It was painfully obvious what a terrible idea it would be.

However, Emilia countered Subaru's pleas by drilling into him with her earnest eyes.

"It's no use even if you pretend to be upset. The only time it bothers me when you're angry is when I've done something wrong. It's not me who won't listen to reason right now—it's you, Subaru."

"Argh…"

Seeing those violet eyes staring straight at him made Subaru falter.

On top of that, while Subaru was at a loss for words, Emilia pleaded with him.

"Subaru, I understand that you're doing this to try and protect me. But that just means you'll get hurt again, so I absolutely refuse to turn a blind eye to all this. If you're fighting, then I'm fighting, too. If you're fighting to protect someone, then I'll help, just like you've been protecting me all this time, Subaru…"

"____"

"I want a chance to protect you, too, Subaru. I mean, look. You seem like you might cry at any moment."

He couldn't let his resolve waver, yet Emilia's pleas pushed him to the limit.

Subaru had to summon his own courage to keep her away from danger. He needed a heart of steel that could withstand any and all hardship.

And yet in that moment, Subaru was afraid. He was scared. He was terrified.

Subaru had already lost his life three times in a single hour.

Even Subaru Natsuki had never experienced so much death in such a brief span of time. To begin with, even if he had an eternity, it wouldn't be enough time for him to ever get used to dying.

Death was always frightening. There was no getting used to it, nor could he allow himself to become numb to it.

To be robbed of one's life meant losing a future. It was the denial of one's way of life, trampling on their existence, and a defilement of the soul; that was what being killed meant.

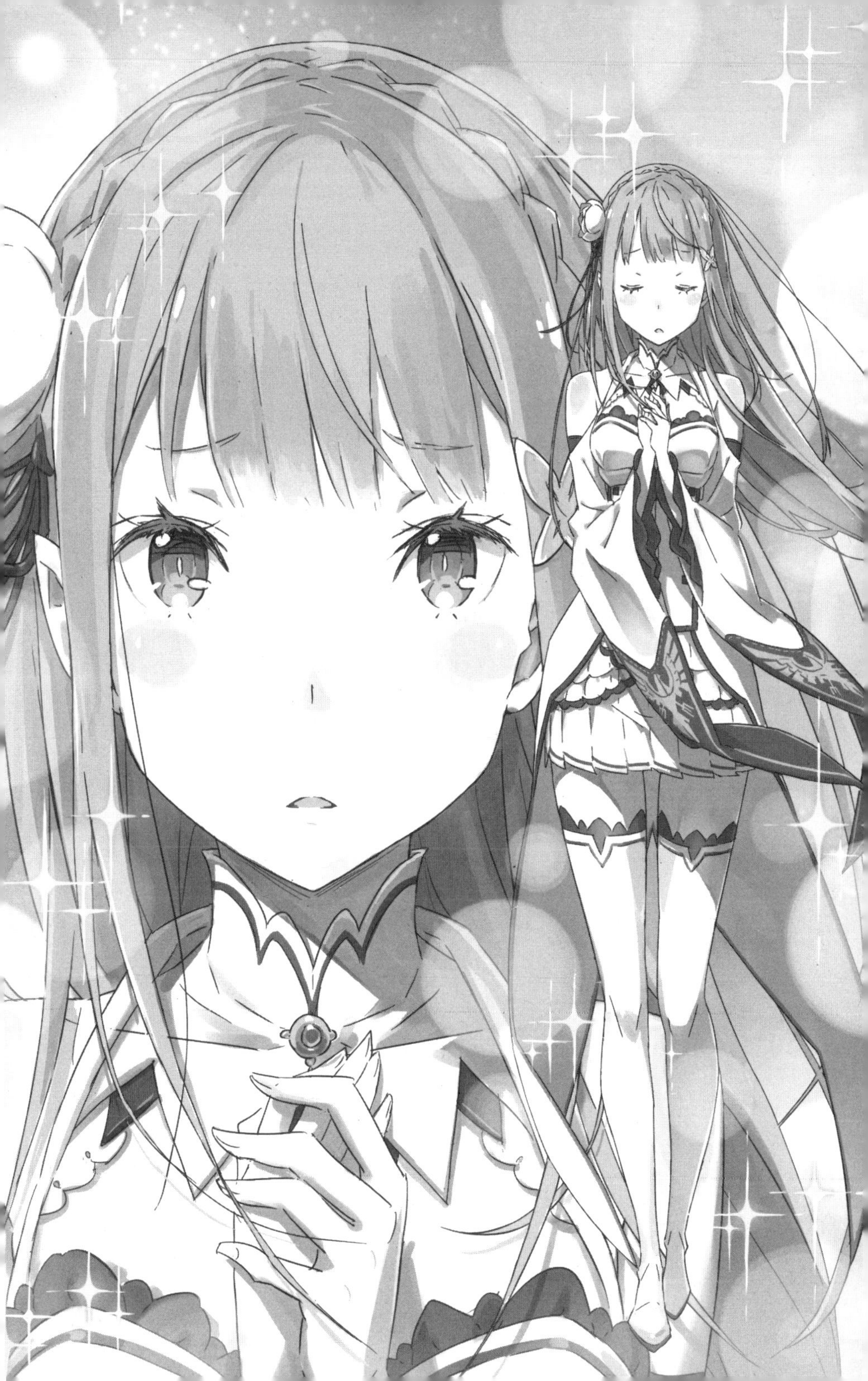

Subaru had suffered that fate over and over again. *I don't wanna die* was the thought that loomed greatest in his mind at any given moment.

No matter how much time passed, Subaru Natsuki was unable to conquer that weakness.

"…Subaru, it's time to give up."

With Subaru unable to mount a sensible rebuttal, Beatrice sighed deeply and spoke for him.

"Beatrice…"

"Don't you know full well how stubborn Emilia can be, I wonder? Now that she's aware, there is little you can do to dissuade her. Besides, I suppose Betty understands how Emilia feels and has no inclination to convince her otherwise."

It wasn't that she couldn't. She simply didn't want to. That was what Beatrice, the crux of the operation, had decided.

Emilia gazed at Subaru earnestly. Beatrice gazed at Subaru affectionately.

Under the pair's gazes, Subaru's heart finally broke.

"…The Witch Cult is probably targeting you. For starters, please put your safety first at all times."

"Mm-hmm, okay. I know that you'll come save me even if I get captured, Subaru."

"Please don't say something so ominous… Also, how much did you overhear?"

A smile of relief came over Emilia as Subaru capitulated to her demands. Her expression immediately sobered when she recalled what a difficult foe awaited them.

"I caught most of it. A bad person from the Witch Cult who uses magic like Nekt is coming. Beatrice is going to use Shamak to counter that, and we have to beat the bad guy in the meantime, right?"

"Breaking everything down like that makes it sound like a Sunday morning cartoon, but I guess that's fine. So I can count on your help?"

"Of course, leave it to me. I've grown lots and lots over the past year, you know."

Putting both fists in front of her, Emilia assumed an adorable fighting stance. She was a little too relaxed, but she had the plan firmly in her mind.

Of course, adding Emilia to the operation didn't alleviate all his worries, but—

"With Emilia-tan and Beako, there's no way we're gonna lose."

Taking uncertainties and problems and turning them into advantages was just how guys like him rolled.

"On that note, we're here. It's time."

Between Beatrice's planning session and an unexpected rendezvous with Emilia, they arrived at the time-tower square right before the mysterious interloper was set to appear. The only thing that remained was deciding where to start the operation.

To rescue Lusbel from inside the tower, drawing Sirius away from it would be ideal.

"Emilia-tan, that weirdo's gonna pop out at the top of the tower anytime now. When she does, launch a preemptive strike with one big shot, would you? It'd be great if you could knock her off it. After that, assuming Beako can get set up, I want you to start combat on my signal. I'll be providing support."

"Yeah, leave it to me. I'll do everything I can."

Emilia nodded, acknowledging Subaru's instructions. Counting Beatrice, the three-person operation was ready to go.

Then right after their plans had been set—

"—She's here!"

—the sight of a dark figure leaning out from the time tower's window made Subaru unwittingly tense up.

A slender form wrapped in a black robe swayed at the tower's edge. Beneath her, no one else in the square seemed to notice that someone was looking down on them from that vantage point.

When seen from a bird's-eye view, it was immediately obvious how fragile the tranquility of a thin layer of ice truly was. With a single action, the stranger peering down from that lofty perch thoroughly shattered the delicate peace.

"————"

Slowly, Sirius spread both arms wide. Though her bandages covered up most of her form, the ecstasy on her face was immediately apparent even at a distance. Finally, just as she was about to bring her two hands together with incredible force—

"—*Ul Hyuma!!*"

—Instantly, a giant icicle appeared directly above the tower and collided with Sirius.

A projectile of ice as thick as five Subarus tied together slammed into the tower. The sturdy wall immediately gave way as the icicle's tip impaled the upper structure of the tower.

The spectacle nearly made Subaru drop his jaw.

"E-Emilia-tan?"

"You said to launch a preemptive strike, so I tried my best… Did I mess up?"

"No, no, good job. You did well… I was just surprised that it was more preemptive than I expected."

It was Subaru's fault for not giving more precise instructions about the timing, but it was the eccentric's fault for being so unguarded that Emilia didn't even hesitate in her initial attack. That took care of their first problem, at least.

Their initial strike had been launched without sparing even a single thought to waiting and seeing what would happen. That was the kind of shock and awe that was needed to score a surprise victory.

"Beako, think we got her?"

"For the moment, I believe the people around us think we did."

When Subaru posed his question, Beatrice also displayed signs of surprise in her reply. Lowering his gaze to see for himself, Subaru concurred with what Beatrice had said.

The people in the square ahead of them were all looking at Subaru and company—or strictly speaking, at Emilia after she'd suddenly committed that act of mass destruction. As far as they were concerned, it was Subaru and the girls who were the real terrorists.

He could claim *This was preemptive attack to prevent actual terrorism* all he wanted, but whether the crowd would believe him was anyone's guess.

"Errr, we didn't mean any harm. See, we're…"

"—It's no use, Subaru. Get back behind me."

Subaru tried to persuade the pedestrians with all the sincerity he could muster, but Emilia pulled him back by his shoulder. Then after she took a step forward to shield him, she raised her right hand and swung it in a downward arc.

Instantly, a *crack* echoed in the air as a blue sword formed within Emilia's hand. It was a beautifully sculpted sword, boasting a slender, icy blade. Emilia trained its tip toward the crowd in the square without any hesitation.

"Whoa, whoa, that's definitely too much! If we talk to them, I'm sure they'll understa…"

"You're wrong. Look closer, Subaru. Their eyes—they aren't sane."

"What?"

Gasping in response to Emilia's tense observation, Subaru studied the various people in the square. After a brief examination, Subaru noticed it, too. This was definitely not normal.

Bulging veins marred the faces of everyone glaring at Subaru's party, and their bloodshot eyes gleamed red, not white. Every last one of them wore the exact same expression.

Their cheeks were twisted, teeth bared like fangs as growls rose from their throats—these were the products of nigh-unendurable emotions of wrath.

"Beako! Is Shamak ready yet?!"

Facing a frothing mob to the front, Subaru called out to Beatrice. However, the girl who was the linchpin of their plan ruefully bit her lip at the sight of the throng.

"…I've made a mistake."

"What?"

"This blasphemy is fundamentally different from Nekt! This is closer to a curse or a hex than any proper magic. I suppose you could call it manipulation of souls themselves! This is not something a mere Shamak can deal with!"

Beatrice's voice trembled with anger and distress. Hearing that, Subaru gritted his teeth.

He didn't understand the principles at work in detail, but it was enough to know that Beatrice had judged that Operation Shamak could not be salvaged.

And the fact that the people in the square were being consumed by a tremendous wave of emotion far beyond the norm meant that—

"—It reeks."

He heard a single word trickle out in a muted voice, like someone was casting a curse.

It was a vicious word that seemed to resent all existence.

"It reeks. It reeks. It reeks. It reeks. It reeks. It reeks. It reeks. Itreeksreeksreeksreeksreeksreeksreeksreeksreeksreeksreeksreeksreeksreeksreeksreeksreeksreeksreeksreeksreeksreeksreeksreeksreeksreeksreeksreeksreeksreeksreeksreeks! It reeks! It reeks, it reeks, it reeks!!!"

A moment later, cracks ran along the icicle that had slammed into the upper portions of the time tower and impaled itself in the wall. In the span of a single breath, new fissures ran along the entirety of the mass of ice; an instant later, the icicle shattered into glimmering fragments.

Standing among that dazzling diamond dust, which scattered under the rays of the sun, a single eccentric stood.

She was not unscathed. Half of her white bandages were soaked with blood, and the tower's white wall was marred by the ichor dripping from her dangling left arm. As she stepped clear of the fallen rubble, her gait seemed unsteady.

However, the insanity and ferocious emotions residing in the madwoman's eye was nothing like what Subaru had known until then.

"It reeks...horribly... The stench of a woman. The filthy, abominable, awful stench of the half-demon that stole my precious from me. Even though you are not my precious, your fetid odor bears a remarkable resemblance. Aaaah, how dreadful!!"

On the scant remains of the tower's top floor, Sirius clawed at her bloody bandages. He'd never seen her spit blood and send spittle flying as she shouted in pure hatred.

Even if she was just as insane as before, her madness was taking a very different form.

"Have you come to test my love, spirit?! Are you not satisfied with stealing my precious from me, filthy half-demon?!!"

Spreading both arms wide in anger, Sirius screamed and lunged forward.

As she hurtled from the top of the tower down toward the ground, the madwoman spouted flames from both hands as she raised them overhead. The crimson fire enveloped the chains around her hands, tracing a flaming trail behind her as Sirius landed in the square.

Landing on all fours, both of her hands still burning, she lifted her face.

She trained her eye upon Emilia, who held her ice sword at the ready, and Subaru, who was standing stiff— No, she was actually focused on Beatrice, who was standing out front as if to shield Subaru.

The next instant, Sirius shouted in a voice drenched in enough rage to burn the entire world to ashes.

"I am! A member of the Witch Cult! The Archbishop of Wrath!"

Bathed in the waves of heat emanating from those rising flames, the crowd in the square raised shrill voices, and all of them lifted their arms high.

The waves of insanity and flames were completely at odds with Subaru's memories, and within that maelstrom, the madwoman introduced herself.

"—I am Sirius Romanée-Conti!! Shitty half-demon and shitty spirit, I will burn you both to ash, then scatter your remains before the grave of the husband you burned!!!"

2

With crimson flames residing in both hands, Sirius bellowed in rage, her face as fiendish as an ogre's.

She was enveloped by her own dazzling inferno, and the zeal in her eyes burned just as bright. The avatar of Wrath glared at Subaru's party— No, that wasn't accurate. After all—

"It reeks, reeksreeksreeksreeksreeksreeks—you reek, you shitty half-demon...!"

—as Sirius hurled more insults, Subaru's existence didn't even register within her eye.

Sirius's undivided gaze, one that seemed capable of searing someone to death with looks alone, was aimed at none other than Emilia and Beatrice, the two girls standing at Subaru's side.

"The hell's wrong with her? This is totally different from what she looked like every other time..."

Subaru could not hide his uneasiness at seeing Sirius's wrathful transformation and where her hatred was directed.

In a very short span of time, Subaru had confronted Sirius on three occasions, and during each encounter, she had been—though he hesitated to use the word—normal. In those fleeting meetings, even if it was extremely difficult to call her a person who possessed common sense, she had also never acted like a creature that had abandoned all reason.

She'd been logical to the end, a morally bankrupt person trying to impose her pet theories on ordinary folk who failed to understand her vision, and that was it.

The version of Sirius before his eyes now stood in stark contrast—this was Wrath incarnate.

"I burn you and burn you, and still, you keep crawling out like maggots... You must hold some grudge against me, eh?! I am sad and depressed, yet I cannot be allowed to even grieve! Just how much...how much will you take...?!"

"...I don't have any idea what you're trying to say."

When Sirius began sending spittle flying with every word, offering nothing but blame and accusations, Emilia didn't give any ground as she replied. She didn't flinch or pull back a single step from the fiery verbal assault.

She steadily trained the sword of ice in her hand on the crowd lined up behind Sirius.

"If you're angry about something, I'll hear you out. I'm the one

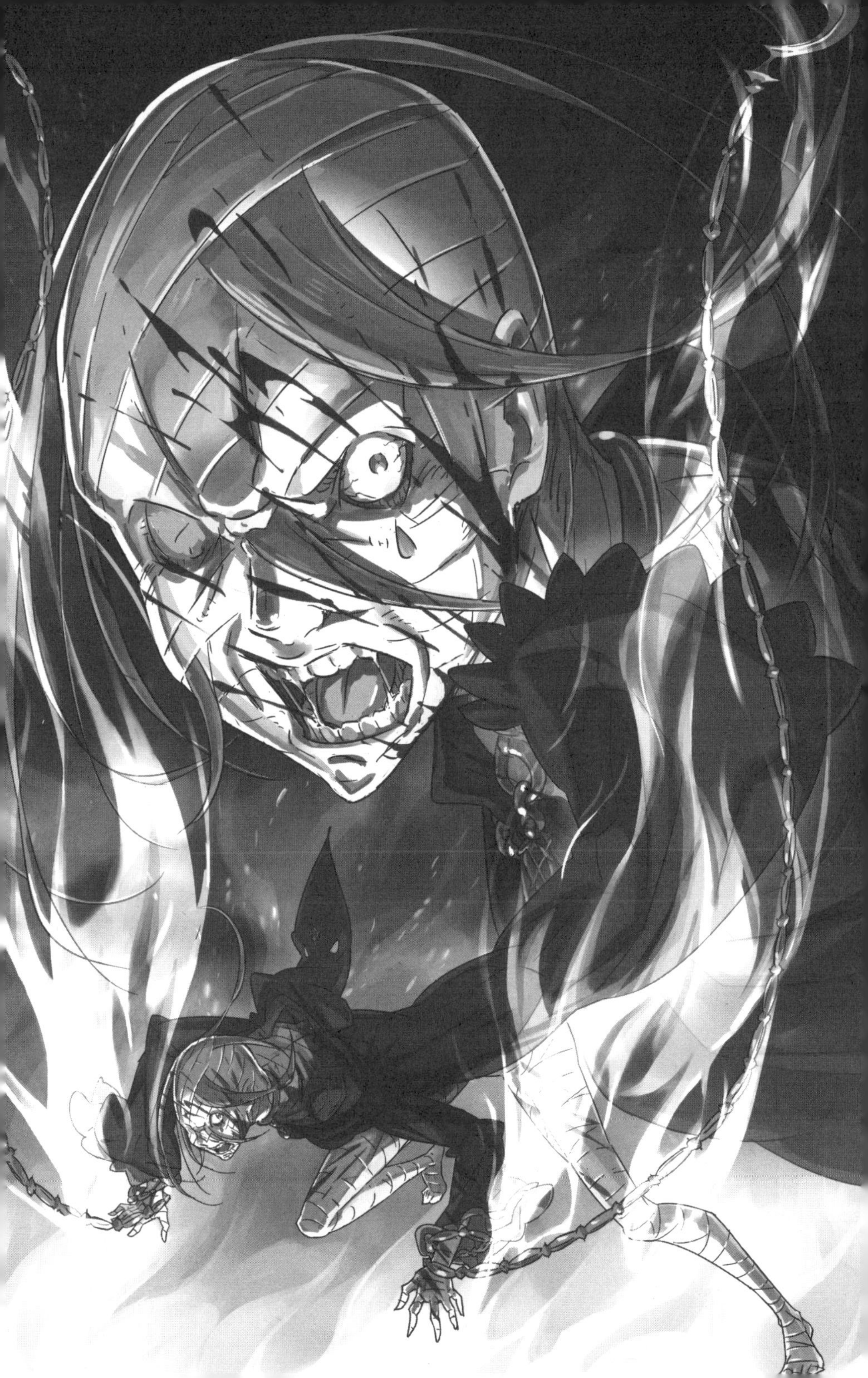

who attacked you all of a sudden, so it's natural for you to be angry. But this has nothing to do with the people around us. Let them go."

"Don't look down on me from your high horse! If you wish for me to yield, then show it through your actions! It's only natural to be angry? Then apologize! Grovel and beg for forgiveness! And then I'll roast you from your ass to your bowels!!"

"Hmm. Words don't seem to be getting through— In that case, I have ideas of my own!"

Enraged, Sirius blinked hard at Emilia's casual change of tone during their brief exchange.

A moment later, Emilia leaped up from the ground, going from a low stance to lunge at Sirius. Emilia's slender body cut through the air as she swung the sword of ice with her arm, tracing a beautiful arc toward the top of the madwoman's shoulder.

"Emilia?!"

"—Tch!!"

Subaru's shout of surprise overlapped with Sirius's sound of irritation.

Seeing the icy blade approaching her left shoulder, Sirius instantly raised her left arm in an attempt to counter Emilia's blow with blazing flames. However—

"You shitty half-demon!!"

"Don't repeat that insult over and over. People will think I'm dirty or something."

—the pale tip of Emilia's blade did not lose to the flames as it collided with Sirius's raised left arm. However, the coiled golden chains enveloped in wreaths of fire gave off a high-pitched creaking sound as the ice sword crashed against Sirius's flaming limb.

But fire and ice battled for only one brief instant. A second later, Emilia's weapon audibly shattered.

"Serves you right!"

Leaving only its hilt behind, the magic blade reverted to mana. Sirius raised a cry of victory and swung her flaming right arm at Emilia. It was a brutal attack with enough force to split stone walls.

The moment it made contact, it would burn and gouge its target, leaving terrible wounds.

In the blink of an eye, Emilia's unmatched beauty would be scarred forever—but something else happened first.

"Take that!"

With a voice profoundly out of place, she knocked away Sirius's arm this time—thanks to what had once been Emilia's ice sword.

"Aah, aaah, aaaaaah! How frustrating!"

Screaming, Sirius crossed both flaming arms above her head. Up above, Emilia was swinging her summoned hammer of ice downward with unspeakable force.

She'd produced a maul of ice with a broad, blunt face to replace her broken sword. Sirius flew from that heavy, crushing blow, only for Emilia to give chase.

"Yah! Hiyah! Yah! Take that! Uraaah! Hiyah!"

"You piece of shit! Half-demon! Maggot! Insect! Whore! Disgusting eyesore!"

With extraordinary body movements and her weapon's centrifugal force, Emilia was displaying far greater close-combat capability than Subaru had ever expected. The swings of the icy maul were weighty, keeping Sirius on the defense. It was a one-sided battle after Emilia completely seized the initiative. Thinking that she might prevail at this rate, Subaru clenched a fist hard.

"We can win this… Wait, right now, that's bad! Emilia! The people in the square are still…"

"Subaru, is it not a bad idea to let your guard down now of all times, I wonder?!"

If Emilia struck Sirius down, the people around them would share the same fate right then and there.

When Subaru tried to point out that danger, Beatrice's expression changed as she scolded him. Wondering what was wrong, Subaru looked back, only then realizing that countless gazes were turned toward him.

"““““"—You shitty insect!!"”””””"

"Aw, crap."

The crowd shouted as they looked at Subaru as one, rage and vilification pouring from their bloodshot eyes. The madness they trained upon Subaru and Beatrice was identical to Sirius's.

It was best to assume they'd been completely soulwashed by Sirius's Authority. Then in accordance with their irrepressible rage, they shifted their hostility toward Subaru and Beatrice.

"So it's not just resonance—she can brainwash people and make them into her own pawns?!"

"This is not the time for such musings. Without a plan, I suppose all we can do is buy some time!"

As Subaru clutched his head over how difficult this situation was, Beatrice jumped onto his back. He supported her light body with his hands as the throng came rushing at them all at once.

"Emilia, buy us some time, please!"

"Don't expect me to do anything too crazy!"

Upon hearing Emilia's dependable reply, Subaru sprang backward to escape from the mob. Fortunately, the movements of people who had lost their sanity were as slow and clumsy as a poorly controlled marionette.

"Whoa! Wow! Cutting through, here! That was close! But now we're all clear!"

Dodging the outstretched arms, Subaru evaded with sideways leaps to keep the throng at bay. The sight of a crowd rushing with empty expressions made it look like a scene straight out of a zombie movie. A similar feeling of terror had soaked into his bones.

"Just running ain't gonna cut it! At this rate, all we can do is wait for reinforcements once people notice the huge commotion!"

"Without a plan to deal with the opponent's power, wouldn't reinforcements only increase the casualties, I wonder? If we inadvertently cause Reinhard to come running, all that will do is turn Betty into a mere adorable little girl."

"Then I'll really become the Moppet Mage… For the moment, no worries about summoning that hero right this moment."

After all, Lachins, the one who would be their best option for sending Reinhard a signal, was currently chasing Subaru, raving at him with a bright-red face. Carried by the rest of the crowd, he looked like he was on the brink of a clash with one or two of his impromptu companions.

When Lachins eventually pushed them back, his fellows immediately tripped over their own legs, causing them to tumble downward. Caring nothing for them, the rest of the crowd walked right over the two fallen while moving inexorably forward. It was a frightening sight.

"I don't think they're feeling pain from all that adrenaline, but it'd be pretty dangerous without that, right?"

"Given the way they are, it doesn't seem strange for them to trample one another to death."

"Well, that's not good!"

Subaru didn't want any casualties. That was the biggest objective he was fighting for so hard.

Of course, Subaru understood that there were things beyond his own reach. Indeed, there were far more people whom Subaru *couldn't* reach.

There were so many things he wanted to protect. But there was a limit to what he could do.

"—Still, I don't have any intention of deciding that limit myself!"

"There's the Subaru that Betty knows best!"

Receiving the greatest encouragement possible from behind, Subaru drew his whip from his hip holster.

He had to save what lives he could. Accordingly, Subaru emotionally resigned himself to inflicting moderate amounts of damage. Charging toward the center of the throng, he locked onto Lachins, running at the head of the crowd.

His target was someone whose face he knew. He couldn't call their relationship a good one, but Subaru's heart struggled with the idea of harming him all the same.

"This is gonna hurt, but better than if it's someone I don't know! Sorry, Larry!"

"Who's Larry?! I'm... Habhhh?!"

As Lachins shouted on reflex, Subaru unfurled his whip, wrapping it around his victim's ankles. Subaru proceeded to yank the whip upward as hard as he could, dragging Lachins, who'd lost his balance, into the people surrounding him.

"Take a time-out and cool your heads!"

Charging toward him, Subaru rammed Lachins in the back, knocking him into the waterway. While Lachins raised a cry, Subaru kicked several others who were tottering down to join Lachins, removing more and more people from the front lines.

"Now that that's taken care of... Lusbel!"

As he whittled down the number of pursuers coming after them, Subaru raced all the way to the time tower. His objective was to secure Lusbel, who was surely still there on the topmost floor—where Sirius had left him, intending to use him in her speech.

"Beako, hang on tight!"

Subaru called out to Beatrice, who was on his back, as the crowd blocked the way before him. Their arms and bodies mercilessly barred the way, but Subaru did not hesitate as he charged into their ranks once more.

"Now I'll show you the improvised parkour that my mentor pounded into me!"

As he shouted, Subaru quite literally slipped past countless legs and bodies as he broke through.

These were the fruits of his daily training at the secret base in the forest. The skills that Clind had drilled into him greatly resembled the style of movement that Subaru knew from his world as parkour. Making use of his entire body, he stayed nimble and flexible to skillfully navigate the crowd, cutting right through it.

Still supporting Beatrice on his back, Subaru tumbled his way into the time tower with amazing vigor.

"I bit my tongue!"

"Sorry about that! But saving the hostage up top comes first!"

After answering his partner's objection, Subaru raced up the spiraling stairs with great haste. The remaining members of the crowd pursued from behind, but all their jostling was preventing them from climbing the stairs easily.

Seizing the opportunity, Subaru and Beatrice stayed ahead of the pack until they finally reached the topmost floor. When he looked around, he saw that because Emilia's initial blow had half-destroyed the place, the wind could now pass through, making the air quality far better than it was in Subaru's memories.

For an instant, his blood ran cold as he considered the possibility that even Lusbel had been blasted to bits, but—

"Nngh! Nnngh!"

—the boy bound by chains was there in a space that had narrowly managed to maintain its original shape. Though it was probably a stretch to say he was safe, Subaru raced over after confirming the boy was alive and in one piece.

With Lusbel's bindings already complete, Subaru undid the painful-looking gag and tried to choose the best words to put him at ease.

"—Behind you!"

"Bwah?!" "Gah, I wonder?!"

Lusbel's teary-eyed warning made Subaru immediately lower his head, taking Beatrice along for the ride. Instantly, he felt the familiar presence of death whistle by his neck as something passed by.

When he looked back, he saw a fox-man who'd leaped onto the uppermost floor to unleash a massive sword strike. The man was one of the people initially at the square who seemed capable of fighting. His white tail swayed as he launched another attack.

"Beako!" "*Shamak!!*"

Giving up on challenging such skill head-on, Beatrice instantly activated a spell that quickly enveloped the fox-man in black mist. The beast person lost all fighting capability while lost in the void—proof that Shamak was effective.

"That's the all-powerful Shamak for you! Doesn't this mean the link to Sirius got cut?!"

"Who said anything about that, I wonder?! Even if he really is neutralized, the link is still active! I suppose it's likely that if that degenerate dies, many others will follow suit!"

"Shiiit, what do we do?"

"I'm thinking as hard as I can!"

Leaving the unraveling of the mystery to Beatrice, Subaru could only trust in her and buy some time.

The problem was how Emilia was shaping up against the real enemy.

"Emilia is…"

Hoisting Lusbel up, Subaru climbed over the wrecked windowsill and raced to the tower's exterior. Beneath him, fire and ice met each other in a furious exchange as Emilia and Sirius remained locked in combat.

Subaru knew that over the last year, Emilia had continually trained herself in between her lessons about governance. Subaru knew very well that Emilia was far stronger than he.

Even so, Subaru was worried for her. It wasn't an issue of who was stronger. To Subaru, Emilia was the girl he loved. That was the long and short of it.

People might call such worries a trifling matter. But to him, that—

"Terya! Soya! Soooi!"

Raising shouts that, as usual, somehow came off as silly, Emilia looked like she was a raging gale as she hounded Sirius with ruthless ice attacks.

"Eeeiiiyah!"

Spinning her body, Emilia danced as she closed in with twin swords of ice. Sirius swung burning golden chains about, shouting insults as she intercepted the blades, only for Emilia to crouch down as she spawned a new spear of ice, which she immediately used to swipe at Sirius's chest.

With a painful cry, the force and impact hurled Sirius across the paving stones, leaving her rolling to a stop on the ground.

—Emilia was making full use of her vast mana capacity, launching high-speed combo attacks, fully intending to destroy her ice weapons in the process.

When she used the martial art that Subaru had dubbed "Icebrand

Arts," the fleeting nature of shattering ice engendered such phantasmal beauty, it was like watching the dance of a fairy.

The remnants of ice that were smashed during the battle danced and scattered as glittering mana set the stage for the pair. Emilia and Sirius—fire and ice—employed contrasting weapons as they continued to pursue their deadly duel.

"Uyaaa!"

Pursuing Sirius as the woman rolled, Emilia twirled her icy spear around, lashing out with its haft. Down below, Sirius used crafty groundwork to evade the butt of the spear, then grabbed hold of it herself.

"It is seething zeal that makes the heart tremble! Aa! Aah! Aaah! Wraaaath!"

"Wha?!"

In an instant, the spear of ice transformed into a spear of flame in Sirius's hands. When the heat made Emilia unwittingly let go, it was Sirius's turn to go on the offensive this time.

The bandaged madwoman twirled the spear of flame, pursuing the leaping silver-haired girl to burn her to death in an aggressive counterattack.

"Those lascivious eyes! That seductive bell-like voice! That licentious, glimmering silver hair! That indecent white skin! That indecent face! Aah, what a filthy woman! Is that how you make men swoon over you so?! Is that how you stole my precious from me, you thieving cat?!"

"Wha?! Wait a— Please do not say such strange things!!"

Dodging the attack by letting it slide just past her chest, Emilia spawned another ice sword in her hand to intercept it. The three-pronged spear of flame was blocked head-on by a broad greatsword made of ice.

The ice creaked as it held against the hungry flame, leaving Emilia and Sirius deadlocked as they glared at each other.

"These eyes, this voice, this silver hair—all of them were praised by the people I love! They're the same as the coolest woman in the whole world! If you say any more strange things about them, I'm going to be angry!"

"Anger?! Anger, you say?! Don't make me laugh! That is mine! That is the treasure that I received from my most precious person! This duty, this name—everything I have was a gift from my precious! To try to take this from me... Stop! Stopstopstopstopstopstopstop!!!"

Sirius's voice gradually became even more piercing still, eventually rising to a tearful shriek.

The spear of flame in the madwoman's arms snapped, at which point she crossed her arms, slamming the shortened pieces together with both arms. To counter the flaming-sword combo, Emilia split her own greatsword in two, turning them into a pair of ice daggers.

But under that torrent of blows, it was Emilia who was on the defensive this time. It wasn't because Sirius had become noticeably stronger. It was the opposite— Doubt had crept into Emilia's heart.

Rage readily mixed with grief, and the surrounding people in the crowd moaned in agony as they cried tears of blood. That sight in the corner of Emilia's vision threw her thoughts off slightly. It was then that—

"—Wah, aaaah?!"

"Emilia?!"

Subaru's eyes went wide at the sight of Emilia raising a shriek and dropping her twin daggers of ice. When Emilia fell on her knees to the pavement stones, Sirius laughed loudly with both blazing arms raised high.

"Look! This is love! This is love! People loving one another, the ideal of the many becoming one! Bonds are forged by our shared feelings, so that we might experience one another's joy and sadness! That is why this ending has been preordained! O pitiful half-demon, doomed to never obtain love—here, you shall burn!"

"...What love?"

"What?"

As Sirius crowed over the turning of the tables, Emilia's words brought her pealing laughter to a halt.

Before the madwoman's fixated, wide-open eyes, Emilia looked squarely at her opponent's face and continued without fear.

"If I am hearing your words correctly, you seem to think I am mistaken... Why?"

The question that Emilia posed was born from her particularly acute sense of curiosity. But such an earnest plea only poured more fuel on the fires of Sirius's wrath.

"That is because you do not even know the great truth! You filthy half-demon, living without even knowing what love is. And so you must perish! The very existence of a half-demon is a sin! Your birth was a mistake. It was a mistake for your father to meet your mother! When shit and an insect come together, a shitty insect is the only possible result. Your shit-smeared tale will now come to an end!"

"!"

These were insults that even the kindhearted Emilia refused to pass unchallenged. It was absolute slander, condemning not only her existence, but even her parents for giving birth to her.

"Ooh..."

A trail of light drew a tiny voice out of Sirius as she backed up a step.

Emilia had held her ice sword down low and slashed upward. The pale sword grazed Sirius, sending the fasteners of the madwoman's black robe flying.

One more step forward, one lunge, and Emilia would land a clean hit. It was with this certainty that she raised her ice sword anew.

"—Eh?"

"Nnngh!"

—Then she saw the girl wrapped up in chains within Sirius's arms, and time stopped.

"—Tina."

Dazed, Subaru heard that murmur spill from Lusbel, who was still in his arms, and Subaru cursed Sirius for keeping the most sinister form of insurance on hand.

Matching the instant of Emilia's sword attack, Sirius had suddenly yanked a chain out of thin air. Materializing from seemingly nowhere, a lone girl appeared right in Sirius's arms as her evil gambit succeeded.

The golden chains that were coiled around the girl were the same as those that Subaru had seen wrapped around Lusbel inside the tower, and a flood of tears flowed from Lusbel's eyes—the hostage was Tina, the very same childhood friend whom Lusbel had supposedly been protecting.

Right as Subaru realized the new hostage's identity, anger consumed Emilia as she laid eyes on the crying girl.

"—That wrath is wasted on you."

That was the moment Sirius smiled more wickedly than ever before. She then slammed her right arm against the ground, generating a blast of wind that sent Emilia flying backward.

The resulting shockwave kicked up black dust over the center of the square. Emilia rolled onto the paving stones, unable to break her fall. She came to a rest faceup on the ground with her limbs spread out.

"Ah..."

Emilia squirmed about a little, but she only stirred to cough painfully, barely able to breathe.

Seeing this, Sirius let Tina drop and roll at her feet as she raised both arms to the heavens. At that moment, the intensity of the flames enveloping them made them burn so bright, they seemed ready to split the entire sky asunder.

And with flames still entwining her arms, Sirius boisterously applauded Emilia.

"Such sweet passions are not for insects to embrace. Seeing that is just nauseating— Now then, let me say thank you, and sorry."

Crossing both arms above her head, Sirius increased the potency of the inferno enveloping her.

"Emilia——!"

That instant, realizing that he needed to save Emilia, Subaru leaped down from the top of the tower without hesitation. Trusting Beatrice to soften their landing, he focused only on getting to Emilia as fast as he could.

With Beatrice's magic reducing his body weight to nothing, Subaru safely slowed as he approached the ground. He got ready to charge forward. Or at least, he tried.

"Move, legs, move!!"

Subaru's limbs rattled and trembled, immobilized as if cowering in fear. The same went for Beatrice on his back and Lusbel in his arms. They couldn't stop shaking with fright.

The emotions probably came from Tina, who had fallen at Sirius's feet, spreading from her to them. As she shrank from unprecedented fear, their hearts became one, leaving Subaru and Beatrice unable to shake off the waves of terror.

"...E...milia...!"

With his throat convulsing, his uncontrollable sobbing and nausea left him unable to even shout the name of the girl he loved.

Subaru's voice likely would not have reached Emilia either way.

What was Emilia thinking as she lay there, powerless before the approaching apocalyptic firestorm?

—This, too, would vanish in the hot white of the inferno burning everything to ash, remaining unknown for all eternity.

"_____"

The square was scorched by an incredible amount of heat. The heat wave seared skin and lungs alike.

The spectacle of flame was so awe-inspiring that it could only be considered a true enigma.

"Suba...ru..."

As Subaru fell to his knees before the sea of flames, Beatrice called out to him from somewhere behind him.

Subaru didn't look back. He was still bent forward, every inch of his entire body ruled by fear. He had become desperate even as he denied the reality unfolding before his eyes.

Compared with the desolate alternative, he saw fear as salvation. If he didn't have to sear into his own eyes the worst of all worlds that had ever come about, then it would be better to simply stay there, ruled by fear foreve—

"Suba-Subaru! Subaru!"

Even so, Beatrice continued calling out Subaru's name with even greater urgency.

She smacked his head multiple times, but Subaru shook his head side to side. He couldn't stand. He had no reason to stand.

…Even if, at that moment, the madwoman stood directly before Subaru's eyes, ready to take his life.

"—I made it in time."

The instant he heard that voice, Subaru's heart gave in to his fear of not knowing.

He lifted his head, turning his eyes toward where the flame had fallen onto Emilia and wondering what had happened.

—There was a single man.

Calmly standing on the paving stones, which spewed black smoke, he acted as if nothing was out of the ordinary. And in his arms, the man carried the girl whom Subaru had presumed lost, the girl whom he was sure had vanished.

"Emi…lia…"

The girl whom he had despaired over, the girl enveloped by the flames that he had failed to save her from—she was still there.

Eyes closed, she had gone limp—unconscious. However, her chest rose and fell almost imperceptibly—an unmistakable sign of life. She was not dead. Emilia was alive.

"You're…"

He was now looking at the person who had suddenly appeared to save Emilia from mortal peril.

Subaru was glad to see that Emilia was safe, but even then, the fear tormenting his heart had not subsided as he called out to the man's back with a trembling voice.

In response, the man slowly turned around. He relaxed his lips.

"I have come for her. I am relieved I arrived in time. Truly."

"Come for… What do you…?"

"—I have come to collect my bride. Is that not what one should do as a man—nay, as a person?"

Those unexpected words, spoken as if they were the most natural

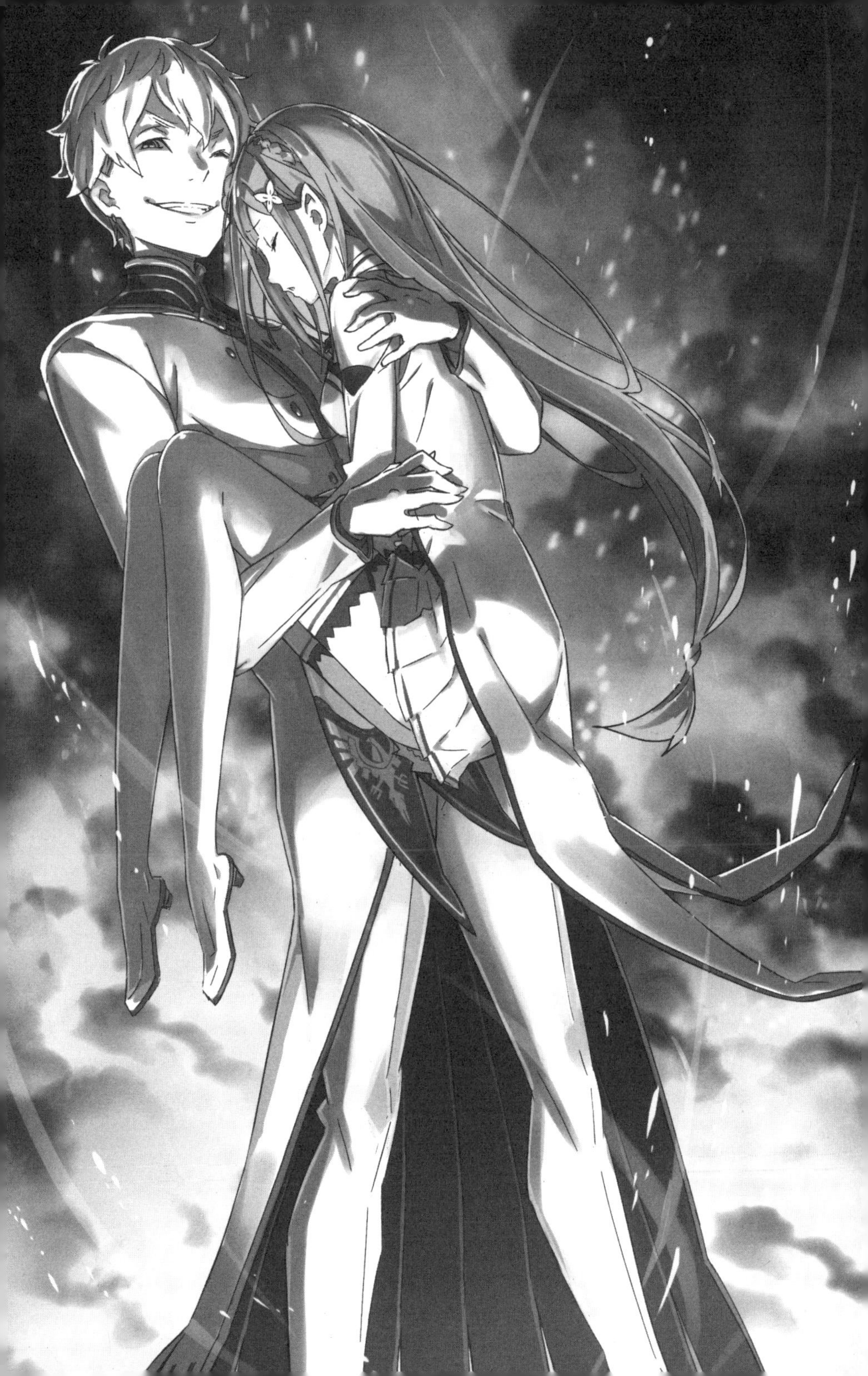

thing in the world, instantly brought Subaru's mind to a grinding halt.

While Subaru was as still as a rock, a thin smile came over the young man with a shock of white hair.

"I am the Witch Cult's Archbishop of Greed—Regulus Corneas."

"As promised—I have come to make her my seventy-ninth wife."

3

The man in white had abruptly intervened in the battlefield of raging fire and ice.

He was neither tall nor short and sported white hair and a symmetrical face that left a somewhat middling impression. His physique seemed to be the theoretical ideal of a man of medium height and medium build. Judging from his outward appearance alone, he seemed to have a weak presence that probably let him immediately blend in with any crowd.

But the young man, who lacked defining features, had a name that could not be ignored.

"The Archbishop of Greed...?!"

Before Subaru's shocked eyes, the man—Regulus—stood serenely in the aftermath of the firestorm in the square.

Regulus was calm after picking up Emilia, who was still unconscious, and enduring Sirius's apocalyptic inferno.

"But I truly must say, I am glad I reached her in time. My lovely bride was nearly burned to cinders. Even I, a person who takes pride in requesting little from others, am not so strong as to stoically accept my lovely bride being turned into a pile of ashes. Well, that is only natural. I am not an abnormal person, so of course, I could not simply bear with such degeneracy."

Looking down at Emilia, who was resting in his arms, Regulus spoke eloquently with an expression of relief on his face. The contents of his words were strangely out of place, but there was no mistaking from what he said that he was already ignoring the urgency of the situation from the get-go.

Unfortunately, since Emilia was unconscious, there was no way for his show of concern to reach her, putting it all to waste.

Watching Regulus take everything at his own pace, Subaru swallowed hard before he spoke up.

"Wh-what do you think you're...?"

"—Excuse me."

Suddenly, Regulus looked toward Subaru and interrupted his attempt to say something.

Irritation shone clearly in his empty eyes as he sighed with a note of exasperated fatigue.

"Do you not understand the meaning of courtesy? I introduced myself first, didn't I? The only considerate thing to do would be to introduce yourself to ensure that everything can smoothly proceed. Knowing each other's names is the first step to establishing a working relationship, yes? I am the kind of person who considers that important, you see, and so I have introduced myself. Of course, this is a basic level of consideration that normally shouldn't need to be explained—am I wrong? I mean, normally, people simply understand. The fact that you did not and could not—is that something you did on purpose? Or have you simply lived until this very day in such an obtuse manner? This is incredibly rude. To drop formalities with another is to express that you do not see the other party as worthy of politeness. In other words, that is denying their individuality. It is nothing less than infringing upon another's rights. You are infringing on *my* rights—me, a rational man free of want or desire."

"...A—all right, I get it. My name is...Subaru Natsuki."

Seeing that Regulus's eyes were becoming more and more tinged with madness as he rambled on and on, Subaru offered his name, heeding the alarm bells going off in his mind.

Instantly, Regulus stopped moving his lips. He slowly narrowed his eyes.

"...Yes, that's good. Respecting others is part and parcel of respecting yourself. Such concerns may be natural, but this is what creates a better world for all parties to live in. One should not yearn for too many things and accept happiness that is appropriate to one's station. By abandoning selfish desires, everyone may live within their means. Such is a wise and praiseworthy way of life."

Regulus laid out his sound argument with such tranquility that it wouldn't be strange for someone to assume he was joking. But the glimmer in both of his eyes proved that this was no game.

Just like with Sirius's logic, Regulus's words sounded like sane if flowery rhetoric at first glance. Yes, his remarks were the same, using superficially sound reasoning to gloss over the abominable statements nestled within—

"Thank you for your opinion— Now burn to ashes and begone!!"

The instant he had the thought, Regulus stood there as a fire resembling an overflowing waterfall assailed him.

The ferocious heat wave from the apocalyptic inferno enveloping the square made Subaru cover his face. Even though Regulus had introduced himself as a fellow Archbishop of the Seven Deadly Sins, Sirius had mercilessly scorched the other away for having interfered with her plan.

And so without any time to counter her, Regulus and Emilia were engulfed by flame once more.

"Subaru..."

Behind his back, Beatrice's voice trembled as she grabbed onto his shoulder with enough strength to hurt. This was a sign of her concern for Emilia. Subaru knew exactly how she felt, so much so that it stung almost unbearably.

But Greed was so off the charts that the pair's concerns held no meaning whatsoever.

"Now just a moment. Who raised you to resort to flames before your words? If you wish to say something, then speak. Or are you a talentless fool who cannot even understand language?"

Waving an arm in annoyance, Regulus extinguished the vortex of scorching flame.

The firestorm vanished like it was nothing more than an illusion, with Regulus standing utterly unaffected at its center. Of course, the same went for Emilia there in his arms.

Even after those flames had surrounded him, he didn't show a single drop of sweat, never mind a burn mark.

"You and I are both Archbishops of the Seven Deadly Sins, yes? I know that you must be touched in the head. I have enough tolerance to overlook a great many things. However, you see…"

Looking back, Regulus lowered his voice as he glared at Sirius. Taking stock of his gaze, Sirius continued to rub together the golden chains wrapped around both her arms as she gritted her teeth in hatred.

"Just now, you intended to slay this girl by fire, yes? It is somewhat unreasonable to ask me to forgive that transgression. Since time immemorial, every story tells us that when the people we love are harmed, it undoubtedly stokes the fires of anger. That is a right that everyone possesses, and therefore, it is only natural that I am justified in seeking vengeance."

"Anger?! Ha, do not make me laugh! A small, superficial man like you should not lightly utter such words! Anger is mine! It is the irreplaceable treasure that my precious bestowed upon me!"

"What is it with you? Are you still obsessed with that fool who went ahead on his own and died? My, my, how creepy. Only a flawed person would cling to a dead man all this time. If someone you love dies, you should proactively search for another. That is a law of the world, the extent of nature, and to disobey makes you…quite the piece of garbage."

"I know you laughed at his death—do not dare to speak such lofty words to me!!"

Showered in detached insults, Sirius sprayed spittle as she flew into a rage.

Giving in to her anger, the madwoman broke a paving stone as she stepped forward to swing her flame-imbued golden chains at Regulus—only for the blow to bounce right off the side of the man's face. The chains made a dull sound as they struck flesh again and again, going left and right as Sirius's blinding rage struck Regulus all over. The flaming trails left in their wake enveloped the young man as he stood perfectly still.

"Begonebegonebegonebegonebegone! Turn to cinders along with that abominable half-demon!!"

The next moment, the cage of fire converged toward the center, enveloping Regulus in a rising pillar of searing flames.

Its height surpassed that of the wrecked time tower. Paving stones melted under the intense heat, and enough melted away at the center of the scorching fire, where Regulus stood, that a crater had formed.

There was no mistaking that these flames were not something a mere human could endure. However, no matter how apocalyptic the inferno seemed—

"—You know, you really should realize it by now. You just don't measure up, you see."

There, in the crater that was burned by flames all over, a sad smile came over Regulus.

Sure enough, he was unaffected by chain or flame. Emilia was intact within his arms as well. Subaru should have been happy to confirm once again that she was safe, but at the same time, he could see an end coming that would be difficult to avoid.

—If the fight continued, Sirius would be slain by Regulus.

If that was the only issue, Subaru would've been fine with it. If anything, having the number of Archbishops of the Seven Deadly Sins whittled down through infighting was something to celebrate—or it would've been if Sirius's death didn't affect all the surrounding people, that is.

"_____"

Even then, the fear racing through Subaru's body was undiminished. His knees buckled, and his lungs were unreliable, racked by pain that refused to subside.

But in this situation—

"Subaru."

—his precious partner called him by name, scolding Subaru Natsuki for shirking and cowering.

"_____"

The warmth that he felt through his back lent strength to his bowed knees. They gave him the courage to defy his fear, to stand and face the twin natural disasters that were the madwoman of Wrath and the villain of Greed.

If Subaru had been by himself, he probably would have long since succumbed to fear. Standing up would've been impossible.

Subaru could only do so now because he wasn't alone. Unlike the people consumed by madness, Subaru had someone right by his side.

That was why—

"…Lusbel. Can you stand and run on your own?"

Putting the boy, whom he had carried in his arms, down on the ground, Subaru released him from his bonds. Lusbel gazed at Subaru, and then he turned to look at Sirius's feet out of concern for Tina.

"I know you're worried. But leave that girl to us."

"…Okay. Please save Tina somehow…"

With teary eyes, Lusbel entrusted Subaru with his hope. Subaru accepted it with a solemn nod—Lusbel's wish was noble. He wouldn't let anyone sully it.

"—Beatrice."

"I know."

Communicating his thought with a single call of her name, Subaru and Beatrice advanced toward the chaotic battlefield.

Fear had knocked him down. The enemy they faced was almost incomprehensibly dangerous. But most importantly, Subaru had a reason to fight.

"Hmm?"

Right as he was busy glaring at Sirius, Regulus raised an eyebrow, having abruptly felt that something was off.

The cause was probably the end of a whip wrapped around his slender neck. After flying through the air, the whip had found purchase on Regulus's neck, tightening along its length to rob him of his freedom.

Taking this as a signal, Lusbel raced across the chaotic square. Watching his back…

"Now stop touching my Emilia like she belongs to you…!"

…Subaru howled, the explosion in his heart triggered by unceasing love.

He had no idea whatsoever how Regulus had fended off the flames. He could only assume it was probably the effect of an Authority, something on par with Petelgeuse's Unseen Hands and Sirius's soulwashing.

It was safe to assume that he wouldn't be able to hurt Regulus. In that case, what about binding him with a whip to hinder his movements?

"*—Shamak!*"

Additionally, Beatrice conjured Shamak, the greatest of all spells, and enveloped Regulus in a black cloud.

Chanting while seated on Subaru's back, Beatrice had plunged the villain's thoughts into the void with perfect timing. If he could only pull the guy down within the darkness and take Emilia back—

"Do you have a death wish? Then you should just wait your turn. Do not make me bother with you."

With a single step, Regulus completely blew away the black cloud surrounding him. It didn't seem like the spell, which was meant to obliterate the victim's five senses, had any effect on Regulus, who now turned his gaze toward Subaru and Beatrice as they raced forward.

Instantly, Subaru felt every hair on his body stand up as he sensed impending death, and so he shouted:

"Beako, now!!"

"I suppose I'm ready!"

Matching Subaru's voice, Beatrice began a complex ritual.

—This evoked one of the fruits of their spending almost every waking moment of the last year together.

"*—E M M!!*"

Howling as he chanted, Subaru sent mana to Beatrice directly from his broken Gate. This power served as the activation key to initiate an original spell, the only one of its kind in the whole world.

This was E M M, one of the three spells jointly developed by Subaru and Beatrice.

Watching it unfold, Regulus looked like he thought he was being pranked as he stretched his right hand toward Subaru. The five fingers he opened without fanfare contained such immense power that Subaru instinctively knew it was the same as death itself reaching for him.

If they touched him, dying was unavoidable. However—

"Huh?!"

—the instant he thought he'd killed the pest, Regulus's fingertips brushed the surface of Subaru's body.

But that was all. There was no blood spatter, nor was Subaru cruelly transformed into a corpse.

This was the effect of E M M—an invisible magic field that covered the entire body, an absolute defensive spell that physically cut a being off from the world, designed to prevent anything from interacting with Subaru whatsoever.

"Uraaah!"

As Regulus blinked hard, Subaru aimed a mighty punch right at his shocked face.

He felt feedback; the punch had undoubtedly landed. But when Regulus recovered from the recoil, there was no mark on his face or any other sign that anything had happened. He had complete damage nullification—in other words, a full-time E M M state.

When Subaru thought about how his own E M M dispelled after taking one hit, the difference in power was staggering.

"I'm still charging!"

Before Regulus could counterattack, Beatrice informed Subaru about her progress toward the next spell. In the intervening time, Subaru was defenseless in a situation where both dodging and blocking were difficult—meaning he would simply have to sacrifice a bit of his soul.

"Do not act so high and—"

"Come!! Invisible Providence!!"

Subaru howled again. A moment later, an invisible fist crashed into Regulus's irritated-looking face from below, slamming into his jaw.

Interrupted by the blow, Regulus was sent reeling. Subaru closed the distance to try and rip Emilia out of his arms—but then he stopped as he felt his intestines churning and a hot nausea rising up in his throat.

"Ugh, ubhhh!"

Covering his mouth, Subaru coughed. Blood dripped through the gaps in his fingers—this was the cost he paid.

The price of using this invisible force, a forbidden art that exceeded his body's capacity, was the corruption of Subaru Natsuki's soul and abject torture for his innards.

"Subaru! Are you all right, I wonder?!"

"*Cough*... Sorry, I messed up. Even though I wanted to get Emilia back right then..."

Heaving up the clot of blood stuck in his throat, Subaru gritted his teeth at the fact that he'd been one step too slow.

In the one year since the time he'd first used Invisible Providence, his cheap knockoff of Unseen Hands, he still hadn't mastered it. The unseeable, invisible black hand coming out of his chest was an incomplete Authority, and the price that it demanded was pain that racked his entire body and the deterioration of his soul.

For all that, the effect was only a single punch—a fact that made him want to cry.

"But I still got something out of it... Getting hit by that guy is bad, but his movements are sluggish. Considering all the people I've seen to date, even Larry, Curly, and Moe could probably beat this guy."

Regulus's style of fighting was amateurish, below even the likes of Subaru; he was barely more skilled than a total novice. His ability to nullify damage was very troublesome, but even lethal blows didn't mean anything if they couldn't connect.

Annoyed by that appraisal, Regulus adjusted his grip on Emilia.

"What petty trickery... What if you harmed my lovely bride, flailing around like that? Even without someone teaching you manners, is it not natural to treat girls with kindness? Are you incapable of even that?"

"You just can't stop grating on my nerves, can you? That girl's the one I treat the kindest in the whole world. What do you think you're doing, going 'lovely bride' this and 'lovely bride' that and all sorts of weird garbage?!"

"I've told you before, yes? Do not make me repeat myself—I have come to take this girl as my bride."

Regulus's brazen reply treated the sacred institution of marriage with such nonchalance that it was incredibly off-putting.

Even as he forced his quest of seeking love onto others, he prioritized only himself. His fundamentally warped logic was chill-inducing.

"Previously, I was unable to uphold an identical vow. That is why I shall not yield this time. I will protect her. I will take her as my wife, cherish her, and enjoy the tranquility that I am due. I do not wish for many things, but if it is for the sake of protecting my small slice of happiness, I will not hesitate to exploit the power that I have been granted."

For the first time, Subaru felt fear coming from Regulus's demeanor as the man shared what seemed to be his genuine thoughts.

Seeing Subaru's reaction, Regulus went, "Ahh," seeming to accept something as he nodded. "I see now… You know, it might be cruel to say this, but it's futile to try and come between destined lovers. It pains me to say this, but everyone knows that it's quite unsightly to pine for someone who is already spoken for."

"Shut up! Emilia-tan is my bride. No way am I giving her up to the likes of you!"

"Heh, so Emilia is this girl's name? It has a nice ring to it. It makes me want to whisper to her, admiring her like a songbird. That name suits this charming girl perfectly, yes?"

"You don't even…know her name…? What do you see in her that makes you ramble on and on about how she's your lovely bride?"

"Her face."

He was stunned. Subaru fell silent after hearing his instantaneous reply.

Regulus cocked his head in confusion as the silence made him wonder if he'd been misunderstood.

"Her face is exquisite. When it comes to love, that is everything, isn't it?"

"Die."

"Would it not be better if he was dead, I wonder?"

Subaru and Beatrice's condemnations overlapped out of simple shared enmity.

Simultaneously, Beatrice tapped Subaru's shoulder from behind his back, indicating that she was done charging. The details of how Regulus's damage-nullification Authority worked remained unclear, but they still had something to try.

This was the third of the original spells from the SubaBeako combo—

"—Whoa?!"

The instant he took his first step forward, the ground between Subaru and Regulus suddenly cracked open, revealing a pit of roaring flames.

The heat wave billowing up at Subaru made him recoil. He proceeded to back away, glaring at the perpetrator who had cut his counterattack short.

—It was Sirius, who had been content to simply observe the fight between Subaru and Regulus up to that point.

"You…! Wait, the girl… Where did you put Tina?"

There was no sign of the girl who'd been taken hostage and ought to have been at the madwoman's feet. However, she did not reply to Subaru, keeping her palms thrust out as she maintained her silence.

He wasn't sure what the nutcase had in mind after observing the battle so far, but having her intervene was exceptionally worse.

Dealing with Sirius herself was already difficult, especially considering how they had to work around her Authority. Sensing that the situation was deteriorating quickly, Subaru wiped cold sweat off his brow— However, the situation had worsened far more than he had imagined.

"—I have found you."

"—Wha?"

Finally, as she stood still, Sirius looked at Subaru, and— No, she was *only* looking at Subaru and him alone as she continued murmuring.

Sirius suddenly seemed as if she'd completely forgotten her bloodlust from moments before. The madwoman was now ignoring Regulus's very existence, giving her undivided attention to Subaru. Subaru's throat dried out instantly when he saw the crazed glint in her eye.

Then the madwoman pulled back both arms, which she had thrust out, and gently pressed her hands against her cheeks.

"I have found you. I have found you. I have found you. Ahh, ahh, ahhhh! Yes, there's no mistake! I am sorry, I am so sorry I didn't notice earlier! But ahh, it really was true!"

"Wh-what the…?"

"You were here all along, darling?! I searched everywhere but couldn't find you, and all your spares had been ripped away, nowhere to be found! I have searched for you for so, so, so, so, so, so, so, long…and now you have finally returned! My darling has returned to my side!"

Her shrill, high-pitched voice was born from indecent passion.

Continuing to press her hands to her cheeks, Sirius wriggled and writhed about, her slender hips shaking as her voice leaped with joy. When it finally dawned on Subaru that every aspect of her voice and her demeanor was a manifestation of seething romantic passion, he was struck with horror.

"My feelings have reached you! Finally, my love has reached you! After all this time!"

Utterly ignoring Subaru's shock, Sirius stretched both hands out toward him.

Then with all the spirit that the madwoman possessed, she pronounced her love in a thundering voice.

"I have been waiting aaaaall this time for you and only you…my beloved, beloved Petelgeuse!"

4

The repulsive zeal in that violet eye was all aimed at Subaru.

The sight of Sirius's ecstatic gaze left him unable to do anything but draw in his breath.

"...She is...staring at you, Subaru."

"...I know, so please don't say it out loud and make me feel worse."

When Beatrice whispered to him from his back, Subaru replied as he suppressed his fear as best as he could.

He'd felt this terrible premonition during the first time around that one loop.

"...This Romanée-Conti family thing almost sounded like an insane joke, but..."

At first, he'd entertained the ridiculous idea of a famous family in the Witch Cult cranking out one Archbishop of the Seven Deadly Sins after another, but reality easily exceeded Subaru's expectations.

"If you have to be a husband-and-wife team of Archbishops, then you should get to pick your bride... Well, I guess if she *is* your pick, there's nothing I can do about it, but..."

"Please do not ignore me, Petelgeuse. You truly are naughty. Always acting so coldly toward me... It just, just, just—frustrates me so much!"

Over a year after they last met, Subaru was finding new reasons to resent Petelgeuse and his awful taste.

Meanwhile, Sirius squirmed and pleaded with him in an ingratiating voice. Just the gestures from the bandaged madwoman were nightmarish enough, but seeing the soulwashed crowd performing the same gestures made the scene an outright comedy.

The fact that their souls were being manipulated to make them go along with the madwoman's delusions really made it more of a tragedy, though.

"And what's her basis for mistaking me for that Petelgeuse bastard in the first place? I don't resemble that jerk at all."

"...Goodness, I simply cannot put up with this. Most likely, she saw your earlier trick, spurring her current disturbing delusion.

She truly does not know the meaning of shame. Strong women are so difficult to deal with when they become convinced of something. It goes well beyond pitiable and simply becomes unsightly."

Regulus, now out of sight and out of mind as far as Sirius was concerned, shrugged with unconcealed disdain on his face.

But Subaru had learned something—it was Invisible Providence that had caused this. Sirius had mistakenly identified that incomplete Authority as Unseen Hands.

What made things worse was the fact that the evil spirit Petelgeuse had the power to possess and hijack the bodies of others. There was no room for doubt that the madwoman thought he was dwelling inside Subaru.

Setting that deduction aside, Sirius's burning zeal from a moment before vanished like a mirage as she glared at Regulus with frigid eyes.

"Yes, yes, thank you kindly. And so very, very sorry. Right now, I am in the middle of something. Do you understand? Comprehension is quite important, and mutual understanding is just as critical. You've finished what you came for, yes? Would you quickly take your leave now?"

"Are you giving me an order? Do not make me laugh. Speaking of making me laugh, you called yourself Sirius Romanée-Conti, did you not? Would you notice already that using your feelings for him as an excuse to take his family name as your own without permission is just downright disturbing? In a sense, that is an infringement upon Petelgeuse's rights. Well, dead people don't have rights, so I suppose it's fine, really."

"He and I loved each other!!"

Regulus's words, filled with bottomless disdain, triggered another explosion of Sirius's emotions.

"I mean, our eyes met over and over again daily! He never scolded me for taking out his things! He let me have his leftover food and said nothing even as I breathed in the air he breathed out! He never grimaced when I slept in the same bed that he had, and he even praised me for skillfully burning half-demons away! He gave me my name! He smiled! For me, me, me aloooone!!"

Sirius's breath had become ragged, her bandages drenched with tears as she laid her feelings bare. The gruesome sight and the contents of her words made Subaru feel sorry for Sirius for the very first time.

In addition, Sirius's indignation resonated, and the surrounding crowd was suffused with roiling emotions once again. Their faces became dark red, and the bleeding from their eyes and noses increased; it was clear from a single glance that their lives were being whittled away.

"S-stop it! If this is for my sake, then don't drag the people around us into this! Behave, please!"

"Behave, you say?"

Thinking about the collateral damage, Subaru clung to a single thread of hope: trying to play on Sirius's yearning.

When Subaru made that dangerous gamble, Sirius stared at him in a daze for a while.

"...Ah-ha, ah-ha-ha, ah-ha-ha-ha-ha-ha!!"

Embracing her slender body, Sirius guffawed at Subaru's words. Her reaction made Subaru tense up. Seeing this, Sirius tore her mouth open to form a crescent moon.

"Even if you wish it, I refuse. I mean, we've finally reunited! We have finally met like this once more. And yet once again, you ask me to endure, to hold back?! How dare you tell me to wait while some spirit I've never seen clings to your back!! I will burn you!!!"

Even as she spoke, her emotions raged as Sirius let out a roar and pointed at Subaru—no, at Beatrice on Subaru's back. Sirius then shifted her other hand toward Regulus.

"Either way, your real objective is the half-demon that man is carrying, isn't it?! Why are you so partial to a filthy, silver-haired half-demon?! Surely, you understand by now?! Why choose that wretched, vulgar, damned half-demon...?! If you love her that much, then I will burn her before your very eyes...!"

"Geez, I don't even understand a thing you're saying anymore..."

Screaming and even coughing up blood, Sirius vented her hatred toward both Emilia and the Witch of Jealousy.

Wasn't resurrecting the Witch of Jealousy the Witch Cult's goal? Subaru couldn't understand why she treated the supposed object of their worship like it was the one thing she most hated in the entire world.

More than that, it meant Sirius didn't share Petelgeuse's long-cherished desire in the slightest, didn't it?

In any case, with Subaru's hope for a breakthrough dashed, the situation had turned into a three-sided battlefield.

That said, the side in the worst state was, without a doubt, Subaru's party. Despite surviving longer than in any other loop this time around, his failure to acquire any information except how dangerous their enemies were left him in all-consuming despair.

But he couldn't simply stand there—he had to save Emilia and the city.

"Isn't it fine either way, I wonder?"

From his back, the sound of a dependable voice bolstered Subaru's decision. Relying on that voice, Subaru moved to boldly leap toward the two Archbishops of the Seven Deadly Sins—

"—Excuse me, I am sorry to interrupt when you are getting so motivated, but it is finally time, you see."

"What?"

Regulus cut in and dashed Subaru and Beatrice's resolve. Still carrying Emilia with one hand, he pointed toward the sky with his empty one.

—The next moment, the sound of a bell echoed in the sky above the City of Water. That tolling indicated that noon had arrived.

Nodding in response, a melancholic smile came over Regulus as he spoke up.

"With this, I no longer have free time to spare for you. At the very least, you should be thankful to the Gospel that... No. It is meaningless to thank a torn page. You should be thankful to me, then, for doing my part in obeying the Gospel."

Leaving these words behind, Regulus turned his back on Subaru and Beatrice, having lost all interest in them. Dumbstruck by his sheer gall, Subaru immediately exploded.

"Hold on a minute! 'Time,' you say? What about the time? What the hell are you talking about?!"

"It is exactly as you heard. My free time has come to an end. We have something that we came to do in this city. Ahh, I do not mean merely me, but also the woman touched in the head over there. Isn't that right, Sirius?"

Replying to Subaru's inquiry, Regulus motioned his chin toward Sirius as the latter stood still.

When Subaru looked over, it was shocking how Sirius, who had been so enraged before, was obediently tucking her chains into her sleeves, looking like she wasn't satisfied with the outcome. Nonetheless, she was clearly getting ready to move on just like Regulus.

What impudent, selfish, completely conceited people were they to do this much and then just drop it all and walk away?

"Ahh, do not lament, Petelgeuse! I understand! I, too, wish so much to burn what is incomplete! To act like this before you… It fills me with such sadness that I wish to tear my chest apart! Is it not the same for you, darling?!"

In stark contrast to Regulus's composure, Sirius clawed at her face in grief. Swallowed up by the madwoman's emotions, the crowd let out sobs and laments that filled the square.

As that painful and revolting scene played out before him, Subaru ferociously broke into a sprint. Regulus was right there, carrying Emilia out of the square as if the conversation was already at an end.

"Wait, you bastard! Don't carry on with the conversation all on your own! Put that girl down! If you don't…"

"You see, a thought occurred to me."

Stopping in his tracks, Regulus turned only his head toward Subaru, smiling.

That smile petrified Subaru's body—almost fatally so.

"It is a lonely thing to have a ceremony without any attendants on the new bride's side, so it would be a little too coldhearted and pitiless of me not to invite you, the illicit lover— Therefore, I will not kill you."

As he spoke, Regulus lightly tapped a paving stone with the tip of his toe.

With a gesture that made it seem like he was only adjusting the fit of his shoe, he shaved the top of the paving stone right off. The resulting debris flew toward Subaru's legs—instantly causing his right leg to explode.

"—Eh?"

A horrid cross section was revealed as if he'd been gouged by a massive beast's claw, neatly exposing Subaru's white bone, pink flesh, yellowish fat, and gray-colored blood vessels, which had been savagely severed.

Incomprehension. Comprehension. A moment later, the pain reached his brain.

"?!! Daaagh! Agaaaagh?!"

His vision went pure white as terrible pain shot through him. It was as if a number of sharp needles had been stabbed into the crown of his head.

Screaming, Subaru failed to break his fall as he tumbled to the ground. He then tried to stanch the leg injury with his hands. It was no use. The wound was too big. Subaru's hands alone could not plug it.

"Subaru?! Subaru! Subaru, hold on! Let me—!"

Beatrice, falling to the ground alongside Subaru, hurriedly activated a healing spell as she realized the gravity of his injury. Seeing the pair reduced to that miserable state, Regulus nodded in apparent satisfaction.

"Your demeanor toward me has been quite rude this whole time, but with this, let us call it even. I hope this pain serves as sufficient motivation for you to reflect upon your actions. Ahh, there is no need to thank me. I mean, this really isn't enough to thank someone for. It is merely a wake-up call that should be natural coming from any reasonable person."

"Aaaaa! Gah, ghh, ugoaaah!!"

That voice wasn't audible anymore. Pain, pain—Subaru Natsuki was ruled by pain alone.

His eyes were cloudy. He was clenching his back teeth so hard that they seemed ready to split in half. His vision was completely red. He didn't have any sense of up or down, left or right. Incomprehension. Incomprehensionincomprehension. He did not comprehend, but there was something he knew.

"Emiliaaa…! Waghhh, urgh, goeee!"

In the throes of excruciating pain, Subaru called out the name of the girl who was the only thing he cared about in that moment. But it was useless. As he gasped from pain, tiny Beatrice desperately tried to keep him from thrashing about as she continued treating him.

However, as if to mock Beatrice's dedicated efforts, the situation continued to worsen.

"…This isn't funny in the least."

"My apologies. But this is no joke. This, too, is a matter of natural consequence."

As Beatrice murmured despondently, Sirius replied from somewhere behind her in a melancholic voice.

All around Sirius, people were writhing in pain. They were screaming from the crippling pain in their leg, identical to Subaru's wound. It was as if they'd all been maimed by the same beast.

"If my beloved Petelgeuse had a chance to share a few words, he would say this: Pain makes us savor life, and life exists so that we may prove our love. I believe this to be true as well. That is why I have this wish! After all, love is the wish to become one! To see the same things, to feel the same things, to pass the time together, to end our lives together—for love is all about joining with one another!"

Spreading both hands wide, Sirius brought them together before her chest, producing a loud, explosive sound resembling applause.

After indulging in the suffering of others with an expression of pure ecstasy, Sirius turned a hateful eye toward Beatrice.

"Everyone should taste the same life as my precious. But I shall allow no such thing for you or for that filthy half-elf. Who would knowingly allow you to share anything with my precious?"

"…Would you cease being so crazed with jealousy, I wonder?

Betty has long become one with Subaru without turning into anything like you. Is Betty not Subaru's, I wonder?"

"—!"

Beatrice gave a retort, conceding nothing to Sirius and her manipulative words.

The spirit and the madwoman sternly crossed gazes. But the madwoman quickly averted her eyes from the staring contest.

"For now, I leave him to you, for the instructions of the Gospel must take precedence. Yes, I have little choice in the matter. So sorry. My apologies. But I will come to see you again soon. Yes, very soon indeed."

To the end, Sirius directed her mad feelings of love toward Subaru, even as unbearable pain stripped him of conscious thought. On a final note, the madwoman gave Subaru a long stare of yearning before departing from the bloody square with a single leap.

Beatrice could not even keep her eyes on Sirius's back as she faded into the distance. Before she realized it, all sight of Regulus, and Emilia with him, had vanished from the square.

"—Subaru."

Subaru was unconscious, vomiting stomach fluids mixed with froth.

Touching his leg, she continued to treat the still-bleeding wound. The site of the injury was large and deep; if she let her mind wander, he would almost certainly die of blood loss. Subaru's life was Beatrice's first priority.

There were nearly fifty other wounded besides Subaru in the square. Thanks to the Authority of Wrath, they had suffered the same exact wound as him, but the effect of Beatrice's healing was not being shared. It was an abominable Authority.

"—Subaru, I am so sorry."

Diligently tending to Subaru's health, Beatrice murmured frailly as she tried to stay strong.

A tear fell from her one of her wide-open eyes, leaving a line as it coursed down her white cheek.

"I am so sorry. Could I be any sorrier, I wonder…?"

Beatrice apologized over and over, even though she knew that her voice could not reach Subaru, who had passed out from the pain.

Even though she knew that her words changed nothing.

"I am so sorry, Emilia...!"

Sirius of Wrath had toyed with people's hearts, creating a long list of casualties in the process.

And after a display of overwhelming might, Regulus of Greed had abducted Emilia.

—Two Archbishops of the Seven Deadly Sins had been unleashed upon the Water Gate City of Pristella.

CHAPTER 3
WITCH CULT DISASTER RESPONSE HQ

1

—*Dong, dong, dong.*

The low, weighty percussions of gongs seemed to come from everywhere at once, near and far.

The flow of his blood had slowed—it was an unpleasant feeling akin to having mud coursing in his arteries. His internal organs barely seemed to be working, and his guts felt like they were a rough collection of clay work; these kinds of mismatched sensations dominated his body.

Oxygen wasn't traveling to his brain properly, either, making it hard to form thoughts, and what thoughts did form were unreliable.

He felt a feeling of loss, as if his body was no longer his own—

"—Ah."

Abruptly, he felt his fading self being pulled back from the brink as raspy breaths trickled out from his lungs.

Instantly, his hazy consciousness miraculously pieced itself back together, and Subaru Natsuki slowly opened his eyes.

After becoming accustomed to darkness, his eyes were not ready to fully accept the white light now shooting into them. A shadow crossed right and left across his indistinct vision. It took him thirty seconds to realize that these were human silhouettes.

He sensed the presence of hastily moving people, a dirty ceiling, and air that seemed to have a whiff of rust to it—finally, he found that he was lying on something hard and that he was staring at those silhouettes in a daze.

"—Ohh, looks like ya woke up, Bro."

Just when Subaru returned to reality, someone abruptly peered at him from close-up.

This person was wearing a jet-black steel helm. From that gear alone, some might have taken him for one of the city's heavily equipped guards, but considering how much skin he exposed from the neck down and his obvious lack of one arm, those characteristics immediately told Subaru this was someone he knew.

"Al...?"

"Yep, it's Mr. Al. See me once, and you can't forget me even if you tried. This is still one helluva situation, though."

The man in the steel helm—Al—shrugged and chuckled at his own words.

As Subaru continued to grasp more and more of the situation, his mind began to whip around chaotically. What was a mercenary in the employ of the Priscilla camp doing there? —No, to begin with, where was he?

Then just as that question occurred to Subaru—

"Aah! Subawu woke up, didn't he?! I told you to call me if he woke up, *meow*!"

A loud voice rose as someone rushed over with a swift patter of feet. The newcomer thrust a finger not at Subaru, who was lying down, but at Al, who was standing beside him in his familiar steel helm.

"You need to do as you're told, *meow*! Really, you're useless if you're just going to stand around, doing nothing helpful!"

"Aren't you bein' a bit harsh? I'm the one who did all the work hauling Bro and the young lady over here, y'know."

Al shrugged at being chewed out so much, but the one lecturing him didn't pay that the slightest heed. Instead, this person—a lovely girl, or rather, a young man dressed like one—turned to face Subaru.

"Even Ferris…"

"Yes, yes. It's Ferri, beloved by one and all. Okay, Subawu Natsuki, let me explain. This is a field hospital, and you were brought in with heavy injuries. Still with me?"

Upon speaking those words, Ferris gave him an adorable wink. That cute gesture was very much at odds with the blood splatters that marred his white cheeks and outfit, a sight that conveyed in simple terms that the conditions here were nowhere near normal.

Once he looked around, spurred by Ferris using the term *field hospital*, Subaru realized that what he first guessed was the scent of rust was actually the heavy odor of blood. He could see a whole slew of faintly moaning casualties. There seemed to be so many that even the gravely injured were lying on nothing more than sheets of cloth. Subaru belatedly found that he was in the exact same state.

"What…is this…? The hell happened…?"

"It seems you're still a bit confused, *meow*. Take it slow and remember what went down before you fainted. If you can recall that, then you'll have your answer."

Ferris spoke to the confused Subaru in a hard and unkind tone. However, this wasn't an effort to dismiss Subaru; it was just a sign of how pressed Ferris was.

As healers went, Ferris possessed peerless skill. With such a large number of wounded needing help, it wasn't hard to imagine just how critical his power was.

In the first place, what kind of terrible incident could have produced such a large number of casualties—?

"!! The Witch Cult!"

"That's right… Honestly, they're just the worst, *meow*. I knew that already, but this made me feel like I didn't really understand until now. I never imagined they'd go this far."

Biting his lip with regret, Ferris affirmed what Subaru had realized.

Subaru understood his anger toward the Witch Cult. But as his memories gradually returned, Subaru had something even more important that he absolutely had to know.

"E-Emilia?! What happened to Emilia and Beatrice?"

"———"

"Both of them were in the square with me, and then…"

Sitting up, Subaru grasped Ferris's slender shoulder when his words failed him. This was because from the way Ferris averted his eyes, Subaru could tell he was right to be worried.

"Calm down and listen, okay?" said Ferris as a preamble to Subaru. "First, you absolutely need to rest, Subawu. You were badly hurt… As for Lady Emilia, we can't get in touch with her. From what you said just now, it doesn't seem like…you got separated because the city's in chaos, huh."

Sure enough, Subaru's energy faded as Ferris gave him what could hardly be called good news.

Emilia's safety or lack thereof was completely unknown. Paired with his memories from just before fainting, he certainly hadn't been wrong to think that Emilia had been whisked away by Regulus of Greed. Subaru had been helpless to stop him.

As for Beatrice, if she was in the same place as he—

"Bro, if you're worried about your partner, she's sleepin' soundly over there."

"!!"

Al sat cross-legged, pointing toward Subaru's right side as he spoke. When he turned that way on reflex, he saw a curtain covering the space immediately beside him. He rushed over and practically tore it down.

On the other side of that curtain, he spotted a girl wearing a dress, slumbering on a sheet of cloth.

It was Beatrice. She lay faceup with her eyes closed. He couldn't spot any external injuries. When he took in the familiar sight of her sleeping adorably, Subaru let out a sigh of relief.

"Beako…! Ahh, I'm glad she's safe. Really, I… Er, gyaaah!"

"Ferri said to *rest*, yes? Do you understand what '*absolutely need to rest*' means, *meow*?"

Ferris was on him in moments, poking at Subaru's right leg and berating him in a voice that quivered in anger. Instantly, Subaru screamed, feeling as if a thunderbolt had struck the crown of his head.

The back of his eyes flickered from pain that was intense enough to make him taste blood inside his mouth. When he looked down, wondering what was up, he saw that there was a thick bandage wrapped around his right leg.

"Bro, when I found ya, it was so grotesque that I got cold, cold feet. Your leg was hangin' by the smallest flap of skin. A little bit more, and you would've ended up one limb short, just like me."

Al revealed some information about what transpired after Subaru had passed out, indicating his own missing left arm with a flippant tone of voice for a bit of emphasis. His explanation, plus the thick bandage around his leg, made Subaru's hazy memories come back with a vengeance.

—Regulus.

That man, the white-haired villain who spirited Emilia away, had launched an attack as he was leaving, gouging and ruining Subaru's leg as a parting gift. That was the source of the pain that had rendered him unconscious.

"So you see, lovely Beatrice grafted your torn leg back together, and Ferri treated you on top of that. It should be just about healed right up, but you can't do anything crazy for a while, you hear me?"

Crossing his arms to form an X, Ferris sternly forbade Subaru from straining his body. Subaru nodded listlessly at the instruction, as he was more preoccupied at seeing Beatrice asleep.

"Beatrice...?"

Having spent most of the last year in the same bed as her, he could tell that Beatrice was sleeping very soundly. But he had to wonder if this sleep was a little too deep, even for her.

Though he had shrieked right beside her, she hadn't stirred in the slightest.

"Is she really...sleeping? She didn't even twitch, did she?"

"...*Sleep* might be the wrong word. Her state is closer to a coma than real sleep."

"A coma?!"

Upon hearing that far more dangerous-sounding term, Subaru hastily touched Beatrice's sleeping face. It was cold to the touch. Not a single cute reaction stirred her eyelashes or her lips.

The echo of the word *coma* grew more credible as all traces of blood seemed to drain from Subaru's head.

"It's a reaction from using every last bit of mana she had to spare. I told you, didn't I? Lovely Beatrice desperately grafted Subawu's leg together using healing magic."

"That's… But even if she's been almost out of gas forever, I never thought she'd slip into a coma."

"That would be true if Subawu was the only one hurt, right?"

Ferris narrowed his eyes as he watched the pale-faced Subaru inhale sharply. Taking stock of the pair's conversation, Al used a finger to toy with the metallic parts of his steel helm as he spoke.

"By the time I got to the square, they were all rollin' on the ground with the same wounds as you, Bro. That moppet managed to treat all of 'em with healing magic. Damn impressive, I gotta say."

Subaru recognized the faces of the other patients who were lying down on sheets of cloth all around him, just like he was.

The fox-man, the eyepatch woman, blood-drenched Lachins, and more, all of them with wounds on their right legs just like Subaru—No, the wounds weren't merely in the same locations. They were identical.

—The resonance that came with Sirius's soulwashing had mauled everyone in the square the same way.

Beatrice had wrung strength out of herself to heal not only him, but also everyone else as well.

"Is Beatrice all right? You think she'll get better if she keeps resting like this?"

"…To be honest, I think there's little hope of that. I might be the top healer in the kingdom, but spirits are outside my specialty. I think the best we can hope from letting her rest like this is maintaining her current condition."

"!"

Ferris's explanations made Subaru harden his cheeks. If that was the most they could manage, then that meant she would have to remain asleep. When he heard that, the first thing that came to mind was the girl he'd left at the mansion despite how much he'd wanted to keep her near him.

Seeing that remorseful reaction, Ferris realized his own slip of the tongue. "Sorry," he apologized. "I shouldn't have spoken like that just now. But I should mention that letting her sleep won't help her recover, and unlike an injury, it's not something Ferri can heal. The reason she's asleep is because she lacks mana, so if she gets supplied with some, she should awaken, but..."

"Supply her with mana? If I could do that, things would be easy..."

His insufficient mana supply was a chronic problem that had plagued him and Beatrice ever since they first forged a pact.

As a special type of spirit, Beatrice could not accept mana unless it was supplied by Subaru, her contractor. And Subaru, the source of that all-important mana supply, was a louse who was incapable of properly storing sufficient amounts of mana.

Subaru's helplessness was always a burden on Beatrice. He already owed her enough that it'd take a lifetime to pay her back, yet his debt to her seemed to constantly be growing.

"It's not just about Beatrice, either. Emilia also needs my help... but here I am, stuck like this...!"

His connection to Beatrice ran deeper than one nearly torn-off leg. Beatrice was also Subaru's connection to the possibilities beyond his reach, to his few fleeting hopes.

Emilia was in peril. The city was in peril. He had to do something. If it was for their sake—

"Am I an idiot? Nah, I'm definitely an idiot. If I have time to cry about it... Mnghhh!"

"Okay, that's far enough!"

When Subaru tried to ignore the pain in his leg and stand, Ferris clamped both his hands down on his face. Ferris then forced Subaru to turn his head toward him, bringing their faces close, until they were only inches away from each other.

"Why does it always have to be zero or a hundred with you, Subawu? Getting all mopey-dopey is bad, but running around willy-nilly puts everyone in a bind, too. Don't you get that?"

"Mopey-dopey? Willy-nilly…?"

"It's true, though, right? You don't even have little Beatrice to stand by you right now, so what can you do running off all by yourself? You are absolutely not allowed to waste the life you've been given."

The way he said it might have sounded silly, but Ferris's words were infused with powerful, sincere feelings.

"_____"

After hearing Ferris's plea, Subaru felt the strength drain from his legs as he stopped trying to forcibly stand up. Then he heaved a great big sigh and decided to stay put while sorting out his feelings some other way.

"Sorry. I got too restless… Come to think of it, I didn't thank you for the leg, either."

"I don't really do this for words of thanks, you know. Though it's always nicer to hear some than not."

"Thanks, really. You're a lifesaver. I owe you."

"You are very welcome, *meow*."

When Subaru piled on the thank-yous, Ferris gave a curt reply and finally took his hands off Subaru's face.

"Al, you were a huge help, too. You carried me and Beako all the way here, right?"

"Yep. By the way, I wanted you to thank me properly, too. That said, there's someone else you really oughtta be thankin' here, Bro."

When Subaru tilted his head, wondering what that could mean, Al amusedly motioned with the jaw of his steel helm. When Subaru glanced in that direction, he saw a boy holding his knees as he slept in a corner of the room.

"Lusbel…"

"The little guy called me over with tears in his eyes, so I just couldn't ignore him. I followed him to the square that got painted red, red, red with Bro's and everyone else's blood, y'know? Seriously, I wanna praise myself for not blacking out then and there."

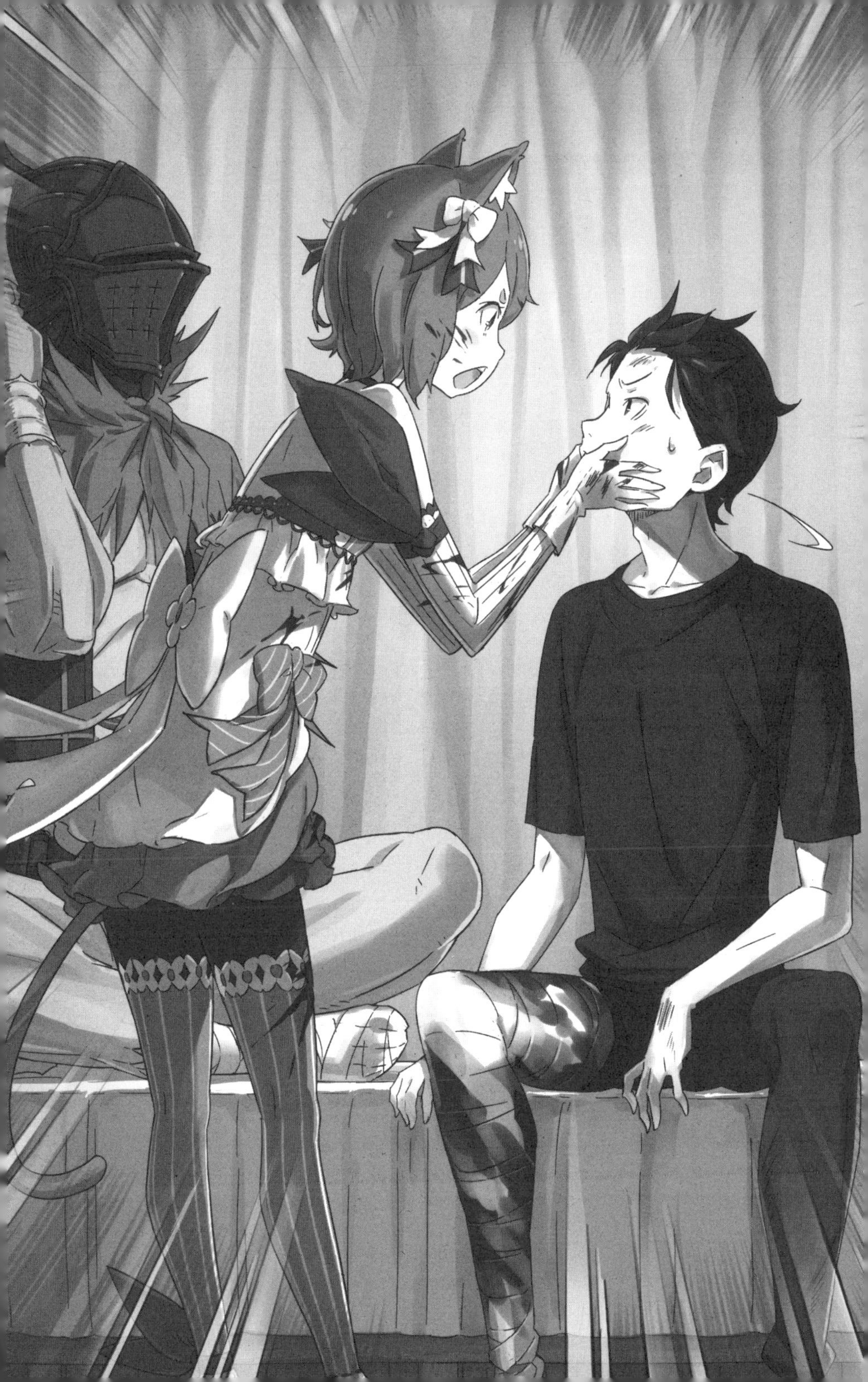

It was in Al's nature to talk about everything like it was all a long-winded joke, but Subaru really did owe him a great deal. The same went for Lusbel, who had bravely returned with help. Even if he was with an adult, Subaru truly respected the boy for deciding to head back to that terrifying square, knowing full well what awaited him.

It was thanks to Al and Lusbel's help that Subaru could hold Beatrice's hand as she slept.

"So Beatrice's condition isn't going to deteriorate right this minute or anything, right?"

"That, I can guarantee. All I'm saying is that we can't help her wake up right this minute."

"Got it… Please fill me in on what's been happening. How's the city right now, and what is the Witch Cult up to?"

Striving to maintain calm, Subaru tried to get a grasp on how things had been developing. When he posed that question, Ferris and Al exchanged looks, wondering where to begin. Before they had a chance—

"—It would seem your timing is very good. I was just about to speak regarding precisely that."

The new voice carried well and was backed by an undercurrent of strength. When he turned, Subaru caught sight of the speaker now arriving at the entrance to the field hospital. Long, green hair danced around her as the refreshing beauty came to a halt—

"Lady Crusch! This place is full of wounded… You didn't have to go out of your way to come here."

"I am sorry, Ferris. I had no intention of invading your battleground. However, I heard that Master Subaru has awakened. How could I possibly ask him to come to me in his state?"

As she explained her thought process, Crusch approached the cloth where Subaru sat. As opposed to what she had worn earlier in the morning, her attire retained vestiges of elegance while prioritizing ease of movement.

He couldn't help but recall that this was very close to what Crusch looked like before she lost her memory—

"Seems like you're geared up for a fight, too, Crusch."

"The circumstances being what they are, I made some preparations. Master Subaru, how is your leg injury?"

"Thanks to your Ferris, me and Beako made it through somehow. If I tried hard, I think I could jump a couple of times without crying."

"That is good to hear...or is it?"

After hearing Subaru's irreverent quip, Crusch innocently tilted her head in apparent confusion. Out of the corner of his eye, Subaru could see Ferris silently mouthing the words *You have to reeeeest!* Subaru donned a proper and serious look.

"So can you tell me what's going on in Pristella right now?"

"Of course. However, there is something I must ask of you first—Master Subaru, is there no mistaking that you encountered the Witch Cult's Archbishops of the Seven Deadly Sins?"

"...Yeah, no doubt about that. My leg injury, and Emilia... Her kidnapping was all their doing as well. I saw them with my own eyes, and no one goes around pretending to be those guys."

Surely, no one would be so suicidal as to falsely claim the title of an Archbishop of the Seven Deadly Sins. Regardless, Subaru had also seen part of Sirius's and Regulus's Authorities. And considering their revolting personalities, their identities were almost certain.

After hearing Subaru's reply, Crusch murmured, "So Lady Emilia really was..." as she lowered the tone of her voice before continuing. "...It would seem we should indeed think of that broadcast as fact."

"Broadcast?"

Crusch drew herself up as the unexpected term reached Subaru's ears.

"Well, there was a broadcast about one hour ago. Just like the morning broadcasts, it was conducted by using the metia in Pristella's city hall."

"...Wait, it was the Witch Cult that made a broadcast? Did they hijack the metia there?"

When Crusch had trouble picking her words, Subaru asked about the worst case he could think of. Crusch, Ferris, and Al nodded in silence, confirming his suspicions.

"The broadcast was sudden, but the culprit's identity is clear. They were considerate enough to openly announce who they were, you see."

"Announce... Right, that's exactly what they do. They always announce themselves before doing anything."

Crusch's words, filled with righteous indignation, drew a deep nod from Subaru.

Thinking back to the Archbishops of the Seven Deadly Sins whom Subaru had encountered to date, all of them had stated their names and titles without fail. It seemed like it was the one rule that was actually observed by these morally bankrupt people who were unable or unwilling to uphold any other societal norms.

Was it Sirius who'd seized the broadcast, compelled by her incoherent delusions and a twisted desire to enter the limelight? Or was it Regulus, who cloaked himself in self-deception like a suit of armor?

"—Capella Emerada Lugunica, the Archbishop of Lust."

"...Eh?"

When a totally unfamiliar name made a sudden entrance, Subaru was dumbstruck as he looked at Crusch.

She met his gaze head-on, the intensity in her amber eyes only growing stronger.

"The broadcast made this declaration: The Water Gate City of Pristella has fallen into the hands of the Witch Cult."

2

"So you woke up, Natsuki. I'm glad; that's such a relief."

Anastasia flashed Subaru an elegant smile the moment she saw him come in, with Al lending his shoulder for support.

Unlike Crusch, she was wearing the same outfit as earlier in the day: a kimono and her white fox scarf wrapped around her neck. Combining that with her calm outward demeanor, she seemed to be the only one who was acting like this was just another day— No, even she couldn't manage that. Subaru could see faint traces of fatigue pulling at the fringes of Anastasia's face.

That only made sense. She was one of the concerned parties that was deeply affected by the Witch Cult's mayhem.

"Sorry for oversleeping, Anastasia. Do I still have a seat?"

"Not to worry, I have arranged a spot just for you. It's critical to talk to you about the people you ran into as soon as possible, Natsuki. So come on—sit, sit!" Anastasia beckoned him by hand.

Subaru favored his right leg as he walked to the round table at the center of the room. Borrowing Al's assistance, he plopped down into his chair, taking a breath as he scanned the room.

"*Whew*, that's a lot comfier... Uh, so this is where we're gathering?"

"This is the Witch Cult Disaster Response HQ. It is a bit seedy-lookin' for that, though."

Chiming in after Subaru, Al played with the metal fixtures on his helm as he heaved a hearty sigh. Overhearing his murmur, Anastasia put her hands on her hips and closed one eye as she scolded him.

"Come now, don't be like that, Al. I can appreciate how worried you are since your precious princess isn't here."

"Well, not so much worried as scared. She'll definitely be angry that I'm not by her side in a situation like this."

He shook his head in dread. The roster of attendees at the meeting certainly made his fears seem credible.

They were inside a conference room, which was wide enough to accommodate twelve people. Multiple royal-selection candidates, including Anastasia, had assembled, but Al's master—Priscilla—was not among them.

Of course, she hadn't been present when Emilia was whisked away by Regulus, either.

"Come to think of it, my party's way too short on people. Not even Otto or Garfiel are here."

"Unfortunately, it wasn't possible to gather everyone involved in the royal selection. On my end, Mimi hasn't come back since last night, either. Hopefully, Garfiel's with her." Anastasia touched a hand to her cheek, concerned that she didn't know the whereabouts of the girl whom she seemed to treat like a precious daughter.

"If they're together, then there's no need to worry about them running into trouble… Anyway, why meet at this place?" Subaru gestured at the building in general. "Al called this the Witch Cult Disaster Response HQ, and that really does seem to be spot-on. The situation in the city sounds serious enough to warrant it, too… But why is the HQ set up inside the Muse Company?"

Subaru finally asked the question that had been bugging him for a while now.

Indeed, Subaru and the others were currently inside the Muse Company building, which was located on the affluent main boulevard of the city.

He'd visited the magic crystal trading company's main store just a day earlier, and now it was operating as an emergency shelter. The wounded were being treated underground, while refugees were given guest rooms. With the state of his leg, Subaru, too, had been carried underground, where it was so overcrowded that coming up to the conference room had been quite a journey.

"It's a nice, big building, so I get the appeal of using it as a shelter when push comes to shove, but a company's still a company, right? They're not usually the first choice for setting up a response HQ."

"That's what you'd think at first, right? But there's a good reason. The biggest one is that Kiritaka is on the Council of Ten, which runs Pristella… Really, when you get down to it, he's the leading member of the city's top ten most influential people."

"Are we talking about the same Kiritaka? Seriously?"

Subaru's face tensed up as he recalled the not particularly pleasant run-in he'd had with the man just the day before. Of course, judging from Kiritaka's station and how much everyone seemed to trust him, Subaru figured that he possessed a talent that matched his status.

It was just that his first impression of the man and the latest incident from the day before were difficult to reconcile with this new information.

"—Master Kiritaka is an upstanding and capable man. There's no reason to be concerned, Master Subaru."

Crusch had read his thoughts right as she joined them in the conference room.

Having split off midway up from the underground treatment area to fetch Wilhelm, she'd returned with a freshly dressed Ferris and the Sword Devil in tow.

"Thank you for coming, Crusch. What about Kiritaka?"

"It would seem he is too busy with the evacuation and dispatching of personnel to attend at this time. He said he would join our conference once matters calm down a little."

After hearing Crusch's reply, Anastasia went, "I see, I see," with a nod. Watching the exchange, Wilhelm glanced at Subaru in his seat and the bandage on his leg.

"Sir Subaru, what is the condition of your leg?"

"About as good as it looks. Sorry for the pitiful state I'm in. Wilhelm, you're…"

"I originally came to seek Sir Kiritaka's opinion on how to best allocate the city's forces. Having completed that bit of business, I am currently escorting Lady Crusch. That man is quite accomplished for his age."

"Hnnngh… At this point, that's the only thing I can say…"

With both Crusch and Wilhelm vouching for him, Subaru could only conclude that his doubts about Kiritaka's ability had been misplaced. But if that was true, then just how important was Liliana to Kiritaka if she was able to provoke him that much?

He brushed those pointless thoughts aside when Crusch called his name.

"Master Subaru, it was immediately after hearing the broadcast that Lady Anastasia immediately suggested we relocate here. Thanks to our acquaintance with Sir Kiritaka and this building being designated as a shelter, Ferris has been able to use his abilities where they are most needed."

"The fact that we were able to keep Subawu's leg in one piece was also thanks to that decision."

Apparently, Kiritaka was so reliable that he was the main reason

Anastasia had suggested they set up here. Crusch and Ferris both seemed to concur with that assessment. From the way they put it, Subaru had lucked out, given the terrible ordeal he'd been through.

"Worst-case scenario, I could've bit the dust right then and there and taken Beako with me…"

"But that didn't happen. That little girl did everything she could to get ya outta there. You're a lucky dude, Bro."

Subaru managed a smile at Al's lighthearted take on things. If Subaru actually had any luck, he would've made it through the day without dying multiple times.

Sadly, reality was not so accommodating. That was why Subaru didn't trust fortune even a little.

—Subaru Natsuki's good luck dried up in a back alley on the same day he'd been summoned to another world.

"I'm all out of luck, so the only thing I can do is stay steady and work with what I've got."

Even now, it was only thanks to Beatrice's sacrifice that he had any moves to make at all. Subaru had to rise to the occasion.

"Incidentally, is everyone here? Setting aside Crusch's crew for the moment, Anastasia's team seems way more understaffed than usual…"

Focusing on the matter at hand, Subaru mentioned the missing faces that he expected to be attending. Otto, who should've been at the Muse Company already for follow-up negotiations, was concerningly absent. Additionally, Julius, Ricardo, and the Iron Fangs, who served as Anastasia's main combat forces, were nowhere to be seen.

On top of all that, neither Felt nor anyone associated with her was anywhere in sight.

"Julius, the big doggy-man, and the Iron Fangs escorted Ferri over here. After that, they left to check on the other shelters."

"They've been instructed to contact Ferris if they happen upon anyone gravely injured in the hopes of saving even one more life."

"Gotcha. That's… Wait, what do you mean, 'contact him'?"

In a world where cell phones weren't widespread or really available at all, there shouldn't have been an easy way to stay in touch remotely. However, Ferris responded to Subaru's doubts by saying, "Look," and raising his hand. In his palm was a folding mirror—or more precisely, a metia that looked like one.

"A conversation mirror?!"

"Heh-heh, that's right. It's the same one we seized after the battle against the Witch Cult a year ago. Lady Anastasia has been keeping it safe, and she let us take it out for a spin."

Ferris winked as he held up the metia that made it possible to communicate with anyone holding its opposite. It really did perform the same role a phone did.

A year ago, this had been part of the spoils of war acquired after the battle with Petelgeuse, the Archbishop of Sloth. Now these metia were apparently seeing use again in another battle against the Witch Cult.

"The ones that can connect with three mirrors at once are rare. It'd be a waste not to break them out at a time like this."

"So the other ones got distributed to the guys out on patrol—gotcha."

It was karma that metia once owned by the Witch Cult would end up being used to fight them. Anastasia was incredibly well prepared to have them on hand, ready to go.

"Okay, all that makes sense. But Otto's not involved in that, is he?"

Subaru asked about Otto, who probably would've been irritated that he was being treated like an afterthought.

It was none other than Subaru who'd proudly refer to Otto as a domestic adviser who could hold his own in a fight, but compared with Julius and Ricardo, he was overwhelmingly outclassed as a warrior.

Subaru figured there was no way he'd be part of the crew that went out on patrol, but his question made Crusch lower her eyes.

"Unfortunately, Master Otto is not here. He was nowhere to be seen by the time we arrived. He might be at one of the nearby shelters…"

"Th-that guy's bad timing is just legendary…"

Subaru cursed Otto's inability to be at the right place at the right time despite the fact that he was already supposed to be at the Muse Company to begin with.

Regardless of where he was or what he was doing, it would be a serious problem if he wasn't safe and sound—

"—I guess there's no need to worry. He's the last person I expect to slip up, so I'll save him for later."

"I-is that really fine? Perhaps you should worry somewhat more…"

"Nah, it's all good. In terms of pure fighting strength, he can't hold a candle to a guy like Wilhelm, but…when it comes to staying alive, Otto's basically second to none."

"…You must…really trust him a great deal."

"It's actually kinda embarrassing, so don't tell him I said that, okay?"

If nothing else, Subaru fully intended to take that secret with him to the grave.

Either way, he decided to trust that the patrolling unit was on the right track and that Otto was safe for the moment. The same went for the absent Garfiel. He'd worry about the lack of combat strength later.

Setting them aside, the concern that suddenly came to mind was—

"Are Patlash and Fulfew still back at the inn? Both of them are sharp, so there's probably nothing to worry about… Come to think of it, Priscilla's one thing since she's staying in a different inn, but where's Felt and her people?"

"We currently don't know the whereabouts of either party. I heard Lady Felt left the inn on some errand, but there is one element of uncertainty."

"And that would be…?"

"Apparently, she was planning to have a chat with a certain red-head who ruined the mood this morning."

A troubled expression appeared on Anastasia's face. Subaru's was much the same. However, the one with the most concerning face of all was Wilhelm, who found it difficult to maintain his composure for obvious reasons.

Seeing Wilhelm harden his cheeks as he went silent, Anastasia let out a little sigh.

"That being said, Felt has Reinhard with her, so we shouldn't worry too much… Still, it's scary to not have any idea what that other little princess is up to."

Changing topics, Anastasia pressed a hand to her cheek as she pointedly tried to probe Al for information. Al simply went, "Gimme a break…" as he responded with a throaty voice. "A guy like me can't tell what the princess is thinking. Well, I don't think she's gotten herself in trouble or anything, but my guess is that she ain't gonna just patiently sit and wait this out."

"Come to think of it, Priscilla was with Liliana at the park in the First District. After we split up, I bumped into the guys who turned my leg into a chew toy, so I'm not sure what happened to her after that, but…"

"The princess was in First District? …That ain't too far from here."

Processing the new information that Subaru had offered, Al rubbed his steel helm's jaw and sank into thought. Of course, the proper thing for a retainer to do after learning of his master's location would have been to rush out to her side.

"Well, the princess probably has thoughts of her own. No need to dash off in a panic or anything."

"Are…are you sure?"

"Didn't you say so yourself, Bro? It's all about that trust, man. This is embarrassin', so make sure you don't tell the princess I said that."

Subaru made a face when Al took his words and turned them around on him. Subaru's reservations aside, both of them understood the thought process behind the other's decision.

"All right, sorry for making you bear with me while I took time to figure things out. Let's get to the topic at hand. Since we're in the Witch Cult Disaster Response HQ, tell me—what's the plan?"

"First, we're waiting for word from the unit we dispatched.

However, the very fact that the Witch Cult broadcast originated from the government office's metia means..."

"There is no mistaking that the city's four control towers have been seized."

As she said that, Crusch stood by a window and gestured outside with her hand. Following where her fingers pointed, if Subaru squinted, he could make out a stonework tower connected to the city's exterior wall—that must have been one of the control towers.

These structures were administration facilities that regulated the amount of water as well as the flow rate of the city's always-running waterways. They occupied the cardinal directions, with one each in the north, south, east, and west. Only one of them was visible from the conference room, but—

"—What's that flag I see up top?"

In the distance, there was a fluttering banner rising over the tower. Subaru didn't remember seeing one while wandering around the city that morning or the day before. The flag had some kind of strange symbol traced on it using red dye.

The eye pattern pricked at an unpleasant part of Subaru's memories.

"That is the symbol of the Witch Cult. It's rare for them to engage in such public displays, but..."

Like Crusch said, that symbol was the same one that marked the signature black outfits of the Witch Cultists. The robe that Sirius had been wearing sported it as well.

And now it was on a flag flying over the control tower—the message was crystal clear.

"Let me guess: All four control towers have the same flag?"

"That is correct. Now that they have seized the control towers, should they wish it, our enemies can submerge Pristella in water at any moment... Action must be taken immediately."

Crusch made it obvious what an awful situation the city was currently in.

This was like if a baby was holding the detonator for a nuclear bomb—what made it far worse was that unlike a baby, the Archbishops of the Seven Deadly Sins understood perfectly well the value of the switch in their hands.

"Are the city's residents panicking? Hearing that the Witch Cult has taken over the control towers can't be good news."

"Thanks to Pristella's extensive preparations for floods, chaos in the city has been kept tamped down to a surprising degree. However, evacuating the city is no simple matter."

One of Lugunica's five largest cities, Pristella had a population of roughly a hundred thousand. It wasn't impossible, but conducting a major evacuation of that many people without sparking a panic was far from easy.

Factoring in the Witch Cult only made matters even more complicated, since it would be essential to avoid drawing their attention.

"The city's main gate is the only real way in or out of the city, and one of the control towers is very close to it, so the enemy's really got us by the scruff of our necks. Speaking of those guys…"

"—The three Archbishops of the Seven Deadly Sins, huh?"

Taking Ferris's meaning, Subaru highlighted the reason that the situation was so dire.

Judging by the reactions around the room, everyone else was up to speed. It certainly wasn't good news, but it wasn't particularly surprising, either. They were simply wary of the threat that the enemy posed.

"There's Wrath, who wounded me along with the other people in the square; Greed, who carried off Emilia; and Lust, who's apparently broadcasting from the municipal offices… An all-star team of assholes."

"You seem unexpectedly calm about this, Natsuki, even though Emilia was kidnapped and everything."

"That's exactly why. If losing my cool and going berserk would get her back, I'd raise enough hell to make it into the history books. But it doesn't work that way, so…"

Subaru had already made one blunder by losing his cool. The price was Emilia's abduction. Beatrice had settled the tab in his stead.

He couldn't afford any more screwups. He needed a heart of steel so that he could take back everything.

"Sir Subaru's feelings are admirable. I shall do everything in my meager power to assist you."

"Thank you so much, Wilhelm. That's super reassuring."

Wilhelm, who was incredibly invested in helping the two troubled lovebirds for personal reasons, had just pledged his support. That was alone was a big comfort. The Sword Devil's strength was indispensable if they wanted to last in a direct fight.

"? What is it, Al?"

It was then that Subaru abruptly noticed that Al had been watching the exchange between him and Wilhelm in silence. But when Subaru posed the question, Al offered a noncommittal "Nothing, really" and shrugged. "I was just thinking that you're pretty twisted in your own way, Bro— Anyway, let's push on to the main topic."

"R-right, suppose we should. Uh, so about that broadcast…"

Even though what Al said bothered him, Subaru turned his attention back to the room as a whole to bring up something that had been bothering him since the initial discussion.

Namely—

"—This Archbishop of Lust called herself Capella Emerada Lugunica? What's up with that?"

3

—*Capella Emerada Lugunica.* That was the name the Archbishop of Lust had used to introduce herself.

Subaru hadn't personally heard the introduction, but the name alone was more than enough to catch his attention. In particular, he couldn't simply dismiss the *Lugunica* part.

"The only people with *Lugunica* as their family name should be in the royal family, right? Why claim that name?"

"Isn't it just to mess with us? The royal family all dyin' of illness is a pretty famous story, y'know?"

"There must be some kind of scheme behind it. I believe it would be hasty of us to dismiss the matter as nothing more than a prank in poor taste."

Al and Crusch aired their respective opinions about the doubt that Subaru harbored.

Given this was the Witch Cult, either explanation was entirely possible and worth considering.

"—One thing does come to mind."

It was then that Wilhelm raised a hand, cutting in with a new perspective.

"And what might that be?"

"While I do not have anything to add about the name *Capella*… there was most certainly a member of the Lugunica royal family who went by the name of *Emerada Lugunica*."

"!!"

Everyone blinked in surprise at this unexpected reveal. Wilhelm touched his chin and half closed his blue eyes as he rummaged through his memories.

"Lady Emerada was alive prior to the Demi-human War…over fifty years ago. I have never met her personally, but records mention that she was a woman of exceptional beauty and wisdom."

"So is this a case of them impersonating someone who actually existed? Maybe it's an attempt to ruin someone's good name?"

That would be a rather petty and spiteful thing to do, but such an unsavory pastime was far from unthinkable when the Archbishops of the Seven Deadly Sins were involved.

But then Wilhelm retorted with a quick "No," shaking his head at Subaru's remark.

"I do not know the opponent's aim in doing this…but Lady Emerada was not someone who passed away with great deeds to her name. If anything, it is the opposite."

"You mean…"

"Lady Emerada succumbed to illness at a young age. However, not only was her death not mourned by the kingdom, but she was also denied a state funeral, as would be standard. The stated reason was that conditions at the time were too dire to hold a formal ceremony. However, the real reason is that the kingdom's people had no desire to do any such thing."

Wilhelm's explanation left Subaru with such a disturbing sense of foreboding that he said nothing. Noticing this, Wilhelm let out a tiny sigh.

"Lady Emerada was a terribly beautiful and wise person…but she was also reportedly cruel in the extreme, and constantly shrouded in an unfathomable darkness. As such, though she was part of the royal family, she was branded a heretic, and even news of her passing seemed to have been suppressed for some time."

It must have been painful for Wilhelm to speak in uncertainties that reflected on the dignity of the kingdom he once served with his sword arm. He had sounded increasingly tongue-tied by the latter half of his tale.

In contrast, choosing to go by the name of *Emerada* seemed to be a comment on the poor character of Lust after this revelation.

"…There's no way it's the real person, so Lust is almost certainly just pretending to be Emerada."

"Claiming the name of a royal who fell victim to illness is most likely an indirect form of harassment aimed at those who knew Emerada. I believe that most who masquerade as a member of the royal family do so to invite suspicion and mistrust."

Wilhelm's conclusion made everyone present sigh with unsettled looks.

Unlike Subaru and Al, who did not feel any particular allegiance toward the kingdom itself, Crusch and Wilhelm seemed stricken by what was happening.

However, the strongest reaction came from someone besides them.

"—That's unforgivable."

"Ferris?"

Murmuring in a low growl, Ferris was shaking a fist.

Though Ferris usually seemed ever aloof, rarely concerning himself with anything besides Crusch, he currently wore a mask of raw anger. The sight shocked Subaru.

Lust's evil intentions were tantamount to spitting on the faces of the royal family of Lugunica. There was no doubt that to Ferris, a knight of the royal guard, this was a desecration of the highest order.

At the same time, Subaru sensed that there was another reason for Ferris's rage that had nothing to do with fealty for the kingdom.

"—Ah."

As Ferris harbored such deep, silent anger, Crusch moved close, gently taking his hand. Instantly, Ferris gasped and lifted his face, only to be met by Crusch's steady gaze and soft smile.

"I-I'm sorry, Lady Crusch. I shouldn't have lost control like that..."

"It is fine, Ferris. I am the one who should be sorry, for I suspect your anger is largely on my behalf."

"____"

From the way Ferris lowered his head, Crusch's words must have hit the mark. It was probably true that Crusch's lost memories were the source of his aggravation.

That they could not share that burden gnawed at him, undermining the powerful bonds that should have connected the liege and her retainer.

"Yes, yes, let's all simmer down. Getting worked up at every little bit of mayhem our opponents cause would just be playing into their hand."

It was then that Anastasia gathered everyone's attention with a resounding clap. As Subaru had surmised, she was quite accustomed to presiding over meetings with large numbers of people. She looked at everyone in the room before continuing:

"Whatever Lust might be planning doesn't change the fact that she's our enemy. And it doesn't change the fact that she holds the control towers, which means she has us by the scruff of our necks."

"Man, you change up fast... No wonder you're the one Princess pays the most attention to."

"Why, thank you. The way you put it wasn't the most comforting, though."

As Anastasia restored their focus and cleared the air, Al praised her by using his own frame of reference, drawing a troubled smile from Anastasia. Then he twisted his neck and said, "If anything, these Archbishops are so messed up in the head that trying to find the logic in their plans is probably a waste of time. More importantly, what are we gonna do about their demands?"

"Demands? Wait, wait, this is news to me. What demands?"

"Ahh, right, I was just about to bring up the contents of Lust's threat to get you up to speed, Natsuki."

Subaru voiced his surprise at Al's mention of demands, and Anastasia confirmed that an explanation was coming. Her word choice hinted at the menace they were facing.

"The Witch Cult took over the control towers and the city hall, but it would seem their objective is different than, say, destroying the city or massacring the residents. According to Lust, they're searching for something, and threatening the populace is simply a means to that end," Anastasia explained.

"Then…in other words, they've taken the city hostage as some act of terrorism?"

The reason he hadn't ever considered the possibility of the Witch Cult doing this sort of thing was simply because terrorists took hostages as a means of negotiation. Such rational acts of evil didn't match up with Subaru's internal idea of what the Witch Cult stood for and how they operated.

"Natsuki, are you all right? You seem startled."

"Nah, nah, I just didn't see that coming from their crew… Sorry, getting sidetracked. Anyway, what are they looking for?"

It probably wasn't anything decent. There was also the possibility that with Emilia already secured, they had already gotten what they came for, but from the looks of things, that was unlikely.

As Subaru made those deductions, Anastasia gently stroked the white fox scarf around her neck before she replied:

"—The Witch's bones."

"…What?"

That answer was so far beyond Subaru's expectations that his brain was unable to process those words. While he was reeling, Anastasia spoke up again.

"The Witch's bones. That's why they came to this city."

"―――"

When that incomprehensible fact was thrust in his face once more, Subaru's words failed him.

Trying to imagine what the Witch's bones were and their significance was a demand far beyond Subaru.

In the first place, the very notion of the Witch having left her bones behind as some sort of relic sounded like a complete hoax. After all—

"The Witch of Jealousy, who swallowed up half the world long ago, was never destroyed and continues to slumber in a land far to the East, still coveting the world—or so goes the tales that have been passed down for generations."

Still holding Ferris's hand, Crusch directly addressed the source of Subaru's agitation. Swallowing, he simply responded with a "yeah" and a nod. "I heard that from Beako, too. The Witch of Jealousy isn't dead; she's just sealed away. But if that's the case, then how would she leave bones behind?"

As he spoke, he couldn't help but remember his fleeting encounter with the Witch of Jealousy in the Sanctuary.

She was a black shadow of a woman who exchanged only several scant words with him in the span of a few moments—but for some reason, Subaru's heart rejected, stubbornly, the notion that she was dead in any way. He had no choice but to reject it.

Subaru's soul wanted to cry out: *It's impossible for her to be dead. And someday—you will come to kill me, yes?*

Yes, those words, which were not a real promise, demanded and begged for him to reject the possibility that the Witch was dead.

"That's right. There's no way that's true. It can't be..." The uneasiness filling Subaru made his breathing uneven.

"—Calm down, Bro. Look, about these Witch's bones... It's not like they have to belong to the infamous Witch of Jealousy, right?"

"—Wha?"

Al grasped his shoulder, speaking those words in an effort to soothe him. Everyone else in the room turned their eyes on Al, though they couldn't see his expression under his steel helm.

"So how about it? Like Bro and the young duchess were sayin', the most famous Witch was sealed away and all, but there were other Witches, too, right?"

"There are beings besides the Witch of Jealousy who we call witches as a term of convenience. During the Demi-human War, magic users cooperating with the Demi-human Alliance were often called witches as well, and they were greatly feared."

"Meaning there's a precedent. Then…"

"Well, it's a little different for this city. If a witch is mentioned here, then it must be about a real one rather than some imitation who's only a witch in name."

Wilhelm had been the first to answer Al, but Anastasia's follow-up confidently drew a conclusion that Subaru found difficult to accept.

"From that manner of speaking…I take it that Lady Anastasia has something in mind?"

"Even I wouldn't be talking like this if I wasn't almost certain. The reason I wanted to meet up with Kiritaka after hearing Lust's broadcast is because of that same hunch, even if it meant going out of my way to make it happen."

Anastasia narrowed her light-blue eyes as she divulged what she'd kept hidden up to that point. She then surveyed everyone's faces all at once.

"Anyone can find this out with a little digging, but does everyone know how this Water Gate City came to be?"

"…I heard that way back, this was originally supposed to be a trap for catching something."

Subaru recalled that upon first arriving in Pristella, Beatrice had given him a history lesson as he admired the beautiful urban landscape. She hadn't elaborated on exactly what was supposed to be trapped, though.

"That's correct," said Anastasia, nodding at Subaru's reply. "Apparently, this city was a trap set for the Witch. The Witch met her end here when the entire place was flooded. According to legend, her bones remain somewhere in this city, even today."

"But the Witch of Jealousy was sealed and…"

The full story about the city's past had been revealed in an unexpected fashion. Still, nothing seemed to add up.

As Subaru began to disagree—

"—Typhon drowned in a flood, right...? So this is where that happened, huh?"

—he was interrupted by a faint, halting murmur that originated from inside a steel helm.

"_____"

When Subaru looked over in surprise at the unanticipated mention of a certain name, Al was blithely playing with the metal fixtures of his helmet, having fallen deep into thought. But Subaru had no doubt that he'd just said the name *Typhon*.

This was the name of the Witch of Pride, one of the six other Witches from the same era as the Witch of Jealousy.

"The answer to your question is simple, Natsuki. There are Witches besides the Witch of Jealousy. There are almost no records remaining, but there certainly are oral legends. And one of them states that in this city..."

"—This is where the bones of the ancient Witch remain."

Neither Anastasia nor Crusch heard Al's murmur as they steadily advanced the conversation. As a result, Subaru missed his chance to investigate deeper into Al's cryptic remark.

Of course, when he took a moment to consider their current priorities, it was obvious this wasn't the time to get sidetracked.

But if what Al murmured under his breath really was true, the Witch of Pride, whom Subaru had encountered at the Sanctuary—the Witch who was a bundle of youthful innocence—had perished in the very city that Subaru currently stood in.

The thought alone made Subaru's chest ache.

"What is the connection between the Witch's bones and Lady Anastasia making haste to meet with Master Kiritaka?"

Returning to the topic at hand, Crusch once again asked about Anastasia's true intentions. Anastasia began her reply by winking.

"The existence of the Witch's bones is a closely held secret in the Water Gate City...and the only people familiar with the legends and supposed whereabouts are on the Council of Ten. I figured I might as well try asking one."

"Meaning only the big shots of the city have any idea… Anastasia, does that mean what I think it means? That you think it's better to give in to Lust's demands?"

"Of course not. Complying with someone who threatens people to get what they want will only end with you being taken advantage of every single time. Anyway, I just wanted to confirm the current location of the bones… There's no guarantee that one of the Council of Ten won't do something stupid and tell Lust where they are, right?"

"…I suppose that's true."

Unlike Subaru's shallow mindset, Anastasia's assessments were swift and accurate.

Negotiating with terrorists often did make things worse. In their current situation, the Archbishops would almost certainly flood the city the instant they recovered the Witch's bones.

That was how assured Subaru was about their deceitful character.

"See, I was looking into the details of this while you were asleep, Natsuki. When Kiritaka makes it up here, we can talk about these bones in more detail. Then we can decide on a proper response."

"By 'response,' you mean…"

"—Whether to fight or to flee, of course."

There was quiet determination in Anastasia's low voice. It was as if an angry blue flame had been lit within her.

"I'm the one who called all the royal-selection candidates here to Pristella. Of course I feel responsible for the way things have turned out… I need to extract some compensation from these unexpected visitors after all they've done."

Anastasia was the owner of a major company who didn't have any notable ability in combat worth speaking of. And yet her soft-spoken pronouncement made Subaru feel like a great beast had just clamped its fangs down on his neck.

This was a sharp reminder that Anastasia Hoshin was one of the last people he wanted as an enemy.

"—Ahh, wait, wait. The conversation mirror's responding! It must be Julius and the others."

Just as the conversation reached a lull, Ferris raised a hand with a look of surprise. He was holding the metia up, showing how the mirror's surface glowed white in search of a response.

Setting it down on the round table so that everyone could see, Ferris gently touched the surface of the mirror with his hand.

"—It seems that Ferris and…everyone else is over there. I take it you can see me?"

A tall, handsome man with purple hair rose to the mirror's surface. It was Julius Juukulius, who had gone out into the city to save lives.

As soon as it was clear that Julius was on the other end, Anastasia rushed to place herself in front of the mirror with a rapid patter of feet.

"Julius, I was getting worried after you didn't get in touch for a while. How's it looking outside?"

"I am very sorry to have troubled you. The situation in the city is chaotic. The residents are becoming increasingly enraged by the Witch Cult… More importantly, there is something I must urgently convey without delay."

Quickly cutting his reunion with Anastasia short, Julius instantly vanished from the mirror's surface. Displayed in the mirror in the stead of the tall, handsome man was a little cat-person wearing a monocle—TB.

It turned out that he, one of the three sibling lieutenants of the Iron Fangs, had been accompanying Julius.

"TB? What's wrong? You seem upset…"

"L-Lady Anastasia, this is very, very bad. Has my older sister returned yet?"

Interrupting Anastasia, TB asked a frantic question. Bewildered by his disheveled appearance, Anastasia answered with a quick no, shaking her head.

"Mimi hasn't been back. I was worried about her, too…TB?"

A profound sense of dread could be felt from the other side of the mirror. However, there was still more to come. Suddenly, what looked like a ripple glided across the conversation mirror's glass surface.

"Excuse me! Is Lady Anastasia there?! This is bad! Hetaro says that Mimi's in trouble!"

An instant later, the third of the linked conversation mirrors connected to the call. Displayed on the mirror's surface was the dog-man Ricardo, staring into the mirror with his mouth wide open. But as soon as the image became clear, Ricardo's head was immediately pushed aside by a teary-eyed kitty-person.

"Lady! Lady!! Big Sis is— She's…!!"

The one pleading in a tearful voice was Hetaro, TB's almost identical-looking brother. While the boy normally wore a meek expression, his face now was twisted up in abject sorrow.

"Hetaro, calm down. What happened? Speak slowly and clearly."

"Th-the effects of our blessing— It's flowing from Big Sis and into us! Sh-she must've gotten hurt really bad… At this rate, Big Sis won't…!"

"'Blessing'… You mean the blessing of thirds, yes? In other words, Mimi got injured at some point, and it's affecting Hetaro and TB, too? Do I have it right so far?"

Hetaro and TB nodded simultaneously to confirm Anastasia's deductions.

Listening to the conversation from behind, Subaru recalled hearing from Mimi that the blessing of thirds—the one that tied the three siblings together—made them share wounds and fatigue.

Once upon a time back at the Roswaal Manor, a sudden change came over Ram when Rem had been in danger. This was similar to what Mimi and her brothers had—which meant Mimi was currently in trouble.

Urgency raced through everyone present, including on the other ends of the conversation mirrors, as they grasped this new development. Just as they processed the striking revelation that one of their own was clearly in mortal danger—

* * *

"*Yoo-hoo, yoo-hoo-hoo, yahoo-hoo!*"

—a brash voice that seemed to not care about the situation at all reverberated throughout the city.

"What the...?"

Subaru, unsure how to react to this abrupt announcement, instinctively turned his face toward the ceiling. The voice was coming from somewhere above. Not from the ceiling, but quite literally from the sky itself.

This was the work of a metia that reached every corner of the city—and the one using the municipal office's facilities to make this broadcast was the same Archbishop of Lust who had come up in conversation several times already.

"*To all you meatbags in the city: Are you having fun? Have you gotten hammered and horny from hearing my lovely voice for the umpteenth time today? Bwa-ha-ha-ha-ha!*"

It was a high-pitched, grating laugh. That haughty voice paid no heed to the feelings of those who were forced to listen. This was an assault on the ears of every person in the city.

It had only taken Subaru moments to come to a realization—the person making this broadcast had a vicious, ugly character.

"So this is Lust... Man, does she have perfect timing or what?!"

"*Now then, all you meatbags who can't help but get hot and heavy at the sound of a beautiful girl's voice, I have a very important announcement from your oh-so-gentle and merciful broadcaster! So listen up! Pay attention! Cleaned out your ears yet?!*"

In contrast to Subaru, who was unable to conceal his restlessness, those hearing this kind of broadcast for the second time displayed a variety of reactions. Wariness, anger, hatred—in any case, they were not nearly as shaken while waiting for the words that were bound to follow.

What was the owner of this maddening, agonizing voice going to tell them?

"Soooo it turns out that even though I asked you so, so nicely, a couple of people who clearly didn't get the message decided to target the municipal offices... This upsets me so much! Really, I can't exaggerate what complete and total morons you ignorant meatbags are!"

"...We're not putting up with this anymore. Ricardo, Julius, listen closely: Go back to the municipal offices with Hetaro and TB and have them find out where Mimi wen—"

As the broadcast continued, Anastasia decided to address the most pressing issue. She gave orders to her knight and her loyal hound through the conversation mirrors to try and secure Mimi's safety.

However, even as Anastasia strove to maintain her calm, the change in the situation made sport of even her.

—And this came in what was, to all concerned, the worst of all possible forms.

"—Who goes there?!"

Abruptly, Wilhelm shouted sharply toward the entrance to the conference room. As the Sword Devil readied his now-drawn blade, Subaru and the others turned in the same direction.

An instant later, the door practically burst open as a lone figure raced into the conference room.

For a moment, the sudden appearance of an intruder startled Subaru and the others, but the first to shed his surprise and raise his voice was none other than Subaru himself.

"Garfiel?!"

The familiar voice made Garfiel, out of breath and slick with sweat, lift his face.

Noticing Subaru's presence, he drew near with a tottering, uncertain gait. Subaru only belatedly realized the cause of this uncharacteristic behavior and the strange atmosphere that had befallen the room.

Garfiel was carrying something in his arms.

No one was able to speak a word as Garfiel stopped before Subaru. Once he got that far, Garfiel crumpled to his knees, lowering his head as if clinging to Subaru.

Then when he presented what lay in his bloodied arms, his throat trembled.

"I'm sorry... I'm so sorry, General!! I'm...! I'm useless! Worthless...!!"

There was a shriek. Garfiel howled in grief.

Cradled in his bloodied arms was Mimi, who was visibly at death's door.

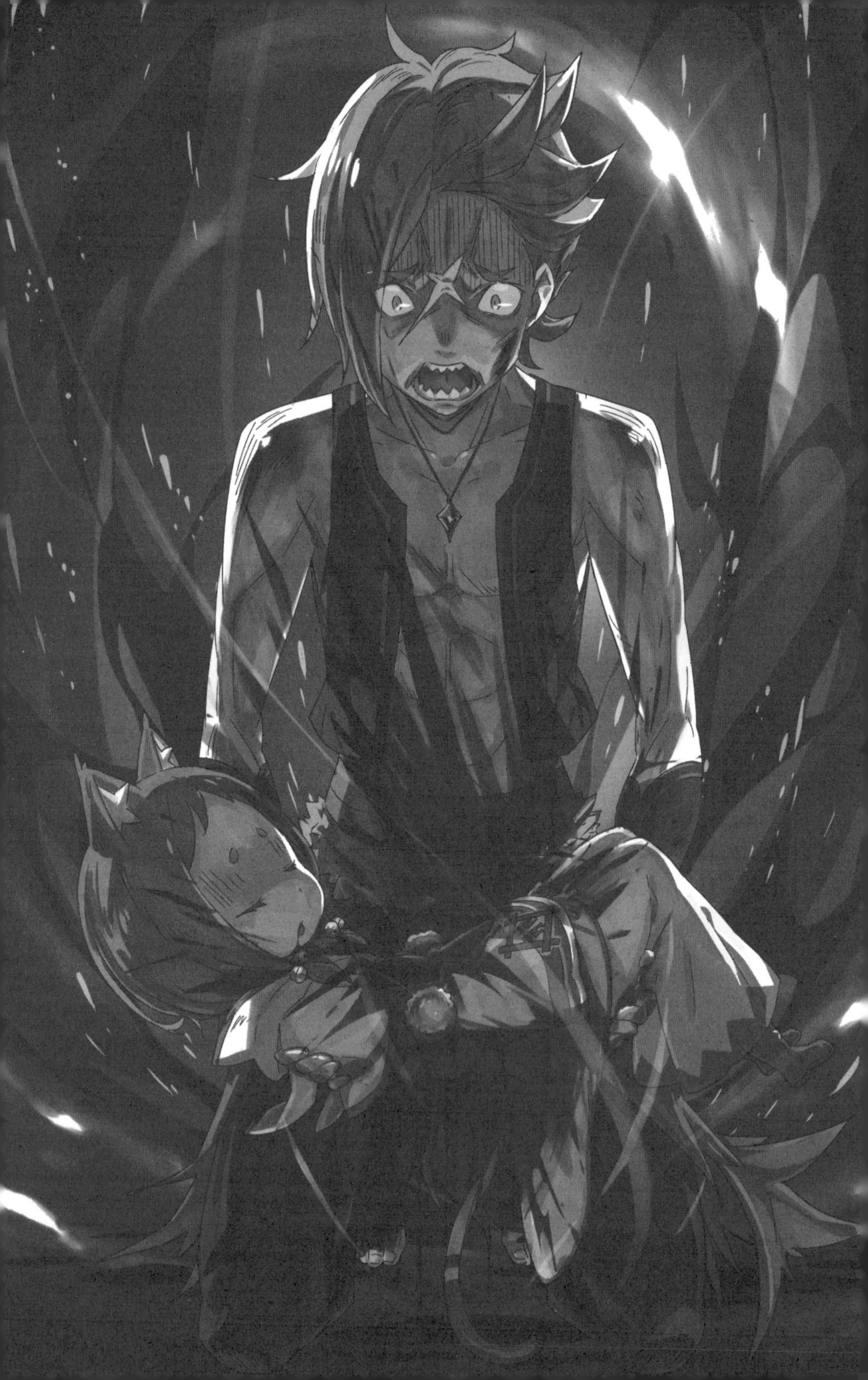

CHAPTER 4
GORGEOUS TIGER

1

Rewinding time to the day before Garfiel raced into the shelter—

"―――"

As he walked along a city street at dusk, Garfiel's breath caught when he abruptly noticed someone's gaze on him.

Standing at a street corner on the other side of a crowd was a black silhouette of a woman. Her reflection swayed gently on the water's surface.

She was a familiar figure whom he saw at the edges of his vision from time to time—though Garfiel knew full well this was not a real person, but the phantom of a woman who had once existed.

He could not smell her.

Given Garfiel's nose, it was impossible for him to miss picking up the scent of someone within eyeshot—never mind the scent of blood that had hung around that woman, so poignant that it was ingrained in his nostrils, never fading no matter how much time passed.

That was why Garfiel could speak with certainty: This woman was a phantom.

Besides, he had also been the one who killed her—Elsa Gramhilde—with his very own hands.

"_____"

But all that time later, the woman's phantom continued to stare at Garfiel.

Her smile had been so blackish red, like the darkest blood, that he could almost swear that he smelled the colors. Those lips made his chest ache to this day.

The first time he'd noticed the wraith was about two months after leaving the Sanctuary.

Right after an incident involving him as well as Subaru and Otto in a certain town, Garfiel started seeing her flickering into the edges of his vision every so often.

Somehow, he understood the cause—this echo reflected the weakness in Garfiel's heart.

Garfiel had never properly put that incident behind him. Even though he saw himself as nothing but a coward, Subaru and the others kept saying over and over again that Garfiel had done well.

When he thought back on it, he realized they'd always done that. His companions always overlooked his faults.

But Garfiel had not forgotten everything he had done to the people who were now his comrades.

One wrong step, and he surely would have ripped into Subaru and Otto with the very claws that he used to protect them. Even if he lacked the courage to do so, it would have become all too easy if he had fallen into despair.

That was why Garfiel could not forgive his own weakness or his cowardice.

Accordingly, Garfiel had accepted that he was seeing Elsa—the first life he had ever taken—because she was the manifestation of his weakness.

The phantom's blood-colored smile mocked Garfiel the instant his heart foundered—

"Hey, Garf, are you listening? Right now, Mimi's talking about some really good things! Mimi really is!"

A bubbly grin entered his view, blocking off that blood-colored smile in the distance. If this girl brought her beaming face any closer, he'd be able to feel her breath. Garfiel recoiled.

"…Uh, right, I'm listening."

"Good! Anyway, Hetaro and TB are such spoiled kids. It's really hard on me as their big sister!"

Garfiel's reply was listless, but judging by her cackling laugh, the girl hadn't noticed.

She had orange fur and round eyes that were overflowing with innocence. For whatever reason, the cat-person Mimi, a member of a rival camp, kept hanging around Garfiel every chance she got.

At present, Garfiel and Mimi were taking an evening stroll through Pristella together.

Garfiel would have preferred to be alone, but he'd blundered by letting Mimi find him and tag along. There was no way she had the ability to pick up on subtle social cues.

Somehow, ever since arriving in Pristella— No, ever since their first meeting at Roswaal Manor, she'd been particularly fond of him. At first, he'd assumed this was a vigilant investigation of a rival candidate's combat strength, but the way she talked and acted had made his initial suspicions fade. At this point, he assumed she'd simply taken a liking to him.

Without any idea of why she might think that, he usually agreed to go along with most of her whims.

"Grrr! Garf, you're making a weird face! Did something funny happen?"

"Does this look like a happy face to you…? I don't wanna talk about it, and I got no obligation to."

"You shouldn't use hard words like *obligation* and *courtesy* the way Joshua does, okay? Mimi thinks it's good to use regular words. Plus, smiling like an idiot like you always do is way cooler, Garf!"

"The hell did you just say to my face?!"

Perhaps she was sincerely trying to praise him, but Garfiel just got irritated and bared his fangs at her. The girl cried out with a "Waaah!" and smiled as she broke into a run. After going a short distance, Mimi came to a stop, grinning as she waited for him to catch up—and the phantom who had surely been there earlier was nowhere to be seen.

Garfiel had rushed out of the Water Raiment that evening because of the lingering effects of his interaction with Reinhard the Sword Saint.

The current Sword Saint was known as the strongest not only in the Kingdom of Lugunica, but in all four of the great nations.

Not only had Garfiel heard the run-of-the-mill rumors, but he'd also heard about the man directly from Subaru, who had met the living legend. That was why Garfiel had been longing for a chance to meet him in person someday.

He'd firmly believed that this was a necessary rite of passage for him to become the strongest.

To Garfiel, being called the strongest held a special meaning.

He was sure that anyone who was born a man must have dreamed of being the strongest at least once. And everyone who had that dream forgot about it at some point over the course of a long life, yearning for that which they had abandoned. Garfiel did not want to forget that dream.

That title was an absolute necessity for the cowardly Garfiel to protect the things that were most important to him. With that thought in mind, he chased after it without rest.

That was why the fact that he had subconsciously backed down the instant he was face-to-face with the strongest was currently driving him to despair.

He'd lived for a scant fifteen years, yet Garfiel had spent the majority of his life in training. He poured all his effort into mastering the martial arts, proving he could uphold his oath to protect what was precious to him with his own two hands.

The instant he yielded ground in the face of real strength, it felt like he had betrayed his oath.

Before he could make the Sword Saint draw his sword, before he could make the man brush away his honed fist, Garfiel had already lost.

Garfiel, worries or not, you're damn strong.

That was how Subaru tried to console Garfiel as he struggled in the quagmire of defeat. Those words ate at him so much that he thought it was an achievement he wasn't wailing pathetically that very moment.

Provoked by those feelings, which were swirling in his chest with no outlet, she became visible—the woman he had slain. Unable to ignore her presence, he'd raced into the Water Gate City at dusk all by himself.

That had been the plan anyway.

"Garf! Garf! Look, look! Hey, you can really see the sunset on the water—it's so red! That's amazing! Look! So pretty!"

Running around all excited, Mimi tugged on Garfiel's sleeve, pulled on his hair, and even leaped onto his back. His self-styled companion seemed not to know the meaning of thoughtfulness or mercy.

Thanks to her, he couldn't even find a moment to wallow on his own.

"Hey, simmer down already! Don't you get that I'm down in the dumps?!"

"Hmm, nooope!"

"Who answers right away to a question like that?!"

Grabbing onto his arm, Mimi kept on tugging him along, forcing Garfiel to accompany her wherever she pleased.

He could have flung her away and fled if he was of a mind to, but that would only end with her chasing him through the city. He wanted to avoid causing trouble for Subaru and the others.

Ram and Frederica had also given him a strict warning before the group had set off for Pristella. He was to make sure his eccentricities bothered no one save Otto, who was an expert in cleaning up other people's messes.

"Mm? What's with the gloomy face, Garf? Some kind of anvie... anpie...anmiety?"

"Are you tryin' to say *anxiety*?"

"That's right, anxiety! So what is it? Tell me, tell me!"

Then and there, Mimi went, "Mm! Mm-hmm!" as she thrust a fist out to emphasize her request. Seeing the girl so eager for conversation made Garfiel clack his fangs, feeling like all the bitterness had simply drained away.

Garfiel turned his gaze toward the waterway, narrowing his jade eyes.

"...I guess the scenery is nice, eh?"

"Yeah, for sure! It's amazing! It's super amazing! I wish the young lady could see it, too!"

He only half listened to her rambling, but the sight of the sinking red sun reflected on the waterway was undeniably beautiful.

With the sunset drenching the world in cinnabar red, its rays left vivid patches of yellow and white on the water's surface, burning that sweet, dazzling scenery into the hearts of all who laid eyes upon it.

"_____"

As that scene mesmerized him, Garfiel realized that his heart had become oddly peaceful.

He should have been all alone, wallowing in the feelings of helplessness oozing out of him due to his disheartening defeat, but the sunniness of the girl by his side had kept Garfiel from sinking into a pit of despair.

"Hmm, hmm, hmm."

Standing next to Garfiel was Mimi, the girl in question, humming in high spirits. She tugged on Garfiel's loincloth as she swayed her head back and forth, clearly enjoying herself.

All of a sudden, he realized that her hair and tail were the color of a vivid sunset. When he unwittingly reached a hand out and stroked her head, Mimi stretched her body up in apparent delight.

"Fluffy, huh? Our lady does that a lot, too. She says it has heawing properties!"

"Ahh, the general talks about *healing properties* and stuff, too. I feel like I kinda get what he means now."

"Hey, Garf. Is feeling up Mimi's fluffiness good for you?"

"Hold on, you made it sound really wrong just now!"

Mimi only went, "Huh?" and innocently tilted her head, causing Garfiel to burst into laughter.

The exchange made what negative emotions were still swirling in his chest dissolve and go away. He could tell that his competitive spirit, presumably dampened by humiliation and a sense of defeat, had defiantly rebounded.

"...No one becomes the strongest overnight. Me, I'm still in the middle of climbin'."

"Oooh, that hill to become the strongest sounds really, really tall!"

"Heh, you understand surprisingly well, don't ya? Yeah, that's right. That's what the road to becoming the strongest is like."

When Mimi thrust a fist upward, Garfiel touched the white scar on his brow and clacked his fangs.

He hated to admit it, but he'd regained his competitive spirit thanks to Mimi. If he'd brooded over things all by himself, who knew how long it would have taken for him to reach the same conclusion?

"—Ah! Garf, over there!"

Right as he realized he felt grateful and couldn't bring himself to openly admit it, Mimi tugged hard on his sleeve. Her gaze was trained on a waterway that was glimmering bright red. When he looked over there, Garfiel saw it, too.

A boat was moving by itself in the Great Waterway, which cut through the city. Some rope that had been keeping it moored to the opposite shore must have come undone. But that wasn't the real problem.

"Those kiddies!"

Mimi shouted in alarm at the vessel sitting in the path of the small boat that was running adrift. Five children were playing on the moored craft, unaware of the approaching boat.

Upon hearing Mimi's voice, people in the vicinity of the waterway quickly recognized the danger of a collision. The nearby boat owner hastily ran toward the children, but he wouldn't make it in time. Noticing the ruckus, the children's faces went pale as they finally saw the approaching ship as well.

At this rate, mere seconds remained until disaster—

"—Hey, runts. You better thank that big sister over there for bein' the first to notice."

"Garf!"

Clearing the waterway in a single bound, Garf landed in the vessel that the children were aboard. The children's eyes went round with amazement at how Garfiel had appeared on a vessel in the water almost without making it sway at all.

Taking advantage of their surprise, Garfiel scooped up all five children in one go, leaping once more to escape. Hardly a moment later, the two ships collided and foundered in the waterway.

"There we go!!"

Caught up in the capsizing of the two vessels, other boats began tipping over like dominoes. Having dropped the children off by the bankside, Garfiel grabbed hold of the rope connecting the remaining ships to the docks and pulled on it hard to right them by force.

"Well, that's that!"

As the force of the waves lessened, Garfiel meticulously retied the slackened ropes and flashed a smile at the children, who were now safe and sound. Afterward, he helped recover the two capsized vessels, and the boat owner bowed his head several times over in gratitude for Garfiel's strength and for keeping the damage to a bare minimum.

Patting the shoulder of the unlucky boat owner, Garfiel paused to take a breath. It was then that—

"M-mister, thank you very much!"

—the children he saved spoke words of thanks all at once. When Garfiel looked over, he found that their gazes no longer contained surprise—they were filled with awe.

It was as Garfiel was having his moment with those children that applause began pouring down from all around.

Enduring this with an embarrassed look, Garfiel lightly rubbed the scar on his forehead.

"Don't even mention it. It was just coincidence I happened to… The damp evenin' wind told me, that's all. If someone in this Water Gate City started cryin', these waterways would overflow!"

The sounds of applause suddenly dwindled when Garfiel responded with pride.

For some reason, the voices of acclaim became distant, and the cheering became sparse and awkward. But unlike the other people around them, the reactions of the children remained just as dramatic.

"Th-that was crazy!" "So cool!" "No retreat! No surrender!"

"Ohh, that's a good one! Just like *The holy lady's fist splits the ground asunder!*"

"Mister, what's your name? What should we call you?"

As Garfiel puffed out his chest, one of the children posed that question.

Instantly, Garfiel bared his sharp fangs, revealing a ferocious smile.

"I'm no one important enough to be givin' out my name. If ya gotta call me somethin', then... Me, I'm a tiger. Yeah, a golden tiger. So people call me—Gorgeous Tiger!"

"Gorgeous!" "Tiger!!"

When Garfiel struck a pose, stretching both arms up at an angle toward the heavens, the children got even more worked up, and they all imitated Garfiel.

"Garf, that's amazing! Super cool!!"

It was then that Mimi, running a roundabout route about the waterway, met up with Garfiel and the children at last. Her eyes glimmered like the rest of the group as she joined in, making the same mysterious pose.

"Gorgeous!" "Gorgeous!" "Gorgeous Tiger!!"

With all applause and cheering long gone, the boat owner was the only other person still on the waterway, his cheek twitching as he observed in silence.

2

After quickly taking a shine to the children, Garfiel ended up buying them food at a nearby stall. Then he stood tall and triumphant as he strutted around the city.

"And then I said this: 'I've seen through your evil deeds, third-raters. Your wickedness and wicked faces ain't gettin' by my general and my bro!'"

"Wow! That's so cool!" "Whoa! I got goosebumps!"

As the fast-approaching night began to color Pristella's sky, Mimi and a blond boy cheered Garfiel on as he spun his tale. The latter was only six or seven, and he was one of the children whom Garfiel had saved on the waterway.

The story that Garfiel was telling at the time was the cursed-goddess-statue incident, the one that had left the deepest impression upon him out of everything that had happened in the last year.

At any rate, the trio of Subaru, Otto, and Garfiel had soon gotten deeply involved, and as a matter of course, they encountered the owner of a metia. Needless to say, a great deal of trouble ensued.

Garfiel clacked his fangs cheerfully at having an audience so happy to listen to his stories. All three were currently on the way to the blond boy's residence; they were escorting him home.

After taking the children to a food stall, Garfiel had a responsibility as the eldest person present to safely return them home. He'd already delivered the other four safe and sound. This child was the last.

"Gotta say, for little runts, you kids sure went a long way from home."

"Errr... Actually, we went to the park in the First District to hear the Songstress..."

"The Songstress, huh? Accordin' to the general, she's got one hell of a singin' voice..."

Garfiel crinkled his nose at the innocent admiration coming out of the boy's mouth.

The boy was talking about Liliana, the famous Songstress of Pristella. It had been brief, but Garfiel had met the real deal at the Muse Company. To be blunt, she seemed like an extremely willful person, and he felt like she had fatal flaws irreconcilable with the rumors that she was a songstress of uncommon talent.

"Garf, you haven't heard the Songstress sing? What a shame! Somehow, she's reaaally good!"

"What, you actually got a good listen?"

"Yeah! I didn't fall asleep till the very end! That's a huuuge achievement! Mimi's incredible, right? Praise me!"

When Mimi presented her head, Garfiel gave her a perfunctory pat. Mimi went, "Yaaay!" anyway, racing forward with great delight as Garfiel turned toward the boy.

"So did ya get to meet this Songstress you admire?"

"Nah, seems we were a little too late… I wonder if my sister will be upset."

"Sister? Why would she be upset?"

"…Because I…left without telling anyone."

"Ahh—"

From the boy's sullen face, it appeared that the plan was to keep his promise with his friends a secret from his family. But because he would be returning home later than expected, he couldn't help but be afraid of how his family would react, particularly this older sister of his.

Garfiel understood that feeling painfully well. Older sisters were powerful creatures. He might even go as far as to say they were formidable walls that little brothers could never surpass. That's how it was for him when he finally reunited with his own sister even after spending ten years honing his body. One look at the young boy they were escorting home, and it was obvious that even contests of strength were hopeless. There was a despairing difference in power between older sisters and their younger brothers.

"Got it. Just leave it to me."

Though worried, the boy blinked hard when Garfiel reassuringly patted his own chest.

"I know how scary big sisters can be, y'see. Me, I got a big sis, too, and the woman I love has a younger sister too. Kid, if your sister is upset, I'll listen to her lecture with you."

"Gorgeous Tiger!"

Deeply moved, the boy hugged Garfiel tightly. Garfiel hugged the boy back, only for Mimi to latch onto him from behind as well.

Thus, with cargo hanging from the front and back, Garfiel pressed on toward the boy's house with wobbly steps and newfound resolve.

"Gorgeous Tiger, huh?"

The fact that the boy had called him that just then made Garfiel clench his fangs.

The feelings of powerlessness that had driven him from the inn had not completely vanished by any means. He still lacked the confidence that he could bump into Reinhard at the *ryokan* and maintain his composure.

Even so, the female phantom who was dressed in black and symbolized his sense of weakness was nowhere to be seen.

This was probably thanks to the children who now revered him as Gorgeous Tiger, and the incomprehensible energy Mimi had instilled within him—

"—Fred!"

Right as Garfiel was beginning to dive into sentimentality, his ears shuddered when he heard that sharp, high-pitched voice.

When he lifted his face, he saw a small figure racing toward him. Her long, blond hair flapped about as the stranger closed in on them like a comet.

She came straight in, charging toward the boy, who was hugging onto Garfield.

"Ah, Big Si… *Gwah!*"

"Just how much were you trying to make me worry about you?!!"

The boy had been clinging to Garfiel—right up until his sister's kick sent him flying. Garfiel found himself admiring her kicking form and the impressive way she landed.

That instant, the girl swiftly turned about, driving her heel into Garfiel's foot as she howled:

"You shady goon! What were you doing with my Fred?!"

"That hur… Well, I guess it don't actually hurt, but could you get off my foot, runt?"

He'd already had his fill of runts, but Garfiel called the girl that nonetheless.

From her silent reaction, the girl was a little taken aback that her preemptive strike had been ineffective. Perhaps looking at Garfiel's face up close made her suspect that she'd picked a fight with a violent person.

Garfiel was similarly taken by surprise. To think that there existed another older sister besides Frederica who'd attack her younger brother without so much as a warning the moment they were reunited.

Incidentally, Mimi leaped to catch the flying boy with a "Pwah!" and both of them ending up rolling to a stop, unharmed. All the same, Garfiel felt compelled to comment.

"Can't really compliment a big sis kickin' her own little bro!"

"Argh… W-well, sorry about that, but what's your deal anyway?! Just so you know, I won't let you lay one finger on Fred or me! I'm scary when I get angry!!"

Garfiel's choice of words made the girl clench her teeth as she acknowledged the error of her own ways.

She may have been the boy's older sister, but the girl was only about ten years old herself, give or take—right around the age when kids got too big for their britches. Taking Garfiel for a street punk based on appearances alone, she'd challenged him while wringing out all her courage with tears in her eyes. She was probably doing her best to divert attention away from her little brother.

However, things were not going to go according to plan.

"G-Gorgeous Tiger…please don't eat my sister…"

The younger brother wedged himself between the tiger and his teary-eyed older sister. The pleading boy's words made the shielding girl open her eyes wide. However, the girl clenched her teeth and stood firm at her younger brother's side.

Garfiel wasn't exactly sure what was happening, but this brother and sister had a beautiful, caring relationship.

"Not that I approve of ya treatin' me like the villain here!"

"Bad, bad! Garf, you can't be a bad guy! You're Garf! You're Gorgeous Tiger!"

Joining back in after a short dash, Mimi bounded up and poked Garfiel in the forehead. It didn't hurt, but he felt like he shouldn't just ignore it, either.

As Garfiel mulled over how to clear his name—

"—Dear? Did you find Fred?"

It was the sound of someone entirely unexpected that shattered the stalemate.

It was the soft, gentle voice of a woman. The instant he heard it, he thought the sister and brother before his eyes might glance at each other's faces, but instead, they broke out running toward it in great haste.

"The hell?"

Right as Garfiel blinked in a daze at their sudden vigor, a new figure appeared from across the way. When the individual rounded a corner and came into sight, the siblings leaped into her arms.

"Mommy!" "Mom, there's a scary stranger!! That Gorgeous something or other was holding Fred, and I…!"

Catching the two as they tearfully clung to her was a casually dressed woman with long, blond hair. Going by what the siblings said, this was their mother, but Garfiel dearly hoped the mother didn't go by their words and assume he was someone suspicious. It would probably become incredibly complicated if she took her daughter at her word.

Either way, having an adult capable of rational conversation come out was a huge help. Garfiel stepped forward, wanting to explain the situation before someone called the city guards—

"—Huh?"

With the children still clinging to her, the small smile she turned toward him stopped him dead in his tracks.

"Garf?"

Garfiel's jerky movement made Mimi look at him with a mystified face.

However, Garfiel could not respond to Mimi's call. He was too preoccupied. His heart and eyes were filled with bewilderment.

He was a storm of emotions, and his thoughts had fallen into utter chaos. Of course that was what happened. It was only natural.

"Um, it seems that you were looking after my children. If you like, could we speak more at our house? It's very close by."

Gently, the woman spoke with a tone that harbored no misgivings whatsoever.

When the unguarded woman closed the distance, Garfiel widened his eyes at the sight of her. His sharp fangs refused to line up. The woman tilted her head curiously at the clattering sound of his teeth.

That expression, that demeanor, that voice—they shook Garfiel to the very core of his being.

After all, standing there was—

"—Mom?"

That raspy voice was all that he managed to spill out from his throat for a reunion that should never have happened.

3

"I am so sorry. I didn't think we would have guests, so I didn't have a chance to tidy up very much."

"Aww, don't worry about that! It's all right! Compared with Mimi's room, it's waaaay cleaner!"

"My my, you are a girl, so that simply will not do. You must keep your own room clean."

The woman gently stroked Mimi's head as the latter sat on a sofa, waving her feet around. Mimi purred happily and seemed to immediately relax.

Garfiel kept his mouth shut tight as he gazed at the pair.

The woman had long, luscious blond hair, fair skin, and a delicate physique. Her face was gentle, and there was softness in her jade eyes—which, up close, greatly resembled those of Garfiel's older sister. From her youthful appearance, she looked like she was in her twenties, but her actual age had to be in the latter half of her thirties.

After all, fifteen years had already passed since then. In spite of that, her appearance had changed little since he last saw her—a fact that tore at Garfiel's heart with frightful intensity.

"Mr., um, Gorgeous Tiger? Are you not fond of tea? I'm sorry. I went and prepared some without asking what you prefer…"

As Garfiel held his silence, the woman—a woman claiming the name of Liara Thompson—lowered her eyes with a troubled expression. Garfiel replied with "Nah, that's not it" as he hastily raised his cup. "It ain't anythin' like that. I was just a little…surprised at how big this place is."

"My, so that was it? True, our home is quite large. It is very much a chore to clean it every day and takes a fair bit of time… But it's strange, really."

"…What is?"

"I always ask guests what leaves they prefer, but this time, I just went ahead and picked this."

How odd, Liara's smile seemed to say as she pressed a hand to her cheek. Garfiel brought the cup to his lips without a word. The taste and the temperature were exactly to his liking.

Deeply disturbed by this, Garfiel searched for any disparities between Liara before him and the woman from his memories.

Liara's attire and behavior suited someone living in a stately mansion. The woman in Garfiel's memories was a simple person who wore simple clothes and gave off the impression of naivete, knowing little of the world around her. This was one area in which they differed immensely.

And yet everything about her presence—that smiling face, that gentle voice, the tiniest of gestures—led Garfiel astray.

"_____"

She had to be someone else. He was sure this was a different person. Liara treated Garfiel like she would with any acquaintance of her children. Furthermore, his mother wasn't such a skilled actress that she could pull this off.

In his own mind, Garfiel desperately came to the conclusion that Liara Thompson was someone other than his mother—Lisha Tinzel. This woman only looked identical.

Garfiel was still nursing when he last saw his mother. The reason his memories of his mother were so vivid despite that was, regardless of how he felt about it, because the Sanctuary's Trial had shown him the past in normally unknowable detail.

Thanks to that, Garfiel remembered his mother's face, voice—and love.

And that was how Garfiel learned of his mother's unfortunate death, which occurred right after she had separated from her own children.

Therefore, a reunion with his mother was a wish that Garfiel would never see granted. This was just a different person who greatly resembled her.

But if she was a different person, then why was her scent so familiar?

"Mimi, the fur around your ears looks very fluffy. I wonder… May I touch it?"

"Of course!"

When Mimi offered her head, Liara happily patted it, savoring the comforting sensation of her fur.

Her innocent, doe-like smile, the way she didn't know how to doubt others, and the unguarded way she'd invite a suspicious-looking man and a kitty-girl into her own home were really quite something.

Everything about her behavior made Garfiel suspect that this Liara really might be his mother.

—Lisha, the mother of Garfiel and Frederica, was an unlucky woman.

When her family was suffering under a crushing debt, she'd been sold to an illegal slave trader at a young age. After this slave trader was raided by demi-human bandits, she became the slave of beast people instead.

Several years later, the bandits readily abandoned Lisha when she became pregnant with Frederica. Afterward, following one twist after another, she gave birth to Frederica while she was the captive of a different group of bandits.

Garfiel had heard from his older sister, Frederica, that her first memories were of her time with the bandits. His sister had not spoken of what happened during that time, but judging from how they up and disappeared the instant Lisha became pregnant with Garfiel, it could not have been a wholesome environment at all.

Spending her time with one misfortune rolling in after another, Lisha, with a young daughter in tow and a swelling belly, finally entered the care of Roswaal in the peaceful land of the Sanctuary.

Your mother… Lisha, was it? I had few opportunities to exchange words with her, you seeee. She was quite a mysterious woman. Or rather, should I describe her as incoooomprehensible, perhaps? She is a woman who seemed to keep happiness very close to her. I believe she motivated herself by living for tomorrow since she was very young… Ahh, yes. I must have been jealous. This is probably why I—

Those were the uncharacteristic words that Roswaal used to describe Garfiel's mother.

It was the first night that Otto had convinced Garfiel to try alcohol. That same night, Garfiel had gone to visit Roswaal in a drunken stupor. As Garfiel snapped at him with even more venom than usual, Roswaal abruptly spoke about his impressions of the young boy's mother.

Garfiel thought he'd die from his hangover the next morning, but he hadn't lost the memories of the night before. Therefore, his recollection of Roswaal speaking about his mother was still fresh. Garfiel was more than a little grateful to the alcohol for leaving him with that much.

At any rate, looking at the big picture, his mother was apparently an airhead whose brain had probably been permanently set to feel happiness. Had that not been the case, why would she have ever left a place of such peace in search of Garfiel's father, of whom Garfiel had nothing but painful memories?

In the end, she'd ended up dying almost immediately after setting off. What in the world had she been thinking?

—Even after all that time later, he'd still never found the answer to where his mother's happiness had come from.

"Mom, I'm getting hungry."

It was then that the siblings returned hand in hand from their room after getting a new change of clothes.

The older sister looked over the heads of their guests to call out to her mother and promptly hurried over to her side, sternly glaring at Garfiel with her jade eyes all the while.

"Hey, Mom. It's suppertime already, so shouldn't our guests head on home?"

"Oh, how can you say that? Mr. Gorgeous and Ms. Mimi helped Fred out, after all. He was apparently in danger of drowning while playing on a boat."

"Hmph, are you sure about that? Wasn't it really this Gorgeous guy who probably rocked the boat in the first place? I bet he was probably planning on coming here to try and milk us for lots of money."

"That's enough, young lady… But now that you mention it, he did save Fred. We should show him our thanks, so maybe offering some money would be the most proper."

"Mom!!"

Apparently, the girl felt like she had to do everything she could to protect her family. Unfortunately, her fervent efforts weren't quite clicking with her mother; Garfiel couldn't help but feel that she was flailing in the air.

But the heartwarming exchange between parent and child bitterly pained Garfiel, like he was walking barefoot over a path of thorns. It was so agonizing that he could barely stand staying there any longer.

"…Seems like we ain't all that welcome, so maybe we should head on out."

"Ehhh, whyyy? Let's hang out just a little bit more!"

"No way. This is like *sculpting the Kokran*, damn it."

Mimi protested when Garfiel attempted to leave, but Garfiel wouldn't brook any objections as he tried to forcibly drag the girl out with him. Liara made a sad face at Garfiel's assertion, whereas her daughter took the opportunity to stick her tongue out at him as she watched him go. As for the little brother—

"Don't go, Gorgeous Tiger!"

Grabbing onto Garfiel's sleeve, he tried to bar Garfiel's path.

Instantly, Garfiel hesitated to shake off those tiny fingers. He wasn't sure why he paused, but…

"Sorry, kid. I got people waitin' for me. They'll be worried if I'm late. That's why I'm goin', okay?"

Still unable to figure out why he froze for a moment, Garfiel put a hand on the boy's head as he explained.

He'd been welcomed in, yet here he was, making his escape. If this was how it was going to be, he should never have accepted the invitation to begin with.

Regret, regret, regret—the only thing left throbbing deep in his chest was regret.

"Fred, I know you're sad, but you have to let go of Mr. Gorgeous's clothing."

Heeding Garfiel's words, Liara gently removed her son's fingers. Garfiel was relieved to have his sleeve free again.

"We must not cause our guests distress by forcing them to stay. As the saying goes, *For guests, hospitality, and a Sowarie.*"

And then Liara's next words cut deep into Garfiel's defenseless soul.

He had let his guard down after that initial wave of relief, only for that single phrase to shear through them, dredging up his memories.

His sense of defeat toward Reinhard, his sense of powerlessness at having betrayed his own dream, his shock the instant he first set eyes upon Liara—compared with that phrase, those were almost inconsequential.

It was enough that he almost thought that his body was being torn asunder—

"Garf, let's go."

It was then that Mimi, who had been so reluctant to leave, gently pulled on Garfiel's arm. When she proceeded toward the door, Garfiel silently followed along.

Right as the two of them were headed to the entrance—

"I'm home... Oh, we have guests?"

—the door ahead of them opened, and a gentlemanly man sporting a full beard raised his eyebrows at the unexpected sight.

He wore finely tailored clothes and had a lively air about him. His face looked like that of a capable man who was calm inside the home. His position was clear even before the children reacted to his return.

"Errr, I don't believe we've met. Who might you be?"

"Dad, this is Gorgeous Tiger!"

"A shady person!"

"Ehhh?"

The starkly contrasting descriptions delivered by his son and daughter left the man—their father—rather confused. In search of rescue, he shifted his gaze to Liara, who was standing beside the children.

The man's warm gaze caused Liara to loosen her cheeks slightly. That was unmistakably love on her face.

Garfiel had hit his limit.

"We're nobody. Nothin' to worry about. Time for us to be headin' out."

Garfiel swiftly said his good-byes, continuing to hold Mimi's hand as he left the room with her in tow. Pushing past the man, who hastily gave way, Garfiel raced out, fleeing the house.

"Gorgeous Tiger!"

From behind, the boy called out to Garfiel in a sad voice. However, Garfiel had nothing left in him to muster a reply— No, he just wasn't worthy.

—When he glanced over, he saw a black phantom encroaching on the edges of his vision. Smiling at him mockingly was a woman who was surely dead.

Gorgeous? Tiger? Where was the golden tiger in him now?

A tiger was strong. A tiger was mighty. Nothing ever shook a tiger.

What part of him was a tiger just then?

Would a real tiger be broken up over something like this?!!

"Garf! Stop already!"

"!"

Just as his thoughts were clouded in a crimson haze, one voice brought him back to his senses.

When he turned, Garfiel realized that he'd been half dragging Mimi along. She had pleaded in pain. Looking closer, he could see that the girl's slender wrist had gone blue from the grip of his hand.

"S-sorry... I didn't mean to..."

"Garf, are you all right? You've been reaaally weird since earlier. Does your tummy hurt?"

When Garfiel tried to apologize in a shaky voice, Mimi peered at him with concern. This was not a look of resentment over her wrist injury, but one of pure consideration alone.

This pushed Garfiel's already sinking heart to even lower depths.

An awkward silence fell over the two as a damp nighttime breeze blew over them. The sun had already set, and the city streets under the night sky were dotted by magic lamps. As the light of the magic fixtures reflected that of the setting sun, the waterway took on a tranquil, mysterious beauty, but Garfiel had no room left in his heart to enjoy the sight.

"Pardon me, both of you!"

It was then that the voice of an out-of-breath man drew near the pair that was standing on the street at night.

When they looked over, they saw the man from earlier illuminated under the magic lamps. With his coat stripped off, he had finally reached the pair, his breath ragged as he rested his hands on his knees.

"*Haaah! Haaah!* I managed to catch up with you. This really will not do... I had plenty of physical energy back in the day, but I've wasted away since I started doing nothing but desk work..."

"...What is it? You got business with us or somethin'?"

There was a barb in his voice when Garfiel addressed the man who'd caught up with them.

It wasn't to the extent of Liara and the siblings, but there was no mistaking that he, too, was poison so far as Garfiel was concerned. Garfiel didn't intend to converse for long. He wanted to get out of there as fast as he possibly could.

Seeing Garfiel's attitude, the man seemed to pick up that he was not being welcomed with open arms.

"I heard the story from my wife. You two saved my son, didn't you? And yet I let you leave without speaking a single word of thanks. The height of impropriety."

"…Ain't no big deal. Exaggeratin' stuff like that just ends up being a pain in the butt for me."

"Everything about my children is very important to me. Please allow me to thank you. I am Galek Thompson, one of the officials in charge of running this city. If there is anything I can do for you…"

"There really ain't anythin'…"

When Garfiel tried to rebuff the tenacious man, Galek, his words got stuck in his throat.

Suddenly, he had a thought—he, Liara's husband, might know who she really was.

"There's just one thing I wanna ask ya."

"Yes, by all means. If it is something my position allows me to answer, I shall."

Galek nodded toward Garfiel with an amicable smile.

It was the same for Liara and for his son, Fred. Galek included, the Thompson family was far too fond of people. That daughter was the only one with a proper level of wariness in the bunch.

—That was how outside threats like Garfiel were able to take advantage of them.

"Your wife… Is Liara her real name?"

"_____"

Instantly, the atmosphere changed.

When Garfiel posed his question, Galek dropped the smile he'd worn to that point. Both his voice and expression were quiet as he rolled Garfiel's question over his tongue.

"I wonder—what do you mean by that?"

"I mean what I said. *Reid always faced his challengers head-on.* I don't like roundabout stuff. Your wife... Is Liara her real name or not?"

When Garfiel cut right to the point, the expression coming over Galek was one of clear consternation. He opened and closed his mouth several times, breathing hard in search of air and words.

"You... Are you saying you know something about my wife?"

"I'm the one who wants to know about her."

Garfiel replied sincerely to Galek's wavering question.

Detecting the genuine emotion at the core of that reply, Galek went silent, sinking into thought. As Garfiel waited for the words that would follow, he felt Mimi grasp his hand with her opposite hand from earlier.

When he shifted his gaze in her direction, Mimi simply went, "Heh-heh—" with a bubbly smile.

"...It would seem I should speak truthfully with you."

Breaking the silence, Galek uttered those words with a sigh.

A deep weariness infused that voice, along with an unconcealable sense of guilt, causing Garfiel to narrow his brows.

Then as Garfiel maintained his silence, Galek began to speak.

"My wife, Liara...has no memories from before I met her fifteen years ago."

"! No memories, ya say?"

"It was a stormy night. I was just another merchant returning from a business deal when I came across the site of a large landslide. My future wife was caught up in that disaster and had been buried alive."

The terms that Galek relayed—*landslide, buried alive*—made Garfiel's breath come to a halt.

Bubbling up in his mind was the glimpse into the past he'd seen in the Sanctuary. An unsalvageable past, in which his mother had left

Garfiel and Frederica behind, setting off from the settlement only to become engulfed in a landslide and lose her life—

—But had his mother really died? He'd never even considered other possibilities.

"_____"

That terrifying concept made Garfiel clench his teeth hard so that they wouldn't chatter.

He'd thought for certain that his mother had died. Even if his mother had been safe, if she had been tethered to life, he couldn't possibly imagine a reason why she wouldn't have returned to Garfiel and Frederica's side.

"After she was rescued, she hovered on the edge of life and death, opening her eyes several days later just as I came to check on her. Then she spoke these words loud and clear— 'Who am I?' she asked."

Galek lowered his eyes, shaking his head from side to side.

"Perhaps it is a side effect of her heart nearly stopping once. She didn't remember anything. All she knew, from the name tag on the clothes she wore, was that there was a *Li* in either her family name or her given name. And so she took the name of a flower that blooms at night. I have called her Liara ever since."

After that, Galek's gaze grew distant as he spoke, but there was not a great deal to tell thereafter.

After he took her into his care, the bonds between them naturally deepened, and it was not long before they fell in love. And ever since he'd taken Liara in, Galek's business had grown by leaps and bounds.

Galek never questioned his belief that this good fortune was from bringing Liara back with him.

Because of her, Galek had worked in this city as a man, a husband, and a father until the present day.

That was why—

"—I love my wife. I dearly love our children. Once upon a time, her past weighed upon my mind, but not anymore. No matter what happened to her before we met, she is my wife, the woman most precious to me."

Galek spoke those words firmly and plainly with his chest out.

These were the unshakable feelings that Galek felt for his wife, carried through from the moment they'd met to the present.

"_____"

Listening to his tale to the end, Garfiel silently looked up at the murky night sky.

How did the waxing moon and the stars dotting the darkness feel as they gazed down at him in that moment?

As Garfiel chose to stay silent, Galek's lips trembled more than once. He was hesitating. But then he firmly closed his eyes, brushing that hesitation aside.

"I am truly sorry to ask you this. However, I wish to inquire nonetheless."

"_____"

"How…are you related to my wife, Liara?"

Just how cruel a question was that to ask someone?

Confronted by the last thing he wanted to be asked, Garfiel slowly shifted his gaze from the sky back to the ground, and then finally to Galek.

Galek looked at Garfiel with quiet, unshakable resolve in his eyes. Even Garfiel wasn't insensitive enough to miss the significance of those words and the emotions invested in them.

More than that, he knew exactly what response he should give.

"_____"

He opened his mouth once, then closed it. He breathed in and out, in and out, over and over.

His pulse was racing. His eyes felt unsteady. His head throbbed with pain. The urge to vomit kept welling up.

He felt a storm of emotions raging inside as well as the ultimate sense of loss. During it all, Mimi held Garfiel's hand.

"Me, I…"

"_____"

"I don't have…any relationship with your wife."

He did it.

He'd said it aloud.

With those words, the torrent of emotions swirling inside his chest rapidly dissipated. What remained was a yawning, cavernous loss, an emptiness that made his limbs run cold.

"I am...very sorry..."

Lowering his eyes, his shoulders trembling, Galek bowed his head to Garfiel.

But Galek's apology was not something Garfiel wanted.

Enough. Just stop it. Don't hurt me anymore. What went wrong? Who's to blame? Who do I have to smash, to rip to shreds, to send flying, to get over this?

What am I supposed to do with the pain in my heart that just won't go away?

"—Darling! Ahh, I'm so glad you're with Mr. Gorgeous and Ms. Mimi."

"?!"

He wanted to scream.

He was on the verge of wailing like a weak little boy.

In that moment, seeing her was more terrible than any poisoned blade for Garfiel.

"Liara, why...?"

"Because I thought you ran out in such a hurry that you would probably manage to catch them. I thought it was terrible for them to leave empty-handed, too..."

Galek was just as surprised by the sudden appearance of his wife as Liara came over in a little run, passing by her husband's side. Then with Garfiel still rigid from shock, she gently extended a bag toward him.

"These are some Sowarie sweets I made. Perhaps it is not so great a reward, but I have confidence in their taste. Please take this."

"Ah..."

With a perfectly innocent smile, she offered Garfiel the cruelest of gifts.

Galek agonizingly lowered his face at the exchange between Garfiel and his wife. It was too painful for anyone to intervene. No one who understood the true nature of this meeting could do more.

That was exactly why—

"Ohh! Yaaay! I love sweets! I'm gonna brag to the lady!"

Grabbing the bag from Liara's hand, Mimi bore an outgoing, smiling demeanor that was completely out of touch.

It was so at odds with the atmosphere from a few moments ago that it took a short while for Galek to accept what was happening. But only Liara, unaware of the circumstances, greeted Mimi's honest delight with a beaming smile.

"I am so glad to hear you say that. Please give my best regards to this lady of yours."

"Yep, yep, uuuunderstood! Super understooood!"

Taking the sweets in her still-pallid hand, Mimi smiled as she gave a playful salute. Stuffing the bag in the satchel she carried over one shoulder, she used her long tail to thwap Garfiel on the back.

"Time to go for real! Gorgeous Tiger and Gorgeous Mimi will be leaving now!"

"Yes, do be careful. Mr. Gorgeous, take care not to fall into the waterway at night."

When Mimi set off with a big wave of her hand, Liara gave a little wave back. With the pair trading hand-waves, the two men watched the exchange with morose faces.

"_____"

From there, Garfiel followed the pull of Mimi's hand and trailed behind her. Neither Mimi nor Garfiel said anything for a while, continuing to walk as Liara and Galek receded from sight.

Finally, when Garfiel judged that they were far enough, he came to a stop.

"Hey, runt... Er, whoa?!"

"Hiyahhh!"

The next instant, Mimi jumped, stretching Garfiel's arm. Kicking off from the ground in a flash, the pair leaped onto the roof of a nearby building.

After going up three stories in one bound, Mimi stretched her back.

"Mmm!! Amazing! It feels so good!"

"Hey, don't gimme that! What gives all of a sudden...?"

Mimi was enjoying the bracing wind as he drew close. But when she stared back at him with her round eyes, Garfiel was at a loss for words. He was oddly uncomfortable seeing how he looked reflected in her eyes.

With Garfiel pressed into silence, Mimi abruptly tilted her head.

"Garf, you look like you're gonna cry."

"…Huh? What the hell are ya sayin'? No way I'm gonna do that."

"I know you're strong, Garf, but that doesn't mean you have to act tough. Liara is Garf's mom, right?"

"!"

When Mimi stepped into the crux of the matter, Garfiel drew in his breath, utterly unprepared.

"Why do you…think that she's…?"

"I mean, Garf's and Liara's scents are reaaally alike. And the scents of Liara's kids are a little like Garf's scent, too. So I figured just maaaybe—"

She didn't learn of Garfiel's family from the course of the conversation. Mimi had accurately arrived at the truth based on a feral sense of smell and base instinct.

Words could be fabricated or suppressed. But Garfiel had no rebuttal for something based on a part of you that never changed.

"What the hell…?"

Garfiel sluggishly sank down then and there, leaning his listless head backward. Overhead, the stars and moon in the sky stared back down at him, their glimmering unchanged from before.

"So am I right? Is Liara Garf's mom?"

"…I dunno. Is that person…really my mom?"

He didn't know. Truly, that was how Garfiel felt from the bottom of his heart.

But just as Galek had told him and as demonstrated by Liara's own behavior, she had completely forgotten her own past as Lisha.

Having forgotten everything, she'd given birth to children as Liara, living together with them as a happy family.

"Ha. Now that I think of it, doesn't that make those two my little brother and sister?"

He hadn't totally wrapped his head around it yet, but if they were siblings by a different father, then his relationship to them was exactly the same as what he had with Frederica. In other words, that boy and girl were his adorable younger siblings. Always the youngest child, Garfiel finally had the younger siblings he'd always wished for.

—Setting aside that no one wanted such a relationship.

"Me tellin' her who I am ain't gonna help at all…"

Liara had parted with her past life as Lisha.

Even if Garfiel revealed everything he knew, it would not change the fact that she had spent fifteen years as Liara or that Lisha had lost those fifteen years. It would only hoist the burden of fifteen years' worth of guilt onto Liara and elicit a sense of loss over the time that Lisha would never get back.

Galek would have to watch his wife struggle, and her children would no doubt be unable to understand their mother's suffering when they knew nothing of the circumstances.

—All that just for Garfiel's self-satisfaction.

Even if Liara was recognized as Lisha then and there, the only one who would derive any closure from that was Garfiel.

There was no way that Frederica or Ryuzu could have known Lisha had survived like this. If Garfiel did not tell them, then they surely would never know.

Unless Garfiel spoke of it, there was no way for Liara's family to find out about the past, either. Their time as a happy family would remain protected and unchanged, peaceful as ever.

If Garfiel could keep it all bottled up in his chest and just abandon his true desires, that would settle everything once and for all.

And yet—

"Why am I…?"

The resolve to cast them aside, the decision to forget, the courage to lock them away—why is this so hard?

Tiger, where have you gone? Show me the right path, the right way to be.

Show me the strength to bear anything, to carry anything, and to stand up even so.

—Oh, tiger, please tell me... Because a real tiger wouldn't lose to anyone.

"＿＿＿"

Squatting down, biting back what was welling up inside, he felt an intense yearning clawing at his heart. Just when Garfiel wanted to cast everything aside, it was then that he noticed.

"Gooood boy."

Someone was hugging his head against their tiny chest and stroking his hair.

"＿＿＿"

As Garfiel sat there, Mimi embraced him from behind.

Placing her chin against his crown, she gently stroked Garfiel's head with her little palm. It almost felt like the soft sensation was lessening the pain of the raging thoughts crawling around inside his skull.

"The hell...do you think you're doin'...?"

"Mm, I figured Garf wanted to cry, see... But you know, Mimi heard that men don't cry unless you make a place for them to do it, and that sounds like such a pain! That's definitely what the lady told me!"

It was something that resembled an answer, but it wasn't quite all there.

Trying to keep his heart and his voice from trembling, Garfiel had chosen those sparse, halting words with great care.

Still embracing Garfiel, Mimi smiled teasingly at him.

"So I bet you were thinking, *I'm not sure where I am anymore, but it's probably in a woman's arms*? That's what you figured, right? Yeah! A man can cry in the arms of the woman he loves!"

"...Who'd fall in love with a little kid like you?"

The first person who came to Garfiel's mind didn't behave like Mimi at all, acting cold and dismissive whenever he wanted kindness. And then she suddenly treated him nicely when he least expected it, only to punch him twice as hard later. What a dangerous woman.

The girl before his eyes didn't have those things in common with her whatsoever—and yet Mimi continued smiling.

"Mm, but it's all right! Even if Garf hasn't fallen for Mimi, Mimi's already fallen for him! And now you're in Mimi's arms! The arms of the girl who loves Garf! So it's all right to cry!"

"—Ah."

Her opinion was just too stupid.

What is this, some kind of wordplay? A kid making things up as she goes along? This is a convenient excuse—nothing more.

It's nothing, so stop messing with me.

—Tiger, tiger, where have you gone?

Come back inside this chest right now. Let out a ferocious roar, smack this shrinking back of mine, drag me back to my feet, and do something about these unbearable feelings.

If you don't...I won't make it this time.

"Mom..."

Stop, stop, please stop.

I don't wanna cry, I don't wanna be weak, I don't wanna talk in a tearful voice like this.

I'm a tiger. A tiger. I'm the strongest. The mightiest. A stronger, harder shield than anyone else.

That's—

"Mom! ...Mom! ......Mom...!!"

"Good boy."

"Why?! Why did you forget me?! After all this... Meeting you after all this time!! You won't even say my name... You won't...f-forgive me......!!"

"It's all right. Garf, you're a very good boy!"

"Moooooommm... Mooommm... Mooommm...!"

—Tiger, tiger, where have you gone?

What do I look like right now? Stars, moon, sky, won't you tell me?

What do I look like right now?

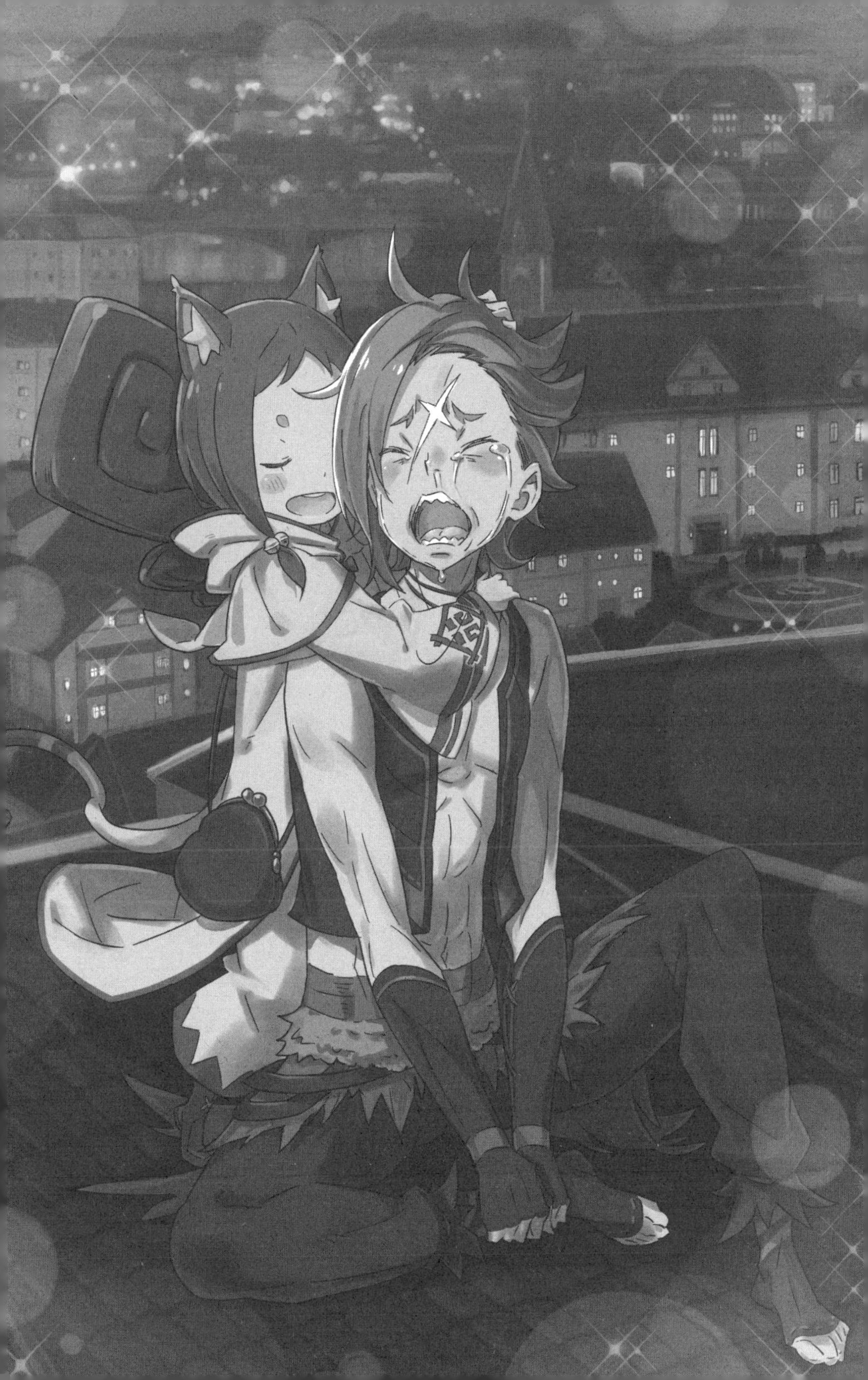

*　　*　　*

If a tiger would never howl in pain, then what do I look like right now?!!

4

"All dry!"

"Shaddap—don't say that over and over!"

The next day, well into Fire Time, Garfiel was wandering through the city alongside Mimi with a guilty look on his face.

Mimi cackled as she tugged at the part of her white robe over her chest that was still dirty from Garfiel's tears, snot, and drool, though it was completely dried now.

"That's filthy. Go wash it off at some waterin' hole somewhere."

"Mm, isn't it fiiine? I'll change when we get back to the inn… I didn't return yesterday, so the lady's gotta be real mad! Hetaro and TB will probably be crying!"

"…Sorry about that."

"Don't worry about it… Mimi told Garf he's a good, good boy and let him cry himself dry—that's all."

Garfiel's meager apology brought a naive smile to Mimi's face. He couldn't lift his head up at all.

He'd made a fool of himself, crying all night long, and before he realized it, he'd slumped down and fallen asleep in her arms. He was somehow remaining calm at the moment, but he couldn't keep up with Mimi's everyday antics at all today.

In the end, Garfiel harbored feelings of guilt and couldn't bring himself to say proper words of thanks.

"So what are we doing this morning? Going to meet your mom?"

"*Pfft…!* Wh-what are you talkin' about?! Meet her…? Like hell I am!"

Garfiel was deep in thought when that explosive suggestion made him open his eyes wide in shock. Mimi simply responded with an "Oh really?" as she tilted her head with an innocent look on her face. "But Liara is Garf's mom, right? Don't you have lots to talk about?"

"You really didn't pay attention to anything that came up yesterday, did you?"

Though she had instinctually cut right to the heart of the matter, Mimi apparently hadn't picked up on any of the finer details.

Mulling over how he ought to explain to her his difficult position in relation to that family, Garfiel quickly discarded the idea. The answer came out with his tears the night before.

"It's fine. Mo… That person is better off not knowin' I'm her son."

"Garf, you're fine with that?"

"It's fine… Ah, haven't thought about if I should tell Sis or Granny, though."

If they knew the facts, Frederica and Ryuzu would probably agonize over it just like he was. If that's really what came to pass, Garfiel might eventually end up regretting speaking to them about it.

But if the situation was reversed, Garfiel absolutely would have wanted to know the truth. After all, even if the only thing that accomplished was sharing that cruel conclusion, both women were still family to Garfiel.

"Mm, that's so complicated! Mimi doesn't even know for sure if she has a mother!"

"…You don't know your own mom?"

"That's right… Mimi and Hetaro and TB—none of us know anything about our parents. Seems like we got abandoned because it was too hard to raise triplets. So Rossi took us in, and now we're with the lady and the captain! We're all family!"

"…That's a pretty big family, huh?"

He was able to glean that Mimi had lived a hard life. From the casual way she spoke, it hadn't been all tragic, but he somehow understood that it certainly wasn't easy.

Mimi didn't let any of that show, however. Without any deep thought behind it, Garfiel patted her on the head.

"—*Wah!*"

Instantly, Mimi brushed his hand aside and hopped backward. Garfiel was surprised by her dramatic reaction. Mimi went, "Ughhhhhh," making noises with a red face.

"For some reason, I've been feeling weird since yesterday. I get all mushy and tingly when I get close to Garf."

"O-oh, I see. That sounds rough… Maybe we should walk a little farther apart, then?"

"I don't wanna. So we should stand not too far but not too close!"

Inching slightly closer, Mimi walked alongside him, just out of arm's reach. He felt that Mimi's face was a little red as she made a beaming smile from that position.

"Ah, come to think of it, we have Sowarie! Let's eat some!"

"Ahhh, right."

Seemingly trying to distract him from the redness on her cheeks, Mimi took the bag of sweets out of the satchel slung over her shoulder. For an instant, Garfiel's chest throbbed in pain at the sight of the bag, but he accepted the sweet that Mimi offered to him, gazing at the treat in the palm of his hand.

A Sowarie was a sweet-tasting baked pastry fashioned out of bread dough with cream and bean jam inside; it was a noontime snack that was tasty and filling. Given the time of day, they were basically having big, round Sowarie for breakfast.

"Mm-hmm! Sweet! Tasty! Yum-yum!"

"…They're good, huh."

Mimi's praise was over-the-top, but Garfiel found the flavor striking as well.

It was impressive—not too sweet and incredibly soft and fluffy. They would've probably tasted even better fresh. If this had been his mother's specialty, perhaps he'd had a number of chances to savor this himself—

"—Man, I'm getting too sentimental."

Clicking his tongue at those lingering attachments, Garfiel stuffed the remaining Sowarie into his cheeks whole. Mimi opened her mouth wide in an attempt to copy him and managed to get cream all over her face.

Garfiel sank into thought once again as he helped her wipe it off. Truthfully, the previous day had been full of ups and downs. Each event had served as a trial, but one unambiguously good thing had happened.

Though he'd put on such an unsightly display the day before, the phantom was nowhere to be seen this morning.

If that phantom was a representation of weakness in Garfiel's heart, it wouldn't have been strange for the events of the previous night to trigger it and bring it into even sharper relief. But that hadn't happened at all.

Just maybe, that phantom might never appear before him ever again. If so, this was an opportunity granted by the sheer presence of the girl who'd stayed beside him—

"—Ahem, ahem! *Can all you meatbags hear this?*"

That instant, a voice suddenly greeted Garfiel and Mimi's eardrums.

"*If you meatbags are listening to my voice, go ahead and shake in your boots, and any meatbags not listening, would you just drop dead and save me a whooole lot of trouble? Bwa-ha-ha-ha!*"

After exchanging looks as that voice continued rambling, Garfiel and Mimi simultaneously turned to the sky. It was because that voice seemed to be calling out to them from there.

"What the hell's with that stupid-soundin' voice…?"

"Mimi knows! This voice is coming from some super-awesome metia! In this city, you can hear singing every morning thanks to it. Yesterday, I slept through it, though!"

As Garfiel questioned the source of the voice, Mimi raised a hand up and rattled off a quick explanation. Garfiel assumed she meant that they were hearing someone via the power of a special metia and not that it was simply a very loud voice.

The whole time that exchange was going on, that high-pitched voice continued pouring down from the sky.

"*So, so, so—did any idiots take me up on that offer and die just now? If there aren't any, then so be it, but it sure would put a damper on my mood after I got all excited to talk up a storm!*"

The annoying voice reverberated across the Water Gate City, drawing looks of surprise and bewilderment from every pedestrian who heard it. Even they didn't seem to have any idea who the speaker was as they, too, stared up at the sky in confusion.

According to Mimi's explanation, the metia was normally used to send singing to every corner of the city each morning, but Garfiel was thoroughly convinced that the owner of this voice was incapable of anything so sensitive.

Her objective was unclear. Her character was vulgar. What he did know—

"*Breathe in, breathe out. That's all it takes for mongrels like you to ruin my mood. You really are pieces of trash with no redeemable value at all, aren't ya?! If all you do is eat, go into heat, and drool without doing anything with your lives, then it'd be better if you were corpses instead! Know what? Just die already! Please just die already! Really, I'm begging you! Bwa-ha-ha-ha-ha!*"

—was that the speaker was incredibly twisted.

"Garf... This is reaaally creepy."

With the speaker's motive still unclear, that unpleasant voice made Garfiel clench his fist in anger. Tugging at his sleeve, Mimi's normal sunniness had been subdued as she gazed at the sky with concern.

Seeing her like that really got to Garfiel somehow. That kind of expression didn't belong on her face.

"*Now then, all you meatbags ignoring my entirely valid opinion, have any of you ignorant slobs finally noticed the purpose of this broadcast? The reeeal purpose?*"

"Hmm...? What purpose is there besides gettin' on everyone's nerves...?"

"*—The fact that my voice is reaching you means that I...or rather, we have taken control of this city's heart, doesn't it? Ah, incidentally, the four control towers at the edge of the city are also in our hands!*"

"!! The control towers?!"

That ominous statement dripped with malice and made Garfiel's breath catch.

He'd heard that the four control towers in the city were crucial facilities for regulating the volume of water across the entirety of Pristella. It was said that their functions were unchanged from when the Water Gate City was used to trap a being of tremendous power so very long ago—and now they had fallen into the hands of this mysterious entity.

It was tantamount to this maniac holding the entire city hostage.

"Now this city is a miniature garden where we can go around amusing ourselves, abusing and toying with you as we please, oh my! You meatbags are just like insects in a cage, aren't you?! No cards to play! No bright prospects! No dreams or hopes! Do you get what that means, huh?!"

Garfiel grimaced as the sadistic voice being broadcast across the city cracked. Simultaneously, the people in the surrounding area were only now beginning to belatedly comprehend the gravity of the situation; disorder and dismay were spreading.

Seemingly pleased at the mounting chaos, the announcer spoke even shriller, becoming more self-absorbed.

"Do you get it? Did you get it through your thick skulls? You're so pathetic, every last one of you running around in a panic as you finally realize what I've been telling you all along! It's too pathetic! Anyway, I, a being of profound beauty and mercy, have happy news for you irredeemable, pathetic bastards!"

"_____"

"My objective is the Witch's bones kept somewhere in this city! I want them. I want them so much that it aches and keeps me up at night, so could you please put in some effort? If you deliver what I ask…I'll probably even reconsider the control-tower thing!"

Having taken the entire city hostage, the speaker now presented her demand. The item she mentioned, the Witch's bones, made Garfiel grimace, but the surrounding unrest only deepened.

The high-pitched voice cackled, as if the speaker had been waiting for that very moment above all others.

"Bwa-ha! Oh nooo, if I don't finally introduce myself, people like you will start trying to escape from reality right about now, huh? That's

why I, one of the wise and marvelous, will point out what's happening loud and clear so that even you can understand it!"

With that malicious voice leading the city by the nose and chaos beginning to swirl around them, Garfiel and Mimi drew shoulder to shoulder, girding themselves for whatever might get announced next.

It was then that the now-familiar voice declared in the broadcast with complete satisfaction—

"I am the Witch Cult's Archbishop of Lust—

"It's me, Capella Emerada Lugunica! Bwa-ha-ha-ha-ha!! Revere, worship, kneel, and beg and piss and shit in your pants as you pathetically wail, meatbags! Bwa-ha-ha-ha!!"

5

—Immediately after that malicious broadcast, the situation began to move fluidly, like flowing water.

The appearance of the Witch Cult and someone claiming to be an Archbishop of the Seven Deadly Sins had sown chaos and disorder, but arguably, the citizens of Pristella were still moving in an orderly manner. Even if they were unsettled, they did as the city's everyday rehearsals trained them; the surrounding people began leading the way toward the nearest shelter.

The citizens guided any outsiders unfamiliar with the procedures. The people close to Garfiel and Mimi called out to them, too, but the pair declined, hurrying to link back up with their comrades.

If they didn't meet up with Subaru and the others at the Water Raiment and put a stop to the Witch Cult's tyranny—

"—Ahh, Mr. Gorgeous!"

"!"

The voice made Garfiel reflexively freeze in place.

When he looked back, running down the street behind Garfiel and Mimi was Liara, who was reassured to have found people she knew. Enduring the aching in his chest, Garfiel turned to face her.

"Ms. Mimi, I'm glad you're safe, too. That broadcast had me worried."

"Yep, I'm all right! Ah, the Sowarie were delicious! We had a feast!"

Since Garfiel failed to respond immediately, Mimi replied for both of them. Garfiel thought it was pathetic of him even as he rested easier knowing that Liara was unharmed.

"Glad everyone's safe and sound. Now get movin' toward the shelter. We've gotta…"

"Yes, I am all right… But, um, Mr. Gorgeous…"

Even when Garfiel bid his farewells and tried to extricate himself as quickly as possible, Liara continued still in an awkward voice. Then she clasped both hands together in front of her.

"Have you seen my children? They went out early this morning to play…but neither of them were at the nearest shelter."

"?!! Those kids?"

Surprised by the unexpected development, Garfiel plucked out one of his own short golden locks in frustration.

"Well, shit, of course you're worked up about that…"

"Y-yes. Also, that broadcast… The metia required to conduct it is at city hall, where my husband works… I'm worried about whether something happened to him."

Voicing her concerns, Liara bit her lip as she looked in the direction of the building.

City hall lay at the center of Pristella, which itself was divided into four districts: north, south, east, and west. It was the place that governed all core city functions. It was also the place that Lust had declared to be under her control.

—Just what kind of damage had the perpetrator of such a cruel, deranged broadcast inflicted on the people at city hall?

Deep in his chest, Garfiel's heartbeat sounded like an alarm bell, and his thoughts were extremely limited.

His unseen younger brother and sister, Galek left behind in a danger zone, Liara running around at that very moment out of concern for her family—where danger to this group was concerned, Garfiel couldn't just calmly sit back and watch.

"General, Lady Emilia…"

Subaru, Emilia, Beatrice, and Otto all appeared in the back of Garfiel's mind.

It was none other than them whom Garfiel had come to the Water Gate City to protect. What good was he if he wasn't at their side then and there? He didn't offer much beyond his fighting ability.

But simultaneously, his heart could not turn from his newly found younger siblings, Galek, and the sight of his mother standing before his very eyes.

—It was time to choose. A decision pressed upon Garfiel that would determine which path his fate would take.

"I am sorry for troubling you like this… Please forget everything I told you, Mr. Gorgeous."

"…Ah."

"I am being exceptionally unfair to you right now. It's quite all right. Those children hear the city broadcasts every day, too, and since long ago, nothing ever slips by that man…"

Liara put on a brave smile to appease the hesitant Garfiel. But her hands, which were apparently folded in prayer, trembled. Her face had gone pale, seemingly drained of blood.

It was a desperate performance. She was trying not to saddle Garfiel and Mimi with duties they were not obligated to take on.

—Just like she'd tried to do when she left him and his older sister in the Sanctuary to search for his father in the outside world.

His heart had swayed between the two choices, but that throbbing memory made him come to a swift conclusion.

"…I'll find your children, and your husband."

"Mr. Gorgeous?"

Liara opened her eyes wide with surprise at his unexpected reply.

Nodding firmly in Liara's direction, Garfiel looked down at Mimi's hand as it gripped his own. During the time he was thinking and the time he was deciding, she'd simply waited in silence for Garfiel to choose.

She had little brothers and other people she wanted to protect, too. He couldn't force her to go with his whims any longer.

"From this point on, it's just me bein' selfish. You go back and... Owww!!"

"As if!"

In the middle of saying his good-bye, Mimi dug her heel into Garfiel's foot. Her body was light, but that kick was angled to provide maximum penetrating force. Garfiel groaned from the pain as Mimi puffed out her chest.

"Mimi's offended that Garf thinks she'll run away after he said something so cool! Mimi's coming, too! Totally coming!"

"Why...? Nah, I get it—sorry."

"—This is where you say *thanks*!"

"—Yeah, thanks."

"You are very welcome! Yay!"

When a silly smile came over Mimi's face, Garfiel smiled back, feeling like a great weight had been lifted.

As Liara watched in astonishment, the pair turned to face her once more.

"We'll find 'em. You go stay at the nearest shelter. Better to stick with the others and wait for us to take care of this."

"B-but...why are you going this far for me?"

—Indeed, why was he?

Liara's shaking eyes pressed Garfiel for the true reason behind his decision. This was not out of worry or doubt. She had a simple misgiving—this was an act of benevolence without any basis that she could think of.

Garfiel clacked his fangs at her words and flashed a fiendish smile.

"Because I'm the golden tiger! I'm Gorgeous! Tiger!!"

"And because Mimi is Gorgeous Mimi!!"

Shouting those words in excessively loud voices, they glanced down at Liara, who blinked in surprise as the pair leaped away as one. With his mother far below, Garfiel turned to face the wind and make full use of his nose.

"Garf, what'll we do?"

"Track 'em by scent. I remember how they smell just fine!!"

"All righty!"

Settling on a plan while almost yelling to be heard, Garfiel and Mimi practically flew as they raced through the Water Gate City.

Mimi was sticking with him in his moment of recklessness as he put off his duties and prioritized his personal matters—even as various factors tried to convince him to reject that choice.

Wrestling with them all, Garfiel touched the scar on his forehead. He decided he would think it through later and simply followed his heart. In the end, this was just faster. There was no reason to pick and choose when he could take everything.

This was the way of the Emilia faction—something Garfiel had picked up over the past year.

"Garf! This scent! It's coming from over there!"

"—Yeah, no mistakin' that! Good work!"

Garfiel belatedly confirmed that Mimi had sniffed out the scents they were searching for. They had found lingering traces of the two siblings. They were leading toward District One—he recalled the conversation he'd had with Fred the night before.

"I get it now! So those two went off to see the Songstress at that park again this mornin'?!"

Meaning the younger brother had risen early after reflecting upon his mistake the previous day, and his foulmouthed sister had ended up going with him as a result. Therefore, he reasoned that they had to be at the shelter located close by.

The park was close to the Water Raiment, and it was a place where they could quickly rendezvous with Subaru and the others—

"—City hall."

A moment before kicking off the ground, Garfiel had caught a glimpse of city hall. There, at the center of the city, which had fallen to Lust, was the final person he was searching for— Once more, it was time to choose.

"Garf, what'll we do?"

When Mimi asked, pressing him to decide, Garfiel asked himself that very question.

Just what kind of person should Garfiel peg Galek as?

Should Garfiel think of him as the hateful man who stole his mother away or see him as the great benefactor who saved his mother's life? Unlike the siblings, who were linked to him through his mother's blood, he and Garfiel were not connected in any way.

If he was basing his choices on blood connections, Garfiel had no duty to rescue Galek. But what would happen to Liara and the kids if they lost him?

A blank space in a family could never be filled—Garfiel knew that better than anyone.

"...City hall—that's where the Archbishop who did that damn broadcast earlier is holed up."

"Mmm, probably, yeah."

"She shook the city all up, and between the general and your little bros, there's lots to worry about... But *a mettore's heart is in its head*. If we smash the cause of everythin', we can settle this real fast."

"! You mean we can save everybody! Amazing! That's amazing!" Mimi leaped at Garfiel as he explained the logic behind his decision. But her long tail immediately rose up, its tip pointing toward city hall. "But is that really all right? I'm getting a sort of bad feeling that's making my hair stand up."

"Can't underestimate intuition. My ears got tired from how many times the general told me that the Archbishops of the Seven Deadly Sins are bad news. Still..."

The only person Garfiel knew who was connected to Witches was the Witch who had a foul personality and was slumbering in the Sanctuary's tomb.

It was a fact that she was imbued with incredible power. But Garfiel never, ever had felt like he'd lose to her in a contest of strength.

Whatever the case, the Archbishop of the Seven Deadly Sins had to be taken down for the city to be freed.

"It'd be great if we could just shut her up. At the very least, I wanna get a good look at the enemy's face."

"You mean ree-con? Mm...okay! Let's go do some ree-con!"

Though Mimi had seemed initially cautious about the dangers, she agreed with Garfiel's plan in the end.

Mimi readied the beloved staff that she carried on her back, and

Garfiel slipped his silvery shields onto both arms. After giving his gear a final check and confirming that the steel was wrapped around his thick arms, Garfiel was ready for combat.

"Let's go."

With that brief declaration, the two broke into a run toward city hall.

The Archbishop of the Seven Deadly Sins Subaru'd beaten a year earlier apparently had a considerable number of followers with him. The combat power of the disciples had been middling at best, but at any rate, there'd been a lot of them. And of course, they were good at blending into crowds.

They'd have to deal with that on the fly and take back city hall by force. Garfiel had presented it as reconnaissance to Mimi for expediency's sake, but in his heart, he intended to overwhelm the enemy with speed and violence.

—At least, that was the plan until he picked up the exceptionally dense odor of blood seeping from city hall.

"____"

As the pair stopped, that thick stench of iron was wafting over from the street right in front of them. If they went straight ahead and turned the corner, city hall would be right in front of their noses. There was no doubting from whence the scent hailed.

"Garf, don't! Don't…!"

The instant Garfiel tried to advance toward the scent of blood, Mimi grasped his loincloth. She shook her head in rejection, almost in tears as she repeated, "Don't."

But he couldn't turn back. If he retreated, he wouldn't be able to fulfill Liara's—Lisha's wish.

"If you don't wanna go, stay here. Me, I'll rip this asshole's head off alone if I have to!"

"Garf!"

Shaking off Mimi's grip, Garfiel raced down the street. Rounding the corner, his vision opened up. City hall was right before him, and when he laid eyes on the square that led to the building—a tragedy awaited him.

"?!!"

The scent of blood was so strong that it made him crinkle his nose, and a single glance was enough for him to recognize the traces of a gruesome slaughter. The square in front of city hall, which was surrounded by waterways on three sides, was overflowing with so much blood that it was almost impossible to tell what color the paving stones used to be.

A great many had already perished, their corpses tumbled into pools of their own blood—based on their equipment, these victims had been Pristellan guardsmen. They'd likely heard the broadcast and had valiantly come running in defense of their city.

Then their lives were savagely torn asunder.

The corpses numbered thirty or so, but even that grisly detail was not what attracted Garfiel's attention most.

—Rather, it was the two figures standing side by side at the center of the square, surrounded by those corpses.

"_____"

The first was a huge man, large enough that Garfiel had to look up to stare at him. He was gripping large swords in both hands, calmly gazing toward Garfiel's way. The other was a figure with a slender, feminine physique, and this one held a long, slim, single-edged blade, her stance exhibiting such beauty that it made Garfiel tremble.

Both were dressed in black outfits from head to foot. Garfiel couldn't get a good look at their faces.

"…But judgin' by the way you carry yourself like a warrior and that smell of blood comin' off ya, you two are the ones who did this, right?"

Garfiel clacked his fangs as he spoke to the two standing boldly in that bloody square. But neither opponent responded to his provocations. He felt the scar on his forehead throb.

"Garf… Those two—they're reaaally strong!"

With a pattering of footsteps, Mimi caught up with Garfiel and stood alongside him. As he had expected, she, too, was floored by the gruesome state of the square, but her tiny form was taut with caution that exceeded her surprise.

His earlier impression that their opponents had shown no reaction had been in error—the moment Garfiel and Mimi stepped into the square, they were struck by a ghastly, malevolent atmosphere and a cutting aura that seemed sharp as a blade itself.

The pair waiting in the square were so dangerous and hostile that it was immediately obvious they were exceedingly difficult foes. Garfiel felt so threatened that his throat suddenly went dry; it was as if the point of a sword was resting against his beating heart.

Their enemies were clearly masters who had stepped beyond the realm of mere mortals—and unless he surpassed these sentinels, he could not fulfill his oath.

"Ha, this is gettin' interestin'…!"

Smiling, Garfiel banged together the shields covering his arms before his chest in an attempt to rouse himself. The screech of metal on metal and a shower of sparks illuminated the beast contained within his timid heart.

But even as Garfiel worked himself up, Mimi spread both arms wide and stood in front of him as she shouted.

"D-don't! Garf! Not these two! They're too strong! Mimi and Garf can't take them alone! Stop!"

"! Can't know till we try it. Ain't no way I'm acceptin' absolutes as set in stone." The words that Mimi used in an attempt to stop Garfiel stabbed at the cracks in Garfiel's heart. Clicking his tongue at his sore insecurities, Garfiel indicated the pair with his chin. "Besides, even if we tuck our tails and run, those two ain't gonna just let us walk outta here. Someone's gotta do this."

"Th-then only once! We go *clang*, pull back, and run. Anything else is no good! Just Mimi and Garf aren't enough! It's hopeless without the captain and Julius!"

Seeing that Mimi still wanted to run, Garfiel firmly dug in and refused.

Mimi's pleas were the right call. Each of the two before them possessed superhuman might—their danger level was equal to, if not greater than, that of the Bowel Hunter. Garfiel largely agreed that facing them unprepared was suicidal.

Or at least, he agreed in theory, but accepting it as fact was a different story.

The two before his eyes were a wall. Blocking his path with overwhelming power, they represented a wall that he had to challenge and overcome. Having lost to Reinhard without a fight, could he really bear to run from his opponents twice over?

He yearned to be the strongest. He had pride in himself. He was aware that he was the shield for his precious comrades. And in a different form than he had wished, he'd reunited with his mother and her new family. To his mother, the safety or peril of the man who had saved her was—

"_____"

Mimi gave Garfiel a concerned stare as these bewildering emotions whirled about inside him. The sight of her waiting for his decision made him recall the night he had spent protected by her warmth.

Instantly, Garfiel shook his head as the obstinacy that held him in place had melted away.

"...All right. We'll do like you said. Give it all we got for just one hit, then we pull out. We'll gather our crew and then come back to mount our real attack—that's fine, right?"

"Mm! Yeah! Let's go and do our best-best!"

Mimi looked relieved that Garfiel had reined in his recklessness.

Now on the same page, they turned as one to face their enemies. The pair opposing them had watched their exchange in silence. It wouldn't have been strange for them to attack during Garfiel and Mimi's debate, but they had not, be it out of pride, mercy, or composure— Garfiel and Mimi would make them regret that.

"!!"

Without any signal, Garfiel and Mimi simultaneously launched themselves at their opponents.

Garfiel ended up matched up against the woman with his strength, and Mimi, the big man with her maneuverability.

As Garfiel drew near with the speed of an arrow, the woman remained calmly poised, not moving a muscle. The distance between them vanished in the blink of an eye, and at five to four paces out, Garfiel initiated the first attack, swinging up with a bestial claw.

—Instantly, a sword flashed with such entrancing beauty, it was enough to make anyone watching lose themselves in it.

"—Gah!"

That moment, Garfiel threw his right shield up to intercept the sword as he kicked toward the woman's open chest. She dodged it without even the slightest wasted movement. As her body twisted away, her blade, which had been caught on his shield, was freed for a renewed attack.

Neck, shoulder, arm—the longsword twisted like a snake to defend them all as a chorus of sword meeting shield rang out. Evading a strike, Garfiel instantaneously retaliated with another kick; the woman blocked this with her scabbard as she was sent flying back.

"The hell?"

Garfiel raised an eyebrow at how light the woman felt.

To his right, Mimi ran circles around her huge opponent and slipped under his massive greatswords, waving her staff to conduct a magic attack. When a blue explosion rocked her opponent and put him on the back foot, it seemed like that was as good a time as any for them to evacuate from the square.

The huge, tottering man wouldn't be able to catch Mimi. It shouldn't be difficult for her to escape unscathed. As for the woman he'd driven back, she was in no position to withstand a follow-up attack from Garfiel.

"For starters, we'll take one down!!"

Therefore, he decided it was time to strike. Garfiel bared his fangs and leaped toward the woman.

With her blade still where the shield had last deflected it, he whipped his claw toward the woman's wide-open torso.

"You're min—!"

He had her right where he wanted her—the instant he was certain of this, death closed in on him from behind.

"————"

The distance between him and the giant vanished. That ghastly aura was the only warning Garfiel got. Curtailing his attack, he flipped his body back and leaped up. Not a moment later, a greatsword swung downward and smashed his body into the ground.

"Gah, arghhh?!"

Caught up in the shock wave, the force blew Garfiel's thoughts away as he hacked up a clump of blood.

After bouncing off the ground, he felt another blow close in on him from the side. He was lucky that his arm made it just in time to catch the greatsword with his shield. Even with the lessened impact, he was still sent skipping across the ground and the surface of the water.

Pursuing Garfiel as he soared through the air, the giant and the woman simultaneously leaped up. Death was near.

Aiming to catch him in a merciless pincer attack, they came in from both sides, keeping Garfiel pinned in the middle.

He deflected the longsword coming from the front with a shield and evaded a savage greatsword swing from behind by kicking the weapon away at the last moment. Guessing the path the sword would take, Garfiel miraculously managed to parry it. But as a shower of sparks scorched his cheeks, Garfiel's body was crushed by greatsword swings that came from above and below.

"Gwuh!"

His hip bones and ribs strained, then snapped. The blunt trauma alone left his vision bloodred as he was pushed to the brink of death.

Even as groans of pain and globules of blood spilled from his mouth, he never stopped searching for a path that would lead him to survival. However, these two powerful foes would permit no such thing.

Still speechless, his attackers turned their soundless slashes into heartless bloodlust as they continued to assail Garfiel.

The woman's swordsmanship was sharp, representing the epitome of how beautiful death could be. The weight of her individual blows could not compare with that of the giant, but the skilled footwork and technique with which she wielded her long blade meant that the slightest misstep on Garfiel's part would inevitably result in a lethal blow slipping past his guard.

The large man's fighting style was crude and violent, but the chaos and lack of polish served to optimize its destructiveness. He swung swords that a normal person would struggle to lift up even with two arms, while he wielded them with a single hand each, raging like an implacable storm of destruction incarnate.

"Ngh! Aaaaaah!!"

On one side, there were dazzling sword slashes that flowed like water. On the other, there were destructive sword swings that would crush anything that stood in their path, like an implacable maelstrom.

Battered by these two very different styles of swordsmanship that sat at the opposite extremes of sound and motion, Garfiel's mind was reaching its limit. He was avoiding and parrying death on pure instinct, only narrowly escaping from multiple fatal blows.

At this rate, he would inevitably be sliced to death or crushed by the sheer weight of heavy sword strokes—

It is because you will kill me that you are my first love, Garfiel Tinzel.

The instant death entered his thoughts, that sweet, dark invitation to what lay beyond life echoed loudly within him.

Instantly, his head seethed as he abandoned those clouded musings. He roared:

"Graaaaaah!!"

His explosive increase in aggression diminished the ferocity of the incoming attacks ever so slightly. The skeletal structure of Garfiel's face audibly changed, and both of his muscular arms bulged in size as golden fur began covering all his exposed skin.

Transforming only his upper body usually lowered his ability to reason and replaced it with an animallike combativeness, but if anything, his thoughts grew clearer.

Roaring at the silent pair, he used his blessing of the earth spirit to make the ground beneath his feet explode. Sending blood and gravel flying as he flew across the gore-drenched battlefield helped interfere with the enemy's coordination.

The sudden change in footing had caused the woman to lose her balance because of her light weight. A bestial claw, sharp as any blade, didn't miss this opportunity. Just before the blow struck the woman's windpipe, the giant got in between to shield her.

A single blow from the mighty tiger was about to rend that thick mass of flesh—

"?!!"

An explosive sound rang out, leaving Garfiel thunderstruck.

Garfiel's blow had been halted by the massive man's arms. However, these were not the same arms carrying the greatswords. Opening up his outfit, the giant had used additional, hidden arms to stop Garfiel's attack with brute force.

All told, four arms were now out, leaving no obvious openings. This overwhelming combination of attack and defense completely stymied Garfiel's counterattack. Instantly, the mighty tiger that should have been the epitome of aggression was brought to a standstill.

In other words, in a battlefield where life and death were decided from moment to moment, his life was unguarded and exposed.

Circling around from behind the towering man, the female attacker closed in on Garfiel from his blind spot, sword at the ready.

Her attack almost seemed like a beautiful sword dance. And in his current state, she could easily lop off Garfiel's head like he was a scarecrow. Even as death approached from behind, Garfiel had no moves to make.

Sensing death coming from the front and the back, he caught a shadowy figure in the corner of his vision flashing him a bloody smile as she laughed—

"Choyasaaa!!"

A powerful shout interrupted, summoning a blue magic wall that blocked the woman's sword.

The wall made a sound like ice cracking as the blade slid across the barrier's surface and thrust harmlessly toward the ground. Mimi had returned to the field of battle, saving Garfiel in the nick of time.

"Garf, you said you'd run right away!"

As Mimi clutched her staff, her first words were a blunt criticism of Garfiel's refusal to follow their plan.

Hearing her voice coming from behind his back in his half-transformed state, Garfiel realized what a fool he had been.

Desperate for results, he'd courted death by misjudging how formidable his opponents were. If Mimi hadn't been there, Garfiel would have undoubtedly met a grisly end—his life cut short without ever achieving his dream of becoming the strongest.

"—Ohooooaaaaagh!!"

Pushing aside the relief that he felt at being saved, Garfiel howled and yanked his arm free from his grappling opponent. Kicking the giant in the chest, he didn't bother to see the results as he leaped clear to rejoin Mimi.

Putting an arm around her slender waist, he poured strength into his legs. It was time to take Mimi and retreat. Following her initial suggestion, they'd gather their comrades and return in force.

"_____"

Right before he could jump, the woman pursued him in a low stance. Mimi turned her staff toward the approaching woman, deploying a triple-layered magical barrier surpassing what she'd summoned before and using the thick walls to bar the woman's path.

Garfiel was glad he had Mimi here with him. She'd saved him time and again.

As that thought occurred to him, Garfiel was already flexing his legs, and—

"—Ah."

There was a soft, strained cry and a light impact. He heard something that sounded like ice breaking.

This caught him by surprise, and he wondered what had happened as he finished leaping away. Paving stones shattered as the half-beast sailed into the sky, seemingly streaming a trail of fresh blood in his wake.

—Fresh blood… Where the hell was it coming from?

"Hey, shorty?"

The moment he called out to her, Garfiel swiftly released his half-transfiguration and returned to human form. However, the chill that ran up his spine was all that occupied him, to the point that he didn't even notice the unsettling feeling of his fur falling out.

Mimi was limp in his arms. When he looked down, he saw that the woman was peering up at Garfiel in the sky, pulling back the longsword she had thrust at them.

He noticed that the longsword was stained in blood along half its length.

"_____"

He could feel something warm spreading across his stomach. The girl in his arms was not moving. Her staff…was falling to the ground.

He landed, then bounded once more. Leaping onto the roof of the nearest building, Garfiel fled without regard for anything else. There was no pursuit. The two foes simply watched as the wounded weaklings escaped.

What their enemies thought of them and their abilities wasn't important at the moment. Jumping five more times to distance them from the square, Garfiel broke the roof of the building that he picked to land on, then set down the girl in his arms.

Mimi's eyes were closed. A great deal of blood was still coursing out of her pierced chest.

Hastily, he stripped away her clothes around the source of bleeding and checked the wound. Fortunately, it apparently missed her vitals. Of course, she was in danger if she wasn't treated immediately, but a user of healing magic was right there with her.

Pressing a hand to the wound, Garfiel poured magic energy into Mimi's body.

Well aware that he wasn't cut out for the role, he'd put his soul into learning healing magic. He wanted the power so that he could manage if something happened to anyone in the Sanctuary. That was why Garfiel had focused his efforts on studying healing magic, and in the process, he had learned a decent amount about treating the wounded in general.

It was time to put all that hard work to use. It was an opportunity to show how far he'd come. This was surely the exact situation he'd wanted to prepare for.

Even a wound this serious would close up in a flash with some healing mana. Touching his palm to the open wound, he could sense the blood coursing beneath the skin, the flesh, the innards, and the healing magic he was pouring in. He poured and poured, but—

—the wound… It wasn't closing.

"Why won't…?"

He heard someone speaking in a very frail voice.

He wanted to kill whoever was speaking in such a pathetic voice at a time like this. Lifting his face, he looked around. There was no one else there. He immediately realized that the voice…had been his own.

I was the one who sounded that weak? Why did I let out a voice like that?

That's just… That's just like…like—

"!! Close! Close, close, damn it! Heal, heal, healhealheal!!!"

He kept pouring all the mana his body could muster into the healing magic. Ignoring his own wounds, he sent waves of healing energy into Mimi's battered body, filling it with gentle power.

And yet the wound that needed to close would not.

"…No…way."

Unable to accept the reality before him, Garfiel spat out in a frail voice once more.

Then he slugged his own cheek, cutting his lip with his own fangs, and used the pain to rouse himself. This wasn't the time to wallow in despair. There had to be a way. There just had to.

He knew it existed. Of course it did. He was just too stupid to realize it.

He had to think. Not knowing was no reason to give up. At any rate, he had to do something to save this girl.

She was the one who'd helped Garfiel cry.

It wasn't right for this girl to die for his sake.

"―――"

Clacking his fangs, Garfiel was still in a daze as he leaped off that roof. Keeping pressure on the girl's wound, he tried to stop the bleeding as he continued attempting his ineffective healing magic.

There was a scent of blood, and death, hanging over the city. He didn't spot another soul as he reviewed all available information in his mind.

I'll take anyone who can help. Please just save this girl. Someone, somewhere, please show me a miracle. Please tell me. If there's anything that I can do, then tell me how to save this girl.

He was so desperate that he was even willing to trade his life for hers if it came to it. Garfiel focused everything on his sense of smell.

The scent of water, the scent of blood, the scent of violence fanned by emotions run amok, the scent of scorched flesh—amid those countless smells, Garfiel's nose picked out the one he wanted.

He knew this one. And it was the one that Garfiel had been searching for.

Leaping over obstacles, racing forward, Garfiel was feverish by the time he finally reached his destination. He arrived at the same building he had visited just the day before and rushed into one of the rooms inside. A large number of people were shocked to see his bloodied form. He had no time to explain. Swiveling his head, Garfiel searched for the man he could rely on.

"Garfiel?!"

Someone called his name. Turning, he spotted the one he was looking for.

He lifted his head. Straight ahead at the back of the room, he saw Subaru. Subaru Natsuki.

To Garfiel, this man symbolized miracles; he was the personification of the ray of light that revealed hope in the direst of situations.

With tottering feet and a heavy head, he raced toward his hope while carrying an all-too-light weight in his arms. Subaru's cheeks stiffened as he got a good look at Garfiel. He had noticed Mimi's limp body in his arms.

"I'm sorry... I'm so sorry, General!! I'm...! I'm useless! Worthless...!!"

Dropping to his knees in front of Subaru, he held up Mimi. Then he despaired, cursing his own foolishness.

He hadn't protected his family. He'd failed to fulfill his oath to serve as a shield. He'd challenged the enemy on his own judgment and been routed, and as a result, this kindhearted girl was now on the brink of death.

"Garfiel, what did...? No, we'll leave that for later! Ferris!"

"I know! Quick, lay her down!"

Taking Mimi from Garfiel's arms, Subaru set her down on the long table. Garfiel simply watched as the nearby, pretty cat-eared girl put a hand upon Mimi's wound.

The next instant, an overwhelming amount of healing mana swelled up. This was incomparable with what Garfiel could wield. If Garfiel's healing magic was a drop of rain, this person's power was a thundering waterfall.

It was so great that even bringing the dead back to life seemed within reach. Garfiel felt like his soul slipped out of his body as he gazed upon such godlike healing power in a daze.

Then Subaru gently rested a hand upon his shoulder. When Garfiel slowly looked up at him, Subaru nodded. He only noticed now that Subaru's leg was heavily bandaged.

"Not gonna sugarcoat it and call this a good situation, but you did well getting this far. With Ferris here, it's the best place you could've brought her. We'll be able to save Mimi thanks to you."

"Thanks...to me...?"

What was Subaru saying?

Thanks to Garfiel, Mimi would be saved? What was he even talking about? Wasn't it Garfiel's fault that Mimi had ended up like this to begin with?

Even so, Subaru had naturally arrived at the conclusion that she'd been saved by Garfiel's good judgment. But that was all wrong.

He felt lost. His thoughts were empty and hollow. The disgust and guilt tortured him and seemed like they would never stop. There was a persistent ringing in his ears that wouldn't go away. He found the insistent pain of his own wounds laughable and out of place.

I want blame. I want pain. I don't want anyone to forgive me for my stupidity.

Garfiel's wish was one that would be granted. After all, the world was not so forgiving.

There would be a price to pay for his errors—but the bill would come in the most loathsome way possible.

"Ferris, what's the matter…?"

Sensing that something was wrong, Subaru suddenly asked a tentative question.

In front of him, the treatment to save Mimi's life was still underway. An incredible stream of mana was flowing. It was so awesome that even the residual energy seemed powerful enough to cure all ills.

And yet the girl employing this breathtaking power had a desperate look about her as she shook her head.

"Why…? The wound…isn't closing! I can't help her like this! I don't understand!!"

As that pained report echoed through the room, Garfiel slumped against the wall and crumpled to the ground. The wall was cold. The floor was cold. He was covered in blood. The wound would not heal.

"_____"

As Garfiel hung his head, the phantom woman in black gazed upon him.

She said nothing. She didn't make a sound. She didn't even smile. Her black, hollow eyes told him nothing.

Nothing except that the price for his mistake was being repaid in blood.

CHAPTER 5
THE OPERATION TO RETAKE CITY HALL

1

"Old Man Wil! Carry her! I can't stop the bleeding here!"

Seeing Ferris change his expression, Wilhelm did as he instructed and picked up Mimi's bloodied body. The two proceeded to rush out of the conference room with urgent steps, heading to the field hospital in the structure's basement.

With healing magic being ineffective, they had no choice but to fall back onto ordinary medical treatments. Fortunately, Ferris was skilled not only in healing magic, but also surgical techniques as well.

If not for that, it was likely that there would be nothing else they could do but despair.

"Has my heartache reached any of you even a little? Really, for beings lower than insects trapped inside a box, how are you so slow on the uptake? I wuv it! Bwa-ha-ha-ha!!"

Even as some of them were making heroic efforts to save a life, Lust continued her menacing broadcast.

In truth, this could no longer be considered a broadcast that was meant to intimidate its listeners. It was simply being used to mock and scorn, to spit upon the valiant efforts of others. It was a sadistic ritual.

"―――"

Under that downpour of malice, Subaru looked at Garfiel, who had flopped against the wall. Covering his face with both hands and hanging his head, Garfiel sported wounds all over his body. They were definitely not the kind that could be ignored.

However, the gravest wound was not to his body, but his heart.

"You scum are even lower than insects! And now that you've deeply hurt me, I really want some payback for this pain to my heart! My heart will be assuaged by what I said before! I expect great things from the smarter meatbags among you!"

Lust redoubled her malice during that time as well. Subaru focused on her voice, searching for a way to land even a single retaliatory blow against this villain who kept rambling without a care for those who were forced to keep listening to her.

Information, weaknesses, clues about the enemy, anything would do—with that mindset, he noticed a particular sound.

Besides Lust's high-pitched, earsplitting voice, there was also the sound of her clapping and stomping her feet. She acted like a child who was struggling to settle down, and that certainly also grated on Subaru's nerves—but he was focused on something else.

He heard…another sound.

The source was most likely right beside the broadcasting metia, unintentionally mixing in with her voice and reaching Subaru's ears through the broadcast.

Then Subaru's sense of reason instinctively rejected the identity of that sound.

Don't pay attention. Stop. You don't need to know— Don't give in to your cowardice.

"!"

Biting down hard on his lip, Subaru used the pain to come back to his senses. He clenched his teeth as he examined the nature of what he had just rejected.

Concentration, rejection, comprehension, rejection, comprehension, comprehension, comprehension—

That was what hummed in Subaru's ears.

The buzzing of an unbelievable quantity of insects was mixed in with the threatening broadcast. It was incredibly anxiety-inducing, the manifestation of a nightmare that provoked an instinctive disgust, and the instant Subaru realized that, he—

"Incidentally, isn't it about time for the smarter meatbags among you to notice something that you really should've kept ignoring?"

"—Ah."

She pointed out with terrifying timing that she'd planned for them to hear it all along.

"Bwa-ha-ha-ha! You should've just been enchanted by my beautiful voice, but now you're paying the price because you just haaad to do something pointless. Speaking of which, the stupid try-hards who tried to force their way in should be having a real bad time right about now."

Subaru was stunned. She had basically just revealed that they were still dancing in the palm of her hand. Toying with their minds like this wasn't enough to sate Lust's malicious appetite.

She smacked her lips and made sure everyone could hear it.

"I'm so deeply hurt that you would slap away the hand that I held out! That's why I figured it's time to stop holding back and time to tighten up a bit around here. And all you meatbags who got excited when I mentioned making things tighter just now, I'll have to teach you what the word *serious* really means! Bwa-ha-ha-ha! Bwa-ha-ha! Bwa-ha-ha-ha-ha! ...Haaah."

Her laughing gradually lost strength, and by the end, only a tedious sigh trickled forth. That sharp drop in emotion made it sound like Lust had decided to forsake everyone else as she continued:

"—I'll start by turning the meatbags at my feet into mincemeat."

"!"

"If you want to avoid that, I've only got one demand. If you're going to surrender, then just get it over with already and bow your heads as low as you can. That's the smart thing to do, right?"

Calmly, with none of the excitement she had shown just moments ago, Lust thrust her demand onto the city.

That sudden reversal and a threat that promised gore made Subaru gasp for breath.

Then Lust's disturbing moment of composure ended with such ease and speed that Subaru could have sworn the change was audible.

"Well, that's all from little ol' me! ...And I said this already, but here's a friendly reminder that we've set up camp in the control towers, so don't try anything funny. The sight of a drowning human's face is so awful, I almost can't bear to look at one again! Bwa-ha-ha-ha!"

With one last screeching laugh, the spiteful broadcast finally came to an end.

It had been a completely one-sided statement of intent that left just as suddenly as it had arrived. Her way of speaking was perfectly in character for an Archbishop of the Seven Deadly Sins—a manifestation of ugliness in a new form.

"M-messing with us like that..."

At the same time the broadcast ended, Subaru no longer heard the buzzing that had put his heart in a vise. His body instantly relaxed, and as soon as it did, the first words out of his breathless mouth were grumbles.

Of course, trash-talking someone who couldn't hear it was little more than the distant whimpers of a beaten dog. Subaru clenched his fist in frustration at his total inability to even say a retort that would reach their enemy.

"—*Subaru, can you hear me?*"

Abruptly, Subaru heard a voice calling his name from the round table. When he looked over, he saw that the conversation mirror, which had been abandoned in haste, had not lost its glow and was currently displaying a morose knight's face upon its surface.

"Yeah, I hear you. You caught the broadcast just now, right?"

"*But of course. Loath as I am to say it, that voice surely reached every corner of the city. There is Mimi's condition to consider as well. TB and I shall return to you. We will speak again once we arrive.*"

"Yeah..."

Once he finished that short exchange with Julius, Subaru closed his eyes once before turning toward the conference-room window.

"...We can talk it over soon."

The red-eyed flag fluttering atop the control tower in the distance looked like it was laughing at the Water Gate City.

2

A short time later, Julius and the others who had ventured outside returned to the designated shelter.

"B-Big Sis, hang in there…!"

"Keep fighting, Big Sis…"

Concerned for their unconscious sister, Hetaro and TB continued calling out to Mimi. Feeling their sister's wounds due to their shared blessing even now, both brothers had pain and grief carved onto their faces in equal measure.

"Every second counts! Keep pressure on the wound to stem the bleeding… Argh! This method is so outdated…!"

Ferris was too worked up for anyone else to get a single word in. Everyone present understood what was at stake. Critically wounded, Mimi could be entrusted to none but him.

"Sir Subaru."

It was then that Wilhelm called to Subaru with an austere expression.

Sensing unconcealable anguish from the man's subdued voice and seeing the deep creases marring his forehead, Subaru nodded. He had a pretty good idea what was upsetting the elderly butler.

"Mimi's wound won't close. It's probably…"

"…It is almost certainly due to the blessing of the grim reaper."

Picking up where Subaru left off, Wilhelm spoke those words with resolve.

The blessing of the grim reaper was a terrifying power that afflicted any wound caused by the bearer of the blessing with a curse that kept it from healing. Based on what they had seen, there was little doubt this was why healing magic had no effect on Mimi's injury.

Additionally, from all Subaru had heard, there was only one individual he knew who possessed such a blessing.

Theresia van Astrea, the prior generation of Sword Saint—Wilhelm's departed wife.

"I'm scared to ask this...but, Wilhelm, is your arm...?"

"―――"

When Subaru asked, Wilhelm stripped off his butler's jacket without a word. The old wound on his left shoulder was concealed under bandages—it was the unhealed gouge that his wife had left upon him.

The bandages wrapping the wound that had been carved in him by the blessing of the grim reaper were faintly red and wet.

"If that's still bleeding, then..."

"My old wound has reopened. It seems that I cannot pretend to be uninvolved."

Putting his jacket back on, Wilhelm quietly murmured. Subaru couldn't think of anything to say to him. However, what dwelled in Wilhelm's eyes was neither hope nor relief, but anger.

Even though he'd discovered the possibility that his wife, the one he had supposedly lost so long ago, might still be alive—

"—My wife passed away fifteen years ago. That fact has not changed."

Pushing down the roiling emotions he must have been feeling, Wilhelm refuted what Subaru had been thinking as he leveled his gaze directly at him. That moment, Subaru thought he could feel a small part of Wilhelm's surging desire to fight.

"Someone out there is involved in her death, in the desecration of her soul. I swear upon my sword and the days I spent together with my wife—they shall pay."

With an indomitable resolve, the Sword Devil had become as tenacious as hardened steel.

Anyone who set eyes upon this man would realize that there was nothing else to be said. Cheap condolences and consolations would only be an affront to his determination.

"―――"

Standing beside Wilhelm, Subaru quietly took a breath.

Ferris continued doing everything he could while Hetaro and TB stayed huddled at Mimi's side. Ferris soon shooed away the rest, sending them to an adjacent waiting room. Subaru and the others continued discussing plans as they changed locations.

He was still deeply worried about Mimi's condition, but the city's situation didn't allow him to focus on Mimi alone. The most pressing issue they needed to discuss was—

"—As you have all heard, the Archbishop made a second broadcast. The lives of the hostages at city hall may not have very long."

One of their group raised a hand and shed the jacket of his white suit as he kicked off the conversation.

He was a man with meticulously combed hair and an elegant face—however, his expression was taut. This palpable desire to deal with the formidable problem left before them belonged to none other than the president of the Muse Company, Kiritaka Muse.

Right up until moments before, Kiritaka had been doing his best to get a grasp on the situation while suppressing disorder across the entire city as one of the Council of Ten, but after hearing the earlier broadcast, he decided to participate in the urgent meeting that was currently being held.

Given that he was a central figure in the city, Subaru had wanted to confirm something with him right at the start.

"There's no time, so I'll get straight to the point—Kiritaka, could you give us an explanation about the Witch's bones?"

It was Anastasia who cut to the chase without the slightest hesitation, taking a position at the front of the waiting room. She discarded the demure attitude she usually adopted, turning a sharp, serious look toward Kiritaka.

Realizing from her keen gaze that Anastasia was serious, Kiritaka nodded and assented to her request.

"I suppose there is no point hiding it at this juncture. Therefore, in brief... The Witch's bones do exist, and they are here in the city. Only the people on the Council of Ten know where they are... Of course, I am one of them."

"...So the bones seriously exist?"

When Kiritaka confirmed as much, everyone present drew in a

small, short breath. It was tangible proof that the establishment of the city four centuries prior had indeed been related to a Witch.

But Kiritaka met their general reaction with a "However" before continuing his explanation. "I must say this bluntly. The Witch's bones absolutely cannot be moved. Accordingly, we cannot comply with the opponent's demand. The bones cannot be used as a bargaining chip."

"Master Kiritaka, is it simply your opinion that they should not be moved?"

"No. I am not saying they cannot be moved due to custom or adherence to ancient history. In a situation where human lives hang in the balance, such things are not even worth considering."

"Then are you saying that…?"

"They physically cannot be moved."

Kiritaka's reply to Crusch's question was firm, but his follow-up to Subaru's words was mostly listless.

It was an oddly roundabout way to ultimately say they could not be moved even if someone wanted to. The Witch's bones—if Al's murmur was to be believed, the chance that they were relics of Typhon was high. She'd been a young girl and barely any different from Beatrice in stature, so it was hard to imagine that the difficulty in moving them was due to size or weight.

There had to be another reason.

"Maybe it's more about where they're currently located or the role they play?"

"That would make sense. If the Witch's bones truly do exist but they're kept a secret from everyone except the city's council, there should be a fairly important reason for it."

Anastasia quickly agreed with Subaru's conjecture. The pair's hypothesis made Kiritaka visibly tense up before letting out a resigned sigh.

"…As you have surmised, special power dwells within the Witch's bones—power sufficient to serve as the foundation of this city. Without the bones, the Water Gate City is unsustainable."

"What happens if they're moved?"

"It seems that all present are aware of how this city was founded. Should the bones be moved, the city will undoubtedly sustain damage on par with that legendary event... No, it would likely be an even greater disaster than that. The result would be the same as if the Witch Cult flung the water gates of this city wide open."

"...I see. And that's why you can't move 'em." As he made that remark, Subaru glanced at Crusch. She shook her head side to side in response.

The power of the blessing of wind reading allowed Crusch to tell whether the words of others were truth or lies. There were a number of loopholes, but it was a pretty safe bet that this meant Kiritaka's statement was not willful deception.

In other words, handing the Witch's bones over was tantamount to destroying the city. By including such a terrible condition in her proposed deal, Lust had clearly miscalculated.

"Or perhaps we should assume that she came up with her terms knowing full well what it would mean for the city."

It was then that Julius murmured an alternative explanation with a faint crease in the brow of his forehead. Having returned with TB and joined the renewed meeting, he swept his hair to the side when he noticed all attention gathering upon him.

"After visiting several shelters, I can safely say that the residents of the city have endured well. Even so, there will be no end to the number of people who find this current situation hopeless. Without understanding the consequences it will entail, some may even demand that the Witch's bones should be handed over."

"You mean Lust is getting off on seeing the city rip itself apart? ... That's a sick joke."

It was a pessimistic bit of speculation, but at the same time, it was difficult to rule out. When Capella, the Archbishop of Lust, made her broadcast, all of them had gotten a glimpse of the joy she got out of sadistically toying with people's hearts.

Perhaps the real objective of making the entire city hear her voice was simply to tyrannize the hearts of others—

"—We ain't handin' over those bones, and we sure as hell ain't entertainin' their stupid demands. It wouldn't change a damn thing."

It was a quiet declaration. The tenor of that voice made Subaru lift his face with a strong sense that something was off.

He found the quietness of that voice deeply unsettling. This was because the one who just spoke was always so strong and spirited— a far cry from the impression of the subdued, muted emotion the voice gave off now.

Sporting charred-brown fur and a large, muscular frame, the demi-human dog-man Ricardo was normally bold with his words and his actions. Like Julius, he had returned from his excursion and now stood in silence with his thick arms crossed, seemingly thinking hard about something.

Then he slowly walked over to the wall and broke the silence again.

"I didn't say thanks yet. Bro, if ya hadn't brought Mimi here, there's no doubt in my mind she'd be dead. I owe you one. Big-time. Seriously, thank you."

Ricardo sank down and sat cross-legged, pressing his head to the floor as he conveyed his gratitude. His words were directed at none other than Garfiel, who was still slumped against the wall, his head hanging like a rag doll's.

"_____"

Despondent, Garfiel had only barely managed to do as Subaru instructed and cast healing magic upon his own wounds. He opened his jade eyes, revealing a frail, clouded gaze filled with bewilderment and remorse.

Based on what Garfiel had wailed when he brought Mimi in, it was clear he felt responsible for Mimi's condition. As her guardian, Ricardo had a right to blame him for what had happened.

And yet instead of accusing Garfiel, Ricardo had chosen to bow his head. Ricardo's sincerity stabbed deep into Garfiel's heart, driving the boy further into the grasping hands of guilt.

"Well? Shouldn't we stop dancin' around the issue here and ask what we need to ask?"

It was Al who pointed out their inactivity from his seat at the long table. Fiddling with the seams of his helm, he surveyed all those present.

"That nutty broadcast earlier can't be unrelated to those two rushing in here all a mess. They're crucial live witnesses who just returned from city hall. That's a big deal, am I right?"

Though wounded, Garfiel jerked his chin up. Al shrugged with a familiar disinterest. His aloof demeanor came off as insensitive, but he asserted that was what the situation called for.

There was no doubt that Garfiel and Mimi had confronted their enemies at city hall. Perhaps that had been a hasty decision, but the two had tried in their own way to do the best they could.

And they'd paid the price—in fact, Mimi was still paying for it even as they spoke.

"Garfiel, it might be tough to talk about it, but please tell us what happened. I get that no chump could've put you through the wringer like that. But…"

"_____"

"…we have to give a serious thrashing to all the morons who attacked this city. We'll need your strength to make that happen. I can't afford to let you stay down in the dumps like this."

He knew it was a cruel demand to make. But Subaru gave it to Garfiel straight and spoke from the heart.

Garfiel had challenged the enemy based on his personal judgment but had failed to protect Mimi. It was easy for Subaru to imagine what crushing regret and responsibility must have weighed on Garfiel's chest.

That was only natural. Subaru himself felt the exact same way Garfiel did.

"…We heard…that broadcast. Me and the runt headed for the center of the city all because I wanted to give that bastard broadcastin' out of city hall a good beatdown."

Haltingly, his face still angled toward the floor, Garfiel began to speak. Suspending his treatment, he clenched a fist so hard that it nearly broke the bones in his hand. That was the only way he could keep his churning emotions from exploding.

"There were a whole lotta dead people in front of city hall. I think they were city guards. The ones who did them in were a pair, a big man and a thin woman. Both fought with swords, and they…"

Garfiel's fangs trembled as his words trailed off. What he had left unsaid were no doubt Garfiel's defeat and the cause of Mimi's wound, which refused all attempted treatments.

What made Subaru want to doubt his ears was that it was a complete mystery who that pair might be.

The fact that they were acting in concert with Lust meant they were definitely Witch Cultists. But as Subaru knew, no Archbishops matched the physical characteristics that Garfiel had mentioned.

They were unknown Witch Cultists who weren't even Archbishops. What's more—

"Both of 'em are a match for… Actually, I think they're stronger than me."

Garfiel seemed weak, seemingly shrinking in on himself as he agonized over that thought. His awe at his opponents' might and his guilt for letting Mimi get hurt left Garfiel looking incredibly small.

"—Looks like ya got a pretty good grasp on the strength and weakness of your opponents."

"Ricardo…"

Ricardo had kept his head pressed to the floor right up until he made that comment. An instant later, a terrifying, ferocious, and bestial presence filled the room.

"Tell me, Bro. Of the two ya mentioned, which one is it? Which one do I cut apart to avenge Mimi?"

If Ricardo's exhaustive thanks were sincere, then he was equally sincere in just how far he would go to rip and tear his enemy to sate his thirst for vengeance.

Taken aback by that daunting show of brutality, Garfiel hesitated slightly.

"…It was the woman who got the runt. It happened when Mimi covered for me."

"That was Mimi's choice. I ain't gonna criticize her decision."

"I get it. I get ya. No one… Not a single person's blamin' me…but I do! That's why I gotta give it to that woman…!!"

Practically flying to his feet, Garfiel wore a mournful look on his face as he shouted his desire for retribution. Rising in turn, Ricardo stared down at the boy across their difference in height.

"That was a good howl. A man never goes back on his word. Now stand up and fight."

"Yeah…yeah! Damn right I will! I'm gonna do it…!"

Garfiel howled as if he was tearing into something with his jaws as the light returned to his clouded eyes. There was some bravado at work, but now angry, Garfiel had sworn to Ricardo that he would avenge Mimi.

Acknowledging his resolve, Ricardo nodded and glanced momentarily toward Subaru. Though it should have been Subaru giving Garfiel that extra push he needed, Ricardo had thoughtfully acted in his stead.

The captain of the Iron Fangs was as good at helping people back to their feet as Subaru expected.

"Thanks to Garfiel's report, we now know the degree of danger that awaits us at city hall…and have learned about the sacrifices made by the guards who fought with the resolve to die in defense of the city. Next…"

Now that Ricardo had lit a fire under Garfiel, Julius pulled the conversation back on topic, faintly narrowing his yellow eyes as he looked at Subaru.

"Subaru, what would you do?"

"…Whoa, that's an awfully sloppy way to pass the reins over to someone else."

Subaru grimaced at Julius's uncharacteristically haphazard manner of speaking. Julius's only response was a smug chuckle.

"I was simply thinking back to the battle with Sloth. I was hoping that you might be particularly effective against the Witch Cult once again. As such, I reasoned that you might come up with a plan that would not have occurred to me."

"Don't get carried away, man. If I was that effective against 'em, my leg wouldn't have ended up like this."

"That is unfortunate. However, there is also the matter of Lady Emilia. Surely, you do not wish to leave her in her current predicament. I simply wish to confirm what you intend to do."

It may not have been the answer he hoped for, but Julius didn't seem particularly disappointed. Of course, he of all people hadn't expected Subaru to turn out to be some kind of mystical Witch Cult killer.

Subaru himself immediately understood that it was the second issue Julius had brought up that was the real point.

"…Greed is the one who kidnapped Emilia. Even now, his selfish pet theories have every hair on my body standing on end. I don't wanna leave Emilia with that bastard one second longer than I have to."

"By that, you mean you are prioritizing Lady Emilia's rescue?"

"*Damn right I am*—is what I'd like to say, but…"

When he tried to give Julius's question a confident answer, Subaru broke off with a sigh.

He did want to get Emilia back as soon as possible. That was, without question, Subaru's true feelings on the matter. The idea of leaving Emilia in the hands of someone with such warped thinking for any period of time made him want to hurl.

But the city's dire state and Lust's demands did not permit Subaru to act out of emotion.

"We can't let Lust do as she pleases. If we don't stop her, she's gonna wreak absolute havoc with people's minds— Plus, that metia is a serious problem."

"Agreed. The metia in city hall is a chain that binds everyone in the city."

A voice that could reach every part of the city was plenty menacing enough. Lust was clearly aware of its efficacy, but Subaru had a different concern in mind.

There was someone else inside the city, someone with an Authority that amplified emotions and made them resonate with those of anyone in the vicinity. If that ability was augmented to a despairing degree by that metia, what would happen?

A pandemic of explosively irresistible madness would spread, and the city would be annihilated.

To save Emilia, they had to prevent the destruction of the city and regain control over that metia. Both goals required defeating Lust at city hall.

Accomplishing this was the first step on the path to rescuing Emilia from Greed's clutches.

"The enemy has seized the four control towers as well as the municipal offices at the center of the city. That said, the priority target is obvious. Getting Lust out of city hall comes first. Plus, if Lust was serious during that broadcast earlier, the lives of the people inside city hall are more at risk the longer we wait."

"I see… A most valuable opinion. It largely matches my own thoughts."

When Subaru detailed his plan, Julius nodded in apparent satisfaction.

In all likelihood, the handsome knight had internally come to the same conclusion much sooner. Perhaps making Subaru say it out loud was to test whether Subaru had lost his cool and reached a hasty conclusion.

"Good, good. Let's review and take stock."

Lightly clapping, Anastasia resumed her self-appointed duty as master of ceremonies. Spreading her hands, she fixed Subaru with her round, light-blue eyes.

"I support following Natsuki's plan. I agree that leaving the broadcast metia in that person's hands is dangerous… The longer we let her be, the greater the chance the city's residents might lose the will to carry on and force our hand."

"I also concur with the two of you. If we allow the enemy free rein, our options shall gradually diminish. If we are making our move, the sooner the better."

With a crisp posture, Crusch agreed with Subaru and Anastasia's conclusion.

Just as she had said, they were currently well staffed and ready for a fight. The Muse Company was currently housing Garfiel, Ricardo, Julius, and Wilhelm, distinguished warriors all.

Adding in the Iron Fangs and Kiritaka's private forces, the White Dragon's Scale, would enhance their strength even further.

However, Kiritaka interrupted that line of thought as he shook his head side to side with a grim face.

"I am very sorry. Currently, my personal troops are carrying out a different mission at my direction. They are securing the members of the Council of Ten and escorting them here."

"Shit, that's… Nah, that's something you need to do. If one of them blabs, the city'll be destroyed by something other than the water gates. That said, I'd love to improve our chances somehow…"

If it was possible, Subaru would've preferred to face the enemy at the same strength they'd been able to field during the battle with Petelgeuse—at minimum. After all, they were currently facing no less than three Archbishops of the Seven Deadly Sins, so by simple arithmetic, he assumed the fight would be three times as tough.

"—Nah, you probably don't need to worry about that, right?"

"Al? What do you mean?"

Al suddenly interrupted Subaru's train of thought. Twisting his neck, he said, "Well, you know?" as a preamble. "Bro, you're worried about city hall turning into a haunt for the Archbishops of the Seven Deadly Sins, right? But didn't they say in that last broadcast that they've set up camp in each of the control towers?"

"? What of it? Is there something odd about that?"

"!! Ohhh, I get it now! Yeah, you're right!"

Ricardo voiced his confusion, but Subaru grasped what he was getting at.

Apparently, they'd each stationed themselves in different control towers—and what did that expression imply?

"The Archbishops took over the control towers at the same time… but I don't think they're working together like a big happy family. They're the kind of people who'd be willing to start turning on one another even as their enemies close in on them."

Subaru pointedly recalled how Sirius and Regulus had nearly gone for each other's throats.

Had it not been for Subaru being in the way, the falling-out in the time-tower square would probably have ended with one of them going down. In the first place, the terms *harmonious* and *group activity* didn't suit them in the slightest.

Could such hyper-individual personalities really rein it in and coordinate properly?

"The fact that no one else spoke during Lust's broadcast seems to support that theory. They're all way too keen on promoting their own causes to leave something like that to anyone else."

"I cannot call that anything other than a very subjective opinion... However, it is oddly convincing."

Subaru's conviction left Julius furrowing his refined eyebrows as the man shut one eye and considered the plausibility of it all.

There was no question that this was the most speculative theory they had discussed so far. However, Subaru was certain in his deductions. Having come face-to-face with three Archbishops of the Seven Deadly Sins and having had indirect contact with a fourth, Subaru Natsuki believed wholeheartedly in their warped character.

Then just as their counterattack on city hall suddenly seemed genuinely within reach—

"—*Whew*. Somehow, I managed to finish the treatment." The door to the adjacent room opened, and Ferris emerged, covered in a sheen of sweat as he tottered forward. Covered in bloodstains despite having already changed clothes once, he wiped his brow with a towel as he gave Anastasia his report. "Lady Anastasia, I have done everything I can. The rest..."

"How's Mimi? Can ya save her? You will, right?"

Ricardo's breathing was ragged as he talked to Ferris over Anastasia's head, hoping for good news. Behind Ricardo, Garfiel stared at Ferris as if clinging to his every word.

With their gazes and earnest pleas focused on him, as well as the attention of everyone else in the room, Ferris lowered his eyes.

"The wound still isn't closed. For now, I did what I could and stopped the bleeding using primitive methods... Then borrowing the power of the blessing shared between Mimi and her little brothers, we're somehow keeping her going for the moment."

"By 'blessing,' do you mean the blessing of thirds? What's that gonna do to them?"

"That blessing gives the power to share wounds and fatigue between the three of them to begin with, right? They forced that bond to strengthen, taking a greater share from Mimi's wounds than they normally would. That's extended our time limit, but..."

"—When Big Sis's life runs out, it means we will die as well, I presume."

From the door to the other room, someone behind Ferris cut in with a voice that was short of breath.

When Ferris moved to the side, everyone could see Hetaro and TB sitting on the floor of the adjacent room. A simple cot lay between them, and resting on it was Mimi.

Their older sister continued to sleep as the two younger brothers gently held her hands— However, their free hands were pressed to their own chests in obvious signs of pain.

"—Ya pair of fools. I swear the both of you don't have a lick of sense."

"...When I think of this as Big Sis's pain, I feel a little bit happy I can share it with her."

"I am not quite as taken with this as my older brother seems to be. Therefore, captain, I trust that you will do something about this as soon as possible— After all, should we die, the three of us will absolutely haunt you."

Shouldering a portion of their sister's wounds, the two little brothers braved the same mortal danger. Their courage made Ricardo's fangs tremble. In an attempt to console him, Ferris put a hand on his shoulder and said, "Don't be angry with them. These kids are just desperate to help Mimi."

Ferris was standing up for the choice that the two cat-people made. But really, his voice was thick with his own regrets over his lack of ability.

"It isn't your fault, Ferris. Besides, I'm guessing those two came up with that idea on their own, didn't they? These children are such a handful. They never stop to think whenever their beloved big sister is involved."

With a thin smile, Anastasia indicated that she understood her subordinates'—her family's decision.

Then Anastasia seemed to slowly bite down on her teeth.

"Ricardo."

"If we're gonna do it, we do it fast. Otherwise, there ain't no point. Am I wrong, boss?"

When called upon, Ricardo replied without hesitation. From his low growl, it was clear there was no one capable of calling a halt to his determination to fight—nor was there anyone who failed to comprehend the feelings urging him onward.

With a click of his heels, Julius straightened his back and gave Anastasia a reverent knight's salute.

"Lady Anastasia, should you command it, all members of the Iron Fangs can move at once."

"Thank you. Our Iron Fangs will secure the route to city hall. After that, ideally, the elites will launch their assault and take control of the building without delay. Our enemies are a looming man, a slender woman, and the Archbishop of Lust."

"On our side, we've got Garfiel, Ricardo, Wilhelm, and Julius, right?"

"—I shall participate as well."

It was Crusch who raised her voice.

Her long, green hair was tied back, and a longsword hung at her hip. She retightened the straps of her boots as she boldly volunteered for the front lines.

"Are you sure you're up for this, Crusch?"

"I may not be as I once was, but I have retrained with Wilhelm as my teacher. I also have the power of the blessing of wind reading. I have no intention of weighing anyone down."

Before she'd lost her memory, Crusch had been mighty enough to be one of the heavy hitters during the battle against the White

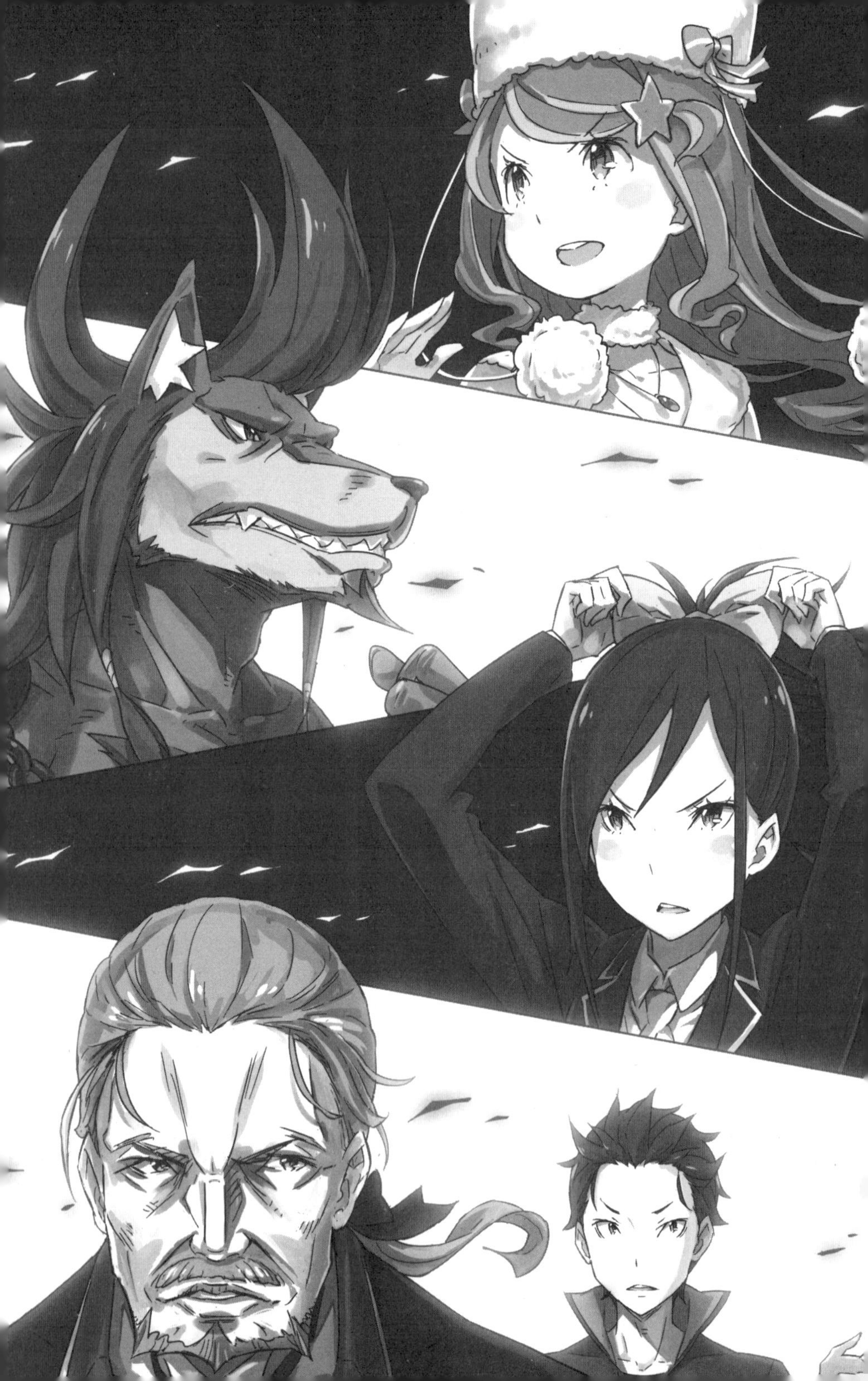

Whale. But now Subaru wasn't sure where she stood in strength. If he was blunt, even her gravitas didn't compare with the old Crusch, and he didn't think her current personality was suited to fighting, but—

"Lady Crusch's natural talents have not waned whatsoever. Her strength with the sword is sufficient. I guarantee it."

Apparently wanting to dispel Subaru's concerns, Wilhelm gave his firm stamp of approval. Touching a hand to the hilt of his own sword, he turned both of his blue eyes toward his master.

"However, please do not overexert yourself. I respectfully ask that you prioritize your own safety."

"It is a noble's duty to stand before the masses, endure the rigors of combat, and shed blood, if need be. Shirking that responsibility in the name of self-preservation would only cause the blameless populace to suffer instead. I will fight, Wilhelm."

"...What a headstrong liege I serve. Of course, this is exactly why I have pledged my sword to you."

Crusch held strong even as Wilhelm cautioned her. Seeing him stand straighter in approval at his master's reply, Ferris swiftly raised a hand.

"Yes! Yes! Me too! Your lovely Ferri will accompany you! Please let me come along!"

"Ferris, go to the other shelters and treat whoever is in need. I am happy you are thinking of me, but even if it is for my sake, do not lose sight of which battlefield you should be attending to."

"Uuuuuuurgh…"

His request denied, Ferris desperately racked his brain for some way to protest. But unable to find any fault with Crusch's eminently reasonable argument, he soon gave in with a tearful face.

"Old Man Wil, take care of Lady Crusch. You absolutely have to keep her safe."

"Of course. I shall see it through, even if it means I will meet my end in this land."

Wilhelm's reply was brimming with powerful, noble determination.

In the end, with Crusch added to the mix, the core force tasked with retaking city hall numbered five people.

Just as he was reviewing their roster, Subaru noticed Al sitting on the stairs.

"Can we depend on you for the coming fight? I've never seen you duke it out, but…"

"Weeell, actually, about that… This pep rally is real inspiring and all, but…"

"? What's up?"

Al scratched the back of his neck as he stood up. Then while pressing a palm against the scabbard of the falchion resting on the back of his hip, he turned his head and looked somewhat uncomfortable.

"Sorry about this, but I can't go to city hall. The situation's changed. I've gotta split off from you guys to go find Princess and link up with her."

"Huh?! The hell are you talking about at a time like this?!"

"I said sorry, didn't I? I really am about all this."

When Subaru was taken aback by his sudden declaration, Al gave a vague apology, but this wasn't something that could be settled with a quick apology. He wanted to know what in the world Al was thinking.

"For starters, weren't you the one who said you didn't need to worry about Priscilla?"

"That was before I got all sorts of new data and had to revise everything. Besides, even if I'm there, I ain't no use in a boss fight at city hall. If I'm just gonna hold the crew back, I might as well not be there. Am I wrong?"

"Y-you…"

When Al asserted his own powerlessness, Subaru couldn't do anything but gape.

Al had been a full participant in the meeting up until that point, so he understood exactly what was at stake. If they didn't take back city hall and send Lust packing, the entire city would be in danger. There was no way he didn't understand that.

"—Sir Al, you will not reconsider?"

Setting Subaru's bewilderment aside for the moment, Julius took the opportunity to pose an additional question toward Al. Turning to address The Finest of Knights, Al simply said, "Yeah," and nodded without enthusiasm. "Sorry, I won't be changing my mind… Unlike you guys, I haven't been able to hook back up with my master."

"It is only natural for a vassal to think of his liege. I shall not criticize you for that."

"That's appreciated. I'm glad you understand."

Al's reply to Julius's elegant words somehow came off as cold. It was just that he seemed guilty for going against everyone's decision and opting to act on his own. Then he looked at Subaru once more.

"This isn't exactly what I was talking about, but you're in the same position, right, Bro? I think I've gotta prioritize a woman who's important to me over going to city hall."

"_____"

"That said, I'm pretty sure there's a limit to what you can do with that leg anyhow."

Al's assertion made Subaru's face crumple as if he'd sustained a painful blow.

In a sense, Al's position was totally reasonable. Whatever spin Subaru might put on it, Emilia's safety was not assured whatsoever. It was completely possible that she was in peril that very moment.

And with his leg so badly injured, Subaru had few sane choices to pick from.

—In response to Al's words, there wasn't much Subaru could do.

"Aaarghhhhhhh…!"

"W-wait—Subawu?! What are you doing?!"

Enduring the excruciating pain in his right leg, Subaru somehow managed to rise to his feet. Seeing Subaru exert his grievously hurt leg so terribly, his physician, Ferris, hastily rushed over and slapped him on the head.

"Owww, that hurts."

"Of course it hurts! I told you, you *have* to rest, so why do you keep being so reckless?! Do you have a problem with Ferri's diagnosis? Because it wouldn't be strange if your leg fell right off!"

"I, uh, wanted to prove my resolve, or something like that. Ferris, you of all people should understand how I feel."

"Uuugh…"

Caught by Subaru's intense black eyes from up close, Ferris pouted and struggled to form a response.

This was Subaru's reply, both to Al's words and to his companions who were heading toward a place of death. If his choices had decreased due to his leg wound, he would simply have to push through on grit and guts alone.

Al had cited his lack of power as a reason not to participate. That undoubtedly applied to Subaru as well. But Subaru had the heart of a trickster. If he could at least support the others with that, then—

"—There's meaning in pushing myself. This is what I can do for Emilia's sake."

"…Are you saying even if you lose your leg, you'll have no regrets?"

"Of course I'd have regrets. But they'd only get worse if I back down here and now."

"*Sigh…* If you're going to go this far, you might as well have kept acting cool right up until the very end."

Sighing in exasperation, Ferris reached a hand toward Subaru, who was breathing hard as he endured the pain. Then he stroked the thick bandage over his patient's right leg.

"I'll use my special trick, then."

"What's that? Er…wait a— *Ow*, that hurts! That hurts a lot! Wait, ow, ow, ow! It really…doesn't…hurt?"

Gradually, his leg was enveloped in the faint light and heat coming from Ferris's hand. Bit by bit, the stabbing pain was drawn out, and soon, it felt better than ever.

"Hey, are you serious…?! If you had such convenient magic all along, don't be stingy and just use it sooner! Yes, yes, yes! I can move! I can…"

With the pain completely gone, Subaru emphatically stomped on the floor several times. After that, he slapped his leg where the wound had been. When he did so, he felt something wet on his palm. He saw that it had become deep red.

His right leg's wound had split open and was bleeding with a fair bit of force.

"Whoa, whoa, whoa, it's not healed?!"

"I never said I healed it. I only asked if you'd regret losing the leg. All I did was remove your sense of pain. If you try hard enough, you should even be able to run around."

Subaru was stunned by how much he was bleeding as Ferris tied a fresh bandage over the wound. Just like he had explained, his leg didn't hurt at all.

It was painfully obvious that this rather unnatural state did mean he could push it to some extent.

"Any strain you put on your leg will absolutely have serious effects, so try to be careful!"

"…Got it. This is a huge help. I owe you."

"…There's absolutely no way Subawu is going to listen to what Ferri says, is there?"

As Subaru checked the condition of his leg and nodded, Ferris puffed up his cheeks and turned away in a huff.

Subaru would have loved to protest and say, *That's not true*, but he had no idea what he'd resort to until the choice was upon him. He had learned not to make promises he couldn't keep.

"All right, I'm adding myself to the team that's mounting an attack on city hall. Just letting you know in advance, there's no use trying to stop me. It's true that I can't exactly contribute a ton in raw power, but even I have stuff I can do…"

"What do ya mean, 'try to stop ya'? A guy like you is worth a hundred men. We're dependin' on ya."

"I can do things like… Wait, what?"

Expecting a hail of objections, Subaru was ready to justify his presence, but Ricardo accepted his proposal without any hesitation. Noticing that Subaru was surprised by his reply, he elaborated and said, "Bro, I saw how hard ya worked, both during our rumble with the White Whale and when we fought Sloth. It ain't just Julius and Wilhelm who rate ya highly."

"———"

Ricardo's unexpected appraisal left Subaru struggling to find words. When he looked around the room, seeking answers, he saw Julius shrugging and Wilhelm nodding deeply.

It seemed that neither had any objections. On top of that, Crusch was faintly smiling as well.

"Needless to say, I would be glad to have your support. By all means, Master Subaru, join us."

"You serious? This seems a little weird, but…"

Subaru was totally confused, unaccustomed to being counted as someone who could contribute in battle without question.

"Geez, you gonna be that reckless here…?"

When that string of exchanges brought a grumble spilling out of Al, Subaru turned toward him.

"I get what you're saying, but I still think this is the best call. I do feel sorry, though."

"No need to say sorry to me. You should just do what you want, Bro. I'll be doing the same— Ah, I will give ya one piece of advice, though."

"Advice?"

When Al abruptly raised a finger and said something unexpected, Subaru cocked his head. Then in a voice that sounded totally emotionless, he said one thing.

"—If Gluttony shows up, don't say your real names."

A shudder ran up Subaru's spine.

That word of caution had come with no warning, and simply hearing it was enough to claw at his heart.

Eyes wide, Subaru stared straight at Al. Glancing at his dumbfounded face, Al shrugged nonchalantly.

"Hope the two of us meet again safe and sound, Bro."

He left him with those carefree words.

3

—The Water Gate City of Pristella had gone so quiet that the events of that morning felt like a mirage.

As Subaru walked along the paving stone–lined streets, a slight glance to the side would have been all it took to get a perfect view of the peacefully crystal clear waterway, belying the crisis currently gripping the city. Looking at the serenely flowing water might have seemed like it could wash away the vortex of chaos swirling inside his chest, but that would be a lie. The melancholy that he felt could not be relieved with such simple means.

"Priscilla and her people always leave a mess behind… Man, did he lay down a real doozy before he left, though."

Subaru was grumbling about the explosive parting message he had gotten right as they were on the verge of departing from the Muse Company.

His surprise at hearing Al bring up Gluttony was no small thing in and of itself, but that wasn't the only piece of information the cryptic man had offered up. Afterward, Al had added one more thing.

"…So it's possible that all the Archbishops are in Pristella right now, huh?"

Now that he thought about it, that was more than plausible.

At present, three Archbishops of the Seven Deadly Sins had already been confirmed to be inside the city. Plus, they knew the Witch Cult had taken over the four control towers on top of seizing city hall.

Given that five places had been captured, if each was under the control of one of the leaders of the Witch Cult, then Wrath, Greed, Lust, Gluttony, and Pride were all in attendance.

"—You are too deep in thought, Subaru. You should calm down a little."

"Argh…"

While brooding over the possibilities, someone abruptly tapped his shoulder. It was only then that Subaru noticed he'd forgotten to even breathe. When he glanced over, he saw Julius was right beside him, staring with an anxious look on his face. Subaru recoiled immediately.

That overreaction made Julius snort with a "Hmph," before continuing to speak. "From the looks of it, you have regained your senses."

"Yeah, I'm actually pretty grateful for that… I really did wade in a little too deep."

"Little wonder. To be blunt, you have too much hanging over you. There is taking back city hall and securing Lady Emilia's safety. And then there is the potential presence of your fated foe, Gluttony."

"———"

"Were I in your position, I would have my doubts whether I could remain as calm as you are. On that score, your efforts are more than sufficient. You should take pride in them."

"What's with you…? Don't creep me out like…"

Subaru furrowed his brows, feeling a chill after receiving that overly considerate compliment. He understood that Julius meant him no ill will, but how his friendly demeanor made him feel was a separate matter.

Still, thanks to Julius's thoughtfulness, Subaru regained enough composure to properly examine his surroundings.

—At the moment, with Subaru included, the six members of the group tasked with retaking city hall were walking through the city.

Garfiel and Ricardo, both boasting keen senses of smell, led the group from the front. Crusch and Wilhelm followed behind the pair, and Subaru and Julius brought up the rear.

They walked in formation, on guard against attacks the Witch Cult might launch, but fortunately, there was no sign of any enemy presence so far, let alone an assault. Instead, what came into sharper relief were the various things smoldering deep inside each of the members of the assault team.

In Subaru's case, the injury to his leg, his fraught escape with Beatrice, and, more than anything else, not knowing whether Emilia was safe ate at him. The added flicker of Gluttony's presence left his mind teetering on the edge.

Much like him, the other members of the party harbored various issues in their own minds.

Garfiel and Ricardo were concerned for Mimi's well-being; Wilhelm's wound, which was left by his departed wife, had deep implications; and Crusch was struck by the possibility that Gluttony, to whom she, too, was tied by destiny, might be somewhere in the city.

Before heading out, Subaru had sworn to the sleeping Beatrice that he'd come back with good news, but his worries did not abate in the slightest.

"On that point, you're pretty much the only one here with a calm and collected mind, aren't you?"

"Considering my concern for Mimi and the others' well-being, I would hardly claim to be calm. I am, however, striving to be as calm as I can manage."

"And I'm thankful for that… Hey, you think we can win?"

Gently, Subaru averted his eyes and posed the question in a quiet voice so that none but Julius could hear. He detected Julius's breath catching ever so slightly.

"…It is rather unusual for you to ask me, in particular."

"I think I'm being stupid, too… I'd rather have our strongest guy here and not have to worry like this, though."

"…In this sort of situation where the innocent could be hurt, it is inconceivable that Reinhard would not move. The very fact that he has not yet revealed himself should be taken as an indication that some kind of commensurate problem has befallen him. This includes the likelihood that he is engaged with Witch Cultists somewhere else."

Even though Subaru hadn't named anyone in particular, Julius listed off all the possibilities he could think of.

As a matter of fact, Subaru had already experienced a lap where Reinhard had engaged the Witch Cult in combat. But this time, the man hadn't been seen ever since the Witch Cult had attacked in earnest.

Naturally, this conspicuous absence and the question of exactly whom he and Felt had sauntered off to meet were major points of concern.

"Gahhh, how long am I just gonna grope around in the dark? If he ain't here, he ain't here. Worrying's not gonna make worries go away, and it's not about whether we *can* win; it's that we *will* win. Time to get my head in the game...!"

Continuously stressing about every concern that came along would summon dark clouds over any warrior.

Subaru slapped his cheeks with both hands, brushing aside his welling feelings of frailty as he let out a strong and sharp breath of air.

Glancing at the sight, Julius narrowed his eyes a bit without a word. Thinking the reaction odd, Subaru tried to press the issue when—

"—Smells of blood. A lot of it, too."

Still on point, Ricardo scouted ahead with his nose. Garfiel nodded in silence.

Right then, the report from their top two trackers confirmed that they were getting close to the tall building visible on the other side of the street—city hall. It was here where Subaru and the others halted for a moment to make their final preparations.

"＿＿＿"

Garfiel equipped his shields on both arms, and Ricardo adjusted the way he carried his large hatchet. And with a look resembling a quiet sea breeze in Wilhelm's eyes, those three projected a sense of incredible tension.

To Garfiel and Ricardo, the opponents waiting for them in the square ahead were targets for vengeance, and as for Wilhelm... exactly what this impending encounter would mean to him was something Subaru just had to know.

"I had my flower buds survey the area, but it seems there is no sign of troops lying in ambush. According to Mr. Kiritaka, the only entrance into city hall is from the front— There is no option save challenging them head-on."

Julius had used a number of his six contracted greater spirits to check the surrounding area; he was enveloped by pale lights as they gave him their reports. Subaru was simply grateful for the news that there was no ambush lying in wait for them.

"Can't you get the spirits to take a look inside the building, too? If we could find out where the enemy is and how they've set up, this'd be a lot easier."

"Unfortunately, I am not inclined to force the ladies to go that far. There is no guarantee that the enemy has not learned from Sloth's defeat and taken anti-spirit measures."

"Yeah, nothing good'll come from them getting nailed and depleting your fighting strength, huh?"

Julius's power was directly connected to the number of greater spirits he had and the number of options they put at his disposal. Plus, Subaru wanted to avoid the risk of them probing too deep for recon and alerting the enemy to their imminent attack.

Above all else, the longer it took them to act, the greater the danger posed to the hostages in city hall.

"Let's go, just like we planned it. The exact details are gonna depend on the enemy's composition and positioning, but basically, we'll stack several people to fight each one. Relying on numbers, we'll focus 'em down one at a time and then take back city hall. But—"

"If we believe we are at a disadvantage, we must instantly make the decision to retreat…correct?"

When Subaru spoke, taking the reins of the group as if by nature, Crusch turned a serious look toward him. Replying to her with a firm "That's right," Subaru surveyed the faces of everyone present.

In his companions, he saw tension, wariness, and, more than anything else, the will to fight. He nodded and gave the signal.

"—Let's go!"

On his call, Subaru and the others broke into a run toward city hall as one.

Rounding a corner, they rushed into the square that sat in front of city hall. Swift as ever, Garfiel ran at the head of the pack, and when the square came in sight, he narrowed his green eyes and shouted:

"The square's full of guard corpses! Don't let it shake ya or slow ya down…"

The instant they charged into the square, the scent of blood that

Ricardo had mentioned slipped into Subaru's nostrils. And filling his vision was a mountain of corpses, just as Garfiel had spoken of—or not.

"—Eh?"

Garfiel had just yelled for them to not stop moving. And yet the instant he set his eyes on that sight, Subaru couldn't help but slow down, dropping the speed of his sprint a notch.

But it wasn't just Subaru. The other five were no exception. That was how completely the sight that greeted them in the square exceeded their expectations.

"———"

According to Garfiel, the square was filled with the numerous corpses of the guards who had fallen in an attempt to take back city hall. And it was true that the current condition of the square seemed to also point to that ghastly truth.

There was a dense odor of spilled blood, and the paving stones were dyed red to the point that it evoked the expression *a sea of blood*. However, there was not even a single corpse lying around. In their stead were bizarre creatures.

They were pink-colored masses of flesh. As far as descriptions went, Subaru felt that this was the most fitting.

Their pink-colored surfaces were glossy, warped, and irregular in form, like mud dumplings made by little children. They were large enough that Subaru couldn't comfortably put both arms around one, and there were at least twenty of them.

The flesh piles of unknown origin formed a sporadic line. The reception put everyone's footsteps out of kilter—

"—It's them!!"

Immediately after, Garfiel, running first among them, looked overhead and howled.

With the shock over the flesh creatures yet to recede, everyone forced their gazes upward. Two figures were leaping straight down at them from city hall's upper level, jumping right toward them with a slash of the swords they wielded.

"! Here I go!!"

As their enemies sailed down before them, Crusch valiantly stepped forward and held her longsword at the ready.

Then she unleashed invisible blades—this was her skill One Blow, One Hundred Felled.

Slicing the air at an angle, this was Crusch's lethal sword technique that took full advantage of her blessing of wind reading. The slicing attack was carried on the air, extending the reach of her sword strikes by tens of yards and providing her with an ultra-long-range option. This slicing attack had deeply wounded even the White Whale, and now it was hurtling forward. A moment later, it scored a direct hit on the two figures in midair.

"You got 'em?!"

"No! They were able to defend! I did not land a hit!"

When Subaru's voice went shrill from excitement, Crusch shook her head with a bitter look on her face.

The pair, a giant man and a slender woman, landed as they fended off the blades of wind with their respective weapons. Paving stones exploded under the huge man's feet; the woman stood quietly in the pool of blood without even disturbing the air around her.

They appeared on the stage as polar opposites, with a pair of greatswords and an uninscribed longsword. The sight of the black outfits covering them from head to toe was emblematic of the horrid fashion sense displayed by adherents of the Witch Cult.

The moment after Subaru took this all in, the two enemy figures leaned forward ever so slightly and launched their counterattacks.

However, before those two varieties of wicked blades could reach him—

"Even if they have fended off Lady Crusch's sword blows, there is no escaping the rainbow's yoke!"

—three different, dazzling colors circled around the Witch Cultists' heads, summoning a cylindrically shaped aurora to seal the enemy's movements.

Of the six greater spirits serving Julius, three acted in unison to catch the cultists. The cylinder of light must have had incredible restraining power, for the Witch Cultists went down on their knees from incredible pressure upon them.

It was then that Garfiel, Wilhelm, and Ricardo launched savage, ferocious attacks.

"!!"

Blunt and edged, each of the respective blows was an attack able to inflict a mortal wound.

Ricardo aimed for the big man's head with his huge hatchet, while Garfiel's fist and Wilhelm's sword aimed at the woman, all of them entering lethal range—

"_____"

The kneeling woman spun around the longsword in her hand, sweeping at Garfiel's and Wilhelm's feet. Instantly, the two leaped to evade her sword, but the woman turned her body to move perfectly parallel to the sword's arc, spreading one of her long legs to snag Garfiel around his neck and forcing him to pull her out of the effective range of the magic spell.

"The hell?!"

With the rainbow-colored force field throwing off his movements, Garfiel was stooped over as the woman broke the bridge of his nose with her knee. She then grabbed hold of Garfiel's arm as he recoiled, using its shield to easily deflect Wilhelm's flurry of sword attacks.

The unbelievable technique left Garfiel raising a painful cry, whereas Wilhelm let out a groan.

The price of that stagnation was a spinning kick that dug into the aged swordsman's abdomen, with the blow causing Wilhelm to bend forward; after a half spin around his stooped body, the woman launched a backward spinning kick that laid him out on the ground.

"_____"

At the same time, the sound of an eruption exploded between Ricardo and the giant.

The large hatchet swinging down at the crouching man was blocked by two greatswords crossed over his head. The screech of steel creaking against steel rang out, at which point Ricardo punched down several times with his unoccupied fist.

The blunt blows hammered the great hatchet from behind, bringing the dull cuts ever closer to the huge man's head. But finding himself this pressed, the giant promptly reacted by unleashing a new pair of arms from the inside of his black robe.

Now using four arms to block his blows, the bizarre creature made Ricardo's face twist up, bringing a savage expression to his face.

"I've heard of your kind before, member of the many-armed tribe! Four arms ain't nothin'!"

Though his enemy tried to block him, Ricardo spurred himself onward, heedlessly banging on his great hatchet. If his opponent had four arms, he'd just have to wring out more power from his two.

But Ricardo's intentions were betrayed when the giant unveiled yet another hidden trick. Two more arms appeared from under the black robe, along with two more greatswords.

"The hell…?!"

Four arms were devoted to defending with two greatswords, while two more arms and greatswords went on the attack. With one turn, the attacker and the defender had switched completely; Ricardo backed up a step as the tide turned against him.

"—Garghhh!"

A seventh and an eighth arm came flying from the giant's back, punching, punching, and punching Ricardo's chin some more. The giant man caused blood to spill from Ricardo, sending him crashing into the far side of the square.

"_____"

The group supposedly had the initiative, but the attacks of all three of the close-range team were intercepted, with the woman sword fighter and the giant launching merciless follow-up attacks.

"As if I'm letting that happen!"

It was then that the slow-footed Subaru finally caught up and made his move.

He launched his whip at a significant range, making a rending sound as it struck the paving stones with force. The snapping sound from the whip, which ripped through the air at close to the speed of sound, caused a moment's hesitation in the two cultists.

"Fusion magic—*Ul Gora!!*"

Immediately after, Julius rattled off an incantation as his greater spirits returned to him, generating a crimson whirlwind in moments. The swirling wind was then engulfed in fire, the resulting flames forcing the Witch Cultists to leap away to safety.

The heat wave of the enormous inferno made Subaru unwittingly gawk.

"The hell is that?! Were you always a hardcore spell caster?!"

"No, this is nothing more than a bluff. It is too unrefined to be used as a proper attack. Accordingly…"

When Julius replied bitterly to Subaru's question, the scene before them proved his words true.

Having fallen back in the face of the flaming whirlwind, the retreating woman lashed out once with her longsword—and that was all it took to sever the wind's core, disturbing the spell's composition and causing the whirlwind to collapse, then vanish.

The frighteningly keen sword sense that the woman sword fighter boasted combined with the giant's four massive swords and eight arms, making them seem like twin heralds of doom. Fear shot up Subaru's spine as he continued watching them pull off superhuman feats that were even more impressive than the ones he'd heard them do.

"Going all out at them and having nothing to show for it is a pretty major shock."

When he glanced over, Garfiel and the others, who had escaped thanks to Julius's backup, were all wiping off blood and catching their breath. But the sense of despair at the fact that their melee fighters had been mostly overwhelmed was not something so easily brushed aside.

However, it would have been wrong to assume they had run out of cards to play.

"We know they're pretty nuts in close combat, but they're seriously wide-open against long-range attacks."

Julius's magic, Crusch's wind blades, and even Subaru's whip had been effective to varying degrees.

It was possible that even if his whiplashes did hit, they would be easily shrugged off and ignored, but there was no mistaking that Julius and Crusch could launch attacks that might make the difference between victory or defeat.

"―――"

The repulsive piles of flesh dotting the surrounding area weighed on his mind, but he tore his attention away from those unearthly objects. The right thing to do was prioritize taking down the two in front of them—

"Everyone, let's attack again. We'll make Julius and Crusch our main attackers, and…"

"—Bwa-ha-ha-ha! You came, you came, you really came, didn't you?!"

"?!!"

Suddenly, the scene was interrupted by high-pitched, silly-sounding laughter that seemed completely out of place on the battlefield.

This incredibly grating voice brought the giant and the woman to their knees on the spot. Simultaneously, as nigh-unendurable terror urged Subaru and the others to hold their breath, the laughing voice still trembled in derisive mirth.

"All it took was a few threats to reel such big fish in. How do you meatbags even live when you're this stupid, ugly, and shallow-minded? I wouldn't be able to deal with that! Bwa-ha-ha-ha!"

"—It can't be."

Searching for the source of the voice, Subaru's gaze wandered when he noticed Crusch gasp right beside him.

Her amber eyes had shot wide-open as she looked toward the roof of city hall. Realizing that the speaker, Lust, had to be over there, Subaru turned in the same direction.

That was when he finally understood the true meaning behind the raspy echo of Crusch's dazed murmur.

"Bwa-ha-ha-ha-ha!! What's with that face?! Such a stupid face! Did you practice it just for me? If you did, I want to reward you!! How about my spit? Would my saliva make you overjoyed? That should literally be mouthwatering for meatbag scum like you!!"

The nonsensical laughter echoed as the speaker standing on the roof of city hall—no, standing above it—gazed down upon Subaru and the others from her vantage point with scorn.

Then she flapped the large, malevolent black wings on her back once.

"Let me reintroduce myself! I'm the Witch Cult's Archbishop of Lust!!"

Her red eyes glimmered with cruel delight as she—Lust—laughed with renewed disdain.

The single, black dragon claiming the title of the Archbishop of Lust gazed down at the surface, laughing scornfully.

"Capella Emerada Lugunica—that's meee! Now die, you rotten sacks of meat!!"

4

—Circling in the sky high above city hall, the black dragon continued its mocking laughter.

It had sharp, ferocious fangs, magnificent black wings that gathered the wind underneath to soar through the skies, plus a daunting face, and it was encased in a hide of rocklike scales—this was well and truly what Subaru imagined a dragon would be.

Some of its features resembled Patlash, the land dragon, but they were incomparable in the size of their frames and the raw power they possessed. If a land dragon was on par with a horse, then the black dragon overhead was best likened to an elephant.

The sight of it spreading its wings and leisurely gliding around brought no words to mind save *nightmare*.

"Gawking at me with those passionate gazes means you're all turned on, aren't you? What, are you animals in heat the whole year? Are you enjoying this chance to ogle me? Oh noooo, whatever shall I do?!"

"…Well, this dragon's so expressive that it gives me chills."

Writhing in midair, Capella—the black dragon twisting its reptilian form into vulgar shapes—behaved in a way that left Subaru unable to conceal his disgust. How could he take anything else away from the mouthy dragon's first impression being this twisted?

It was impossible not to feel repulsed by Capella, who came off as human in all the wrong ways.

"If it was doable, I would have liked to confront Lust in order."

Checking the heft of his knight's sword, Julius peered up at the dragon overhead as he commented in a quiet voice. Mentally agreeing with those words, Subaru saw the pair of sword fighters down on the surface apparently stiffening from awe at the appearance of their comrade, the winged dragon overhead.

The two of them knelt as if in reverence for the winged dragon that was their master, even as they kept an eye on Subaru and the rest of the party without ever letting their guard down. They were such formidable foes by themselves that adding in the black dragon would put the group at an overwhelming disadvantage.

However—

"—When fighting a dragon, the important thing is to break its wings as soon as possible, bringing it crashing to the ground. If we permit it to fly in the sky as it pleases, it will rain dragon breath upon us unopposed. We must avoid this at all costs."

With all of them unsettled by the appearance of the dragon, Wilhelm delivered that bold pronouncement at the center of their formation. His words, filled with such certainty, made Subaru unconsciously glance over toward the Sword Devil.

"From how you said that just now, it kinda sounds like you have experience fighting dragons."

"Once, nearly four decades ago, I crossed swords with Bargren the Black Dragon, who appeared in the south of the kingdom. Compared with that one, this dragon is far too small. Should we lop off her head once, she will surely perish."

"What, once wasn't enough for this Bargren guy?"

"I lopped off all three of his heads."

There is only one to lop off this time, implied his deeply reassuring words.

The evocative tale of that legendary duel to the death bolstered

Subaru's spirits as he adjusted the grip on his whip. Privately deciding that he needed to hear that heroic tale in detail later, he girded himself to rejoin the battle. The others' morale had recovered as well.

Seeing that Subaru and company's hearts were unbroken, Capella went, "Wuh?" as if totally taken off guard. "My, my, a die-hard bunch, aren't you? Normally, after being screwed around with so much, reinforcements arrive, and oh, look, it's the Archbishop!! The usual routine is for weaklings like you to try to run with your little tails between your legs. Or did I mistake you for the wrong kind of insect?"

"—Quit yappin' on and on! I don't care whether you're a big lizard or an Archbishop of the Seven Deadly Sins! Everyone who gets in my way, I'm gonna smash 'em, send 'em flyin', and beat 'em down!"

When Capella made her bizarrely long tongue dance and form such wicked words, Garfiel turned his fist on her. Detecting such incredible hostility directed toward her, Capella went, "Eh? Ehhhhhhh?" and laughed. "Bwa-ha! I think beaten dogs howling in the distance are the annoying ones. Ohh, that's right, you're not a beaten dog—you're a beaten cat, was it? *Meow, meow, meow, meow*, your face went beet red when you cried over that kitty girl dying didn't you? Poor widdle kitty!"

"!!"

Garfiel listened to nearly unendurable words of abuse as they clawed at the weakness in his heart. Seeing the painful look on the side of his face, Subaru took a step to stand in front of Garfiel.

"General..."

With his adorable little brother calling his name out, Subaru glared at Capella overhead without saying a word. Noticing his gaze, the black dragon narrowed its red eyes, clearly finding it unpleasant.

"Huh? What's with you? Even compared with the other meatbags, you have the most out-of-place scent, you know? How did you even get mixed in all this? Did you get looooost?"

"Shut up. The more you talk, the more you're ruining my internal idea of dragons. Also, quit claiming the name of that princess. I feel sorry for her."

"Claiming? What in the world are you talking abou…?"

"Also, you people are so sloppy, it's painful to watch! You big shots should be biding your time and coming out one by one! Who the hell just shows up all at once without paying any attention to the pacing?! Who do you think you are, trampling on people's daily lives looking like that? Are you pretending to be a god?!"

"____"

The caustic words that Subaru unleashed with the force of a volley of arrows made Capella open her eyes wide, taking her aback for a moment.

Seeing a black dragon look dumbfounded was quite a spectacle in and of itself, but that hadn't been Subaru's aim. Of course, he couldn't deny that his tirade contained more than a fair bit of his real feelings, but the actual purpose was—

"That's enough stalling from me! Nail her, Julius!"

"On occasion, I admire your brashness from the bottom of my heart."

As Subaru clapped his hands together, Julius immediately replied from behind, gathering light upon the tip of his knight's sword. When all six greater spirits assembled within the blade, The Finest of Knights swung it like a musical conductor.

"What a petty little trick you're trying to use on…!"

"Burn under the light of the rainbow! —*Al Clauzeria!*"

The tip of the sword, which he thrust out, emitted a rainbow-colored beam, unleashing a swirling aurora. The rainbow attack, which contained the combined might of six greater spirits, shot out in a straight line, aimed right at the black dragon circling directly overhead.

—Instantly, the beam burst apart, enveloping the roof of city hall with an explosion of light.

The sky was dyed in the surreal colors of the beautiful aurora—a purifying ritual to purge all evil. The spell, which had been wielded so fiercely in the battle with Petelgeuse, now bared its fangs at Capella.

"Gaaaaaah!!"

Struck by a direct hit from the rainbow light, Capella raised a high-pitched shriek.

"⎯⎯⎯"

With this strike serving as a signal for combat to resume, the kneeling pair of sword fighters kicked off the ground once more, quickly approaching Subaru and the others.

A fluttering longsword and several whirling greatswords were intercepted by the white-haired Sword Devil and a ferocious golden-haired tiger.

"As if I'd let ya!!"

Making his battered will to fight burn even higher, Garfiel blocked the giant's greatswords with both shields. The vigorous impact rocked Garfiel back on his heels, but he did not retreat a single step.

Beside him, the swordswoman was being pressured by Wilhelm's slashing sword attacks, forcing her backward.

"Do not assume you can retreat with ease! I must know for certain!"

The Sword Devil dealt out more attacks without mercy. However, the woman skillfully wielded her longsword, parrying each and every sword blow while evading pursuit with highly polished footwork.

Her body almost seemed like it was designed for the sole purpose of wielding a sword.

Wilhelm was exhibiting swordsmanship on the same level that he had brought out during the fight against the White Whale. The swordswoman engaging him displayed excellence in technique and creativity, along with a superhuman sense of balance.

Lashing blades whistled through the air and scraped against the ground as they ran along their paths, parrying, redirecting, and defeating each other's blows.

Not even sound could intrude as their incredible sword duel continued, each attack and defense so polished that it was no exaggeration to call it the pinnacle of the sword.

"Uraaaaa!!"

The other battlefield nearby was a cruder scene as half-beast and giant swordsman clashed head-on.

Garfiel raised a battle cry as he and the giant slammed into each other with mighty blows. This was a contest of wild savagery that was incomparable with the elegant battle of sword masters.

The fighting style of the sword-wielding giant could not be cleanly categorized as that of a trained swordsman. Against an opponent employing what was ultimately refined brutality, Garfiel counterattacked with his personal brand of brawling.

Bones creaked, flesh ruptured, and souls cracked in the grand, chaotic battle of titanic blows, with the clashing of shield against greatsword reverberating like a symphony of percussion instruments. Their fight also sent sparks flying everywhere, distracting the eyes as well as the ears.

Wilhelm's duel had gone eerily silent, while Garfiel's battlefield was a roaring thunderstorm.

Lacking the ability to intrude upon any of those matches, Subaru was left alone in the three-sided battle. But there was no time to bemoan his lack of strength. Before he had a chance, a new move revealed itself upon the game board.

And this was—

"Master Subaru, look out!!" "Pull back!!"

Right after two voices called out, Crusch came flying in from the side, tackling Subaru. Pinned under her soft body, he watched as Ricardo stepped forward.

Ricardo opened his large maw and let a howl erupt from the space between his rows of sharp fangs—

"Wahaaah!!"

His howling voice made the very air quake as the resulting sound became a shock wave that was imbued with enough destructive force to reshape the world around them.

It was a Howling Wave—an attack similar to what Mimi and her little brothers had used to great effect during the battles against the White Whale and Petelgeuse. However, the frightening thing was that Ricardo could, on his own, unleash a blow on par with what had required the cooperation of all three siblings.

"_____"

Ricardo's target had been a plume of hungry black flames that was chewing through the aurora and descending onto the surface.

The thick spouts of fire, which was blacker than darkness itself, collided head-on with the Howling Wave in midair. Instantly, the flames were snuffed out by the shock wave without offering any resistance, leaving the lingering embers to scatter here and there all over the field of battle.

But if anything, this helped the black flames become even more effective.

"The hell's with this black fire...? It ain't goin' out?"

The flying black flames continued to blaze ceaselessly, whether they sat atop paving stones, waterways, or masses of flesh. The area that was covered by the wave of writhing flames expanded bit by bit, encroaching upon the world more and more as if they were alive.

Like setting oil on the surface of water aflame, the black flames continued asserting their presence.

"_____"

The downpour of black flames had not touched Subaru or the others, erasing the aurora in their stead by disrupting its magical composition. Julius's wary gaze was still focused on the black dragon, which had spewed the black flames.

Following his lead, the sight of the black dragon entered Subaru's vision as well—

"—Eek! Oh no, oh no, staring at someone from such a harsh angle is turning you on, isn't it? Stooop, don't look! Stop violating me with your eyes! Bwa-ha-ha-ha-ha! If I told you that it's forbidden to touch the dancing girls, are you going to say searing them with magic doesn't count as touching...? Bwa-ha-ha-ha!"

Unleashing another stream of vulgar words, Capella looked fine and well as she landed on top of the city-hall roof. But this was not in the sense of being unscathed— If anything, the effects of Julius's spell had been profound.

As the black dragon rested her wings, both of those wings were still aflame from coming into contact with the aurora, with bone poking out from molten membrane in some places. The damage did not end there; her internal organs were boiling from the scorching heat deep in her seared abdomen, and the right half of the dragon's head had been sent flying, leaving that stupidly laughing tongue in tatters as one of her eyeballs hung freely.

Half-alive and *half-dead* didn't even cover it. From this terrible spectacle, she was already on the brink of death.

However, it was not this alarming sight that caused Subaru to swallow his breath, Julius and Ricardo to narrow their eyebrows, and Crusch to inadvertently raise a feminine-sounding yelp.

—All those terrible wounds were regenerating at a speed that was outright disgusting.

Blood vessels wriggled, flesh swelled up, bones broke audibly, torn tissues mended, and Capella's destroyed flesh repaired itself with swiftness that was a far cry from any norm.

The speed of this healing ability made her cells seethe, vaporizing the blood coursing through them and causing it to rise as a ghoulish red vapor.

"So are you satisfied now that you've caused even my beautiful viscera to be exposed for everyone to see? You're all perverts with such uncontrollable lust that you'd do anything to see even your beloved meatbag's rectum, aren't you? Hey, hey, are you satisfied? Hey, are you totally sweaty because you had your fill?"

"You're… What the hell…is that?"

"Asking something you can figure out the answer to just by looking makes you a fool through and through, doesn't it? But I will reply because of the depths of my compassion. As you can see, I have conquered death! I am a complete being!!"

As Capella embraced herself with her healed wings, her grandiose words rocked Subaru.

A complete being—put another way, Capella was calling herself immortal. And after seeing half her head get blown away only to heal it at great speed without relinquishing life, there was a strong case to be made that she was telling the truth.

One had bodies to spare, one dragged others to the grave, one was an invincible being, and one was an immortal monster—

"! Damned Archbishops of the Seven Deadly Sins!"

"Ah, somehow, I feel like you lumped me in with those jerks just now. Could you please stop that? I mean, come on! People will start calling my character into question!"

When Subaru resentfully clicked his tongue, Capella rejected him with vivid displeasure. In that time, the black dragon, her body largely finished regenerating, slowly raised her heavy hips—

"Oops. Whoa there. Coming through."

The next instant, the distant ring of the time tower's bell echoed across the city's sky.

Hearing this, Capella's motions came to a full stop, and when the black dragon tilted her long head, she let out a languid "Ahh—" as she gazed wistfully at the sky, watching evening approach.

"Seems like it's the appointed hour. Your clumsy faces really aren't bad, but a bigger stage awaits me, so excuse me while I go back inside!"

"Huh?! W-wait!"

"Why should I?! My beautiful voice needs to echo across the sky! How exactly will these fools stuck in the insect cage suffer? Stay tuned for the broadcast and find out! As for you, do entertain my minions and then die and rot as you see fit! Bwa-ha-ha-ha-ha!"

Laughing loudly, Capella unilaterally declared that the time for talk was over and then turned around on the spot. The black dragon's huge body then promptly vanished into the roof. It seemed that Lust was genuinely intent on leaving the battlefield.

Of course, the right thing was to think she was making Subaru and company lower their guard as part of some sort of ruse, but—

"If we let her go, there is no telling what she might finally inflict upon the hostages. We must make haste."

"If she broadcasts it live, morale will crumble, and panic will spread across the city like wildfire. Shit! No way forward except through, huh? Man, we have to chase her in there? In a situation like this?"

It was clearly a bad move, but they had no other cards to play. In the first place, they'd challenged the enemy at city hall because rescuing the hostages and stopping the broadcast was a top priority. If that meant dancing on the enemy's palm, they just had to grin and bear it.

"Guess that's settled, then. Leave the folks outside to me and those two. Julius, Bro, and Ms. Crusch will charge in."

Ricardo announced his plan to Subaru and Crusch as they pondered. Subaru's eyes questioned whether he had any basis for his unwavering judgment.

"Ain't nothin' special. Just intuition, Bro! Intuition! …The mountain of intuition I've built up from surviving a ton of battles!"

"So we're just trusting your gut?! Maybe that's the best thing to rely on…!"

Concurring with Ricardo's judgment, Subaru leaped up on the spot. Then lending a hand to Crusch, who'd saved him from the black dragon's flames, he helped her to her feet.

"You really saved me back there, Crusch. Usually, it's the other way around."

"Let's keep it a secret from Ferris and Lady Emilia."

His eyes went round at the unexpected reply, but he grasped that this turn of phrase was Crusch's way of lightening the mood. As he focused on the task before him, Subaru clenched his teeth then and called out to Garfiel, who was still caught in a battle of frenzied blows.

"Garfiel! We're going ahead to stop Lust! Once we're done here, we gotta go save Emilia! Don't lose!"

"!! Go and get it done, General! Me, I'm seein' this through!!"

Slipping between the gaps of whipping greatswords, Garfiel sent sparks flying as he howled his reply.

"Wilhelm, I leave this place to you!"

"Understood!"

Beside Subaru, Crusch shouted a few brief words of encouragement to the Sword Devil, who replied as he unleashed a flurry of countless silver flashes.

Finally, Subaru and Crusch broke into a run, heading straight for city hall with Julius taking point. Of course, the two warriors whom Lust had entrusted with guarding the place tried to move to bar their way, but—

"Line up like that, and you're basically just food for me!!!"

Ricardo leaped toward them and used his powerful shout to blow both sword fighters away as they attempted to impede Subaru and the others' advance. The giant and the swordswoman used their own evasive techniques to avoid taking any damage from the howling wave.

But the partners of the dances that the enigmatic pair had pulled out from prematurely did not let them escape without a fight.

"Do not be so cold. I am right here, devoted to you every step of the way!"

"Don't go showin' your ass in the middle of a fight! I'll tear your tail fur out and give you a real thrashin'!!"

Sword against sword, and fist against slam—furious blows met again and again, allowing no one in that square even a moment's respite.

The two Witch Cultists were being hindered, and if they insisted on giving chase, Ricardo would stop them by force. With reliable allies covering their backs, Subaru and the others headed straight for city hall, reaching it by the shortest possible route.

"Subaru! I will carve you a path! I entrust Lady Crusch to you!"

On the verge of racing into the building, Julius raised his knight's sword high as the greater spirits gave off a dazzling radiance.

Wondering what was happening, Subaru blinked furiously when, right before his eyes, Julius was enveloped in an explosive wind that materialized directly below him, his mantle fluttering as Julius sailed into the sky.

"Why did yo…?! Crusch, pardon me!"

Feeling the same wind buoying his own legs, Subaru forcefully picked up Crusch as she ran alongside. *Lighter than I figured*, he idly thought; a moment later, Subaru's legs peeled away from the ground as he shot into the air.

"Waaaaaaaaaah!!"

Picked up so suddenly and unsure how to deal with the abrupt weightlessness, Crusch raised a loud yell. The two kept on going, sailing over the wall surrounding city hall and finally flying all the way to the roof.

"Crusch, hang on tight!"

Shouting, Subaru supported Crusch with one hand as he drew his whip out with the other. Holding her breath, Crusch clung to Subaru for dear life as he used his whip and instantly wrapped it around the roof's railing.

Taking advantage of this foothold, Subaru and Crusch traced a large, semicircular arc toward city hall's roof. The instant they landed, Subaru spread his legs wide as he fell to the floor.

"Guhohhhh!!"

Feeling a numbness that was impossible to ignore run through his legs, Subaru heard an improper sound coming from his right leg. Having so swiftly betrayed Ferris's admonition telling him not to push it, Subaru released Crusch from his arm.

"...Crusch, are you all right?"

"I—I am fine. But, Master Subaru, your leg..."

"It's all right—don't worry about it. It doesn't hurt. Also, if you mention this to Ferris, he might kill me, so, uh..."

Genuinely fearful of such a future, Subaru gingerly turned his eyes toward the roof.

What he saw was not Capella, who'd been burned by the rainbow, but only a roof that had been wrecked by the black dragon's movements. The only thing on the roof itself was a single door leading to the building's interior.

According to Kiritaka, the metia was located on the building's uppermost floor. Having moved Subaru and Crusch here and taken the shortest route to pursue Capella, Julius brushed back his mantle and looked at the pair.

Flipping off the handsome knight with his middle finger, Subaru tried to race to the door leading inside when—

"—Ah-ha-ha. Settle down right there, ladies and gentlemen."

Loud laughter stopped Subaru in his tracks. Suddenly, the metal door was kicked apart from the inside, blown off its hinges. A new person came on the scene with the sound of bare feet, stepping upon the door, which had fallen so dramatically.

"_____"

—At a glance, their newest opponent seemed like a young boy.

One thought so because he was small in stature with a youthful face, and the voice they heard sounded like it had yet to crack from puberty. But one glance at the boy's eyes was enough to realize that such sentiments were deeply mistaken.

No proper human being would have such warped eyes that seemed like all the vices of the world were fermenting within them.

"We're so happy. We're so glad. We're so delighted. We're so overjoyed. Happy thoughts help us feel happy! Drink! Gorge!! The longer we have to wait, the emptier our belly becomes! And the more we savor the very first bite!"

His scorched-brown hair was tied up in a braid, and his small physique was wrapped in a long robe, with long hems, cuffs, and sleeves that hung about. There was a sadistic smile plastered onto his youthful face, and his smile showed that he had teeth like a shark's.

All these characteristics matched the identity of someone Subaru had heard about before.

"Hmm? Why do you look so annoyed, mister? Could it be that you have some kind of grudge against one of us guys? We're tryin' and tryin' to remember, but we're really bad at faces. Really, we're no good at remembering at all…"

Enduring Subaru's withering gaze, the boy adopted a cruel smile that was reminiscent of a cat toying with a mouse. This attitude grated on Subaru's nerves as he exhaled, striving to remain calm.

"Hey, you shitty brat. If you just walked in here because you have no sense of direction, now's the time to surrender. That's pretty stupid, but it's forgivable. Still…"

"We are the Witch Cult's Archbishop of—"

Subaru did everything he could to remain calm. To try and keep a cool head. He tried and tried and tried.

"—Gluttony, Roy Alphard!"

Attempting to maintain his calm any further was impossible.

"Gluttonyyy!!!"

The instant the boy openly declared himself as Gluttony, Subaru unleashed the fastest and mightiest whip blow of his life.

The tip of the whip tore through the air, mercilessly scoring the face of his greatest foe. A direct hit should have peeled the skin back and rent the flesh, leaving a scar so severe that anyone who saw it wouldn't dare look at it twice, and this blow—

"—Well, lots of people hold a grudge against us because of our feeding."

Catching the tip of the whip with his teeth, Gluttony spoke those words without a single ounce of shame.

5

Subaru's merciless blow, literally the greatest blow he had ever mustered in his life, had been stopped cold without much fanfare.

Still biting the tip of the whip, Gluttony—the one who had presented himself as Roy Alphard—waved his hands in the air as if appealing to the audience. Faced with this foe, Subaru could feel his thoughts boiling.

This Archbishop of the Seven Deadly Sins was the key to awakening the still-sleeping Rem.

"Your luck's run out!"

"You shall not escape! Prepare yourself!"

Standing at Subaru's side as he shouted, Crusch unleashed her One Blow, One Hundred Felled skill at Alphard of Gluttony.

The raging blade of wind sliced through the still air of the rooftop, allowing the resulting violent gales to engulf the air in its wake. This scattered shock waves in all directions, and of course, the slicing attack bore down mercilessly upon Alphard—

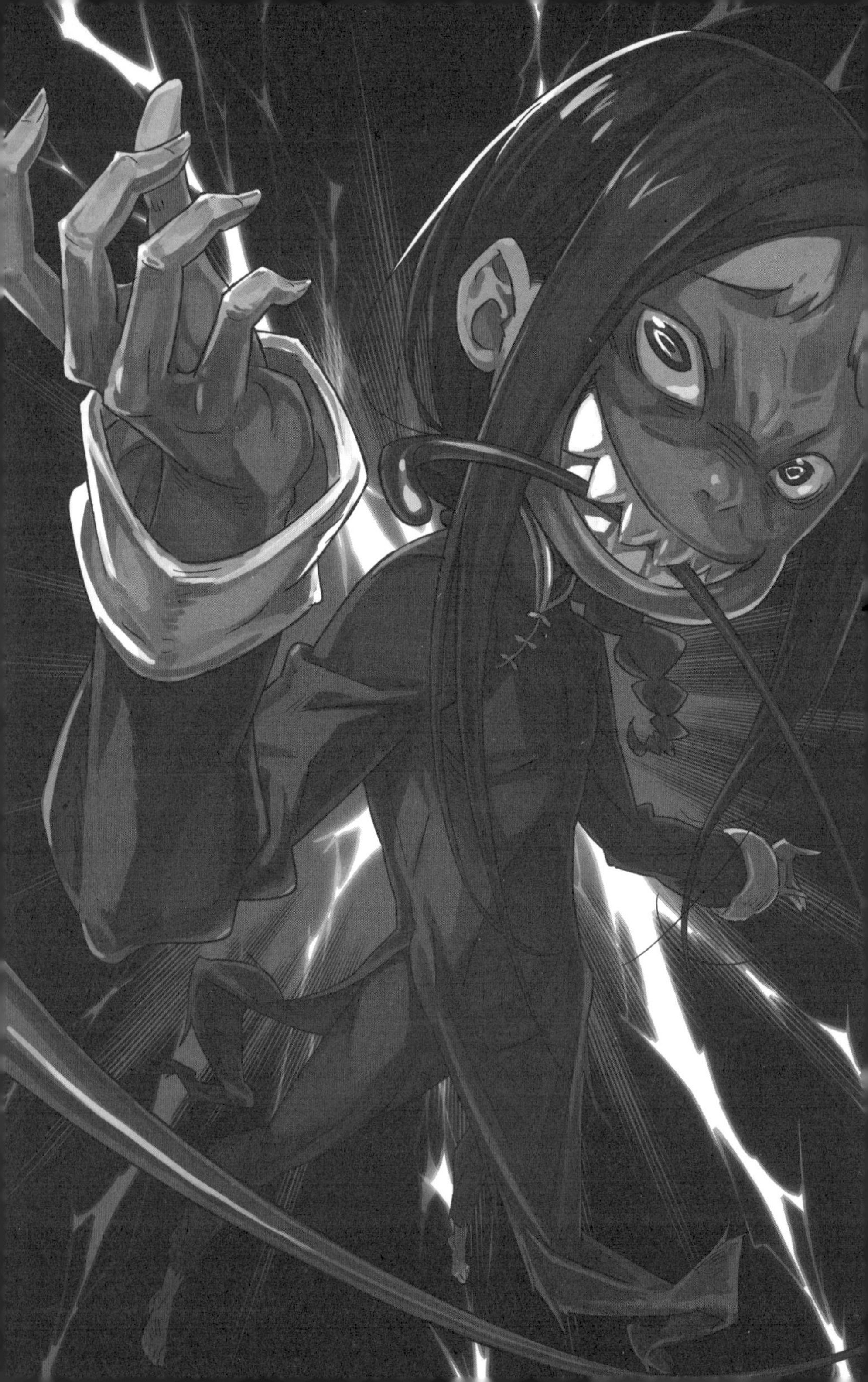

"Ha-ha-ha, that's really something! As a funny parlor trick, that is."

"!!"

Alphard went low, dropping onto all fours to evade the invisible blade of wind. He proceeded to bend and fold his short limbs, licking his chops as he turned to fully face Crusch.

"From the feel of that move of yours, your flavor might be right up our alley!"

The instant after he spoke the words, Alphard shot up like a bullet, exhibiting enough explosive force to smash through the roof.

Unhinging his yawning jaws, the sight of his bare, sharp fangs made Subaru think of a feral, starving beast. But the level of danger that this boy posed was incomparable with any mere animal. This was one part of the nightmarish chaos that had befallen the city.

In contrast to Alphard, Crusch put her hips into her sword attacks, unleashing a thrust that was too fast to be followed by eye. Her target was the enemy's face, aiming to mercilessly impale the brain behind it—

"Good form! But! Not enough polish!! As you are now, you're barely gonna be an appetizer to us!"

As he howled, Roy Alphard rotated his arms disturbingly, as if he didn't need to bother with his joints. Instantly, a fierce scratching sound tore through the blue sky, and Crusch's arm was immediately thrown back.

This was thanks to the concealed weapons known as tiger claws, which Alphard had equipped on the fingertips of both hands.

"As if I'll let you!"

A moment before Alphard could claw out Crusch's beautiful face, Subaru wrapped his whip around her slender hips. "Eep!" cried Crusch as Subaru yanked her over to safety, pulling her right out of the range of the claws.

But dismayed at having his prey snatched from him, Alphard altered his route with a single bound—

"Good, nice, great, wonderful! Did you think you could escape?! If anything, we'll get you and your pal over there, too! Drink!! Gorge!!"

Carrying Crusch, Subaru fell back, with Alphard drooling in hot pursuit. The chase made Subaru twist up his face.

"I didn't think...my role is..."

"—To always play the decoy. Even now, you are incredibly effective!"

"Whaaa?!"

By wholeheartedly pursuing Subaru, who looked like an easy target, Alphard had left himself wide-open in turn—Julius, now in midair, had waited for that moment to pound his rainbow-sword blow home.

Instantly twisting his body, Alphard attempted to evade the glimmering sword flash. However, the brilliant arc of The Finest's sword strike homed in on his foe and drew fresh blood from Gluttony, who rolled onto the floor.

"Gaaah! Now that's a surprise! Er..."

"Then I shall provide you with further surprise. Blossom, my lovely flower buds!"

When Alphard slapped the floor and leaped to his feet, Julius pursued him with a merciless follow-up attack. The six greater spirits swirling above the knight's head glimmered like a rainbow as they swept across the roof in a beautiful display.

"Don't push yourself too much, spirit mage!!"

"Formally, I am a Spirit Knight. I have heard rumors that you are a gourmet, but will you grant my lovely buds a warm reception?"

"Oh, I'll give 'em a real passionate welcome! I'll rip 'em apart like the annoying pests they are!!"

As the approaching aurora seared his vision, Alphard brimmed with slavish appetite. To seal off his enemy's avenues of escape, Julius pursued Gluttony with seemingly endless sword strikes from every angle.

Subaru would have liked to support him without a moment's delay, but Alphard's almost-feral movements, which had him darting all over the roof, prevented Julius from landing a clean hit. He had to do something with Gluttony—with Alphard right there—

"—Remember your objective, Moppet Mage!"

Just then, a voice's shout reached the rooftop, calling out with a completely inappropriate moniker.

"———"

In accordance with Al's warning, Julius had concealed Subaru's true name while communicating with just his yellow eyes whenever he could. As the knight continued with his rainbow swordplay, Subaru didn't need him to spell everything out to understand his intent.

—Julius was saying to let him deal with Gluttony while Subaru went to stop the slaughter and broadcast.

"Hey, hey, hey, hey, you sure about runnin'? Pal, you have a grudge against us, don't ya? Destined foes always, like, taste the richest. The ultimate in deep delights? To eat, gnaw, eat, lick, nibble, eat, bite, tear, crush, gorge! Drink!! Let me do all that, okay?!"

Leaping around, Gluttony hurled insults, trying to draw hesitance out of Subaru.

In fact, Gluttony had. To Subaru, defeating Gluttony was the singular goal he had pursued for over a year. He'd dreamed of this day so many times that he'd stopped counting.

Defeating him would save a girl. Subaru would be able to see her again. He'd come this far believing that.

To just let that chance slip through his fingers—

"—Master Subaru."

Subaru's melancholy was shattered when Crusch looked up from his own arms and called out to him. From up close, he could see a powerful, powerful conviction and an ever-so-slight sway of regret.

—It was none other than Crusch who had as powerful a link to Gluttony as he.

To her—someone who had her memories stolen by Gluttony, someone who was forced to go forward groping through a world that was blank when it shouldn't be—the foe before them was the key to getting her memories and her old self back. Even knowing that, she had chosen to fulfill her duty over helping herself.

They were badly lacking both time and the strength to soundly defeat their greatest enemy. Subaru and Crusch's standpoints were the same. That was exactly why Subaru was the only one able to fully appreciate how noble her decision was.

He was hesitant. He was reluctant. He'd probably regret this. But—

—Sorry, Rem. Please wait just a little longer.

"—Damn it all! Fine, I get it! Hey, Juli! Don't you dare lose on me!"

"That is my line. Make sure to fulfill your duty as the substitute knight of the Valkyrie!"

"Let us entrust this to Master 'Juli' and go, Master 'Moppet Mage'!"

Scratching his head, Subaru set his rueful thoughts aside and took Crusch's hand. Then relying upon the boundary lines generated by the aurora, they escaped Gluttony's attack range.

Their destination was the door leading inside—or not. They would have to veer toward the rooftop's bent railing. Vaulting it in one stride, Subaru supported Crusch as he took one last look at the battle unfolding behind them.

"—Go!!"

However, noticing his gaze, Julius wouldn't permit him to waste time worrying about him until everything was settled.

Internally clicking his tongue at that annoying attitude, Subaru swore to complain to his face later. Then grabbing Crusch by her slender hips, he launched himself into the air once more—

"—Crusch, plan B!"

"Pl-please do not let go!"

Ferris'll kill me if he hears about this, Subaru mused as he crouched, holding on to Crusch tightly and then leaping down from the roof of the city-hall building in one go.

Naturally, gravity pulled on them, and soon, they were plummeting headfirst toward the square. Halfway through the fall, the whip, which had been anchored to the railing above, reached its limit and brought them to a stop, leaving Subaru bearing the weight of two people on his shoulders.

"—Nghhh!"

Enduring the pain of his creaking bones with sheer willpower alone, Subaru and Crusch traced a large curve through the air as they swung toward the wall. Then with both feet extended toward the glass window in their path, Subaru slammed into it and broke right through.

"Raaaah!!"

"Eeeep!"

Glass fragments flew all over the place as Subaru and Crusch rolled into the room they'd aimed for.

Pushing hard on the floor with one hand, Subaru let up a second cry as he released Crusch from his grasp. Instantly settling down, the pair looked around, confirming that this place was indeed their objective.

This was the room on the topmost floor of city hall, in which the metia for broadcasts was placed.

The assault team had worked out beforehand that they would fly to the uppermost floor. Of the various methods Subaru had devised, he'd ended up using the most dramatic, but with the exception of what happened to his leg, the operation had mostly gone off without a hitch.

Subaru pictured Ferris's indignant face in his mind as he glanced toward the back of the room, for the enormous presence of the device set into the wall stole his thoughts.

Even in this city, this was the most precious and important thing—

"—So this is the metia?"

It was the most peculiar metia of all the ones that Subaru had seen to date.

The device he spotted was designed for expanding and enhancing the user's voice, increasing the range of its reach. Relying only upon magic crystals for its power source, this was a "machine" shaped like a pipe organ.

And while Subaru was unwittingly letting the metia steal his attention—

"—Master Subaru!!"

The sharp cry and the shock wave erupting from a savage collision of sword and claw behind him brought Subaru back to his senses.

His body went rigid as he turned around and saw Crusch engaged in a mesmerizing sword dance, delivering a painful blow to the scales of the black dragon sitting at the back of the room.

Howling in agony was the black dragon of Lust, the culprit of repeated acts of evil that targeted the residents of the city.

"—Capella!"

Leaving Subaru behind as he shouted, the black dragon and the Valkyrie engaged in a ferocious back-and-forth that covered the entire room.

The room contained not only a metia, but also a conference table, chairs, fixtures, and the like along the walls. Naturally, these furnishings were quickly blown away one after another by the powerful shock waves that marked the furious battle, leaving the items broken beyond recognition.

But in this back-and-forth, Crusch's masterful attacks held the upper hand.

In that room, the dragon was clearly at a disadvantage, unable to freely swing her large frame about. This was probably because the black dragon had never expected Subaru and Crusch to come flying through the window.

The black dragon had probably been keeping watch over the room's proper entrance, its flame trained toward it the whole time. While she was busy guarding that side, Subaru and Crusch launched a surprise attack by coming in from the roof—this was their plan B.

"Yaaaaah!"

Freed from her fear of high places, Crusch raised a valiant battle cry as she drove her sword home again and again.

Crusch's wind attacks exhibited their true might not in long-range combat, but up close. In an enclosed space with nowhere to run, the invisible blades mercilessly bit into the black dragon's hide.

"—Orrrggghhh!!"

"Look out! Get...down?"

Caught up in the moment, Subaru did his best to roll and flee when the dragon bellowed and breathed a stream of pitch-black flames. However, in the middle of his dramatic escape, Subaru realized something.

—There was a bound, squirming girl wriggling under the bleeding black dragon's feet.

"_____"

Instantly, Subaru felt the urge to vomit as he realized Lust's lowly scheme, in which she cunningly used a hostage in the same way that Wrath had. In the end, the Archbishops of the Seven Deadly Sins resorted to similar means to make their opponents falter.

He'd been defeated by the same ploy before, and as a result, Emilia had been whisked away from him.

"Uooooh!!"

With that fact lighting a fire in his heart, Subaru exhibited his greatest level of concentration as he slid directly under Capella's feet.

Ducking under her head, he slipped between her legs, resolutely sliding over broken glass as he went straight to the girl. Picking up her trembling body, he also slammed his whip into the black dragon's back. It did no apparent damage, but it did certainly make him feel better.

However, Crusch followed up with a sword slash that was not nearly so gentle.

"!!!"

"No quarter! Pay for the wicked deeds that are bringing calamity and disorder to the city!"

As the black dragon clutched her head in a show of fear, Crusch sliced her blade down at her from the front.

Perhaps the Archbishop was just that brittle when forced onto the defensive, for Capella continued to endure a stream of attacks, seemingly helpless against the steel blade. Her wings were rent, her fangs were broken, and the scales of her long neck were shorn, making the dragon scream from the pain.

Crusch raised a long, slender leg, delivering a powerful kick to the dragon's torso. The force must have been far greater than any kick Subaru could muster. The strength of that attack pushed the huge dragon backward, forcing it toward a still-intact window.

Hers were not the actions of someone with a chance of victory. She was simply buckling under the weight of Crusch's strength.

"—It ends here!"

"!!!"

Not lending her ears to Lust to the very end, Crusch slammed her blades of wind into the black dragon's torso and wings, sweeping across her neck and slamming her massive body into the wall again. Finally, the window gave way, and Lust was completely blown outside.

Plummeting with the remains of the window, the black dragon instantly spread her wings, but one wing was broken at the root, and the other was ineffective due to countless lacerations. Her regeneration wasn't fast enough—and so her fall was inevitable.

A few seconds later, the sound of Lust slamming into the ground reached them. It was a heavy, wet *splat*, like meat being slammed against a wall, or a wet mop being dropped on the floor.

"I shall check and keep watch. Master Subaru, please see to that girl."

"R-right, gotcha."

Crusch walked over to the window that the black dragon had fallen through, never lowering her guard. Feeling reassured as he watched her from behind, Subaru gently released the captive girl from her bonds.

"Auuugh..."

"It's all right. Just now, that strong, beautiful lady over there taught the bad dragon a lesson. We can't really afford to take our time, so let me cut to the chase... Do you know what happened to...the other people?"

Subaru spoke to the girl, who still seemed disoriented by the sheer fear and bewilderment that naturally came with getting caught up in a battle between a warrior and a dragon. Kneeling to talk to her at eye level, Subaru posed his question as gently as possible.

The young girl blinked several times, not responding right away. Then slowly, she seemed like she was gasping for air as she moved her lips several times.

"Th-the room over there... Everyone's in there."

Her voice shaking, the girl pointed to a door on the other side of the room that was still marred with the fresh signs of combat.

Setting his eyes upon that door, Subaru somehow refrained from putting to his lips the question that immediately rose in the back of his mind—whether the captured people were dead or alive.

But asking the girl such a thing was far too cruel, and far too thoughtless. But seeing as how there was no sign of activity or life of any kind after the massive battle that had just occurred, he was not very hopeful.

"_____"

Patting the still-worried girl on the head, Subaru slowly turned toward the other room.

His limbs grew heavy and cold. Subaru keenly felt the sheen of sweat forming on his back. He wanted to believe that this being a broadcast room, no sound was leaking out simply because of soundproofing.

"Master Subaru?"

"It's all right. I'll check in a sec... What about Lust?"

"...There is no problem over here, either. For whatever reason, there is no sign of her moving from where she fell."

Crusch replied as she warily kept an eye on Lust below. Hearing this, Subaru took a deep breath and stood before the door. Then he reached his hand out to the knob.

It was possible there were still Witch Cultists lurking behind this door as well. Despite that consideration, Subaru had no better option than to simply check.

However, for some reason, he was convinced that there was no need for such concern. And as a matter of fact, he wasn't wrong. There were no Witch Cultists standing guard inside the room.

—After all, the room didn't need guarding.

"___""___""___""___""___""___""___""___""___"
"___""___""___""___""___""___""___""___""___"
"___""___""___""___""___""___""___""___""___"
"___""___""___""___""___""___""___""___"

Gazes. They were gazes. Gazes, gazes, gazes, gazes. gazesgazesgazesgazesgazesgazesgazesgazesgazesgazesgazesgazesgazesgazesgazesgazesgazesgazesgazesgazesgazesgazesgazesgazes.

—As Subaru screamed, he saw countless, wordless gazes.

—No, it was nothing more than Subaru's impression that they were looking at him. Subaru had no way to know if they actually observed the world around them. He could not comprehend such a thing.

All he could do was scream. This was what *being at a loss for words* truly meant. His mind had frozen over, unable to assemble even a single thought. However, he did know one thing.

—Now he knew the true nature of the ear-grating background noise he'd heard during Lust's threatening broadcast.

"…What…is this?"

When an incoherent voice finally managed to trickle out, that noise filled the room all at once.

What greeted Subaru was endless buzzing that brought feelings of fear, delight, rejection, and many countless others.

Within that dimly lit room, a vast quantity of multifaceted eyes glowed red as they wriggled, moving to and fro as they stared at Subaru, who stood perfectly still. These were…flies. They were, without a shadow of a doubt, flies.

—The room was jammed full of…a huge number of human-size flies.

"!! Master Subar… Ah."

"?! Crusch?!"

Subaru, his brain bleached white by the revolting sight, turned back when he heard a sudden scream. Even as the buzzing of the flies' wings pervaded his ear in response to the scream, Subaru looked and saw what happened.

—He saw Crusch crumple to the floor, and the wretched smile coming over the girl, who was kicking her.

The girl stroked her short, blond hair with her palm, her red eyes gleaming and glimmering as she stared at Subaru.

"Bwa-ha-ha-ha! Really, how can you be such suckers? Did you

really think you were getting one up on me? Me?! That's not even worth a laugh! Bwa-ha-ha-ha-ha!"

As Crusch lay prostrate in a pool of her own blood, the girl stomped on her, cackling in a high-pitched voice—a voice that Subaru only realized then was familiar to him. There was no doubt.

"It's me, your dear Capella! Bwa-ha-ha-ha-ha!!"

Sticking her tongue out, Capella winked and posed for effect, laughing with utter disdain at Subaru for his impudence.

6

Behind him was the giant insect cage, packed with flies. A pool of the black dragon's blood, which had splattered inside the room, spread farther. Standing amid the gruesome spectacles she herself had brought about and trampling all over Crusch was the small girl—no, the Archbishop of Lust.

A fang-like tooth poked out of Capella Emerada Lugunica's mouth as she continued to laugh.

"Wha-what the hell is this...?!"

"It's pointless for meatbags like you to even think about it! Ain't the best thing just accepting the facts in front of your own eyes? A beautiful girl trembles and quakes before you, but behold! She is actually an Archbishop of the Seven Deadly Sins!"

Subaru was unable to hide his inner turmoil as Capella danced before him, sticking her tongue out in a vulgar fashion. Crusch had fallen at Capella's feet, and her eyes had rolled back. Her convulsions were a dangerous sign of her current condition.

No noticeable external wounds caught his eye, and he didn't know exactly what had happened to her. But those were grave symptoms. If he didn't get her out of here immediately, it would soon be too late.

"Your heads aren't much for thinking to begin with, are they? In this situation, why would there be a little morsel of meat just sitting around here at city hall? How you can even live with that stupid, moronic *Ahh, a girl's in trouble—I have to save her* mindset is beyond me!"

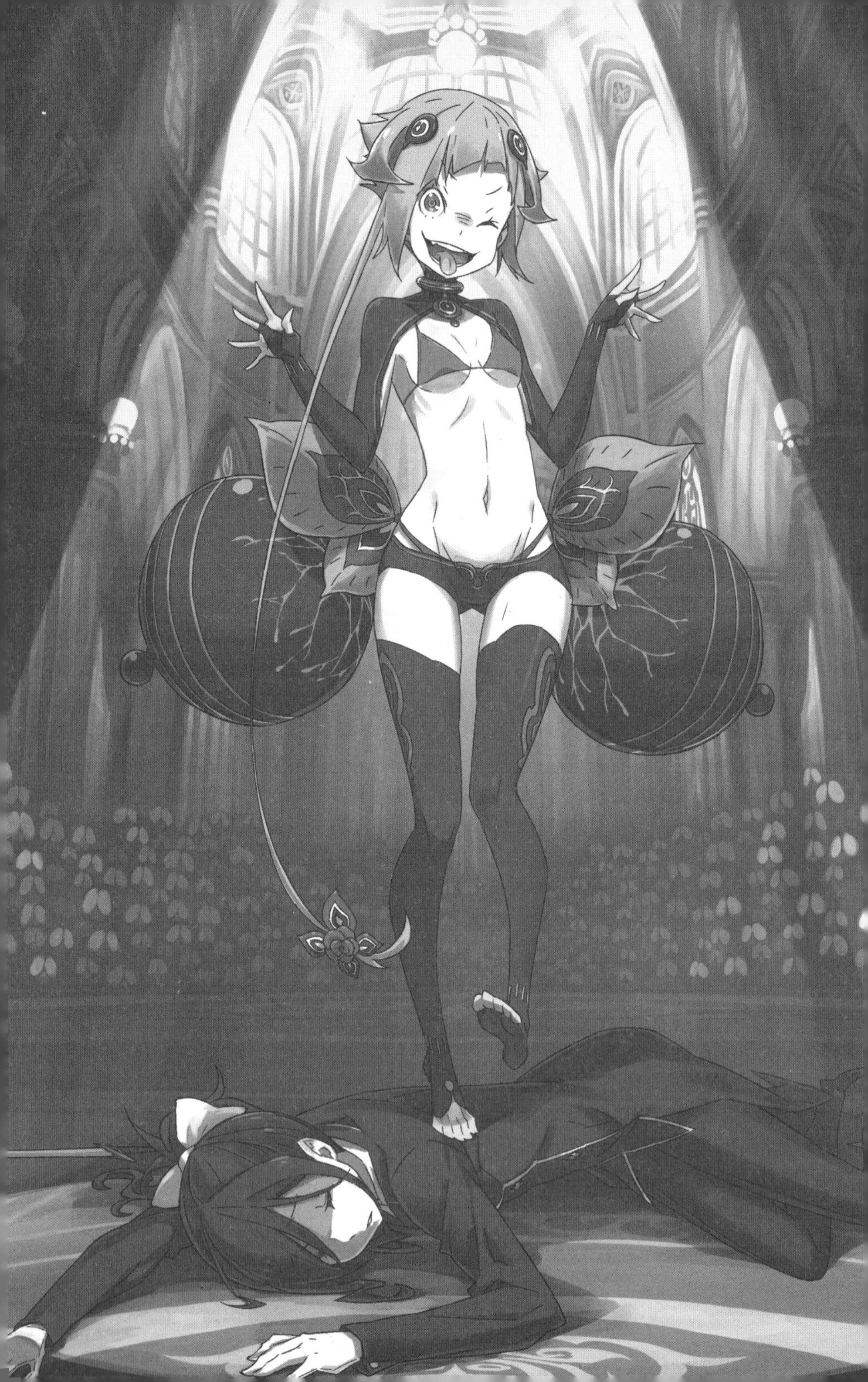

"Sh-shut it. There's all kinds of things I wanna ask you right now… but first, get your feet off her."

"Huh? Aren't you so glad to see my bare feet that you're breaking out in a sweat? Or do you have an obsession with the slab of meat currently savoring the soles of my feet? I do have such an erotic body, after all. You just can't get enough of me, can you? Bwa-ha-ha-ha!"

"!! She's not someone a person like you should be stepping on!!"

Capella stepped on Crusch's chest, grinding her heel in. With her acts of casual violence and mocking laughter driving him past the boiling point, Subaru's emotions raged as he rose off the ground, whip at the ready.

"Ohh?"

Raising a voice feigning ignorance, Capella opened her eyes wide as she watched Subaru move.

Subaru swung his whip, aiming not at Capella, but at a piece of the rubble that was a by-product of Crusch's fight with the black dragon. Subaru deftly entwined his whip around a handful of stones, twisting his wrist to launch them at Capella's head.

"_____"

Not knowing his enemy's means of attack, close combat would be the height of idiocy. In the first place, Subaru lacked the power to directly engage an Archbishop in combat. Even though the blood was rushing to his head, he was still painfully aware of his own powerlessness.

That was why Subaru needed to prioritize not the annihilation of his foe, but finding a way out of this situation.

—He needed to recover Crusch, get away from this place, and link up with one of his comrades.

The debris that he hurled had more than enough mass to cave in an unprotected human skull. Whether his impromptu projectile was blocked or evaded, he couldn't get Crusch up and moving while she was still firmly under that girl's feet.

So his plan was to create an opening to collect Crusch and then—

"Come on, hit!"

"Fine by meee."

"?!"

When Subaru shouted to rouse himself, Capella shot back with a calm and measured reply.

Immediately after, he heard the sound of something hard breaking flesh and bone. Then blood began pouring from Capella's head as it snapped back.

Struck on the defenseless side of her skull, the girl had her forehead torn open; her blond hair was stained a dark crimson. The girl's face, lovely and sweet, was cruelly crushed and deformed as he watched on.

"—Uuugh."

Having the left eye from that half-smashed face stare at him was a startling sight that unexpectedly seized Subaru's heart. He'd only meant to create an opening. He'd just done what some might have called the most foolish thing possible.

"Why do you all hate dancing in the palm of my lovely hand this much? I just adore how you're all such hopeless idiots. Bwa-ha-ha-ha!"

"—Grrraaahhh!"

The instant his thoughts froze, Capella's mocking laugh and a black whirlwind slammed into Subaru from the side and sent him flying.

Struck on the entire right side of his body, as if he'd been slapped by the hand of a giant, Subaru skipped across the floor, taking a desk in the room with him as he tumbled away. Completely battered and beaten up, Subaru came to a stop when he bumped into the far wall. Coughing, he lifted his head, wondering what had happened. That was when he saw—

"Bwa-ha, what's with the face? Am I so beautiful that your voice won't come out?"

"...What...are those?"

"Mmm? Ah, you mean these. Well, well, well. I wonder what they look like to a meatbag like you?"

When Subaru forgot his pain, his voice barely coming out, Capella turned her back to him and amusedly waved her butt back and forth.

There was something strange jutting out from the shapely behind she thrust out toward him, something that did not belong. This was a black, thick reptile's— No, it was a dragon's tail. A dragon's tail protruded from her backside.

Having reached that conclusion, he belatedly realized that it must have been that tail that had hit him earlier.

"Don't tell me you're a…dragon taking human form?"

"Yes, there it is. The irrational argument that you can't help spouting because of your low brain capacity and a total lack of critical thinking! I've been so kind to sprinkle these breadcrumb clues, but it turns out scum like you need a good *kick* to see the whole picture!"

Her mood souring from Subaru's apparently incorrect deduction, Capella swung at him with her huge tail once more. Instantly evading with a quick jump to the side, Subaru watched as she crashed her long tail into the floor and created cracks. Then he took a breath of—

"Letting your guard down at this point just makes all your other effort pointless!"

"—Gah!"

A huge fist slammed into Subaru's wide-open face without warning. When he rebounded off the floor from the force of the impact, he was then launched into the ceiling by the tail, which had been waiting for him. His body collided with the ceiling then, and as he helplessly spun and fell, countless bladelike feathers tore him up on the way down, scattering droplets of blood all over.

"Gngh, gaaaaah!!"

A painful cry escaped his throat as his back was slashed and gouged. When Subaru hit the floor again, he desperately tried to get his mind working again. He'd just been slugged, thrown, and cut up—what did that mean?

Subaru's face had been punched with the massive arm of a beast. He'd been tossed into the air by the black-dragon tail, and he'd been sliced open by sharp, bladelike bird feathers—and all these had spawned from the body of the girl, who was looking down at Subaru as he wheezed in pain.

"Shouldn't you be able to figure out the answer by now?"

A huge bestial arm, a black dragon's tail, a monstrous bird's wings. Each could only be described as grotesque.

As he set his eyes upon her form, no other words could come to mind. If something came to mind other than words, it was physiological disgust at encountering an unnatural being that shouldn't exist.

She was a grotesque monster, a fiend, et cetera. Her true nature was—

"Transmutation, transformation…!"

"Bwa-ha!"

For the first time, Subaru's muted reply drew a laugh of genuine satisfaction from Capella.

"I am the Archbishop of Lust, Capella Emerada Lugunica— I exist to monopolize all this world's love and admiration for myself. I, the one who deserves to be loved the most, can answer anyone's perverse desires. I am the ultimate manifestation of any aesthetic that exists. I can even transform into a beautiful girl according to your tastes. I am a devoted woman, after all! Bwa-ha-ha-ha!!"

As she said whatever she pleased, Capella freely altered her form in front of Subaru.

She shifted from her grotesque form to that of a rustic-looking boy, then immediately lengthened her limbs and turned into a voluptuous femme fatale. In what seemed to be the blink of an eye, she changed again, becoming the apparent epitome of an unfortunate village girl, and an instant later, she took the form of a very young girl, an obscene smile rising to her cherubic face.

"See? So which me do you like the most?"

"——"

He was speechless. Words refused to form. All his heart comprehended was that this was the worst thing possible.

Her morals were seemingly nonexistent. Though a plain and simple ability, Lust's Authority allowed her to violate and trample upon anyone's system of values. It specialized in putting herself on display.

When he looked, the terrible wound that had been caused by the hurled debris was already closed, and there was no sign she was ever hurt. Perhaps she had covered up the scar with her incredible regenerative ability or used her transformation ability instead.

Either way, he'd uncovered the trick behind the black dragon and the little girl, the two forms Capella had taken. At first, he'd suspected she had a Petelgeuse-like ability to possess others, but—

—If this was the case, the whole incident with the black dragon getting blown outside city hall through a window didn't make much sense.

"The fact that it did nothing except breathe fire should've been an obvious clue. Also, setting aside that I left the lizard in the exact spot you'd expect a trap to be, where'd all your doubts go when it didn't immediately move to respond to your intrusion and it didn't speak with my beaaaautiful voice?"

"…Wait… Waitwaitwait, wait up a second."

Reading Subaru's thoughts from the minute changes in his facial expression, Capella cackled with contempt.

Her form became that of a graceful woman with long, swaying hair, then a gentleman with a crimson mustache and beard; even the tenor of her voice changed, leaving him questioning whom he was talking with.

But the instant that misgiving spawned inside his chest, it led to an appropriate, logically consistent deduction that refused to vanish.

If Capella's Authority of Lust allowed her to freely transmute and transform—then what if this wasn't limited to her body alone and could be used on others as well?

"Even with your head and its limited blood flow, you should understand where that lizard and those flies really came from, right?"

Touching a hand to her mouth, Capella acted like a malevolent stage performer as she pressed Subaru for an answer.

Aware that he was forcibly following her script, Subaru replied, his teeth shaking at their roots.

This most awful, most terrible, most wretched of nightmares was—

"—All of them are people in city hall who were transformed by you?"

"Yes, that's correct. But you're too slow, so no prize! You're a slow, clumsy bag of meat, and whatever purpose you exist for, shockingly, is beyond even my understanding!"

"You can't…understand? —That's what I want to say to you, goddamn it!!"

Capella had confessed to her cruel, monstrous actions with an expression that didn't have the barest pangs of conscience.

In the dimly lit room, the multifaceted eyes glowed red and stared at Subaru as one. They flapped wings that they could not use to fly, desperately broadcasting that incessant sound.

Probably because they were crying for help.

"I don't get it! Turning people into…into flies? What's the meaning of that?!"

"Are you saying it's repulsive?"

"It makes every hair on my body stand up! You…! You people are just…!"

"Well, can't be helped if it makes you feel bad. *You can't avoid feeling disgusted*—is that what you're saying?"

"!!"

There were no longer words that could accurately describe what Subaru felt.

Changing people into flies, toying with their lives—it was far worse than merely killing them. It was the worst. It was the lowest.

In a span of a few hours, Subaru had met four Archbishops whom he would never be able to coexist with even if he had a whole eternity.

Sirius of Wrath toyed with other people's emotions and was a madwoman obsessed with her own self-centered love.

Regulus of Greed forced his own values onto others and was a villain who placed himself above all others.

Alphard of Gluttony was a blasphemer who stole the names and memories of people, trampling upon the proof of their very existence.

And Capella of Lust was a monster who spat upon and blotted out the values revered by ordinary human beings.

Each and every one was accursed, beyond saving, and stark raving mad.

The gap between him and them absolutely could not be filled. That conclusion alone made Subaru's vision go red. However, Capella gazed upon Subaru's anguished expression of righteous indignation as she continued:

"—Yes. You hate what you find repulsive, what makes you feel bad. So what of it?"

She smiled, as if there was nothing that could make her happier.

"———"

He didn't understand what she was getting at. He didn't have the means to understand it to begin with. They might as well have been the words of an alien from outer space.

He couldn't understand. Her values and her very way of life were just too different.

"When you saw all these stupidly huge flies, you felt an instinctive revulsion. You thought it was disgusting. Well, you're right. No one could love creatures like that. It'd be unnatural."

She continued changing her form left and right, talking in a jumble of voices as she kept altering her speech alongside her rapidly shifting appearance.

"They're ugly and creepy to anyone's eyes. I changed those piece-of-trash meatbags into filthy insects that are too pitiful to even look at. You can't love any of them, either. Of course you can't."

The monster before him had pitch-black eyes, eyes that saw nothing, eyes filled with bottomless darkness.

"People are creatures who can't live without loving someone. But since they're creatures who can't love something that's strange or revolting, then by process of elimination, they can't live without loving something they can love."

Capella spoke with a passionate voice, almost as if she was speaking about how ordinary lovers fell in love.

"———"

Subaru's mind had gone blank. He could not understand the confession of the monster tilting her head, acting like she had made the greatest discovery of the modern age.

He wanted to get away that very moment. He didn't want to breathe the same air as her for a single second longer. He didn't want to be anywhere he could see her. He didn't want to feel her on his skin. He didn't want to hear her voice.

—After all, this monster loved Subaru Natsuki.

It wasn't just Subaru. The victim she turned into a black dragon, the great many people she turned into flies, Crusch, whom she was even now trampling underfoot, Julius fighting above them, Garfiel, Wilhelm, and Ricardo, and the giant and the woman they were fighting in the square, all the people in the city—she loved…all of them.

It was because she loved them that she did everything she could think of to make them love her. To this monster, that was simply how love worked.

"So you see, I am kind and deeply compassionate, and I am simply a woman drowning in the love of the many. I monopolize all the love and admiration in the world for myself, but that means I can't slack off in my efforts to be loved, you see. To be loved by you, I'll turn into whatever version of me best suits your tastes. To make you look at me, I'll rob you of all interest in anything else. I don't mind if you loved someone else to begin with. After all, this is the end for you. You'll come to love me. I'm giving it my all to make sure you do, see? My personal charm only goes up and up and up and up and up and up and up! The charm of the meatbags who aren't me only goes down and down and down and down and down and down and down!"

"…Just…kill me now."

"Hah? Why? I'm all about making people love me. I wouldn't even dream of doing something so barbaric. Even if you're a completely useless sack of meat, you have value so long as your love is focused on me… My desire for recognition is just a tiiiny bit stronger than most people's. That's why I want even one more person to tell me one more word of affection and to love me for even one more second. Get it? That's all I'm asking."

———.
———, ———, ———.
———, ———, ———, ———, ———.

"Got it."

"Ohh, you finally came around? Well then, put your love for me into words, dissolve in love right there, and turn into a mass of flesh to my liking…"

"Die."

Lacking the luxury of free thought, Subaru wished only for the death of the monster standing before him.

This was his enemy. He didn't want or need any more information.

He swung his whip, slamming it at his feet. Taken aback, the monster instantly backed away, finally freeing Crusch. Subaru crouched down and picked her up.

How many times had he done that today? Her light body secure in his arms, he immediately leaped away.

Realizing what had just happened, Capella's eyes filled with powerful, all-consuming hatred.

"So in the end, you're just a male piece of meat that's obsessed with female meat, huh? Don't even bother denying it. You can put whatever pretty spin on it you want. Ohh, you love a girl because she's pretty. Oh, you love a girl because she's cute. You love soft things that make you feel good, don't you? Don't get all high-and-mighty with me!!"

"Whoooa?!"

Glaring at Subaru as he drew away, Capella let spittle fly as she reached out with both arms.

One arm transformed and grew a serpent's head while the other formed a lion's head— The grotesque limbs stretched out to chase Subaru, weaving through the room to sink their fangs into him and tear him apart.

His right leg was bleeding again. He didn't feel any pain, and at this point, he sincerely didn't care if it tore off in the process. Putting the entirety of his soul into protecting the warmth cradled within his arms, Subaru focused all his athletic ability into evading Capella's pursuit.

"Is that breeding mare really that important to you?! Then you'd better hang on to her tight in the next life, hugging her and never letting go! That body of a filthy temptress! Those eyes that invite sympathy! Those lips whispering sweet nothings! That nice-feeling fleshy flesh-flesh! You just can't get enough! That's why you're trying so hard, right?!"

"! You ass, stop putting words in my mouth! That's not how it is between me and her!"

"Oh, shut up! There's a heady, female scent coming from that female meat! That goes the same for the male scent coming from your male meat! Did it really never come to mind? Can you swear you haven't had even one indecent thought for just one second? If you have, even for a second, that means you're just a male slab of meat desperately searching for a female slab of meat! How am I wrong?! Just try telling me how I'm wrong!"

A serpent's fangs, a lion's maw, a dragon's tail, enormous bestial arms, and monstrous bird feathers were tearing the room apart.

Letting out an anguished cry, Subaru searched for the remotest chance for victory in that raging storm of destruction. Even if he tried to escape, Capella was barring the room's entrance. Her form was in flux, swelling and contracting and constantly shifting between woman, girl, boy, and elder, creating an anomaly so ugly that it scarcely seemed real.

"You haven't stroked her hair? You haven't touched her lips? You haven't embraced her body? Haven't you adorned those tawdry, sweaty thoughts of yours with that pretty word—*love*? Give me a break. You're just mistaking love for something else. You all just went off on your own, smugly dressing up carnal desires with such flowery words and phrases."

There was a glower of madness in Capella's eyes as she stared at Subaru, transforming into her most repulsive form yet.

Her hair was long and silver, glistening in the moonlight. Her eyes were violet, like encrusted gemstones. Her skin was white, reminiscent of powder snow. Her limbs were long and slender, her body amply curved. Some fine details were different, but what appeared there was—

"You just don't wanna be open about all your carnal passions out in public! Don't go dressing them up with words like *love*. How about it? How's this, how's this? This is how hard I'm working to be loved by you! Look at this! Can you still speak? Do you still have something to say? Tell me your promised, inevitable denial!"

Taking the form of a beautiful silver-haired girl, the monster howled as it made a face that *she* would never, ever have made.

"—I love her because I was attracted to her heart! I was attracted to her nobility, her gentleness, her compassion, her open mind, her smiling face when she looks at the sky, her devoted way of life, her stubborn refusal to brook any unfairness, her weak side that she only shows to me, her determination to always do what she can and try her best, her voice that puts my heart at ease, her affectionate eyes, her gaze that tickles my heart, her lips that whisper love, hands that warm mine, her touch that makes my heart beat faster, and her beautiful hair that flutters in the wind! I believe with all my heart that we were destined to be together. Because she was the only one who acknowledged me. Because she was the one who stayed by my side when things were hard. Because she was the one who taught me what was truly important. Because we've always, always been together. Because I want to live the rest of my life seeing and feeling the same things as her. Because we promised. Because I'll never forget that promise. Because she knows the version of me that I can't show to anyone else. Because she's the only one who knows the real me. Because she's the one whose eyes I'll never be able to fool. Because she knows how deep my loneliness goes. Because she's the one who lets me forget my bitter memories. Because she's the one who taught me how to love. Because you were the one wiping the tears I cried. Because you found me in the middle of everything else that was happening. Because you showed me things I'd never seen before. Because you're the only one who truly understands me. Because I can't live without you. Because you're everything to me. Because you make my chest run hot. Because when you're around, all the colors in the world seem brighter. Because without you, I can't feel happiness. Because I can't live without you anymore. Because in the middle of a life full of lies, this is the only feeling that's real."

Rattling off the words like she was chanting a curse, the silver-haired monster's expression died a little with each additional phrase.

But as she rambled on and on about all the reasons one might claim to love another, Capella raised her head, her beauty and charm and obscenity all twisted up in a strange, bizarre expression of adoration and hate as she shouted:

"—Those are just flowery words—every last one of them!!"

"_____"

"Don't think you can just use words that sound nice and leave out the rest! All this stuff about what's on the inside, blah blah, personality, blah blah, our natures are compatible, blah blah—it's all just noise! External appearance, facial appearance—the only thing that attracts your meat to other meat is visual stimulation! If love really tied two people together, then why don't you try dressing things up with those glimmering words, stare with those glimmering eyes, and talk about your glimmering future after your lover's been turned into a fly?! Can you love her? Of course you can't! It repulses you, doesn't it?! It's disturbing, isn't it?! You can't help but feel disgusted, right?! You're the one who said that to me, loud and clear!!"

Her crazed, feral, abusive words, her persecution complex, her jealousy, her hatred, and her profound delusions were how she kept herself from falling apart.

Spraying her spittle as she ranted, Capella seemed to be losing even her tenuous grasp on her sanity, destroying more of the room as she wailed hysterically.

The great serpent hissed, the lion roared, and soon, Subaru could no longer hear Capella's shouts.

They became a storm of noise, and the room crumbled in multiple places. Caught up in the shock wave, Subaru couldn't figure out where to move or even where to look beyond the hovering cloud of dust particles.

Were his feet still touching the ground? Was his half-torn leg still in one piece? The only thing he was sure of was the beating heart of the woman resting in his arms. That one certainty suffused his body with courage.

But this valiant struggle suddenly came to a crashing halt.

"Meatbag, look at meeeee!"

"—Gaaah!!"

Plowing through the dust cloud, the lion head wildly charged at Subaru and sank its fangs into his leg.

His right leg was already barely hanging on, so when the lion tore into it, the limb came off at the femur and flew into the air. Exceeding the effects of Ferris's special technique, the intense pain of losing the leg made his brain boil, and his vision went red.

He hit the ground. Crusch spilled out of his arms. He flailed around, his blood pouring out in great, big surges. Putting pressure on the wound was out of the question. His leg was gone. His lifeblood flowed out like he was a waterfall.

His near-shattered mind vaguely understood that all that red represented what little remained of Subaru Natsuki's life.

"Haaah, my head hurts. My oh my, it seems I lost myself in a moment of arousal. How embarrassing. Bwa-ha!"

Subaru was lying faceup, the whites of his eyes showing as he weakly convulsed.

He'd managed to put his palm on the wound, but it was not up to the task of stanching the flow. But the force of the bleeding was gradually lessening. This was because all the blood in his body was draining quickly.

"Oh no—somehow, you seem to be dying. Seeing a meatbag in such agony makes the pain in a person's heart too easy to understand. It's too bitter a sight for me, really."

"Ah, aah, ah—"

"The female meat will probably die, too, huh? How regrettable. Her body suits me just right, so there were all kinds of things I still wanted to try— Ahh, that's right—"

He could see nothing. He understood nothing. Something…was breathing close by…

Crouching down at Subaru's side, the smiling monster gently put a hand on his leg wound.

"Well, I suppose I should see just what kind of unsightly mass of meat I can turn you into, huh?"

Capella held her own wrist in the air, using her opposing hand to slice it at the wrist and causing it to bleed.

The pitch-black ichor spilled out with incredible force, flowing toward the wound in Subaru's right leg. Blood mixed with blood. Subaru's red blood and Capella's black blood were coming together, dissolving into each other and causing a festering scent to rise.

A moment later—

"?! Ooh, aaaghOOAO?!"

"Bwa-ha-ha!! Does it hurt? Hey, tell me, does it hurt? My blood is so much more highborn than the likes of yours. After all, it's mixed with the blood of a dragon. It's gonna be really something if you lose to the curse in the blood. Between you and the female meat there, I wonder who's gonna hold on longer?"

Capella made an amused sound in her throat, but it was impossible for Subaru to reply.

In a state close to death, a point where even pain was a vague concept, he'd received a sudden shock. The black blood that had been poured onto him wriggled on top of Subaru's wound, ever so slowly penetrating deeper into his body.

He was being overwritten by something that was not him. This was different from pain or agony. It was fear that originated from another dimension entirely— Yes, *fear* was the only word that fit. It was scary. Scary. Terrifying.

He didn't understand. He wasn't even being allowed to die.

Crusch or him, the monster had said. If so, was she undergoing the same torment as him? Subaru was just so weak, unable to do… anything.

Crusch, Beatrice, Rem, Emilia, everyone, everyone, everyone—

"Eh, iii, aaagh—"

"Bwa-ha-ha-ha!! Oh my, oh my, once again, you reject my love. That means you'll be reborn as an unsightly pathetic piece of meat, doesn't it? Now, it's finally time for me to…"

Gazing adoringly as Subaru fainted in agony, Capella slowly rose to her feet.

Her form returned to that of the blond, red-eyed girl once more—whereupon Capella suddenly looked back.

There, where the glass window and the wall had been broken, a crisp breeze was blowing in—

"Heh, you're one tough customer, aren't you?"

"——!!!!"

Crawling up from ground level, to which it had fallen, the black dragon let out a roar upon sighting its hated foe and released a stream of black flames straight at Capella from its wide-open maw.

—The next instant, the upper floor of city hall was engulfed in pitch-black flames.

7

Sensing someone calling her name, Emilia felt her consciousness flitting back to reality.

When she slowly emerged from her slumber, the first thing she noticed was something smooth enveloping her. It was a pleasant sensation, as if she was embraced by an animal with warm, soft fur.

Previously, this was a feeling she could savor on a daily basis, and it was something that made her hazy memories throb.

"—Ah."

The nostalgia left her eyelids damp and heavy.

Wiping those teardrops away with the back of her hand, she cut her lingering attachments to that warmth and chose to wake up instead. Slowly, she opened her eyes, which were rimmed with long eyelashes, and took in the world around her with her large, round, violet eyes.

She saw a tall ceiling, and a room with unfamiliar furnishings.

It wasn't a place she had ever been to before. She was atop a bed, wrapped in blankets that felt high-class.

"Where...am I...?"

With a shake of her still somewhat fuzzy head, Emilia slowly sat up.

She felt a bit languid, but she couldn't feel any pain or distress troubling her body. The familiar feeling of sluggishness was an aftereffect from using too much magic and abusing her Gate, which she was not yet used to exerting.

Then having remembered that far, Emilia recalled exactly what had happened.

"That's...right. I was in the square, fighting the woman in the bandages..."

If she closed her eyes, she could almost see the madwoman, her entire body wrapped in bandages—the one calling herself the Archbishop of Wrath. A shudder ran through Emilia as she remembered the hatred and the terrifying combat capability that had been directed her way.

Emilia had held the advantage for a time during the fight, but the tables eventually turned, and she had been assailed by an overwhelming flame—

"I...fainted after that. But I'm still alive and well."

There was no mistaking that she'd been on the losing end of that battle and had subsequently faced mortal peril. Surviving despite such dire straits meant that someone had to have saved her. Of course, Subaru's face was the first that came to mind.

The leading candidate was surely Subaru. If anyone was going to come and save Emilia, she hoped from the bottom of her heart that it would be him.

Though if she had lost out to Subaru after so much grandstanding, it'd be too mortifying to bear.

"Mmm, this isn't the time to be in the dumps. I'm so far behind already; I don't have time to stop and reflect. I'll think about it while I walk."

Touching her hands to her own pale cheeks, Emilia roused herself and slipped off the bed.

Given the bed and the blanket, someone had definitely been nursing her. She reminded herself to thank that person, find out what had happened since she was last awake, and figure out what had happened to Subaru and the—

"Uhhh, why am I naked?"

Just when she was about to boldly set off, Emilia realized that she didn't so much as have a shift dress. With her naked body fully exposed, Emilia tilted her head as she wrapped the blanket around herself like a cloak.

She looked around the room, but nothing else wearable was there to be found.

"Mm, what'll I do? I believe it's considered unladylike to walk around like this, but…"

Bashfully reserved was a phrase that Puck had pounded into her during his time as her father figure. Now that Puck was gone, she had continued her studies with Annerose serving as her substitute mentor.

According to Annerose's teachings, Emilia was clearly a failure of a student for wandering about in her current, nearly nude state.

"But I'm worried about everyone else right now, and it's an emergency situation, so she'd make an exception, right?"

She had to confirm as soon as possible whether things had been settled with the Archbishop of the Seven Deadly Sins. Citing those circumstances as her just cause, Emilia left the room with a single blanket over her.

Exiting into the hallway, she confirmed that this was definitely a building she'd never seen before. It was just that the interior of the room she had woken up in clashed badly with everything else. A cold, antiseptic atmosphere seemed to permeate the corridor and the rest of the building.

It was probably the room with the bed that was the only exception.

Thinking this, she quickly accepted the mismatch between the atmospheres of the building and the room. This building was not for living in, but rather, it was supposed to be a place for work.

The proof was in the faint, lively sound of water, and the mechanical sound of some kind of gears turning—

"—Ahh, it seems that you have awakened. I am truly glad. I feel heartfelt relief knowing that you are safe."

When that voice was suddenly called out to her, Emilia felt a twinge of surprise as she turned around.

As she did, she spotted a lone young man, whom she had previously bumped into on the city street, now standing there in the corridor. While he smiled as he watched Emilia, she noted his white hair and his nearly all-white clothing.

The young man still had a friendly smile on his face as he casually walked over to her.

"But I cannot commend you for walking out as soon as you awoke. You put a great deal of stress on your body in various ways. If something happened to you, it might be an issue later, would it not? I would sincerely like you to take proper care of yourself. I mean, that body is no longer yours alone."

"Errr, and you are?"

Emilia's eyes went round at the sheer force with which the young man spoke in such rapid succession.

They were surely strangers, and yet the way he closed the distance to within a single pace of her felt a lot like how she would interact with Subaru. However, the decisive difference between him and Subaru was the warmth—or lack of—in their words.

Subaru's consideration for others was one of his cowardly virtues, but the young man standing before Emilia possessed none of that whatsoever. Where his own words and actions were concerned, it was clear that he did not spare a single effort toward the flattery of others.

Emilia had been getting such a strange impression of the young man since that single exchange.

The young man gave a generous nod in response to her question, with Emilia's internal thoughts left aside.

"Ahh, that's right. Sorry, sorry. I was able to gaze upon your sleeping face, but this is the first time you are looking at me, yes? Ahh, strictly speaking, it is not the first time, but there is little point in speaking of that. Even if you and I share a relationship of future blessings, I cannot be careless about the proper order of events. I apologize without reserve. See, I am a person capable of such a thing."

"Er, uhh…"

The eloquent words that the young man used without pause left Emilia feeling like any reply she could muster would be rather awkward.

This was partly due to her being overwhelmed by the firmness of his demeanor, but more than that, a growing suspicion that something was deeply wrong kept eating away at Emilia. It was pleading to Emilia from a distant corner of her mind.

—She just couldn't shake the feeling that she knew this young man from somewhere.

"It is unfortunate that such an important event is taking place in such a dreary corridor. Yet surely, you will look back upon this as a special memory of ours as well. People are filled aplenty with small bits of everyday happiness. I think that will be especially true in my time with you. Don't you think so, Emilia?"

"I…don't remember giving you my name… So who are you?"

"Oh, I'm sorry. It is a bad habit of mine that I lose sight of everything around me when my feelings swell and crest. Even I think my own overly sensitive personality is lamentable when it gets all like this. This time, I was daydreaming too much while conversing with you, perhaps? Ahh, yes, my name."

In a truly convoluted, roundabout manner, the young man's words finally arrived at the topic at hand.

The unease that Emilia felt about him personally, and her odd, persistent foreboding that accompanied his strangely familiar presence—both lit a fire within Emilia, leaving her unable to pull her eyes away from the young man's actions.

Emilia instinctively understood that whether she lived or died was directly linked to the slightest move of his hand.

The young man suddenly spread both arms wide, reverentially bowing to her.

"My name is Regulus Corneas. I work for a certain organization. However, that is not important where you are concerned. To you, there is but one thing you need to know about me. I am your precious husband, and you are my beloved seventy-ninth bride."

"...Eh?"

The young man, who introduced himself as Regulus, seemed enthralled as he spoke these words, but she did not understand their meaning.

Emilia was perplexed as she furrowed her delicate brows. However, Regulus did not even notice her subconscious refusal, as he simply gazed at Emilia and the single layer of fabric wrapped around her body.

"That outfit is poison to the eyes. Wait, I will have fresh clothes brought to you. Rest at ease. Your dress will be changed by my wives, others in the same position as you. They are accustomed to dressing someone in bridal attire."

"Wait, what do you mean by that? No, more importantly, what do you mean by 'your bride'...?"

"That's right, I forgot something very important! Oh, what was I thinking? That was a very close call."

Regulus, who literally had ears yet did not hear, grasped Emilia by her shoulders. Emilia grimaced at the strength he put into his fingertips, but the young man did not pay her discomfort the slightest heed.

All he did was bring their faces so close that their foreheads nearly touched as he peered into her violet eyes.

"I forgot a very, very important question. The wedding ceremony comes after. Emilia, this is very important, so I want you to answer me straight from your heart. It is very important for our future."

"_____"

The bizarre level of intensity made Emilia hold her breath as she maintained her silence.

Regulus smiled, perhaps taking Emilia's silence as tacit consent.

As he smiled, he asked, "Emilia, are you a virgin? That is the only truly important thing, you see."

<END>

AFTERWORD

Let Mr. Regulus's creepiness reach one and all!

Hello there, it's Tappei Nagatsuki, the Mouse-Colored Cat! And good-bye to any more changes to the afterword format!

Thank you very much for sticking with me through Volume 17 of the main series! I'm going to assume that you've already read the previous volumes, so if not, consider this your spoiler warning!

Now then, today's topic is the theme of Arc 5! With the royal-selection candidates and the Archbishops of the Seven Deadly Sins lined up, I wonder if everyone gets that this arc is like a huge, chaotic all-star showdown! The protagonists have been getting driven into a corner in a fairly one-sided manner, but that's just the difference when the fully prepared and the unprepared clash.

Either way, with gates closed on every side, this work is all about how the protagonists will rise back up from rock bottom, so definitely don't overlook the battle in the next volume!

As usual, there's a lot of things going on all at once, but right around when this volume comes out, the theatrical version of *Re:ZERO* should be released to the public, the comic version of *The Love Song of the Sword Devil* is starting up, and also, there's a collaboration novel between *Re:ZERO* and *Mushoku Tensei* (manga version, too)! In any case, there's lots and lots of stuff going on! You get to see a lot of Subaru and Rudeus in the same scenes, which is really interesting, so definitely check it out! See, Mago, I did some publicity, too!

* * *

So after that brief promotional break, let me charge straight into the customary thanks!

To Editor I, sorry that this time, the schedule was even tighter than usual! Who was it who said Arc 5 would be a breeze compared with Arc 4, hmm? Thank you in advance for your help with Volume 18!

To Otsuka, the illustrator, we've finally seen nearly all the Archbishops of the Seven Deadly Sins! Given that we started with "Well, she has no fixed form…" for Capella and her Authority, you did a fantastic job drawing her! But it just wouldn't be okay to have a swarm of flies for the cover! That's just a bridge too far! I'm looking forward to working on the next one together as well. Thank you very much!

To Kusano, the cover designer, this time, like last time, it's just one great illustration after another, but since we'll probably be continuing this pace for a little while longer, please keep sending your amazing work! Thank you very much!

And to Matsuse, who charged forward in the aftermath of the comic version of Arc 3, with Tsubata Nozaki joining in for *The Ballad of the Sword Devil* series that's just starting, thank you for your hard work on the manga version of *Re:ZERO*!

To everyone else at the MF Bunko J publishing department, all the distributors and bookstore employees, and all the other involved businesspeople, I have truly been taken care of by a great many people. Thank you very much as always!

And around when this volume hits stores, the theatrical version of the series will be gearing up for a public release as well! To all the animation staff, truly, truly, thank you so much! It's thanks to the OVA that I've managed to get past Volume 17!

Finally, my inexhaustible thanks to every one of you readers who have always supported me!

August 2018
<<Struggling with a finicky
SPACE key on my laptop>>

Capella

Her bangs on the right side are long.

Makes it seem as if her entire body is made of liquid metal. These parts are used to adjust her mass when she transforms.

Bwa-ha-ha-ha

Lusbel ♥ Tina

Eh? Where? Where?

There's a weird woman in bandages coming closer...!

Galek

- Fortyish
- Slightly chubby
- Naval uniform

City Hall

High-ranking official

"Ahh, so it turns out me and her are doin' this next-volume preview, I guess."

"Ohh, the next-volume preview! I know this! It's that thing the lady did! Mimi, too! Mimi wants to do it, too!"

"Daaah! Pipe down! I'm sayin' you *and* me are gonna be doin' this. Don't be all *mad dogs have no ears for hearing* and listen when people talk!"

"Ohh, gotcha! So? What kind of announcements are we making?"

"First, the next book, Volume 18, is expected to go on sale in December. I'll be honest—we all got pasted pretty good back there. Ain't my style not to get some payback real soon."

"I get that! I really do! Uhhh, after that, what's this thing happening on October 6? Looks like there's gonna be an oh-vee-ay or something!"

"That must be the public openin' for the theatrical OVA. Sounds like another mansion story before I joined the crew. Means we'll get to see the general and Ram on a real big screen… Crap, why ain't I there, too?!"

"Garf, reflections later! The announcements are reaaaally important!"

"It don't sit right havin' to hear that from you, but I guess that's true. So 'round the same time, there should be a Lady Emilia birthday event, and an OVA public screening at Shibuya Marui."

"Plus, there's gonna be cake and stuff! And lots of other stuff, too! Mimi, too! Mimi wants to eat that, too!"

"And *The Love Song of the Sword Devil* series is gonna start goin' on sale on September 27 in *Monthly Comic Alive*. That's the story of the Sword Devil and the Sword Saint. Me, I'm real interested in it, too."

"Ohh? But wasn't the real Sword Devil that old man right there at the *ryokan*?"

"Y-you moron! Like I can just walk up to the real guy and talk to him face-to-face. If I don't prepare for that first…"

"*Haaah*, Garf, are you scared?"

"Wha—?"

"Garf is a scaredy-cat, huh? But that's okay. Juuust okay. It's not like Mimi's disappointed or anything, so it's noooo biggie!"

"Who are you callin' a scaredy-cat?! I'm not scared! Oh, that's right! I'll prove it to ya and give the Sword Devil a piece of my mind face-to-face, right now!"

"Cool! Garf, you're so gutsy, it's super cool!"

"Oh, well, that goes without sayin'! Me, I'm Gorgeous Tiger!"

"And I'm Gorgeous Mimi!"

HAVE YOU BEEN TURNED ON TO LIGHT NOVELS YET?

IN STORES NOW!

SWORD ART ONLINE, VOL. 1-23
SWORD ART ONLINE PROGRESSIVE 1-6

The chart-topping light novel series that spawned the explosively popular anime and manga adaptations!

MANGA ADAPTATION AVAILABLE NOW!

SWORD ART ONLINE © Reki Kawahara ILLUSTRATION: abec
KADOKAWA CORPORATION ASCII MEDIA WORKS

ACCEL WORLD, VOL. 1-25

Prepare to accelerate with an action-packed cyber-thriller from the bestselling author of *Sword Art Online*.

MANGA ADAPTATION AVAILABLE NOW!

ACCEL WORLD © Reki Kawahara ILLUSTRATION: HIMA
KADOKAWA CORPORATION ASCII MEDIA WORKS

SPICE AND WOLF, VOL. 1-22

A disgruntled goddess joins a traveling merchant in this light novel series that inspired the *New York Times* bestselling manga.

MANGA ADAPTATION AVAILABLE NOW!

SPICE AND WOLF © Isuna Hasekura ILLUSTRATION: Jyuu Ayakura
KADOKAWA CORPORATION ASCII MEDIA WORKS

IS IT WRONG TO TRY TO PICK UP GIRLS IN A DUNGEON?, VOL. 1-16

A would-be hero turns damsel in distress in this hilarious send-up of sword-and-sorcery tropes.

MANGA ADAPTATION AVAILABLE NOW!

Is It Wrong to Try to Pick Up Girls in a Dungeon? © Fujino Omori / SB Creative Corp.

ANOTHER

The spine-chilling horror novel that took Japan by storm is now available in print for the first time in English—in a gorgeous hardcover edition.

MANGA ADAPTATION AVAILABLE NOW!

Another © Yukito Ayatsuji 2009/ KADOKAWA CORPORATION, Tokyo

A CERTAIN MAGICAL INDEX, VOL. 1-22

Science and magic collide as Japan's most popular light novel franchise makes its English-language debut.

MANGA ADAPTATION AVAILABLE NOW!

A CERTAIN MAGICAL INDEX © Kazuma Kamachi
ILLUSTRATION: Kiyotaka Haimura
KADOKAWA CORPORATION ASCII MEDIA WORKS

VISIT YENPRESS.COM TO CHECK OUT ALL THE TITLES IN OUR NEW LIGHT NOVEL INITIATIVE AND...

GET YOUR YEN ON!

YEN ON
Yen Press

www.YenPress.com

THE Eminence IN Shadow

ONE BIG FAT LIE
AND A FEW TWISTED TRUTHS

Even in his past life, Cid's dream wasn't to become a protagonist or a final boss. He'd rather lie low as a minor character until it's prime time to reveal he's a mastermind...or at least, do the next best thing—pretend to be one! And now that he's been reborn into another world, he's ready to set the perfect conditions to live out his dreams to the fullest. Cid jokingly recruits members to his organization and makes up a whole backstory about an evil cult that they need to take down. Well, as luck would have it, these imaginary adversaries turn out to be the real deal—and everyone knows the truth but him!

YEN ON For more information visit www.yenpress.com

IN STORES NOW!

KAGE NO JITSURYOKUSHA NI NARITAKUTE !
©Daisuke Aizawa 2018 Illustration: Touzai / KADOKAWA CORPORATION

The Detective Is Already Dead

When the story begins without its hero

Kimihiko Kimizuka has always been a magnet for trouble and intrigue. For as long as he can remember, he's been stumbling across murder scenes or receiving mysterious attaché cases to transport. When he met Siesta, a brilliant detective fighting a secret war against an organization of pseudohumans, he couldn't resist the call to become her assistant and join her on an epic journey across the world.

...Until a year ago, that is. Now he's returned to a relatively normal and tepid life, knowing the adventure must be over. After all, the detective is already dead.

Volume 1 available wherever books are sold!

TANTEI HA MO, SHINDEIRU. Vol. 1
©nigozyu 2019
Illustration: Umibouzu
KADOKAWA CORPORATION